15/-

D1493430

WHITE SAND AND GREY SAND

When the baby is found on the sand dunes, only her unusual Christian name, Ydette, is legible on the identity label tied round her. She grows up with the Maes family in the cathedral city of Bruges, becoming a creature of strange beauty, captivating Flemish and English friends alike, and surrounded always by the mystery of her heritage. The key to her final destiny lies in her own nature.

WHITE SAND
AND GREY SAND

by
STELLA GIBBONS

London
HODDER & STOUGHTON

AUTHOR'S NOTE

There is a Sintmariastraat in Bruges, but the house of the Maes sisters will not be found there. And none of the characters in the story are drawn from living people, with one exception only: some years ago I met the horse Klaartje in the (very comfortable) flesh and simply could not resist describing his occupation and appearance.

To
Ena and Donal Lenihan,
affectionately

"**M**ARIE. *Marie.*"

There was no reply to the low, angry call. The blue sky glowed, the white dunes glared in the sun, and hidden behind them the sea hissed and rustled in the high tide of noon.

There hovered in the air an extraordinary, confused murmuring; a threatening, rumbling, muffled sound that seemed to come as much from the cloudless sky as from the green land spreading rich and fruitful to the horizon. Jakoba Maes heard it, in the uneasy quiet that settled again over the dunes after her call, and she wrinkled her face into a grimace of vulgarity and violence; if her mouth had not felt so dry, she would have gone farther. She muttered something, then looked angrily around.

There was no one there, not even any of the poor fools who were running away; not a soul in sight—though they were making enough noise on the road down there behind the dunes —and as for the beasts themselves, of course they were miles off yet; even at the rate they seemed to be coming, they couldn't be here for days, if they ever got here at all. So it was still safe for a woman to shout out loud in her own country if she wanted to, and she shouted.

"Marie!" No reply. "You silly old fool, if you've . . ."

The mutter died away into a threatening silence, as she plunged down the steep slope, which re-filled her sabots, which she always wore into the country, with sand at the first step, and made her way as fast as she could across the hollow lying beneath, with her long shadow following. In spite of the heat, her head was covered by a black shawl, framing her broad brown face and protecting her wide shoulders in their black stuff blouse from the sun; she was sable as some big bird of the meadows; black, and solid, and angry, as she strode

9

forward against the drifting silver sand. There came from it every now and again, when the wind blew over the ridges, the softest imaginable sound, a kind of lonely whisper, dying off into silence and leaving the strangely ominous, empty sky, and the white dunes, to quietness again. But it did not last for long; it was broken by a far-off drone that swelled to a roar and three aeroplanes hurtled seawards. Jakoba flung herself beneath one of the stunted pines and lay still, with her fingers dug hard into the hot sand, as there came from the swooping machines a sharp, chattering noise.

It passed. They roared on towards Oostende (Ostend), and in a moment, lying with her face still pressed into the sand, she heard three thuds that shook the ground. The clamour from the road had grown louder, and there were screams.

She sat up, brushing the sand from her face, then scrambled to her feet and went on. She did not dare to call, now. There might be one of their men hiding in that thicket on the top of the dune, dressed as a woman or as a British soldier. And perhaps they had got Marie . . .

But as she toiled up the final slope, cursing the Germans and her sister below her breath and not letting herself think what she might find up there at the top, a figure appeared amidst the trunks of the pines, also dressed in black, but smaller than Jakoba, and with no shawl over her head. The arms waved, the other wide brown face showed a gleam of white, yet there came not a sound. And now she was beckoning. What for? Fool, can't she see I'm coming as fast as I can?

"Oh, thank God, thank God you're all right, Jakoba. . . . I thought they'd got you. . . . Our Lady heard me!" Marie gasped.

"There's no need to bring her in . . . I'm not one of your old Sisters round at the Béguinage," Jakoba retorted sourly, as she came up with her. "Why did you go off like that?" She wiped her forehead with one great freckled hand, and stood still, staring.

"I had to. I had to go behind a bush . . . and Klaas wasn't asleep . . ."

"Klaas! I should think *he's* known you long enough not to worry whether you go behind a bush or not . . . listen to *that*!" turning, with the colour leaving her face, towards the general direction of the east as there sounded five faint but tremendous explosions, "they're getting it in Ghent, I suppose . . . and our turn next." Then the blood rushed back into her face, turning it dark crimson under the tan, and she gritted her teeth. "Well, come on, come on, what are you . . ."

"Jakoba, I've found . . . look here. Look what I've found," Marie said.

Jakoba had noticed that she was not wearing her shawl. Now, staring, ready at any instant to drag her sister away, she turned quickly as Marie pointed to something lying on the ground amongst the glittering brown pine-needles scattered thickly over the sand. It was her shawl; it was rolled up into a bundle.

Jakoba took a step or two forward . . . it might be some clothes, or a ham, or something else worth having, people were leaving all kinds of useful things all over the place these days.

Then she saw what it was, and made an angry sound of disappointment.

"A *jochie* *?" she demanded, and knelt down, bending over the bundle, "is it dead?" She stared curiously at a gleam of white showing amongst the black folds; she did not like to touch it.

"Dead, no, bless her. She's asleep." Marie knelt down beside her sister. "Look," she whispered, drawing aside the shawl, "isn't she a little darling?"

"That's a good silk coat," was all Jakoba answered; "and look at her hair . . . that's been taken care of . . . her people must have money."

"She was all wet when I found her, Jakoba. I think," Marie was still whispering, and as she spoke the wind went through the dark green branches of the bowed and twisted trees overhead, with a soft sighing sound, "she'd been in the sea." The long quiet murmur died away in silence. Jakoba,

* Kid; brat.

turning her head, looked off towards the expanse of yellow-green water rolling below that was visible from the top of the dune. There were no sails of fishing-boats to be seen today. The horizon was veiled in a mist of heat. About a mile out, distinct against the broad sparkling pathway cast by the sun, something long and dark was lifting and falling lazily to the outward pull of the tide. Jakoba wrinkled her eyes against the glare; she could not be sure whether there were some objects scattered round the overturned boat; limp things, drifting along half under water.

She turned again to stare at the sleeping child. She seemed to be about two years old; thick, straight dark hair, tied on either side of her round forehead with white ribbons, framed her face. The lashes lying on her cheeks looked like miniature black fans. She had been crying.

"Well . . ." Jakoba said, "we'd best be getting on."

She stood up, and looked across the dune which she had just crossed towards another scanty thicket of pines, where a figure wearing a blue blouse and a black cap with a peak could just be made out, sitting well back in the shade, and smoking. Behind him, and out in the sunlight beyond the trees, there could be seen a bulky object the colour of well-polished copper; as Jakoba stared, it moved forward, revealing itself as a very large horse, standing with patiently drooping head. Jakoba waved, and the figure in the blue blouse responded by a gesture made with his pipe.

"Yes, better be going," she repeated.

Marie sat back on her heels, and, without taking her eyes off the child's sleeping face, said in a low voice: "All right . . . but what'll we do with . . .?" and she jerked her head at the shawl.

"Leave her here," was the swift, hard answer, then, as her sister lifted her head and looked at her, "Well, good heavens! what else do you expect me to do? Take her with us? Aren't we a big enough target as it is, with Klaartje the size he is, and ten kilometres to get to the farm and keeping off the roads all the way . . . where our own soldiers'll get us if the German planes don't . . . without you expecting me to . . ." she broke off, and turned away, wrapping both thick arms tightly in her shawl.

She stood in silence, with both feet in their black-painted sabots set wide apart, staring away across the distant dunes. A number of people were wandering about, little black figures against the white slopes, or lying in exhausted sleep, or crouching down swallowing a hasty meal in the shelter of the low scrub. People from Oostende and Zandeburghe on their way to the country, Jakoba thought. Oh, they're ready enough to run out to the country now the bombs are coming down on the towns . . . and what a state they're in down at Zandeburghe this morning! Her eyes swept along in the direction of that distant cluster of steep grey roofs, and the *digue* with its row of handsome white hotels . . . dashing in and out of the shops, milling around in their cars . . . serve them right. They'd all been much too rich for years. *Now* let them see what good their money did them.

Away to the east, looking across the flat land divided by lines of willow trees and poplars wearing the rich green of the early Flemish summer, there weren't any roads to be seen any more. There were only long, black lines; jerking and crawling along under the merciless light of the sun that showed up every movement to the prowling planes. That was the refugees; pouring in from Holland, from Luxembourg, from the villages and towns beyond the Albert Canal, all making for the open country and the sea.

Well, it didn't do any good to look at that. Jakoba turned away, and faced round and stared at her sister and the child. Marie was standing up with the black bundle in her arms, bending over it.

"I'm not going to leave her," she announced at once, without looking up. "You can go if you like. But I'm not going to leave her."

"Well, well, we'll take her down to the road and see if we can find anyone who's lost a child," said Jakoba impatiently, beginning to plunge down the slope of the dune. "But suppose her people come back to look for her? Wasn't there anyone about when you found her?"

"Not a soul. I looked for a long time. But there wasn't anybody. She was sitting playing with the sand, bless her, as damp as a mussel . . . her pretty coat's all sandy . . . you'll see . . ."

She was following her sister down the slope now, keeping her voice subdued so as not to awaken her burden.

"H'm . . ." Jakoba's eyes strayed towards the gap where showed the vanishing yellowish line of the sea. The black object was still just visible, drifting steadily out of sight, into the calm, glittering pathway cast by the sun, into the unknown. She kept her thoughts to herself. If she told Marie about that boat, Marie wouldn't be content until she'd got Klaas rowing out after it . . . and who wanted to sit in a rowing-boat on the open sea this morning? But the elder sister kept her eyes fixed on the sea until the rising curve of the dune hid it from sight; it was comforting, somehow, the sight of the sea; it didn't seem to be taking any more notice of *what was happening* than the countryside did.

"I expect her people sat down to rest and she wandered away," Marie was saying, "and then she tumbled into the waves . . ."

"That's about it," Jakoba said. "We'll hand her over to the police," she thought. But she also thought that there weren't any police nearer than Zandeburghe, and that was half a kilometre away, and she didn't want to go back there. Towns, especially on the coast, weren't healthy places just now. So that meant taking her back to Brugge (Bruges) with them. An much time anyone at Brugge would have to spare on a lost child. But perhaps Uncle Matthys at the farm would have her? He had promised to take Klaartje if . . . ever anything happened . . . and now it *had* happened and they were on their way to him, with the horse. Oh, they would find somewhere to leave the brat. But the main thing *now* was to get on; away from the open roads and the coast; into the shelter afforded by orchards and rows of willows and poplar-shaded lanes, which the Government hadn't bothered to patrol with soldiers turning you back from wherever you wanted to go. The brat could be disposed of later.

As they came to the top of the slope where the man and the horse waited, the former turned to look at them. His face appeared strange in this hot, shimmering air hovering above the dazzling sand, because his skin had a bluish tinge, seeming to belong rather to the frozen winters of the harsh Flemish coast than to this morning of May-heat. At once, his small, bitter-looking eyes of a light blue became fixed on the bundle in Marie's arms.

Jakoba did not waste time on saying where she had found the straying Marie (who had wandered off while all three were snatching a brief rest after the walk up from Zandeburghe), and she said no more about her sister's discovery than a brief "Marie's got herself a baby!", accompanied with a loud laugh, before she seized the bridle of the horse, and began pulling the great animal purposefully past the thicket, and down a rough path that led direct to the Oostende road below.

That road! Marie, feeling the weight of the still-sleeping child warm and heavy against her breast, almost shut her eyes with terror at the sight of it. And they'd got to go down into *that* . . . and across it . . . because the road to Sint Niklaas and Uncle Matthys' farm lay directly through the meadows on the other side. The hooting, and the shouting, and the crying of the children, and the shrill, frantic, continuous ringing of hundreds of bicycle-bells that rose up from it, curdled her stomach; it was the voice of sheer terror; she felt sick. And there was the smell from the packed, shaking, jerking cars; the stench of hot oil. She shut her eyes for a minute.

Jakoba's eyes were fixed on the road as she tramped steadily down the curving sandy path between the white hillocks where dark grass grew sparsely. It is like the Hell, she thought; once as a child she had been taken to see the paintings in the City picture gallery in Brugge, and she had been stirred to a kind of gloating wonder by the precisely-painted devils in one particular picture, with their smooth dry skins and their flat knobbed heads, who were dragging down the warm, weak bodies of the sinful into unimagined depths. Much of the horror of those depths, for Jakoba, had been that they would be *crowded*. Down there, the bodies would be packed close and tight and hot, and there would be no room to move, and there the wind from the sea would never blow. . . .

The road to Oostende was like that. The two lines of frantic refugees had met, and jammed; those who were trying to get out from the city, which had been bombed again that morning, becoming inextricably tangled with the masses of people and vehicles pouring coastwards from the invaded cities and villages in the east towards the sea and, perhaps, a boat and safety. The flat roofs of the cars shining through the choking dust were almost touching. The cyclists waited, supporting themselves against the side of a car, a cart, anything that was at hand, while they jerked . . . halted . . . jerked . . . halted, a couple of feet forward at a time. White faces looked through the windows of the cars. Some of them were asleep with their mouths open. Some were crying. "Holy God," Marie whispered, "Holy God."

"Wait till I say 'Come on', and then make a dash for it." Jakoba had stopped with the horse at the edge of the road, and was standing still, looking down at it, and Marie, clutching the child closer in her arms, came along to her.

Motionless as two scarecrows in their black, the sisters stood side by side looking down on the confusion and the uproar below, and behind them the man, with his pipe gripped in his teeth, stood impassively, occasionally saying something in a low, harsh voice to the horse as if to soothe him. The noise did not seem to trouble Klaartje, but something did, for once or twice he moved his great bulk in a backward direction and jerked his head. But at the sound of Klaas's voice he became quiet.

Gradually, as the sisters stood watching as if in a trance, while the wind fluttered the ends of their black shawls and the dust rising from the road settled on their shoulders, they forgot their purpose there, and their faces became, rather than terrified, brooding, and grave. They resembled, in their apparent detachment from the hurrying, desperate, jostling throng below, two statues of Flemish saints standing high amidst the wheeling daws and the changing lights and winds of some ancient cathedral; both flat, brown faces wore just that open-eyed and pitying expression, mingled with wonder; but Jakoba's, for all its calm, was also fierce.

One or two people glanced up at them, their anxious, wandering gaze caught and held for an instant by the two black figures standing high on the white dune against the sky, but, although Marie had uncovered the baby from her wrappings and both sisters half-hoped that someone might suddenly run out of the crowd and claim her, no-one paused in the agonized and headlong flight. The eyes glanced away again; they had already seen too much; if ever they reached safety, there would be more things that they had already seen than it would be possible to remember; on, let's get on, anywhere away from here, on to safety.

"Now!" Jakoba said suddenly, while some farm-carts crammed with children and chickens and bedding crawled across the road.

She plunged downwards and the others followed; for an instant they were choking and coughing in the dust and the stench of the petrol and Klaartje was snorting with terror and disgust; then they were across; they were on the other side; and walking in short, rutted grass that led towards a lane bordered by poplars. There were people going down it, but not many, and it led into a maze of orchards and slowly-moving dykes and meadows, away from the road running beside the coast, into the country.

No-one spoke to them. They tramped on, Marie holding the baby more loosely now, and Klaas walking with bent head and his pipe cold between his teeth, and Jakoba stalking by the head of Klaartje, who had to be restrained from pausing to tear up grass from the side of the lane, and gradually the clamour from the road died away. Once they passed a meadow from which the horizon could be seen, and Jakoba nodded towards the open vista; on the farthest visible limit of sight, three faint, dark

fingers pointed upwards into the tender mist of early summer:
the cathedral, the belfry and the church, the Three who have
watched for centuries over the city of Bruges. They seemed a
very long way off this afternoon, and the sisters would have to
get right up to them before they were at home, for they lived
actually in the shadow of Our Lady's spire.

The lane became narrower, and presently Jakoba, who was
stalking ahead leading the party, turned aside and crossed a
small bridge that spanned a slowly flowing dyke. It led into an
orchard; the near distance was veiled here by a light curtain of
green leaves and pink-and-white blossom supported on the
black trunks and went off into a confusion of sunny light and
dappling shadows, and there seemed to be no path. One or
two people who were tramping silently, bent under the possessions they carried, in the same direction, glanced after the
little party as it turned aside, but doubtfully; there was no
path; surely it was safer to keep to a path, it might lead to a
village or a farm where you could lie still and be quiet for an
hour: and no-one followed them across the bridge; soon they
were walking at the unhurried pace which they had kept up
ever since leaving the dune, in the green light cast by the
blossom and leaf-laden boughs, in a silence. The clamour from
the roads had died away. The air smelled sweet and the bees
droned peacefully in and out of the apple blossom.

"My feet . . . they feel red-hot," Marie murmured, but
neither of the others answered, and they kept unhurriedly but
purposefully on.

Whenever they could see between the trees there were the
big, calm meadows: so flat that it was possible for the eye to
travel unimpeded on: round the outhouses of sturdy, whitewashed farms, across dykes whose limpid, slow-moving course
was revealed by the double lines of old pollarded willows
bordering their banks, past rows of lofty poplars whose feather-
duster heads of light green nodded against the great sky, into
the gentle, rich, tranquil distance. Tranquil, but not idle.
Every foot of this land was at work; if not feeding the small
fields of greening corn and sprouting vegetables, then it was

pasturing the black-and-white cows, the clean pigs and few sheep and the big horses coloured, like Klaartje, a rich cinnamon, that grazed companionably together under the sapling trees or beside some small humpback bridge. Every visible object—soil, foliage, grazing animals, buildings—displayed a calm, ponderous, fruitful charm satisfying alike to the utilitarian compulsion in man and to the human eye. Flanders impressed the beholder as fertile and hard-working and content. To walk in this countryside was like strolling through the lines of a poem by Virgil bodied forth in facts.

And that was not going to save it from ravishment.

The wind must have changed; there were ominous sounds coming to them again; rumblings and jarrings of the earth beneath their feet and once, away to the east and very high up in the cloudless sky, a long falling scream followed by a tremendous explosion. Marie stared upwards while her work-worn brown fingers moved across her blouse in the sign of the cross. Oh, what was happening over there towards Holland, what kind of a thing was it that screamed high up in the air with a falling sound that died away?

She couldn't keep quiet any longer; she must talk to someone; if only someone had been here who *did* talk and *liked* to talk; not Jakoba, who didn't ever talk much and made it clear she didn't want to; Jakoba, who would suddenly throw her shawl across her head and stride out of the house and down the street to the nearest café, there to sit drinking and laughing with male neighbours until the place shut up for the night . . . and sometimes go off alone to walk along beside the sea in her best Sunday costume, coming back all over dried salt from the spray, and sandy, and tired out . . .

Marie reassured herself, by a glance inside the shawl, that the child was still sleeping. Then she began to think with resentment about Jakoba . . . for all those years she had been telling her, Marie Michiels, *what to do* and exactly *when* and *how to do it*. And it wasn't as if she was married, even if she *was* the eldest one. Marie was the married one. Even if it was twenty-five years ago since Jan had gone off, singing (so young, he had been; just twenty-three), to fight the Germans, with his rifle wreathed with flowers from their garden. Well, he hadn't come back, and she had never really known how he had been killed, though there had been the letter from the Government, and the money they gave her . . . and Jakoba was the spinster, the unmarried one, and she didn't treat her married sister with proper respect.

. . . Jakoba; she was undoubtedly a slavedriver, too, a tireless worker herself and determined that everybody else should be. Marie's friend at the Béguinage, Mevrouw Schotte, who took the money and the tickets from the tourists who came to see the place . . . Gabrielle Schotte had more than once said that if Marie hadn't sometimes stood up for herself when Jakoba was about, she would have become a slave, like one of those black people who waited on the *Wijzen uit Den Oosten* * in the pictures painted by the famous old ones. Of course one should try to please Our Lady, and to do the will of God always, but Gabrielle had let it be known that Sœur Teresa herself— and she wasn't the only one at the Béguinage by any means— thought that it mightn't always be altogether displeasing to Them up in Heaven if people sometimes stood up for themselves. . . .

Marie looked up anxiously. Jakoba was stopping. What was the matter?

"Listen," Jakoba said. They stood still, Marie holding the bundle tightly to her breast, and Klaas Impens cocking his head back to stare upwards, with his pipe clenched between his black stumps of teeth. Yes, Marie could hear it now; an increasing, throbbing, beating sound, of a peculiar intensity and majestic menace, that was beginning to fill the curved, whitening dome of the afternoon sky. But they could see nothing.

They stared at one another. Marie began to tremble. Jakoba was looking keenly about her. Plenty of trees, but what use were they? You wanted something underground; a cellar.

"Lie down, lie down, can't you?" she said quickly and harshly, and stretched herself under the nearest willow at her

* Wise Men From the East.

extended length. Marie followed, lying carefully on her side so that the child might not be crushed. But Klaas stood by the head of Klaartje, ready to soothe him if there came an explosion, and very slowly began to pack with fresh tobacco his short, blackened pipe. His face looked as bitter as a quince.

Nothing happened. Feeling angry and sick, they lay there until the sound, having swelled until it was tremendous and almost unendurable, died slowly away towards the north in the level reaches of the sky. Still they had seen nothing. But there were clouds up there now, hiding everything.

Klaas made an ugly sound of laughter that showed his teeth, and gave a jerk to Klaartje's rein. The sisters stood up, dusting their skirts, and the party went on.

Marie was walking now at Jakoba's side. The wish to talk to someone was coming back. After another glance at the child (she looked better now, less tired; she had some colour in her cheeks) she said:

"Do you think she's . . . what do you think she is? French?" looking down at the peaceful face, no wider than a hand's span, framed in the black folds of the shawl.

"Might be. She's very dark. Perhaps she's a *jodin*, one of them that *he's* making it so hot for over in Germany," nodding towards the east, with a rough laugh.

"And come all this way . . ." Marie murmured, playing for a moment with the idea, but then she said, no, she didn't think the baby was a tiny Jewess. "Though her people had money, that's certain," she went on; "look at her shoes," uncovering; "real white kid . . . and she's so clean and cared for . . . perhaps she had a *nanni*."

Jakoba nodded. In ordinary times . . . even so short a time as three weeks ago this awful summer . . . they were accustomed to seeing hundreds of just such rich-looking little monkeys as this one . . . perhaps a bit older, but not much . . . hopping or staggering in and out of the sea at Zandeburghe, in smart bathing-drawers or as naked as they were born. This was the kind of child that careful parents or *nannis* lifted into the blue-and-yellow cart which was drawn by Klaartje to make the

excursion à la mer, at one franc each a ride; down to the sea and
back, in the blue-and-yellow cart, with herself or Marie walking
at Klaartje's head.

Not any more, now. The long beach of grey sand was
empty. Empty . . . at the beginning of May. It was like a bad
dream. Not for twenty-five years (and they had had the three
bathing-huts and the blue-and-yellow cart at Zandeburghe for
nearly thirty years now, they and their parents before them) had
there been empty beaches at Zandeburghe in the beginning of
May. And so far it hadn't been such a bad season, in spite of
those rumours that had kept pouring on in from the east,
frightening the American tourists away, and all the men . . .
seven hundred thousand of them or some such number, so she'd
read . . . called up and waiting to see what those beasts were
going to do . . .

"What?" she said impatiently to Klaas, who was jerking his
thumb eastwards as he walked beside her holding the rein.
"Yes, I can hear it, I can hear it; it's the forts at Liège; I'm not
deaf."

"At Liège? A hundred and fifty kilometres away?" said
Marie incredulously, but neither answered, though Klaas
slowly turned on her a look as if she were one of the children
who had been frightened by his bloodshot eyes and his habit of
growling "Come on, that's enough, get down" during the
season. Those eyes lingered, now, on the face of the child
asleep in the shawl, and presently there came a mutter of sound
from his thin, purplish lips shaded with frosty stubble. He was
nodding his head as he walked, staring down at the glimpse of
stiff, but crumpled, white dress, and the dark hair tied with
white ribbons, and the hand like a minute white starfish that
had crept out of the black folds. A grin began to steal across
his face.

"What?" Marie glanced at him. She didn't like him, but
neither did she ever think about him. He had been attached
to their family almost since she could remember; a hanger-on,
a silent helper and a sharer in the good times and the bad, ever
since she and Jakoba had been big, raw-boned girls with red

cheeks and masses of thick hair, and he a lout in a blue blouse, with big shoulders and a sly, malicious grin, whom her father had paid a few francs now and then to help with the roughest jobs: sawing logs and dragging them back over the fens for the stove in winter, tending the horse that pulled the cart and the wheeled bathing-machines; the dirtiest and hardest work had always gone to Klaas.

"What's the matter?" she asked now. Even saying something to Klaas was better than walking in silence through this quiet, sunny place that made you almost forget the war—until you heard the far-off thundering of the forts of Liège.

He jerked the stem of his pipe towards her shawl.

"Met die manieren van een damen!"

"Ladified. Yes, bless her, like a lovely little doll, isn't she?" said Marie, looking down hungrily at the sleeping face while her flat, strong, ageing body yearned towards it.

She had borne a child once, but it had died of some illness during the first war. She hadn't even got that to remind her of her dead young husband. The body of this child whom she had found sitting in a heap of sand at the foot of the dune, playing with the silvery stuff, seemed to penetrate her own body with its soft warmth, and as she cradled it she was swearing to herself that, whatever Jakoba might say, she would never let it go. They must be fifteen kilometres, by now, from the place where they had found her, and between them and Zandeburghe there were hundreds—thousands—of refugees in cars and carts, and tramping the road with perambulators and boxes and bundles; everything was in an awful and terrifying confusion; turned upside down; people swarming out of their houses like mad things; strangers you'd never seen before in your life sitting by the side of the road and calling out to you with dead bodies lying across their knees—she wouldn't forget *that* in a hurry—was it likely that anyone, even if they were to go back now, this minute, would have time to look at a lost baby girl? Was it likely they'd ever find her people, even if they looked from now until midnight? They might be dead. Probably were. That raid when she and Jakoba had laid down under the trees wasn't the only one there'd been that morning; they'd seen some others of the beasts flying over towards the sea while they had still been a long way off from it, on their way out from Brugge . . . and then they had heard bombs dropping . . .

"*Met die manieren van een damen!*"

"Well, suppose she is? Nothing to laugh at, is it?" she said to Klaas in her surliest voice. Slowly the grin left his face and it changed. Shut in and glum now, with that bitter glare on it that she knew so well. Leave him alone and he'd get over it. But she looked at him for a moment rather curiously, before she nodded in reply to Jakoba's remark that they were drawing near to Matthys Maes' farm. Klaas had been sitting up there in the wood amongst the pines with Klaartje, waiting for them, for a long time before they got there. Had he seen anything?

"Nothing to laugh at, is there?" she said, rather threateningly this time. "What do *you* find so funny? Did you see anything while you were up there this morning?"

He did not even trouble to shake his head. With that bitter scowl on his face he tramped on, keeping his eyes fixed ahead on the whitewashed walls and green shutters of the village of Sint Niklaas, which they were now approaching; and she said no more, for she knew better than to try to get anything out of Klaas if he did not want to talk. If he knew that you wanted to get anything out, he would keep his mouth shut until the Last Day.

She glanced at Jakoba, who was saying something in a low tone. They could see through the lofty archway of whitewashed stone into the farmyard now, but although the chickens were pecking about as usual and the young tomato plants growing against the white brick looked healthy, this year, and it did you good just to see the place, *they* were there. The refugees. A handcart piled up with some neat bundles, from which protruded stiff, shining folds of brocade, stood near the front door, and on the bench beside it sat two nuns. One was drinking from a glass of water as though she could never stop, with her veiled head flung back in a position of gusto that seemed to deny her habit and betray her stout Flemish blood, and the other was sitting with her head in her hands, her face hidden. And all the doors and windows were open. That wasn't like Uncle Matthys, who was over seventy and who liked to feel that he *was* indoors, when once the work he did on the farm allowed him to get there. There were voices coming out through the door of the kitchen.

The party came to a halt in the middle of the yard, and Klaas pulled Klaartje up with a jerk, and then they all stood still. Marie gently eased her feet inside her sabots, wincing, and Klaartje whinnied and moved his head impatiently as he smelled the stables.

"What's that?" asked a child's voice behind her, and she turned round. Her uncle's grandson, Jooris Gheldeere, stood there, pointing at the bundle in her arms; he was a thin boy of six or so, with a long nose in a red face, blue eyes and hair as silver as the sand of the dunes.

"Hullo, Jooris, what are you doing here?" she asked, then, as he stared at her but did not reply, "That? That's my baby. I found her in the dunes this morning. Having a holiday, are you? Where's Grandpa?"

"We've come to get away from the bombs," he said. "He's in the kitchen. What's its name?" He was leaning forward and peering at the face in the shawl.

"I don't know what her name is . . . I must sit down or my feet'll fall off . . . here, you take her," and she gently shoved the bundle at him; then, as he accepted it without displaying either reluctance or alarm, she settled it, wrapping his short arms about it, and limped off to the bench, where she sank down beside the nuns with a great sigh of relief. She did not look at them and they did not look at her; the nun who had been drinking was staring around her with a dazed expression, and the other, the one who had been sitting with her face hidden in her hands, had shut her eyes and was telling her rosary. Presently she opened them, and turned on Jakoba a look that seemed to come from a very long way off; then they moved to the cart near the door. She murmured something to her companion, who got up heavily (she was a stout old woman) and went across to the cart and inspected the protruding folds of brocade, trying to hide them under their coverings. Jakoba had gone into the kitchen, and Klaas, at a word from her, was leading Klaartje across the yard to some buildings amidst the flowering apple trees where the stables were.

The air was quiet, and it smelled sweet. There were the usual noises that Marie always heard, without thinking about them, when the sisters came out to see Uncle Matthys, and because the farm, like the village of Sint Niklaas itself, stood in a wide, very slight depression in the flat countryside, this served to muffle the soft, distant rumblings from those forts. . . . Yes . . . Marie looked about her and sighed again, wiping her forehead with one of the small pieces of clean rag which she always carried about with her because they were useful in a dozen ways . . . there might almost not be any war, here; it might almost be an ordinary afternoon, one of the thousands that had passed during the last twenty-five years, with the light sloping down over the great plain running in from the sea and the meadows beginning to smell of evening.

But the voices coming from the kitchen weren't peaceful; they sounded loud yet tired, and a child was crying in there in a terrified, snorting way as if it couldn't stop. Bombs . . . the word was repeated over and over again. They must come from Aalst; they'd had bombs on them, there . . .

"Jooris?"

A young woman was standing at the kitchen door and looking anxiously out. When she saw the boy, sitting on the bench with the baby in his arms, she looked relieved, and, catching sight of Marie, she smiled. "Hullo, I didn't see you . . ." She came across the yard and stood in front of her. She had very fair hair, and a sweet, round, stupid face with placid thick lips and red-rimmed blue eyes. "Oh . . ." she let out a long sigh and lowered her head, "isn't it awful . . . I can't believe it now . . ."

"When did you come?"

"Yesterday. Father came over and fetched us. (By train, he had to come. The roads were terrible. But the train was full of soldiers, too.) *I* didn't know what to do. There was a bomb on the house across our street and our apartment was all blown in . . . all over dust . . . and the floor gave way. . . . Thank God we weren't at home, I'd gone shopping . . . and all my things ruined . . . I couldn't stop crying . . . 'Pierre', I kept on saying, 'Pierre' . . .''

"Is he still away?" Marie asked. She didn't want to hear about the bombs. Already, after only about three days of it, she had stopped finding this kind of story worth listening to and she wanted to hear a bit of good news.

"Oh yes. Oh Marie . . . he's in the fighting. Round Rotterdam.'' Mevrouw Gheldeere nodded, and the tears rushed back again. "He is. And they've been landing the Germans by air, you know, up there . . . dropping them out of the sky . . .'' She took out a handkerchief and wiped her eyes in a business-like way; then they strayed to her son. "Why, he's got a little girl there,'' she said, in a quite different voice; "whose is that? What a little love.''

Marie turned round. Jooris was stooping in the dust, carefully supporting the newly-awakened figure, so much smaller than himself in its crumpled white dress, and setting her on her feet. She was deeply flushed and her cheeks were creased with sleep but she did not seem inclined to cry; her very dark, very large, and long-shaped eyes were fixed unwaveringly upon his face.

"Why, she's awake!" Marie got up and went towards them. "We don't know *whose* she is. We found her this morning, up on the great dune outside Zandeburghe, sitting playing with the sand,'' she said, over her shoulder. "We reckon her people must have sat down to rest and she wandered off.'' She knelt down in front of the little girl. "Well. Had a good sleep, darling?'' she demanded. The eyes languidly left Jooris's face, and fixed themselves upon her own. The mouth was the colour, and rather the shape, of an apple-blossom bud.

There was a rush and a pounce, and an exclamation of "Bless her little heart!" and Mevrouw Gheldeere, sweeping past her elderly cousin, scooped the baby up into her arms.

"There, there . . .'' she crooned, pressing kisses over her face and into the warm, small neck. "Oh the love, did they lose her, then? oh the darling . . ." The caresses were accepted passively.

Marie, after this had been going on for some moments, turned to Jooris. "You going to stay here?" she demanded.

She did not like watching Janine Gheldeere going on in that way; it was all very well for her, she still had a chance, Pierre might come out of the war and then she might have another . . . only what was going to *become* of them all, with bombs, and the Germans getting nearer every hour? . . . Anyway, she didn't want to look. She stared severely at Jooris and repeated her question.

"We're going to stay here until Father comes back. Grandad says so. And I'm going to help him. I'm going to milk the cows. And I can ride on the van that takes the vegetables into Brugge."

"Do you remember . . . you came to see Auntie Jakoba and me? And you had the doll down from the attic?"

He nodded, staring at her grim brown face that looked as if were carved from wood; was, in fact, not unlike that of the Dutch plaything just mentioned, which wore a full, old-fashioned costume of faded threadbare velvet that had once, no doubt, been the covering of a chair, and was the only toy surviving from many quiet childhoods passed in the shelter of the Maes family. That had been a good day at the Aunties in Brugge. Although Auntie Marie hadn't let him step into the house until she had put down sheets of the *Brugsch Handelsblad* on the clean, tiled floor, she had let him eat as much as he wanted, and later on, when they all went to Zandeburghe, he and his father and mother and grandad, the aunties had let him ride on Klaartje. Suddenly Jooris did a handstand, with his silvery hair in the dust of the yard.

"Jooris!" his mother shouted threateningly, but absently, "mind what you're about." She was sitting down now, with the baby girl perched across her wide, warm knees, and deftly unfastening buttons and tapes. The two nuns were murmuring together over their cart, looking at the sky, and then in the direction of the road, as if they were meditating going on; no-one was taking any notice of them.

"Haven't you undressed her?" Janine Gheldeere called to Marie, who turned, and strolled over unconcernedly.

"Not properly, we haven't. There wasn't the time. And . . ." she checked herself. She didn't want Jakoba to overhear a remark about not knowing what they were going to do with the kid. Jakoba's loud voice could be heard in the kitchen, exclaiming over the stories told by them from Aalst: good thing if she'd forgotten their find, for the time being; the nearer home she, Marie, could get the little thing, the better it would be.

"There'll be a mark on her clothes, perhaps," Janine was saying.

She whisked off the stiff little full-skirted dress with its embroidery of white flowers, pausing to scan the work. "Hand-done," she pronounced. She laid it down carefully beside her on the bench; already her face was less strained, and her eyes looked calmer, "good, neat work, too," she added, not possessing *fairy-like* or *exquisite* in her small store of expressions.

The child gave a funny little shudder as the frock was drawn briskly across her face and head, then sat quietly, while the hand-made white petticoat and the tiny drawers (from a shop, these) were whisked off. Then Mevrouw Gheldeere gave a cry of triumph. Round the small, naked body was a narrow white ribbon, and attached to it a card on which was some writing. Together the fair head and the one with severely arranged iron-grey hair bent over it. But the words were hopelessly blurred; they had run into one another.

"She's been in the sea; I thought she had; she wasn't quite dry when we found her," Marie murmured, removing the very utilitarian spectacles which she had taken from her pocket. "Can you make out anything?"

Janine shook her head. "There's something . . ." she said doubtfully, "it looks like a big 'y' . . . and then a 'd'. Here . . ." She straightened herself and sat up, passing her hand across her warm forehead; she had forgotten the war. She looked across the courtyard. "My Sister," she called in a respectful voice, "could you help us, please? . . . we can't quite make this out."

The younger of the two nuns, a very pale creature with absolutely colourless lips and sandy eyebrows and lashes, came swiftly and lightly across to them. When she saw the baby, she did not smile, but looked at her steadily, and Marie saw her face become if possible even paler. Ah, thought the older woman, yes, it's going to be a bad time for the children, God have mercy on them all. But I'm sticking to this one. Here's *one* that's going to be safe, until they kill me.

The young Sister did not touch the child. She bent over her, with a guarded, shrouded expression, studying the card. In a minute she said:

"Ydette."

"Ydette?" Mevrouw Gheldeere repeated slowly.

"Ydette?" said Marie Michiels.

"Yes." The nun stood upright. "That's all I can make out. The rest of it must be her address. But it's hopeless. The card has been in the water." She glanced at the child and seemed about to ask a question, but she did not.

"I never heard that before," Mevrouw Gheldeere murmured. "Ydette . . ." The name, with its initial sound seeming to echo from the stateliness and ceremony of a former age, and its final syllable containing the prettiness and the simplicity of an idealized peasant world, sounded softly on the soft air of afternoon; soft, even when spoken in those peasant voices.

"I suppose it *is* her name," Marie said, in doubt. "It's outlandish, isn't it? Isn't it outlandish, don't you think so, my Sister?"—respectfully.

"Oh yes, it must be her name. It isn't a usual name, but I have heard it before. It's good Flemish," the nun said.

"Perhaps it's the name of a house," suggested Mevrouw Gheldeere.

"It's a girl's name," repeated the young nun. Then she smiled remotely at them and turned away, not aimlessly, but with an air of recollecting some duty to be done, and went across to her companion. The latter had wandered out of the yard and away to the left, where a meadow was separated from the road by a dyke, and was standing on the brink of the water with her black skirts amidst the yellow kingcups and grass, staring down the lane. Suddenly she called out, and began to run as fast as her size would permit across the little humpbacked bridge; then she turned back, waving and calling, and the other nun, tucking her hands into her sleeves, literally sprang away after her; gliding across the grass like some black mechanical toy, following her towards the road. Mevrouw Gheldeere and Marie stared towards it, and saw a big car bumping slowly forward over the ruts, overflowing with black habits and white coifs and pink faces and bundles and holy images and pictures and golden banners and long, blue, holy ribbons. All the faces were smiling, but some were crying too. The car stopped. There was a great exclaiming, and some of of them climbed out, and then back sped *their* nun, the young one with the sandy eyebrows, and darted at the cart in the corner and began to tug out the bundles. Two more were hurrying after her across the bridge. The air, quiet now, except for the distant thudding and thumping, was full of the low, orderly chatter of their voices. . . .

"What's up now?" demanded a strong old voice at the kitchen door, and Matthys Maes looked out, with Jakoba peering over his shoulder.

The old man looked gruff, as usual (he was never easy to get on with), and his eyes moved authoritatively about the yard as if to collect everything that had happened in his absence, and control it. But there was a kind of helplessness in them, and a bewilderment, beneath their habitual expression, and he was very pale; the red of his cheeks and the tan looked almost as if they were painted on, under the white stubble.

"You'd better bring *her* in and give her a drop of milk," he said, nodding towards Ydette, who, re-dressed and set down with a kiss, was making a slow progress round the yard with Jooris as protector against the chickens, from which she decidedly shrank. "You going to keep her?"

Marie almost held her breath.

"S'pose so, for the time being," said Jakoba indifferently; "it'll be more trouble, just now, getting anyone to take her off us than it'll be to keep her. Besides, Mother'll like to see her."

"She won't be the only one that's lost," said Mevrouw Maes; "at least one of them'll be taken care of."

"No . . . God knows. And she seems good," put in Marie casually.

"Jooris, you go indoors with Grandpa and he'll give you a drop of milk for Ydette. And then you can see she takes it," his mother said.

"And then we'll be off," said Jakoba.

"The sooner we're home the better," Marie added, thinking with fear of the ten kilometres to be got over before they were safe under the shadow of Our Lady's tower; "we'll go and have a look at Klaartje, and then we'll be off."

Jakoba was wondering whether at the last moment her uncle would suggest that Klaas should stay behind at the farm, to look after the horse.

It would be better there; that shed in the sandy field on the outskirts of Zandeburghe, where he had been living for the last ten years, wasn't going to be a safe place from now on. Come to that, nowhere was going to be. But the farm would be safer than anywhere near the sea, and there would be food there . . . if there was food anywhere. A kind of black panic rushed up inside her, but she drove it down with anger, and as the good hot rage rushed through her veins she felt better; she absorbed it, as if it were nourishing food.

They went back into the kitchen, after they had stared at the car laden with the nuns driving slowly away between the apple trees, and stayed just long enough to eat a bit of bread and drink some coffee; the afternoon sunlight shone in between the white curtains and the red geranium blossoms at the window, and the tiled floor was so gratefully cool to the sisters' feet (they had both slipped off their sabots as they sat at the long table) that Jakoba's eyelids began to droop, shutting out the long faces and the dishevelled, hastily-dressed figures of them from Aalst, sitting all round the room holding their coffee-bowls as if they could never let them go . . . where would *they* be tonight? She didn't know and she didn't care; perhaps, if they all went off somewhere, Matthys would ask Klaas to stay. After all, he wasn't like an old man, he could still do a day's work with anyone.

Both sisters knew that they should be moving, yet they lingered. The child who had been sobbing had dropped asleep at last, the loud, tired, excited voices of the family from Aalst spoke less and less frequently; an exhausted silence crept into the low, sunny room where the faint rumbling and shaking of the air outside was muffled by the thick old walls that had been built before Waterloo was fought; they were accustomed, these walls, to absorbing the sound of distant gunfire . . .

"The van'll come as usual tomorrow, then." Her uncle's voice awoke Jakoba; her eyelids flew open and she sat up.

"Very well, Uncle." She began to count off items on her fingers. "Fifty cabbages, twenty-five bunches of spring onions, thirty pounds of peas, four bunches of Sweet Williams . . ."

"Flowers? Who's going to want them, with all this going on?" demanded Marie, looking up from feeding Ydette, who was sitting on her knee, with fragments of bread and butter.

"Madame van Roeslaere, for one," said Jakoba, with her laugh.

"*They* won't be here when we get back; Sophie said they were going off this afternoon," said Marie.

"The chimneys down at the hothouses haven't been smoking since before yesterday," said Matthys Maes, "and I saw young Lombaers' car go by this morning, full up. They've gone off, like all the rest."

"Is old Lombaers going?" Jakoba asked.

"I didn't see him. I don't expect so. He's like me—too old a dog to learn new tricks," and for a moment his broad wrinkled face with the wide chin covered in white stubble showed a spasm of rage; it shook him, sending the blood racing protestingly through his narrowing arteries. "He'll want to keep an eye on the hothouses," he ended.

He did not add, *so far as he can*, for what was the use? What

c

was the use—when all of them here who were over fifty could remember the Uhlans, and this new kind was said to be worse; much worse? And in the last one there hadn't been the bombs.

He got heavily to his feet. He was glad, now, that his wife had died a year ago.

"We'll take a look at that horse of yours," he said, and they followed him out of the room.

Jooris had lifted up Ydette and was making quite a good effort at carrying her; he staggered a little from time to time, but he had shown her how to clasp her arms around his neck, so that she should contribute to her own safety, and he was enjoying the experience; he liked the clean smell of her hair and skin and dress; and from time to time, as they went across the yard towards the stables, he kissed her and blew into her neck, causing her to give a silent, writhing movement accompanied by an equally silent smile as she stared down at the chickens. Marie glanced back at them once or twice and shook her head at him: why, she did not quite know, but it never did any harm to warn boys.

They found Karel, who worked for Matthys Maes, milking the six cows in the warm, dark, reeking stable, while Klaas sat on a heap of straw silently wiping the last crust of what had been nearly half a loaf round a bowl that had held coffee. Trust him; he can look after himself, thought Jakoba, when she saw that her supposition (it had been too slight to be called a fear) that he might go unrefreshed had been groundless. He had simply edged into the kitchen amidst the uproar and confusion, and helped himself. Well, he had had to; Uncle Matthys never had been one to do anything for Klaas. Didn't think much of him. And she hadn't been going to ask for a bit of something for him. Catch her.

Klaas looked up as they came in, and his frosty blue eyes saw everything that was going on. But he didn't speak, and Matthys Maes didn't look at him. Klaartje was in the far corner of the long, whitewashed shed, with the two horses belonging to the farm. He was a much finer animal than either of them, standing above them by a good two hands, and the curve of his long, banana-shaped nose seemed to show that he knew it. He acknowledged the words of Jakoba and Marie with an indulgent movement of his head and a droop of his lashes.

"He's all right," Marie pronounced, running her hand over the warm flank covered in skin like a breadth of cinnamon satin.

"It would take more than a walk from Zandeburghe to upset *him*," said Matthys Maes dryly; so he should be all right, with nothing to do all day but pull a cartful of children down to the waves and back, wasting the good money belonging to their parents. His eyes strayed to the figure of Klaas, dressed almost in rags, sitting hunched up amidst the straw. *He* wasn't going to stay here. He, Matthys, had said that he would have the horse if anything were to happen, and he would keep his word to his brother's daughters, but that Klaas, no . . . let the blue, dried-up little monkey go back to that bit of land he'd been squatting on for the last ten years outside Zandeburghe, and do for himself there. There would be plenty of better use for what food the Germans would leave on the farm.

They stayed for a few minutes, looking at the animals with the unsentimental eyes of people accustomed to work them for profit; Jooris, who would have liked to pat Klaartje and talk to him, remaining near the open door with Ydette in his arms because she had shrunk back from the dark entry and the big, stamping shapes in the dimness. He was entertaining her by making faces. Here, in the afternoon hush, they could all hear the hooting of the cars jammed inextricably in one long, creeping line with vans and carts and pedestrians on the road half a mile away, and sometimes a hoarse distant shout. There did not seem to be much to say.

At last Matthys Maes said to Jakoba, "You'd better go. You want to be home by dark," and they all made a move towards the door.

When they were standing at the edge of the yard, they hung about for a moment, looking at one another. Klaas was slouching away already; Jakoba knew that nothing would be said about his staying, now. Mevrouw Gheldeere had taken Ydette from Jooris and was kissing her, and crying. "Good-bye, good luck," Marie suddenly shouted after the disappearing figure of Klaas, and he just looked back over his shoulder and made a movement—it was hardly a wave, it was a mere sketch of a gesture—with the hand that held his pipe. They saw his blue blouse moving slowly in and out of the trunks of the apple trees for a few minutes, then they couldn't see him any more.

"Well"—Marie was still staring after him, reluctant to move, wanting to prolong the last few seconds while they were still in this place of refuge—"God knows if we'll ever see *him* again . . ."

"He'll be all right; that sort always is," her uncle pronounced; "he's managed to do not too badly for himself all these years—" (He, too, didn't want to see them go, and yet, the fewer people there were at the farm the easier it would be; he could start hiding things, and getting ready . . . Christ, ready for *what*? How could you know? At any instant there might be a bomb. . . . what was the good of . . .) "He'll manage," he went on. "I suppose he gets a bit out of you for grazing the horse and looking after it, and there's his vegetable patch—not bad, for a squatter." *And a dirty, surly, sly sort at that,* he finished inwardly.

"He pays his rent," said Jakoba. "The land belongs to Mjinheer—can't think of the name for the minute—lives at Doorwaden. Klaas sends the money off regular every month." Her pale eyes were glinting like the winter sea as she looked straight into her uncle's. What right had he? He'd already been an elderly man when she and Klaas were young—what did he know about it?

His face did not change, and when they had stared at one another for a few seconds in silence, she added roughly, "We'll be getting along, then," and turned away. She nodded to Mevrouw Gheldeere, while Marie muttered something about Pierre coming back safe and lifted Ydette from her arms.

"We'll expect the van as usual tomorrow, then, Uncle," Marie said "all right, kiss her if you want to . . . there, that's enough," as Jooris stood on tiptoe and imprinted several smackers on Ydette's face, held obediently forward, but with the eyes gazing indifferently anywhere but at him, "she's used to being kissed, you can see that; she knows what to do." Her voice, fainter-sounding and more elderly than her sister's, died off into the quiet. In another moment they were on their way.

They looked back when they got to the edge of the orchard. The three were still standing there, looking at them; the plump young woman in white blouse and black skirt, the long, thin boy with silver-fair hair in the shabby clothes which were all that his mother had been able to find in the ruins of the flat, the old man in his black peaked cap and rough working dress. He slowly lifted a hand and waved, and Jooris frantically flapped both hands.

Soon the sisters were tramping through the afternoon quiet of the orchard, under the motionless boughs, alone. You could hear the gunfire louder here, and there was cheering coming from the hidden road. British troops, perhaps. They were pouring into the country across the frontier, the wireless said. Perhaps they might save everybody, yet. But it was no use thinking . . . get on. Get home. Then there'd be something to do to keep your mind off it.

"Let's go in and see old Lombaers, shall we?" Marie suggested presently; "we have to pass there anyway."

"What for?"

"Well"—Marie sought for a reason that should successfully conceal her real one, which was to have a word with someone else beside her tall, rough, silently-striding sister—"he'll tell us if them at the big house have run off. If they have, there's one of my best flower customers gone."

Jakoba shrugged her shoulders, implying that none of that was going to matter anyway, and soon the chimneys which in ordinary times supplied heat for Mijnheer van Roeslaere's greenhouses appeared through the trees, standing up black and smokeless amidst the whitewashed, sloping glass roofs. At the end of a neatly kept ride stood the villa which he had had built for the Lombaers family, managers and overseers to the business since the 'eighties.

Hubert van Roeslaere's grandfather had in those days indulged in a fascinating hobby which had developed by the turn of the century into a profitable business. Camellias, orchids, stephanotis and other exotics grown by the company, which remained a family affair, found their way to corsages, bouquets and festal tables all over Europe and the Americas. Much of the plant was new, for substantial additions to the original buildings had been made by the present owner in the mid 'twenties, when he had inherited from his father; the twelve acres or so which it covered were surrounded by a low brick wall above which could be seen the corrugated-iron roof of the long shed where the flowers were packed for export, mostly by women workers from Bruges and Doorwaden and the villages round about. The place stood conveniently close to the direct railway line to Brussels and the flowershops and market of Ghent, and behind it ran the great Astrid Canal.

"Doesn't seem to be a soul about," remarked Marie, as they approached the white gate set in the wall; "seems dead, everywhere."

"Probably gone off."

"Like everyone else."

"Crazy fools . . . dashing off like that . . ."

They were talking to keep their spirits up, for there was something singularly depressing about the smokeless chimneys, the silence and the quiet sunlight lying over the deserted path leading up to the shuttered windows of the porter's lodge. It was not like the feeling of Sunday afternoon, either. It was a threatening hush, and even their sturdy nerves responded to its faint, eerie pressure.

"What do you want?"

Both started as the grudging, unalarmed voice spoke behind them. Old Lombaers had come up undetected and was standing there, with the keys of the place swinging in his hand. "Jakoba Maes and Marie Michiels," he went on, rather as if reading from imaginary papers of identity; "come down to see your uncle, I suppose."

He was a spare, dried-up, very neat man of seventy or so with the severe eye and straight shoulders of the former regular soldier. That eye now moved to Ydette, who had been set down by Marie at her side and was standing spiritlessly looking at nothing in particular, and it remained there. When they had exchanged a few comments on the late afternoon news and Marie had explained why they had come out from Brugge, and had satisfied his curiosity about Klaas Impens and Klaartje and the Gheldeeres and the bombs on Aalst (they had known him for forty years as a man who liked to hear all the gossip), he pointed at Ydette.

"Who's that? Where did she come from?" and then, when he had been told rather briefly by Marie, "What about a drink of milk for her?"

"Milk!" said Jakoba, not gratefully. What was there about this dwarf in a white frock that made everybody so eager to give her milk? Milk costs money to produce, and if you were sharp enough you could get it back again, with a profit. People should think twice before they threw milk about. "Water will do, if you must give her something," she said.

"She can have milk; I've got some; Moritz and the girl and the child went off this morning," the old man said, beginning to unlock the gate. "I don't drink the stuff, I like my coffee black."

"We haven't the time," said Jakoba curtly. She had shaken off her shawl impatiently and her head, with the sandy, greying hair in a large knot, held with pins worn steely and smooth by time, was bare. She didn't thank him; throwing milk about...

"It's not far, up to mine. You come along, and I'll . . ."

The explosion was tremendous; it stopped him in midsentence and sent the colour flying from the women's faces.

"God in Heaven," Jakoba said, moving at last, "where was that?"

It had sounded so near; it couldn't be more than three or four miles away. Marie had begun to cry. Ydette was staring up at her contorted face.

"Oh, you don't want to take any notice of that; if it had got *you*, you wouldn't have heard it," the old soldier said. But he

had moved behind the gate, and was locking it after him.
"Don't ever forget that; if you can hear it, the odds are that it
won't hurt you."

He paused, not irresolutely; he was seeking about for other
comforting superstitions, collected during fifty years of soldier-
ing in theory and in fact and stored away in a mind as neatly
arranged as some quartermaster's ideal domain. But somehow
the words would not come pat, for there was something about
this war that was different; it was only beginning; he could
only faintly smell the difference in the air; but it was there.

"So don't you forget," he ended briskly; "and now you'd best
be getting home. That's the best place for the women and the
little things just now." He shook the gate to test that it was
locked, and turned away. Apparently he had forgotten about
the milk.

"Is that what Mijnheer van Roeslaere's doing?" Marie
called after him; the explosion had jarred the very earth on
which she stood, but she was still capable of feeling curiosity.

"What?" Old Lombaers' hand was curved round his ear.

"Mijnheer van Roeslaere. Staying at home."

"No, no. They're gone. Gone off to England. They were
going this morning," coming back a little way along the path.

"And the little boy, Mijnheer Adriaan?" Marie asked, wiping her eyes with one of her pieces of clean rag.

"Of course, and the Mevrouw. All of them. *He* was out here
late last night, giving me the orders."

The orders . . . he talked as if he was still in the Army.

"Good night," she called, turning away, and Jakoba echoed
her, but he had already moved off down the path and out of
earshot. They watched him for a moment; look at him, he
was marching like a sentry; anyone would think he was on
guard.

So Sophie had been right, Marie was thinking as they walked
quickly on: the van Roeslaeres had gone . . . the little boy too
. . . it would be strange not to see him coming out of the door of
the big house, with his *nanni* carrying the water-wings and spade
and pail, on their way to the sands; fat legs in those short blue

linen pants, smart striped blouses, black hair; a great fat boy
for six years old, and spoiled already . . . gone to England. She
shifted Ydette wearily in her arms; the child seemed ready to go
to sleep again; just as well, for there was another good two
hours' walking before they were home. Marie's feet burned and
throbbed as if they were on fire. Up and down, up and down
they went in their sabots, but thank God the city was drawing
nearer at last, and the Three were so much closer that she could
almost see their windows. Soon she would hear Our Lady's bell,
the sound that was like a holy, high, comforting voice, and she
would be gladder to hear it than she had ever been in her life,
for now the roads were becoming worse.

They had left the meadows behind and were getting into the
suburbs of new houses outside the city, making their way
through the groups standing about anxiously talking, and the
pale men hurrying by with suitcases and mattresses and saucepans, the laden cars standing with throbbing engines outside
houses with their front doors open, the silent, staring children.
Last sunlight touched the neat villas, where the snowdrop and
the iris were pictured in long panels of glazed tiles on the walls;
it was all clean and tidy as usual; there wasn't a dirty curtain in
sight—and then suddenly there would be a great pile of bedding
lying on the pavement, or a ham—it was like a bad dream. Oh,
to be home, with the door shut and slippers on, and the potatoes
frying for supper, and the bell tolling, high up in the last light
of the day, from Our Lady's tower!

They were approaching the Ezelpoort, one of the old gate-
ways which lead across the medieval ramparts and moat which
encircle the city, when they were hailed by a voice that soared
easily above the confused uproar of throbbing engines and
human clamour.

"Hullo!" A hand almost as large as the ham they had seen
in the road, and rather the same raw pink in colour, descended,
not lightly, upon Marie's shoulder.

"Hullo," said Marie, rather glumly. "I thought *you'd* gone
back to Blaankenburghe."

"Not me . . . haven't you heard? Parachutists tried to come

down there—course, they couldn't—but I was turned back on the road—I went by bike . . . 'Sides, it's too near the sea.''

Sophie Bouckaerts, kitchenmaid to the van Roeslaere family at the big house, did not enlarge on the disadvantages attendant upon this situation, but in the mind's eye of the fifteen or so people within range of her voice, a submarine silently surfaced.

"No, I'm staying with Auntie; be company for her,'' she went on. "Where've you been, then, and whose is the kid?'' looking with good-natured curiosity at the sleeping face cradled in the shawl.

"Aren't you staying in the house?'' Marie wished they had not met her; there was enough row and fuss and noise going on, without having to listen to Sophie's voice. "Oh, I found her on the big dune outside Zandeburghe this morning . . .''

"Not me. Marieke is. At Zandeburghe? Didn't you go to your uncle's, then? You said you were going along to your uncle's, to take the horse to him. Didn't you go?''

"Yes, we *did*, but we went to Zandeburghe *first*, to see Klaas, and see that the bathing-huts got up all right to his bit of field, and *then* we went on . . .'' Marie swallowed and didn't trouble to keep the goaded note out of her voice. She was so tired. She held Ydette a little closer as she tramped doggedly on through the milling, pushing, shouting crowd; Sophie's great pink face was as fresh as a shrimp's . . . came of being only twenty-five . . . when you were getting on for sixty it was a very different thing.

"Found her? Just fancy! What a little love, isn't she? Wonder who she belongs to? What's her name?'' Sophie was striding alongside them, her big body in a too-short dress of flowery cotton easily bumping aside those who got in her way. Her hair was pulled back into a tight knot like Jakoba's, but it was braided as well, and light brown strands blew around her low forehead in the evening breeze.

"Well, I suppose bang goes my chance of a kid of my own next year,'' she shouted, not waiting for Marie's answer, "André's gone off, the Lord only knows where; saw him Sunday for the last leave and he said *then* that all this might come off, they was all saying so in his lot, he said. . . . Oh, we had such a cry . . . both of us, he was as bad as me . . . and hugging—he nearly cracked my ribs. But I gave as good as I got." Her protuberant eyes, the yellowish-green of the Flemish sea, filled up, and she gave a great snort, "and of course I haven't heard a word since . . . and them at the big house have gone, too," she ended, scrubbing away the tears.

Marie nodded her head slightly. "Old Lombaers said they were going."

"Yes. About eleven this morning. In the car. We was all out in the *plaats* to see them go. Marieke was that upset. But she wouldn't go. Wouldn't leave her sister and the place."

"She's never staying on in that great barn all alone?"

"She is, though. (It isn't so big, not when you're used to it.) Tell you what, you come along some time when she's gone to her sister's at Enghien, and I'll show you the china ladies with the lace petticoats. I'll show *her*." She lifted the shawl aside with a big, gentle hand and looked down at the small, white, composed face. "Little love, isn't she?" she said again. "You going to keep her?"

"Don't know." The answer came in a hard, indifferent tone. Marie was fiercely pleased that she had got Ydette almost to their own front door without Jakoba suddenly deciding to hand her over to the police, and she did not want to remind her sister, stalking ahead, that the child was still with them.

Sophie said suddenly, "Let me have her a minute," and before she could protest, lifted Ydette from her arms. "There . . ." she said, settling her against the full swell of her breast, and looking down at her, "Little dear; lucky she's asleep."

"Don't you wake her up," Marie said dourly. She was relieved to have her arms free for a moment (how they ached, as she stretched them wearily) but she didn't want anyone else to carry Ydette.

The traffic and the crowds were becoming less, and, as they left the Ezel Straat behind and made their way along the narrow streets paved with small round cobblestones which go winding round and around the belfry, the church, and the cathedral into the medieval heart of the city, they felt the fresh, strong breeze which had blown along the ramparts with almost a breath of the sea, falter, fail, and die gradually away. The air became still. Twilight was falling. The clamour and murmur from the roads came muffled by distance, and although there were lights burning in the window of every house they passed, and signs and sounds showing that the occupants were busy, the ancient streets were empty. No-one was sitting on kitchen chairs outside the front doors this evening; that faint, faraway, terrible thundering towards the north-east had driven people indoors. The whole city was in the grip of silent terror; the warm, still, darkening air of the silent lanes seemed heavy with it.

Down the Sint Jacob Straat and through Geldmunt and Zilver Straats they went, and when they came to the Sint Salvator Kirk and the beginning of Heilige Geest Straat, Sophie thrust Ydette back at Marie and announced that she must be off, auntie would be expecting her. In spite of the unnatural hush brooding over everything, their farewells were casual; somehow, Marie and Jakoba—who now turned back impatiently to nod to Sophie for the first time—did not believe that they would never see her again . . . Marieke, the cook at the big house, wouldn't want much more than a bit of cabbage tomorrow, but Sophie, who was going to help with the clearing-up there, would most likely be across to buy it.

The *charcuterie* kept by Sophie's aunt, Mevrouw Bouckaerts, was still open, with all its lights burning, but the trays and porcelain shelves gleamed white and spotless and empty.

"Been and bought up everything," said Marie, watching Sophie cross the road. Good Lord, what a great lump, the figure of a woman of forty. Not that she was fat. You couldn't say that Sophie Bouckaerts was exactly fat; no-one ever did say it.

"Mother'll be sold out, too."

"Sure to be. And it'll be the same tomorrow."

Then they were both silent. Tomorrow?

Deeper into the shadows they walked, over the cobbles damp

with falling dew, leaving the shops and the cafés behind. A few ancient lamps were alight now, throwing their faint glow on some little statue of Our Lady standing in her niche high on a wall or at the corner where two winding alleys met, smiling her mild, gentle smile above her tribute of primroses or wall-flowers or daffodils glimmering in their paleness against the rough brown surface of the bricks. Higher up, the stepped gables were nearly black against the blue, darkening, transparent sky.

"Ah . . ." almost whispered Marie, on a satisfied note: the blessed sound; Our Lady's bell.

It was tolling so high, in the last of the fading day, that it seemed to come from a long way off, although in fact the church was now very near, and as always, since she had first become aware of it almost as she lay in her cradle in the little, dark, clean house in the church's shadow, it sounded to Marie like a holy, comforting voice: deep, and touched by the immense height at which the bell clanged and swung, with unearthliness. The lonely and authoritative sound seemed to her to come down from heaven: it had always seemed to; and tonight it comforted her as only once before—on that evening in the summer of 1914, when her young husband had gone off to fight the enemy which, for the second time in her life, was coming down on her city. She was afraid, now, as she had not been that other time when she was young, but she was also comforted, as she had not been in those far-off days, by the familiar sights and sounds all about her; even a harmless breath of stagnant water drifting up from the canal, their own canal, that ran along the back of their house at the end of their bit of garden, assured her that they were nearly there. The reflection of dim lamp and fading sky in dark, unmoving water, the small, square *plaats* of old houses with stepped roofs and bands of white stone round door and window that glimmered softly through the twilight, the cobblestones drifted over with the grey sea-sand on which the foundations of Bruges are built—even the discomfort these gave to her tired and burning feet—all spoke to her of home.

How the child slept. It was a mercy that so far Jakoba hadn't said anything about her.

And there, thank God, was the shop; not bombed, looking just as it had when they left it at dawn, and the light was on (them who saw to the black-out would be after Mother, it was getting near the time for all that fuss to start) and there was Mother herself, sitting safe and sound as if she hadn't moved since morning.

The vegetable shop was an archway, deep rather than shallow, and roofed by one of those ancient walls of brick, found throughout Bruges, which are probably part of some former nobleman's or prosperous merchant's dwelling, and have in course of centuries become through rebuilding and incorporation part of the ordinary houses of the city. These particular six hundred dark-red bricks, weathered and flaked by time, were attached to the little house—in spite of its smallness it was unmistakably a house and not a cottage—in the Sintkatelijnstraat which had belonged to the Maes family for nearly a hundred years, and through the left wall of the archway a stout door, with comely iron lock and bandings that could not have been less than four centuries old, led directly into Mevrouw Maes' kitchen.

The lamp was a single electric light, dim both from motives of economy and from obedience to recent instructions from the Government, and by its light the sisters could see that their mother, sitting directly beneath its weak glow, was surrounded by denuded baskets woven of withies, bare shelves and empty boxes that had held the day's supply of fruit; there was not even a cabbage leaf on the floor; not a sellable thing was left; save for her own stout, small shape, and the stand on which her lace-making pillow was supported, the shop was cleared out. Her hands were clasped across the black apron covering the small mound of her stomach and she was staring down at the strip of worn carpet on the stone floor at her feet.

"Sold out," said Marie, on a satisfied note.

Jakoba nodded. She wasn't fool enough to be glad about that; tomorrow, money might be worth exactly nothing. It had been, before.

When they got nearer they saw that Mother was crying. It was disturbing; she wasn't one of the crying sort; and they looked at each other in silent dismay, two tall, strong, ageing women, feeling for the moment as if they were awkward girls again.

The faint thundering in the air overhead seemed to fill the silent, twilit little *plaats*, pressing down into it, crushing it, and there sat Mother, with bent head, crying without a sound. They didn't know what to do.

Suddenly Ydette, perhaps aroused by the cessation of movement, stirred in Marie's arms and began to cry too. Up came Mevrouw Maes' head at once, and she demanded:

"What's that?" and pointed.

"That's Marie's baby; she found her on the big dune," and relief made Jakoba's voice even deeper and more carrying than usual, so that the few last neighbours who were about, hurrying dejectedly homeward with food bought in terror and at monstrous prices, had to exchange faint smiles; whoever else might have run away, the Maes sisters hadn't, and somehow that was comforting.

Mevrouw Maes got up briskly, and at once a detailed inspection was carried out on the now howling Ydette; she was turned almost upside down for laundry-marks and birthmarks and hypothetical flea-bites, the decorations on her dress were held up to a pair of black eyes that could still see as clearly to embroider the traditional design of a lily in its pot on a background of net lace as they had for nearly seventy years and her little head was vigorously searched—"yes, she's clean enough" —"But good Lord, Mother, she's as clean all over as a new loaf," from Marie—while throughout the business the old woman asked questions; not the idle and wonder-feeding questions of the pop-eyed gossip, but clear, sensible ones which you had to have your wits about you to answer.

Unlike her daughters, Mevrouw Maes was round and plump, and in her sallow face a girl was imprisoned; a girl who sometimes darted out a glance through the prison bars of weariness and the seventy-odd years of hard toil that shut her in; she was not a particularly pretty girl, nor even a sweet-seeming one; she was only irrepressibly alive, and young. A necklace of heavy silver links was worn round a neck so short as to be a mere memory, and higher up a pair of embossed silver ear-studs occasionally threw back a demure gleam at the light.

"We'll put her into your bed, Marie," the old woman announced, when the inspection was concluded; Ydette, crying no longer, was now sitting upright, encircled by a pair of short, stout arms which already, after only seven minutes' resumption of an almost forgotten posture, held her less awkwardly.

"Yes, Mother." Why, Marie wondered, had she troubled herself about what Jakoba would do with Ydette? She ought to have remembered that her mother liked children; didn't she listen with interest to stories about the more troublesome ones who rode in the cart? Marie didn't even trouble to ask if Ydette was to stay, now. She knew that she would.

"Then I'm going down to Our Lady's, later," Mevrouw Maes went on.

She set Ydette gently but firmly down, and kept an arm around her, so that she stood close against her knee, and Ydette was quiet, looking up steadily at the light burning high in the brown curve of the rough brick roof. "What do you think?" Mevrouw Maes went on; "an American tourist took my photo."

"A photo? At such a time? But they're all mad, tourists," Jakoba said resignedly; she was stacking the fragile, empty containers into neat piles, and thrusting boxes away under the trestle counter, while Marie had gone through into the kitchen, keeping the door between it and the shop open so that she could hear what was being said while she prepared supper.

"Well, perhaps she wasn't a tourist," Mevrouw Maes shrugged. "She was young, and she had a painted face and"—with a swift movement she indicated the swell of a too-noticeable bosom—"all showing. The photo was for an American newspaper, she said."

"With coloured pictures," called Marie, from the kitchen.

"Yes, I daresay . . . so she made me sit on my stool here and sell a cabbage to Mevrouw Kamiel, and then she made all the others stand round and look at the vegetables; she wouldn't tell us when she was taking the picture and we couldn't see; it was a very little camera. She stood and looked at us all, and she told us to think about the war."

Marie came to the door and stared; Jakoba stopped sweeping, with her broom suspended, and stared too.

"To think about the war?" she repeated in a dull voice; "why was that?"

"I don't know." Mevrouw Maes shrugged again. Then she bent and said to Ydette, in a confidential undertone more soothing to a child than the slightly disturbing urgency of a whisper, "You watch, they're putting the boxes to bed: look, that's their bed, under there. And soon you're going to bed too, all nice and cosy and warm, with a drink of milk." She paused, studying the little face lifted to her own, "Does she understand French?" she asked.

"Don't know. I don't think she can talk at all. Marie thought she said 'merci' when we told her to say thank-you when she had the milk at uncle's, but *I* didn't hear it. . . . We've asked her what her name is in Flemish and French and German and Italian and Swedish, and Marie said, 'Whadda *you* call yourself?', in English, like we say to the American children," (the sisters had picked up the phrase in almost every European language during the more than a quarter of a century that they had been coaxing shy or rebellious or reluctant customers in and out of the blue-and-yellow cart), "but she doesn't seem to know."

"She might be Spanish," Madame Maes said consideringly.

"So she might be Walloon. Might be anything." Jakoba yawned, throwing a last keen glance round the tidied shop.

"Ydette . . ." said the old woman in the same confidential and calming tone, bending closer to the small, still, uplifted face, "Ydette?"

Suddenly the mouth that was like a bud of apple-blossom parted, showing minute points that really were more like the pearls of the old poet's rhyme, than anything else, and Ydette

D

smiled. "*Maatje*," * she said, so softly that Mevrouw Maes was not sure she had heard the word.

"What, darling?" She bent closer.

The dark eyes looked at her, solemnly now. "*Maatje?*"

"You come to me," the old woman said, and lifted her up into her arms.

She held her tightly, while her eyes wandered beyond the faint glow of light thrown by the lamp on the cobblestones, over to the big house across the *plaats*. No light was shining there. Marieke must have put up the blackout curtains . . . all by herself, in that great place. The branches of the tall chestnut tree growing outside threw soft clear shadows against the row of white stone shields, carved with birds and beasts and ancient letters, ranged along the wall above the front door. It all looked dim and shut away and sad in the gathering darkness.

That morning, Madame van Roeslaere had come across to say 'good-bye'. It had been a gracious act; Mevrouw Maes, resting comfortably enough between the twin pillars of the Roman Catholic church and a thousand-year-old feudal instinct, had been gratified by it. All that Madame van Roeslaere had said, in her soft, quick, sensible-sounding voice, as she stood there dressed in the coat and skirt made from cloth which came, Sophie said, from Scotland, and her small cap like an Englishwoman's with the green and black feathers—all that she had said was, "Good-bye, Mevrouw Maes, and God in His mercy take care of you."

Mevrouw Maes had got up slowly and with some difficulty from her chair—unprevented by any gesture on the part of her visitor—and had inclined her stout, rheumatic body in a kind of bow. She had not said anything, because at the moment that she had seen Madame van Roeslaere coming quickly across the *plaats* she had been remembering how she had fainted as she stood in a bread-queue in 1916, and she had been swearing to herself 'Never again', in a rage and determination all the stronger because she knew that she would probably be just as helpless this time, too, and the memory had left her rather full of

* Mother.

feelings; besides, there didn't seem to be anything to say. So she had contented herself with the bow, and a silent nod of her head. There had been no expression at all on Madame van Roeslaere's pale face and in the large pale hare's eyes behind the thick lenses of her glasses, as they looked at one another. Her hair was quite white, although Sophie, that great lump who always knew everything that was not her business, said that she was only fifty; that wasn't exactly young, but it was considerably younger than seventy, and some people—here Mevrouw Maes absently put up her hand, as she remembered the incident, to an intricately plaited and coiled mass of iron-grey—some people were not white-haired even at seventy.

So they had looked at one another for a moment, and then Madame van Roeslaere had turned quickly and gone back across the *plaats* to the big house.

Mijnheer Adriaan had not come to say 'good-bye'. Well, Mevrouw Maes had not expected him to, although he had been a patron of the bathing-huts, under the care of those *nannis* of his who were always giving notice, almost since he was born, and had ridden many a time in the cart with Klaartje; and once he and Mevrouw Maes had had a joke together (that was when he had been a very little boy) about how old Klaartje was, Mevrouw Maes pretending that she knew, but would not tell. (Jakoba firmly kept the actual years of Klaartje a trade secret, for it was good for business, and attracted the children, to say that he had been there ever since the bathing-cabins had stood in their enclosure on the beach, and was as immensely old as he was large and strong. Klaas knew his age, of course, but Klaas never told anyone anything about anything; the tightest one Mevrouw Maes had ever known at keeping a secret, Klaas was.)

Ydette made a weary, restless little movement, and the old woman looked down at her. She had already made up her mind that no-one was going to take her away. She should be kept as safe as they could keep her.

She looked across at Jakoba, who was preparing to fasten the wooden barriers shutting the shop off from the street, and stood up, with Ydette in her arms. The trestles, the barrels and stool and the shelves, were ready for the arrival tomorrow of Uncle Matthys' van with the day's supply of vegetables and fruit, but the scales, and the wooden box that they used as a till, were under Jakoba's arm.

"What right have *they* to go to England?" Marie said suddenly in a bitter voice; she had been staring across the now almost dark *plaats* at the big house, while she rolled up the bit of carpet.

"Ah, they've got money, they're rich; it's all right for them," said Jakoba in a muted, mocking tone.

"*I* shouldn't think it so lucky, going off to a strange country and leaving my linen to be looked after by Sophie Bouckaerts," observed Mevrouw Maes, whose prejudices resembled those of Chesterton's yokel, knowing *no harm of Bonaparte but plenty of the Squire*.

"Marieke will be looking after it, not Sophie, Mother."

"That's better, but it's all the same. No-one looks after your things like you can yourself."

"Sophie says she'll show us the house and all the things one day, Mother, when Marieke's gone to her sister at Enghien," said Marie.

"That's good; I should like to see that—if the Germans'll let me." Mevrouw Maes's voice was pungent with the eloquent irony for which the citizens of Bruges are renowned.

"Oh, everything'll be locked up, sure to be, but Marieke'll have the key." Marie didn't want to talk about the Germans . . . *why* couldn't anybody ever say that they weren't going to get to Brugge after all? Weren't the British here, and the French and the Dutch too?—good heavens, were all those men and guns and aeroplanes going to fall down like sand when the tide comes in without doing anything at all? Why did everybody, even her own mother, seem to take it for granted that the Germans were going to get to Brugge?

"I'd like to see the lace," she said quickly.

"The Germans'll have the lace. Come on, I'm hungry." Jakoba drew the wooden gates together, and fastened their unintricate catch. The shop was almost in darkness now, but a faint light still came into it through that part of the arch above the barrier which was open to the sky. They groped their way across the dim place, Mevrouw Maes holding Ydette close, and reached the kitchen door, which Marie had shut and locked, because that was what they always did, before she returned to help tidy the shop. Now Jakoba groped about near the massive lock, and in a moment there came a small, ancient sound; the heavy iron key, with its decorations of scrollwork on the handle, was slowly turning in its wards.

The noise sounded clearly in the stillness now that the distant clamour from the streets was shut away and the three women were momentarily quiet, and it aroused Ydette. She slowly opened her eyes, as she lay comfortably in the softness surrounding her, half-awakening from the sleep into which she had been drifting, exhausted at last by the sheer length of a day whose beginnings—the milk, the brioche and butter given by a gentle hand into her obediently opened mouth, the sound of quiet tones warm with love, the comfortable feel of familiar lights and shadows and colours and the great green thing surrounded by brightness, towards which her eyes, while she ate and drank, continually wandered, a green thing that showered down onto more green—were already indistinguishable, by her, from hundreds of just such other beginnings to the light of a new day.

Now her eyes, as they looked drowsily upwards, encountered first, cool blueness—spread out above her head, and making her mouth feel less parched. Next, beyond the blueness, and looming so high against it that she had to tilt her head back into the soft, soft, silvery warmth in which she was resting in order to see it properly—there was a blackness shutting off the blue, and then it was all black. And then, deep inside the blue and high, high—oh, higher than all the world and the sky —a tall, tall, tall Person, and it was watching.

It wore a pointed hat; and its immensely long countenance was of a pale, ghostly lilac colour, and it was so enormous that all her tiny store of ideas and feelings, and the little sounds that served her as words, were powerless to express satisfactorily within herself the pressure of its hugeness.

There it was, in its tremendousness; and it was watching. It had no face, and yet it was all faces; it had no eyes, and yet eyes looked outwards and downwards from every part of itself; it was solemn, and strange (the impressions of which these words are only the faint conveyings touched upon her infant imagination in all their primal purity and strength), and it was *watching*. She felt it to be neither kind nor unkind, neither a giver of fear nor a bestower of comfort; she was only unable to turn her eyes away from the monstrous and awesome thing, and, as she looked up into the infinite, darkening depths of blue in which the elongated shape of ghostly lilac reared itself, gradually the impression of terror, that had kept her numbed and silent throughout the day, began to dissolve, as if it were being slowly expunged by the severe, solemn, mysterious downward gaze of the Watcher's myriad eyes.

The terror had begun with a noise; far off, small, droning, like the noise that suddenly darted out at her on hot days from amongst the bright things that smelled sweet, making her jump. It came nearer and louder, louder, louder. Suddenly she was snatched and held close to the warmth and silvery softness and the sound that she liked best. There was a sharp noise coming out of the great loudness, and there was loud crying all round, and suddenly her mouth was full of coldness and salt. She tried to cry too. She crawled a long way in the horrible coldness that ran after her. Then there was warmth again, the softness and silveriness; under her feet, in her hands, warm beneath her cold, wet limbs . . . and then sounds once more, to and fro, going to and fro, above her head, but not the sound she liked best.

Light fell suddenly across her face, and she turned her eyes away from the Watching thing because it had suddenly become dim and far away in a blueness that was almost black. Inside the new light there was a blueness low down, and shadows, and a glow. She turned her face again into the softness and warmth of the silver sand, and her eyes shut themselves.

As she was sinking once more into sleep, a beautiful whispering and a trilling, a sound infinitely high up and far away, began to drift out through the low, far-off, threatening trembling of the air. Scattering outwards and downwards over the roofs of the city, it diffused itself through the winding alleyways and over the deserted, darkening *reis* and the motionless water of the canals; it washed with invisible fingers of music the empty places on the walls of the dark galleries whence great paintings had been taken away to safety, as if to assure them that the departed masterpieces would return, and it drifted outwards across the villas surrounding the city until, over the orchards of Sint Niklaas where old Lombaers waited upright and alert in his villa behind the drawn shutters, it died off into a mere whisper upon the wind. It fell softly and clearly into the quiet rooms where the people of Bruges awaited the enemy, and it came into the little house of the Maes sisters and their mother.

It was the carillon; they were home.

O N AN autumn morning nearly six years later, Adèle van Roeslaere stood at the window of her bedroom and looked, first to the left and then to the right, down the expanse of the canal.

This was the moment towards which her heart and mind had constantly been turning in anticipation during the time of exile, and now, standing motionless in the still, hazy sunlight, she drank in the moment as if it had been water. From the topmost rooms of the big house to those that were on a level with the *plaats*, there came soft rumours of domestic sounds, sober, satisfying intimations that her home was alive and in use again.

But suddenly, as she stood there, she ceased to hear them, and the deep pleasure that they brought to her ebbed away as if it were lifeblood from a wound. The water, lapping gently against the stones immediately beneath her window, was fresh as the realization of her hopes; lively,—for this was one of the wider canals down which currents and ripples flowed—and of no colour but the reflection of light, as water should be, and it danced; in spite of the chill in the air, and the October quality of the sunlight, it was dancing. And she had seen the houses on the opposite side of the canal, and had been looking eagerly at the façades of ancient, richly-coloured brick, for more than a minute before, with a frightful inward gasp and pang, she recollected what had happened in the last six years to her friends and neighbours.

Their windows were shuttered, and the hinges of the shutters were rusted into place, or they were curtainless, and dim with the settled dust of years. She had not been home for as long as a day, yet already she knew that she must live for the remainder of her life with the memories of the van der Goes, the Liedts, the Aadenburgs, who had all gone. Marieke had told her the news

—although it could not be called 'news' in the ordinary sense, because it had all happened years ago. Years ago. For some years, now, Liz and Margot and Henri had been dead or— in one of those places.

Adèle quickly pressed both her preposterously long and milky and slender hands over her eyes. When she took them away again, the still, warm, sunny air gave her nothing: no echo of sedate, middle-aged voices chatting on, while the evening light died off the water under the windows; no pictures of her women friends, wearing the furs of winter and swinging their skates from their gloved hands, turning back to her with laughter. There was nothing left but the quiet, sunlit façades reflected in the water, with their shutters drawn over their windows like the eyelids in the face of one who has been granted a peaceful death.

I should have stayed on and died with them, she thought. Oh, how do people who don't believe in God manage to go on bearing to stay alive? and, turning quickly away from the window, she went with her brisk step across to the narrow bed, a nun's bed in shape, and fell, uncontrollably, with her face pressing against the lace of the coverlet. Using the prescribed words of her Church, she began to pray.

In a moment she assumed a position more reverent and more likely, from mere force of habit, to restore self-command, and was sending up petitions for mercy upon the worn, shaken, shabby city and its starved and haggard, but unbroken, people, who were already at work again. *Grant them to lead the lives of human beings once more*, she prayed.

But she soon checked the measured outpourings of petition, gratitude and praise, and got up from her knees and went across to the dressing-table.

Marieke had arranged the gold and silver trays and jars and mirrors and brushes there, and they looked just the same; no one would think that for nearly six years they had been buried under a stone in the paved garden. Once, they had been a cause of guilt and distaste, in their value and numerousness and luxury, to their owner; now, she scarcely saw them. She looked, with an almost equal lack of interest, at the reflection of her pale face, and mouth with its flattened lower lip. She glanced into the long glass, then her eye lingered on the yellow dahlias that Marieke had arranged around the room, and she remembered how she used to feel, before Father Jozef with his amused and impatient eloquence had convinced her otherwise, that her passion for flowers was a sin.

The new parlourmaid put her face round the door and announced, in a voice livelier than it would be after Marieke had had the training of it for six months, that luncheon was ready; and Adèle went downstairs to eat it. What a great tower of hair the child had, and a skirt almost touching her ankles; it looked like fancy dress.

Well, she could not be more than seventeen, at the most, and they were all dressing like that in the first blessed relief of being able to do, in small ways, what they liked again; all that—and it was harmless enough—could be put right with time. She would be given her dresses for her work. God in His mercy had spared much of the old life, Adèle thought, as she seated herself in the big chair with its leather covering and gilt studs; and this child, Lyntje, must have been under the special protection of some saint, that she hadn't been taken off, like some wretched Austrian girls Adèle had heard of, to a camp where the women were compelled to . . . She inserted a spoon, bright as if it had never shared that six years incongruous interment under the paving-stones with the gold combs and the silver trays, into the dish containing a small quantity of some greenish-white substance.

"Creamed cabbage, Madame," said Lyntje, in response to an enquiring glance. Her young hand looked red against the soft, old gleam of the silver platter she was holding.

"Ah yes . . . does it come from the shop across the *plaats*?" Adèle asked, and there was pleasure in asking the question, and there was fear too, and *that* was to become such a familiar mixture, with its bitter-sweet taste, as the weeks went on.

"Yes, Madame. Sophie went across and got it this morning."

"They're still there, then?"

"Oh yes, Madame."

"Mevrouw Marie, and Mejuffrouw Jakoba, and old Madame Maes?"

"Oh yes, Madame, all of them. And the little girl."

Adèle returned to her cabbage. Thank God they were still there. That was another piece of the old life spared. She could not remember any little girl at the shop. But she might be a relation who had come to live with them. She glanced across at the long windows, where the clear, thick white glass had formerly been diversified by a scene here and there in gold and red and violet, portraying a scene from the Bible or some shield displaying the history and genealogy of her family; from this window you could see across the *plaats* and take in Mevrouw Maes' shop with the rest of the view, but the windows were still boarded over. Good Marieke . . . she had been so angry and distressed because she had not been able to get anyone to repair the damage before the family's return. What reward could ever be made for Marieke's care, and her devotion to the house?

This afternoon, thought Adèle, I'll go through the lace with her; she'd like that, and there's so much to be done that I don't know where to begin first.

She knew that the lace was safe; it was a small family collection of old pieces that the women of the family all used, adding to the general store of collars and fichus and jabots and veils and cuffs as family occasions arose for buying more. Marieke had seen to the disposal of that, too. It had been fortunate that civilians, not soldiers, had been billeted in the house during the first part of the war; they were connected with the administration of the farms outside the city, and then they had been turned out in 1942 to let in some of the hundreds of thousands of refugees who came swarming in from Zandeburghe and La Panne and Oostende and Blaankenburghe when the enemy had made a defensive line along the coast twelve miles deep. But Marieke had still been there, and somehow she had managed to prevent the worst depredations.

Adèle removed her eyes from the boarded windows, where

light was admitted only through the undamaged ones at the top, and let them rove, with a quiet yet exquisite sensation of homecoming and relief, over the walls of pale brown oak; they were hung with red-and-gold Spanish leather, stamped with a curvilinear design of leaves and stems and fruit . . . A thick arm suddenly thrust a blue bowl, containing three small green apples, under her nose, held it there for an instant, then slapped it down on the lace place-mat, with its pattern of peacocks and trees and flowers, in front of her. Certainly, Lyntje was going to need an intensive course of Marieke's training before she was domestically 'fit to be seen'.

Adèle peeled an apple, that she did not want, with a silver knife, thinking about the young grenadier standing on guard by the door. In England they had almost no tradition of domestic service left—and what little they did have, they were all, high and low, doing their very best to get rid of as quickly as possible. That shall not happen over here, Adèle decided, pushing aside the apple-rings and getting up from her chair; it's uncomfortable for *us* and bad for *them*. She was critically pleased to see Lyntje spring like an athlete from the starting pistol to hold the door open for her. But that would have to be toned down, too.

She smoked a cigarette in the *salon*, while she read a magazine because she did not want to look at the façades of the houses across the canal (but that would have to be cured; she would have to pray until she had come to terms with that . . . and after all, if they were dead they were in Paradise . . . but suppose they *weren't* dead? There were places in Russia . . .). She came out precisely at two o'clock, between the pilasters with their freshly gilt cornices, and went upstairs to find Marieke. Over the door of the *salon*, set in the woodwork itself, was a serene landscape of an Italian city with some shepherds in the foreground, under a rich blue sky, and she looked up at it thankfully as she mounted the staircase.

It afforded the greatest comfort and relief to Marieke to make a report, at last, of her stewardship and of the losses which she had been unable to prevent among the objects left in her charge. The severity of her everyday expression relaxed, a very little, while she and Madame van Roeslaere were thus occupied.

There they were, mistress and maid together again; the one sitting in a straight chair with a high back, the afternoon light falling through the tall windows onto the smooth, nutmeg-brown, panelled walls and on her white hair and pain-graven face, and the other standing in her black dress and white apron in front of the lofty press carved with apples, and wheat, and naked babies, where the lace was kept; and Marieke never had many words with which to express her feelings, or even thoughts to offer them relief, and this afternoon she was even more silent than usual. As each frail sheet of ancient creamy net, encrusted with knotted threads woven into leaves and love-knots and birds, was lifted swiftly and deftly from the press and held out for inspection, Adèle felt the peace of the home newly restored beginning to rise about her like a blessed tide. She knew that she must begin to work, and plan, and take up again the many duties dictated by her Church and her conscience that she had formerly performed (and how many more, now, with the entire country in the state it was, there were going to be!), but just for this afternoon, during this hour and a half spent with her old servant, she did not resist the temptation to be at rest.

But Marieke was silent for more than the reasons that she lacked words, and that it was not her place to chatter. She was wondering whether this was the time to tell Madame about Sophie.

She would have to know soon, of course. Everyone did know, and if Marieke did not tell Madame, someone else might, and then Madame would perhaps come to Marieke and say, *what on earth do you mean by allowing Sophie to stay on in the house, when* . . . because even the war didn't make any difference to that sort of thing.

But Marieke did not feel like telling Madame this afternoon. Of course, it was a sin, but it was also a fact, and it was alive, and somehow when a sin took the shape of a great, healthy thing with a voice almost as big as Sophie's own, and a body showing promise of being as large as its father's had been, it did not seem like a sin. Father Jozef was always preaching that sin was ugly; well, Sophie's boy was no beauty, but it did seem a bit hard to call him an ugly sin.

Marieke unfolded a christening veil with a ground of *fond de neige* edged by a Mechlin design of curling flowers, that had covered the downy head of many a van Roeslaere baby, and decided that for this afternoon, at any rate, she would forget little Moritz.

Madame was not asking many questions about the lace; she was going on about quite unimportant people in the town; people whose names Marieke didn't know, sometimes; and how should she know what had happened to that smallest one of all the little boys who sang in the choir at Our Lady's, the one with the spectacles, who strode about with his boots showing under his red skirts? or the old woman in the black bonnet at Sint Saveour's, who sold candles and showed people to the seats there? . . . Marieke still had her own position and her own friends in Brugge, even though the Germans *had* tried to turn everything upside down for six years, and how could she possibly say what had become of such doubtless respectable, but entirely unimportant, creatures?

The afternoon drew on. The light of sunset began to tint the sky and touch with warm colour the two heads, the white one and the iron-grey, as they bent together over the creamy webs. Madame van Roeslaere was asking questions quickly, now, and as the answers—the rumours and the legends and the tales, all with their monotonous burden of *dead*, *shot*, *disappeared*, *sent away*, *killed*—went on, her face seemed to have taken on the yellowish-white hue of the lace. Outside in the *plaats*, cars went by, bells tolled with their high, remote voices, lorries rumbled across the cobbles, bicycle bells shrilly rang and everything sounded natural and right again. A little more lively than it used to be, that was all, and not so busy as it was in the main streets, because the *plaats* always had been rather a backwater, but there was no doubt that the city was busily, *willingly*, at work again, thank God. Only it still seemed . . . you couldn't believe it.

At five o'clock, Adèle said, "Marieke, get me some tea, please. Just tea, nothing to eat." She got up from her straight chair with the hard back, and settled herself in a more comfortable one near the window, and rested, and lit one of the cigarettes she had brought from England; cigarettes were still impossible to get over here.

Marieke went away and roused Lyntje out of the kitchen, where she was yawning over a copy of *Life*. Tea! That French fashion, and so they did it in England, too.

"All comfortable upstairs?" demanded Sophie, who had her great elbows on the table, with her chin sunk in her hands. They were only great, now, because her bones were big; no one would wonder nowadays whether Sophie could be called fat and her small eyes looked out steadily and sullenly from under a forehead deeply and redly scarred. Marieke did not answer, but quietly instructed Lyntje about what to take upstairs on a tray. When she had gone, she turned to Sophie.

"Don't say things like that in front of her. Madame wants her trained to be a good servant."

"Madame ought to know what she wants, after five and a half years living safe in England."

"They had the raids, Sophie. And they didn't know what was happening to everything over here."

"Poor souls! I wonder they're alive; must have been terrible." She got slowly to her feet, easing them in the too-small, fragile, high-heeled shoes that had come in one of those parcels from America, nodded to Marieke and slouched out.

"You coming in tomorrow?" Marieke called sharply after her.

"Why not? Nothing else to do, is there?"

"Then don't be late. You was five minutes late this morning," tartly.

"Indeed I was not, it had not gone the hour from the *Belfort*, not when I was on the doorstep," said Sophie over her shoulder, as she disappeared.

Marieke did not resent this piece of lying impertinence; she knew quite well what was best for Sophie, and she meant to go on doing it, and she was perfectly certain that in time, when there was enough to eat again, and enough to wear, and things were cleared up, Sophie would be what Marieke thought of as 'all right' once more. Come to that, she wouldn't mind a new hat herself, and as for her underclothing—if you'd told her, six years ago, that a woman's underclothing could crumble to rags in her hand, she'd have called you a liar. A black hat with a grey ribbon; broad, tied in a bow . . .

When she came in to see if the tea had been all that it ought to be, Madame van Roeslaere was looking out of the window.

"Who is the little girl?" she asked, without turning, as Marieke came up; "one of old Matthys Maes' grandchildren?"

Marieke moved nearer to the window and looked out; she knew of course who Madame meant, but she liked, so much, to be with Madame again and telling her about the neighbours just as they used to six years ago. You could see right across the *plaats* from this window, and everything that was going on.

She shook her head.

"No, Madam. That's Ydette. . . . Madame knows Mevrouw Marie, the younger sister?"

"Of course I know Marie, Marieke."

"(Yes, Madame. I thought that perhaps Madame might have forgotten.) Well, Marie found Ydette on the great dune outside Zandeburghe, on the very day that Madame left for England, and she brought her home to live with them."

"Ydette? What an unusual name."

"Yes, Madame. But Jakoba (Madame will remember Jakoba, of course) *she* says it's good Flemish."

"And the child's been with them ever since? How old is she?"

"They think, about eight, now, Madame. But of course they don't know for sure, because they don't know anything about her."

She had the tray in her hands now, but she lingered, and together they continued to look through the clear, old panes.

The archway at the other side of the *plaats* received only a reflection of the splendid glow of late afternoon light, and the dim reds and browns and oranges of the vegetables, and the small figure in dark clothes with head muffled in a scarf sitting in patient, motionless guard over the pitifully small mounds exposed for sale, had the appearance—seen as it was through the soft radiance with a hint of autumn mist in it —of a painting. But Adèle van Roeslaere had not the habit of seeing human beings as if they were figures in a painting.

"Don't know anything about her?" she asked, "I suppose they've made enquiries?" But even as she said the words, she felt that they were only an echo from the number of times that she had said them, or something like them, while she was working on those committees in England whose purpose it was to help her dispossessed and homeless countrymen and women. She spoke briskly, hopefully, authoritatively, even, but she knew from experience what "making enquiries" could mean . . . and in Belgium during the last six years there hadn't even been those in authority who were willing to help make enquiries—no, by God in His Heaven and His Mother and all the Angels, there hadn't. Well—the terrible world was all about us, and in it we must love and help our fellow-men. She was praying that one day she might want to love and help the Germans.

Marieke was trying to explain, in her stupid old way, that it hadn't been all that easy to "make enquiries".

"I know, Marieke. But it will get easier, now that so many people are coming home and wanting to make them, and it will get better organized as time goes on."

"They think her people may have come a long way, Madame, and then sat down to rest and then perhaps they were machine-gunned. From an aeroplane, Marie thinks. And then somehow Ydette fell in the sea——" She went on, telling the little that was known and the much that was guessed at—or had been, some time ago, but now everybody living round the *plaats* took Ydette for granted and there had been more to think about, during the past six years, than where a small foundling might

E

have come from. Jakoba had never spoken about the boat that had been floating away into the path of the sun; after all, the dark objects that she had thought she saw in the water near it might have been shadows, pieces of wood, anything; and the day that they had found her now seemed so long ago; in another world; in another life.

"They wouldn't want to part with her, now. They've got used to her," Marieke concluded.

"I daresay they have. But of course if her parents ever *were* discovered . . . is she a good child?"

"Oh yes, Madame. She's made her First Communion. Marie and Jakoba had such a business getting the stuff to make the dress, as Madame will imagine, and . . ."

"And has she been able to go to school?"

"On and off, Madame. Like most of the children. When it was very cold they shut the schools sometimes, and of course Ydette has to help in the shop . . . but she does go to school; the good Sisters teach her, at the school in the Street of the Little Red Lion."

Adèle turned to the window again. The small, patient figure across the *plaats* was at work now, selling something to two figures in black shawls.

"And she's a good child—obedient, and so on?"

"Oh yes, Madame. Madame remembers, I expect, that Marie knows them—the good Sisters, I should say—round at the Béguinage and she often has Ydette round there, and I dare say they tell her things." (Marieke meant things about Our Lady, and the Saints, and the good life; she herself went to Mass regularly, of course, but some people were always on about the Saints, weekdays as well.)

"Yes . . . well . . . I will go across and see her later on, when things are more settled . . . they still sell flowers, I see." There were some late-flowering ones, phlox, or chrysanthemums, probably, in a blue jug on the trestle table just inside the arch; they showed up white amidst the soft shadows under the archway. "And how is old Mevrouw Maes?"

"She's getting on now. But she can still get out to the farm

(Madame remembers the farm, at Sint Niklaas?) at week-ends. It was hating the Germans that's kept *her* going through it all, that's what we think."

Adèle indicated that the inspection of the lace had better be resumed.

She did not see her husband until just before dinner, when he put his head round the door of the *salon* and asked her if she would excuse him and told her not to wait; he would be down in a minute, but he was very dirty; he must get the dust and plaster off himself first. He looked white and tired (after all, he's over sixty, she thought, and although we may not have had to go through what everyone else here has, we haven't had an *easy* war; it would be unfair to say that we have). She was feeling concerned for him, until he came into the dining-room, where she sat at the head of the long table arranged with silver and fine china and a marvellous glowing Chinese porcelain bowl of flowers and a small dish of fish covered in a cheese sauce—then she was pleased to see that he was, in spite of his pallor and the slowness with which he moved to his place and sat down, not noticeably depressed.

"Well," she said, when she had explained that she had had his place set beside her, rather than at the end of the table, because, that way, they both got the benefit from the radiator, and he had nodded his approval, "how is it, out there?"

"Oh—," he answered, slowly eating the fish in cheese sauce, "pretty bad." He put his napkin to his lips. The napkin was neither so stiff nor so shiny as it used to be, but it was quite as white. "Marieke can still cook, can't she? although she doesn't have much to cook with." He held out the napkin, "Is she responsible for this, too?"

"Oh yes. She's absolutely determined—and you know what she is when she's determined—to have things just as they used to be for us, and she's made a start already. But *is* it very bad out there, Hubert?"

He nodded, and she asked no more questions.

He had spent a day out there, with the new manager from Brussels. He seemed a good man; keen, and knowing what he was about; he was young, married and with a young family, and Hubert van Roeslaere thought that his enthusiasm for the villa where he and his family would live was genuine, although some men might have shown pardonable dismay at the sight of all the ceilings on the floor. The walls were standing, and the roof; that was something. The villa, even with no glass in its windows and its ceilings down and the garden that had been old Lombaers' pride a flat and trampled waste, looked more hopeful than the greenhouses: without a whole pane, not one, over the entire twelve acres of them, and their smashed and blackened and scorched frames open to the sky.

It had been a grey morning when they got there, and if he lived to be very old, he would never forget how the place looked under the enormous, indifferent, pale sky with the clouds blowing quickly over it in the cold wind. There wasn't a sound. The paths between the houses were knee-deep in grass. And there was one chimney left standing; just one; the others were heaps of bricks almost buried in weeds; you had to look twice to see where they had stood. When had that happened? They told him in Sint Niklaas, where he stopped the car, that most of it had been done in 1940 when the R.A.F. had been blasting the invasion barges collected on the Astrid Canal. After that, the Germans had used what chimneys and greenhouses were left for growing tomatoes, and then the R.A.F. had blown *them* up in the pre-invasion bombings last year. Standing there, looking at it, he remembered that once he had thought this was the ideal site because the communications were so good.

But towards evening, while they were walking about with the architects and engineers and builders who had arrived after lunch, making notes, the weather had cleared, and when, about half past six, they drove away, the sunlight was making everything look, if not more cheerful, at least less desolate. While he ate, and the sense of being once more at home surrounded by at least some of the beautiful and ancient objects amidst which he had lived for fifteen years was beginning to establish itself as the accepted thing and no longer unbelievably strange, he gradually felt less shocked and dejected. The house was almost un-damaged; some of his fortune was invested abroad; Adèle was sitting beside him, and Adriaan would be home in December from the Link House. In a month they would start rebuilding the plant. He supposed that he ought to consider himself the luckiest man in Bruges that evening, instead of sitting there in a silence partly due to feeling guilty because he had—well, hadn't he?—run away.

He looked across at his wife and smiled and lifted his glass, and she smiled and lifted her own. The smiles were not hearty; each shared the other's thoughts and feelings too closely to permit them to be; but neither were they forced.

"In three months from today I want to bring you the first flower from the new place," he said.

"Oh! I *shall* look forward to it. What will it be?"

"Come, that's asking too much! *I* can't possibly tell. It de-pends on all sorts of things—what the market for bulbs is like, the amount of coal we can get—hundreds of things. But if I can possibly manage it you shall have it, the very first one that comes into bud."

"That will be lovely," she said again.

Afterwards, while they were drinking coffee in the *salon* with the long curtains of faded Lyons silk drawn against the chill of the mist-filled night, she sat looking into the shadows beyond the one light that was burning, remembering the bunches of orchids that he used to bestow with gallantry on any woman who was taken over the hothouses before the war; if she was pretty, she got an even larger and more generous supply of exotic red trumpets, and scented white stars and pale mauve Slippers. Poor Hubert—her eyes strayed to the top of the bald head and the gold-and-crystal spectacles just visible above the sheets of *Het Laatste Nieuws*—how he did love beauty in women, as much as he loved it in orchids, and he had been faithful to her own unbeautiful face and body for fifteen years. Her dignity, her position as his wife, their social life amidst the circle of old friends belonging to the most aristocratic circle in the city, and their unsullied reputation with the clergy at Our

Lady's Church—all these had been, before the war, supported immovably upon the fact of Hubert's faithfulness. How grateful she was to him.

It was a dear little joke between them, her fondness for flowers, because flowers had led to their friendship and then to their marriage: he had become a widower lateish in life, childless and sad because of the loss of his wife (who *had* been beautiful, but, discreet rumour said, neither responsive nor kind), and Adèle had been thirty-five-ish or so; a shy and very well-born young woman living alone with her servants and her charitable work and her pot-plants in the big house in the Sint Maria Plaats after her parents had died; she and Hubert van Roeslare were distantly related but did not move in the same social circles. Chancing to learn that her passion was flowers, he had arranged that she should come to see the hothouses. She remembered the bunch of orchids that he had presented to her at the end of that afternoon of wandering through the long, silent, warm, dim sheds where the only sound was the irregular musical falling of water from the pointed ends of the leaves, and how her friends had teased her about its size. She had made a conquest, they said.

She had been extremely surprised. She had never expected to make one, nor even mused upon the possibility that she might. But now that she had—and as the days went on it became clear beyond a doubt that she *had*—she was pleased. Her life had been lacking in the companionship of men, but she found herself able to be friends with this man without effort, and to enjoy the experience. They became such close companions that Bruges was not surprised, although it was pleased, when they married, and when a daughter, and a year or so later, a son, were born to them, there was happiness indeed—*such* happiness—that the sudden death of the little girl had shadowed for ever.

It seemed very much to belong to that life behind the war—beyond the war—that life now over and never, in spite of the efforts of Marieke, to be the same—the fact that, once, they had both been untroubledly happy about Adriaan.

Adèle looked down at the knitting-needles flashing in her long white fingers. The jersey of finest wool, the colour of that English porridge, was almost finished; it was odd, she thought (resolutely turning her thoughts away from Adriaan, because there would be time for thinking about him when she knelt down by her bed that night)—it was odd that wool of that soft, uninspiring colour could look so well when it was made up. She turned the work about in her hands, looking at it critically. But she was thinking about her starving, weary, exhausted city. There was so much to do. She thanked God that He had let her stay alive, to work for His creatures.

She intended to make a special visit to the shop across the *plaats* and talk to that little foundling, but the days went past so quickly, each one bringing its round of domestic or spiritual duties; she began to go to Mass again every morning at Our Lady's Church, as she used to before the war; and then there were her visits to the old women in the various almshouses throughout the city, comforting them and taking them food and flowers and fuel, and she was going down every afternoon to a room where milk and tinned foods sent from America were being distributed to the children, and although she sometimes happened to glance across and see the white face wrapped in the faded scarf presiding over the trestles and their starveling display, she had never managed to find the time to go across.

Once, standing by the windows of the dining-room, now rid of their disfiguring boarding, she saw, just before Marieke drew the curtains, the creature managing a broom almost as tall as itself. The sisters, evidently, made good use of their waif. Then, in the press of ever-increasing duties, she would forget the child again. And then, on some morning when she was walking swiftly back from Mass through autumn air grown keener and more sparkling as winter approached, she would see the small figure walking along slowly, rather doggedly, on the opposite side of the *plaats*—on her way to school, presumably, for she carried an old carpet bag that might contain books. Adèle had got so far as speaking to Mevrouw Maes about her, pausing one morning on her way homeward to greet the old woman as she too came out from the church, and ask how she was, and say that she had heard they had a little girl living with them now, but Mevrouw Maes had not been responsive. She was growing very old, and although she kept her black eyes fixed steadily on Madame van Roeslaere's face, Adèle was not certain that she could see who was talking to her.

Although the mornings were cold, the days were cloudless and hot. One afternoon about three o'clock, Marie glanced irritably at Ydette. Then, in silence, she handed her an apple. It was the smallest of those sent in that morning by Uncle Matthys, but it had a twig and a brown leaf still clinging to it. Marie asked what was the matter?

"My stomach's talking," was the matter-of-fact answer, given in a voice so soft that it could hardly be heard.

"Well, so's mine," not unsympathetically. "It'll have to go on talking, and so will yours, until tonight. You know that as well as I do. You'd better go into the house and get yourself a drink of water."

A year or so ago, the instruction would have been accompanied by a kiss. But Marie had now passed the emotional stage in the life of an ageing woman, and the charming, doll-like Ydette of six years previously had grown into a dark and silent girl with a white face and shockingly thin arms and legs, whose height and appearance did nothing to arouse any tenderness that might be left in an adopted aunt after endless months of terror and suffering and hunger.

Ydette went slowly through the massive door, shutting it carefully behind her, and drew the water into a pottery mug from the old leaden spout above the stone sink, and drank deeply. Then she sat down at the table and rested her head on her arms.

Auntie would not mind, just for a moment; and her eyes moved, in a sort of apathetic content, round the room while she held the apple to her nose and breathed its fresh juicy smell. It was one of the scents of the farm, and pictures of Jooris's red laughing face came to her; this time, his hands were filled with pale brown eggs. Last Sunday they had eaten a mighty *omelette* made with a dozen and a half of them for their dinner; Uncle Matthys and *Grootmoedertje* and the aunties and Aunt Janine and Jooris and Ydette. Every bit had gone. There was no longer any François to keep guard over the eggs and all the other food at the farm, and make certain that the Germans got it. The people at Sint Niklaas had shaved François' head and then shot him; Aunt Jakoba had told Ydette about it. He had once let Ydette have a drink of milk while hiding her behind a copy of *The Cornflower,** that he was pretending to read. A Rural Guard, François had been. Slowly, carefully, savouring every scrap, she ate half of the apple.

She sighed, a funny little breath that came through her nose. That was better; the pain in her belly had almost gone and the light, singing, droney feeling in her head too. But she didn't want to get up and go back to the shop, and if it hadn't been that someone from the big house might come out of the front door, as they often did of an afternoon, and she might miss the joy of seeing them, she would have wanted to stay where she was much longer. The air was dim and cool, and through the little window, over the stiff white curtain ironed by Aunt Marie while it was still wet in order to hold its shreds in place, the hot sunny *plaats* and the brown chestnut tree in front of the big house were like a picture.

She looked dreamily down at the old sea-blue tiles of the floor, scrubbed as usual that morning by Aunt Jakoba with the grey sand that 'we have to use nowadays' instead of soap, because soap must be kept for washing themselves . . . she could smell the faint freshness of their clean surface . . . she could smell, too, the grey sand in its wooden box beside the sink; a cold, sad damp smell which, ever since that day when Koenraed had pulled up the stones in the street, she had disliked.

Now, turning her head away so that she could not even see the box, she remembered how they had all been playing in the

* Nazi-controlled agricultural paper published during the occupation.

road—though Aunt Marie had told her not to—and Koenraed had begun pulling up the stones, and there was the sand underneath, all grey and crushed and damp and sad, and then the Germans had come. (*You must never, never speak to one or get in their way. When you see one, run home without waiting a single minute. You must never, never say to anyone that they are the wicked Germans. Now promise. Say this Saint's name after me, and promise.*) Ydette had often seen the Germans. They were dressed all in grey, and they looked like men.

Koenraed had spat at them, and dropped one of the big stones on a German's foot, and they had taken him away. He was shouting out bad words, and the Germans had told the other children to put the stones back and go indoors. But there was what he had spat, lying on the grey sand, and Ydette had stood against the wall of a house and hidden her face, refusing to look, while Lyntje, who was a servant now at the big house, had helped the boys put the stones back in the road. The sand was hidden, she could not see it any more, but Ydette knew that it was there, under the stones of the street; the sad, grey, ugly sand lying crushed beneath the big stones that were almost too heavy for all her strength to move. Poor sand; poor, ugly-coloured, grey stuff. She was sorry for it, and yet it disgusted her, and when she had to take some of it in her hands to scour a saucepan or clean the sink, the feel of the moist, gritty grains against her skin set it tingling unpleasantly.

She heard the carillon chime the quarter. She would sit here for another five minutes and then go back to the shop, and she would spend the time in looking at the big house.

That place, and the people who had come back to live in it, charmed and held her thoughts even as did the soaring tower of the *Belfort*, whose pale brown face diversified by the dark eyes of its numerous arched windows watched above the life of the market square, and although, of course, she could not go into the big house any longer, she found such silent delight in remembering the many times that she had followed Sophie through the high, grave, dignified door, that her memories almost consoled her for the loss of the reality.

They used to go while the Germans who controlled the farms round about were still working there, before the refugees from Zandeburghe and those places had spread their beds and things over the floors and Sophie and Marieke had hidden the pretty china ornaments away; the Germans went home at night, so the big house was empty. They would often go in the late afternoon, when the shadows were getting long across the *plaats* (that was in the days before Ydette went to school).

"*Goed hemel*, Sophie, you don't carry that key loose in your pocket? It might fall out," Aunt Marie would ask, while Sophie, standing on the doorstep, hunting in the depths of her ragged jacket amongst ration-cards, bits of knitting, good-luck tokens and love-letters, would retort, "It hasn't yet."

Ydette would look up at the dark red-brick front, admiring the windows outlined in white stones and crowned by half-arches; then, enjoying every moment of the slow ascent made by her eyes, she would tilt back her head and send them high, higher, highest, until they rested upon the tall, stepped façade divided in three places by a gap in its structure which revealed the sloping dark crimson tiles of the main roof lying behind— all seeming to float solidly in a deep sky of afternoon blue. What would it be like to see out of one of those highest windows? One day Sophie took her right up to one of the very highest rooms and she found out: all the roofs of the town were spread out below, coloured red and dark blue and silvery grey and brown and cream and—oh! over them peered the Three, watching her from so much nearer than usual that she felt a strong emotion for which she had no name: it was embarrassment. But here Sophie screamed loudly and pulled her back into the room.

They stood outside the front door while Sophie inserted the key; the door was made of a pale glossy wood and set in a recess and it was overhung by a half-circle of smaller bricks repeating the curve above the windows. Between two of the latter there was a small white statue of Our Lady smiling down upon visitors, and along the brick course above the largest one three shields of arms in weathered white stone were embossed with devices of helmets, mailed gauntlets, mythical birds and snarling beasts with awkward, threatening paws.

It was all a picture, painted in dim soft red and rain-softened white, and when Ydette took a last long stare upwards, for the sheer pleasure of looking, she saw in the final, sweeping wave-shaped white scrolls of the roof . . . something . . . it was something she knew, a very, very long time ago, and it was moving *over* her and *above* her, and there had been the coldness that ran horridly after her, pulling at her, and then the warmth and the silveriness and the softness . . . a long, long, long time ago.

"What can you see up there, Yddy? Birdies? Good Lord, don't sigh like that; you'll blow us all away. You'd better take your shoes off here, put 'em down on that old *Cornflower*, it's good for something else besides you-know-what at last . . . read it? yes, I should think so, I've got something better to do, and it's all farmer's stuff anyway . . . put your sabots on that, Yddy."

Her small sabots stood side by side with Aunt Marie's on the newspaper. Beyond them, the black-and-white marble tiles went away into the distance as far as she could see, and there was a dazzle of brightness striking down through the high dim air. For the sun had come out and was pouring between the black curtains at the windows.

"Come on." Sophie waved a great arm like one of the sails on the windmill on the ramparts, and then she stooped and picked Ydette up.

"No need to carry that great lump, Sophie," said Marie, who had her reasons for not encouraging intimacy with Sophie Bouckaerts. She spoke almost in a whisper, awed by the darkness and the stillness and the aura of the absent Germans, but Sophie retorted that there wasn't no need to whisper, no one wasn't dead yet, thank God, and carried Ydette across the hall to a window where the curtains had been pulled aside to admit the air.

"There. Aren't they pretty? Little babies with wings."

"Angels," said Marie severely; there was going to be talk of babies quite soon enough, with Sophie, without starting now. She looked disparagingly at the cupids from a distance.

"And . . . the lady . . ." said Ydette, almost in a whisper, gazing dreamily.

"Yes; got no clothes on; must be cold, mustn't she? Now you come upstairs and see the china ladies I got put away in my room, they're much better; they *are* pretty, if you like."

Sophie always carried her up the wide, shallow staircase whose gleaming surface was scented with the beeswax familiar to Ydette at home, where it was used on the six tiny steps leading up to the bedrooms, and Marie would creep along after them, in her black stockings, following their indifferently whistling guide. Ydette sat upright, resting comfortably against Sophie's big bosom, and tasting with delight the airy, spacious, richly-coloured dusk all about her, to which no bounds seemed set. Marie, for her part, never lost a sensation of guilt at being there at all (well-founded enough, for Madame van Roeslaere, for all her piety, was no encourager of democratic theories, and would have been annoyed indeed to see decent Marie Michiels creeping in stockings up her staircase—Germans in the big house were one thing, but people who knew their proper place tramping all over it were quite another), and Marie also retained from these visits an impression of old men in queer hats staring disapprovingly down at her from the walls, and bad women in outlandish dresses that showed their chests: all of them—the ones in the pictures, the ones in the big books, and especially the little ones made of china that Sophie and Marieke kept hidden in those old cupboards in the walls of their bedrooms—they were *all* doing this, and Marie wondered whether the sight would harm Ydette? On the whole, she was inclined to agree with Jakoba, who after one visit had said that there was nothing in the big house to interest people like the Maes. But Marie always went there when Sophie asked her to; because she would not trust Sophie alone with Ydette.

For Sophie was no longer a good girl. Marie had long suspected it, and now the contours of Sophie's dress were confirming her suspicions. It was not the baby; had Sophie and

André been married she would have welcomed the baby—with
reservations, it was true; babies made work, babies cost money
to keep—but she wouldn't have disapproved. No; it was all
this shameless whistling, and making no attempt to hide anything, that was so affronting. Sophie did not seem to care what
anyone thought.

"There's a heap of stuff here, Sophie," Marie would say
hoarsely, at last.

"Oh, you ought to see what we got stowed away; *this* isn't
worth nothing," said Sophie, shrugging. Marie glanced at her,
but she knew that the broad, flat lips would reveal as little as
did the round, pale eyes. It was funny; Sophie did not mind
everyone knowing she was going with André, but there were
some things you would *never* get out of her, try as you might.
Marie would dearly have liked to know where Madame van
Roeslaere's gold and silver things were hidden.

"But why do they want so many things?" she persisted, as
they climbed the last flight of stairs; "one, I can understand,
or perhaps two; you put it on your table or on the wall and
everyone can see you've got something worth a lot of money—
but whole walls and drawers and rooms full of 'em . . ." She
shook her head.

"Oh, this is nothing," was all Sophie said again.

"I wonder the Germans haven't had them."

"They have had some—couldn't stop 'em—but not so much
as you might think. They've been told to behave proper, see,
so's we shall get *really* fond of 'em . . . and me and Marieke,
we keep on the soft side of them so's we can keep the place
clean . . . but don't you worry. When the Second Front
comes . . ."

"You think we're going to win then, Sophie? Still?"

"'Course we're going to. Come on, Yddy, now here's
something you'll like."

They were only a few of the choicest china figures hidden in
Sophie's cupboard, but Ydette could have looked for ever at
the monkey musicians fiddling away on violins and blowing and
beating on trumpets and drums, and the shepherd with his

lambs placidly curled at his feet, and the goddess with her tiny bosom gleaming white above her green draperies, while best of all were the three china ladies, those "regular princesses" of whom Sophie had told Ydette long before she had seen them; the dashing belles wearing tricorne hats and dancing arm in arm, with their six pale-blue slippers kicking up saucily under the seven rows of white lace that swelled out their pink, hooped skirts.

"I s'pose, if ever things do come right again, *those'll* all be Mijnheer Adriaan's," Marie said drearily as they went down the staircase again. "Do you *still* believe they got to England all right?"

Sophie nodded her head. "I *know* they did. I've heard the Mevrouw's name on the English—" She checked herself, then hurried on, "oh yes, it'll all go to him, and let's hope it does his temper a bit of good."

"P'raps there'll be another one," Marie tittered. "They'll have time for it . . . if they're safe in England."

"Why, she must be getting on for sixty, Marie! . . . You remember there *was* another one? The little girl? It was a shame they lost her."

Ydette was still resting contentedly in Sophie's arms; there had even been a fleeting impulse to suck her thumb, but she found that she did not like it, and stopped. However, she had gradually allowed her head to droop until it rested upon Sophie's massive shoulder, and through her eyes, half closed, she looked up drowsily at the pink curve of Sophie's cheek.

Marie did not reply. Sophie's voice seemed to reverberate through her bosom into Ydette's reclining body. *There was a little girl but they lost her.* Her eyes opened a little wider, she stared up at Sophie's white lashes touched to gold by the light pouring in through the windows. *You was lost, you poor little thing* . . . that was what Aunt Marie had said. *They lost her. You was lost, you poor little thing. Lost.* . . . The tips of her fingers were tingling softly, through her hands poured a stream of warmth and silvery whiteness, warm and comforting beneath her limbs. . . .

"Hey, don't you go to sleep!" She started up as Sophie gave her a none-too-gentle shake. "It's not bed-time yet, worse luck!" with a grin at Marie, who tried to look disapproving but could not help returning it, "now, you come along to the kitchen and we'll have a bit of something." She allowed Ydette to slide out of her arms and down the considerable expanse of herself, now augmented by André Kamiel's baby. "There. Did you like the pretty ladies?"

Ydette nodded, and while Marie, who did not have the habit of thanking people and in any case would not have thanked Sophie Bouckaerts for anything, was glumly resuming her sabots, she whispered "Dank U."

"That's a good girl. Why, I could eat you up, I could." Ydette staggered slightly under the impact of a kiss. "Now you come on round the back."

"Good Lord, Sophie, how you can sleep here alone beats me; it's as big as the Palais de Justice up at Brussels," marvelled Marie, when, the *pick-nick* of substitute coffee and bread sprinkled with a few grains of sugar being concluded, they were being seen off at the front door. It was early summer twilight now, with a harmless soft rain drifting down, yet there was no peace in the little square surrounded by its beautiful old houses; the air seemed to be silently choking back a scream. Behind the tall shape of Sophie, standing squarely in the doorway of the big house, the black-and-white marble floor and the broad staircase were just visible, going off into stillness and deep dusk.

"Lord, I don't mind," she called back, looking full at Marie with a face even more stolid than usual, "I'm used to it."

She waved a great hand at them and shut the door.

The *plaats* looked dark and sad as they hurried feebly across it in the drifting rain.

"You don't want to get too thick with Sophie Bouckaerts," snapped Marie suddenly.

Ydette looked up at the sallow, sunken face draped in the black shawl. She knew that when people were given their full names by Aunt Marie—Jettje Kamiel, Jooris Gheldeere and so on—she was cross with someone.

"You mean . . . not talk to her or kiss her or . . . anything?" she asked, and if Marie had been accustomed to listening for gradations of tone in voices, it would have struck her that this one was thoughtful rather than timid. But she wasn't accustomed to such refinements, and now she was only half-listening because she was hurrying to get home as soon as possible—it always seemed worse at night—and the English bombers might be over, let alone *them* going over on their way to England— and there were the fried potatoes to get on—that shameless Sophie, no, *she* wasn't likely to be lonely, not with probably André Kamiel to keep her warm—and if she thought that she, Marie, didn't know he was in the Resistance and Sophie too, she was wrong, that was all—there was nothing better in bed than a kind, warm, sleepy man—well, Marie hadn't got her own man now, and she knew it was the Will of God that she hadn't, but she didn't *feel* that it was, and as for Father Jozef and them saying so, what did *they* know, never having been married, about being a widow?

Busy with all this, she did not answer Ydette's question.

Ydette had never in the four years that she had lived with them even questioned an order from the old woman or the aunts, but this evening, hurrying across the *plaats* in the wet summer twilight with her head in the old woollen hood bent down against the rain, she wasn't quite 'her usual self'. That head, already slightly swimming with the hunger which the few mouthfuls of poor food given them by Sophie had scarcely relieved, was now also swimming with drifting sensations of glory and importance and richness; beauty and wonder were wandering mysteriously through it, as if they had been the scents breathed out by those big flowers, shaped like stars and horns, which once lived in the hothouses near Sint Niklaas. Ydette had no name for the wandering glories which were making her move and see and hear as if she were in a trance, and yet feel wider awake than ever before, and their only outward effect was to make her take a second upward look at her aunt—with brighter eyes than Marie had yet seen in her face, and with an expression so prolonged as almost to be a stare—and then to

F

utter, in the softest of her many hardly-audible pipes, the word:

"Why?"

"Why what?" demanded Marie, surprised into standing still in the middle of the now almost dark *plaats*.

"Why mustn't I get too thick with Sophie?"

But that was very soon dealt with.

"Because I say not, and not another word or you'll get a good smack."

Ydette did not say another word, and they went on, at a pace which indignation on the part of the aunt, and other feelings on the part of the adopted niece, turned into an awkward blending of a march and a dawdle.

Getting uppish was how Marie described to herself Ydette's *why*? and the expression on her face as she looked up at her; there's ungrateful for you, was her next thought, and us doing everything for her, but a single glance down at the misbehaving dawdler at her side changed the current of her musings, and she gave a great squeeze to the hand she was rather spitefully grasping. She couldn't bear to think what it would be like if they hadn't got Ydette, and she wasn't a bad little thing (well, so she oughtn't to be neither, she'd been brought up as well as anybody could bring her) and she hadn't moped or made a fuss that day when she, Marie, had told her she and Jakoba weren't her real aunties . . . except that perhaps she hadn't understood. She was a bit slow for her age . . . if six really was her age.

Ydette could remember that day, too, although the knowledge which was imparted to her on it seemed always to have been with her, for, while she felt peacefully content with Marie and Jakoba and old Mevrouw Maes, she also felt that her life with them was *temporary*; as if she were on a visit to them and would one day go back to somewhere else . . . she was not sure where it was, or if she belonged there more than she did in the house in the Sint Katelijnstraat, but certainly—oh, beyond any doubt there *was* a somewhere else, although when she tried to see it clearly, as if looking at a picture, it became dim, and faded away.

Yet there was a window that looked out from a rather dark room, on to a garden, and in the garden there was a big tree whose leaves hung down until they touched the green grass, and always when she went into that room she heard a voice, going to and fro, to and fro above her head as voices always did (that was how you knew they were voices) and talking to her—*to her* —with a sound that made her feel the sensation of warmth and silvery softness and contentment in the palms of her hands. These feelings lived in the small, quiet room; it was rather dark, she came to understand later, because the tree outside in the garden grew near to the window, and filtered the light through its branches, hidden in long, pale-green leaves. Yes, that was the other place; there were several other places in which she was in the habit of resting and wandering about, but this was *the* Other Place, the one where she belonged and to which she would one day return.

It had been a winter day when Aunt Marie had told her that she did not really belong to the aunts—a Sunday, because people were walking along the ramparts in their best clothes (they seemed very fine, these patched, fading, carefully-saved garments, to Ydette), and she and Aunt Marie had been walking along there too; at a pace dictated by the fact that their breakfast had been a drink of hot water and a piece of four-day-old bread. The cold wind smelling of the sea drove the grey clouds low over the roofs of the town and a watery yellow light lay over the frosty grass where, near them, a few people were silently strolling. From this slight elevation (they had stopped in their walk to look up at the sails of the windmill) belfry, cathedral and church were all visible, but today, their towers were dark and almost featureless against the bitter pallor of the sky. The wind pulled at Marie's darned and rusty shawl.

Ydette had tilted her head to look up at the sails. How high! But she knew of three other people living in the town (she thought of them as individuals, undoubtedly related to one another, because of their stupendous elevation and brooding look, and as *living there*) who were even higher.

There was a pinch on her wrist; sharp, because Marie had

already spoken twice without result. Ydette turned slowly, and
looked up at her aunt.

"Didn't you hear what I said?"

Ydette shook her head.

"Well, I'll have to tell you again, that's all (you should
listen). You didn't know me and Aunt Jakoba aren't your real
aunties, did you?"

Again Ydette moved her head. She was not startled, but
neither did she possess the words for that sensation, present with
her ever since she had been aware of anything at all, of being
only on a visit to the house in the Sint Katelijnstraat and its
inmates.

"Well, we aren't. I found you—you lost little thing, you."
She stooped and swiftly hugged her. "You were lying on the
sand, playing with it, as good as gold."

Having slowly and lovingly returned the embrace, Ydette
said, "I don't like the sand."

"I know you don't, and very silly it is too; why, that's useful
stuff, that is; what would we do for soap without that?—no,
it was the other kind of sand I found you on, all white and clean,
down by the sea."

She looked keenly into the face uplifted to hers, to make
certain that she had been understood, but although the dark,
wing-like brows were drawn together in an effort of concentration, the total effect was not one of understanding.

Marie did not feel capable of going into it all again . . . not just
yet, anyway. "Come on . . . freeze if we stay here," she said, and
they went on. "I s'pose," she began again in a moment, "that
you can't remember anything about your mother, can you?"

They had given up asking her that, nearly three years ago.
The gentle stare from the bright, dark eyes, the soft, wondering
note in the repeated *maman* or *maatje*, had become irritating to
the two sisters, full as they were of unslaked curiosity, and only
Mevrouw Maes, usually much quicker-tempered than either of
her daughters, had been patient then with Ydette. But none of
the three had succeeded in making her say that she 'remembered' anything.

Now, she silently shook her head.

"Oh, come on. Not remember anything about your own *maatje*? 'Course you can."

Ydette made no movement this time, and Marie did not observe that she was staring, as if she were rapt, into the dull, silvery surface of the ice on the canal. No; she *remembered* nothing: but the word *maatje* called up within her those memories akin to sensations, which lived in the small, dark room: warmth, a gliding softness, a surprising yet soothing glitter beneath her feet, and all around her a shimmering warmth through which, every now and then, there came walking a beautiful, refreshingly cool thing that softly stroked her face.

"Can't you remember your house? (You must have had a house.) A big house, was it? Like the one across the *plaats* where Sophie takes us?"

"I don't know," Ydette said at last, cold, hunger and a strong disinclination to reply giving to her voice an even softer note than usual.

"Well, try and think . . . was it . . ."

"Oh, can I go on the ice?"

"If you want to. Here, catch hold," and Marie, untroubled by fears of a child's getting dirty or catching cold when there were so many other unspeakably terrible things that might befall it, stretched out her umbrella and watched smiling while Ydette went to its full length on the thick grey ice, and even with a fleck of colour in her cheeks, made a little slide down which she ventured, hunger and cold and dreams forgotten.

But the dreams returned; indeed, they never completely left her; they lived always within the thin-walled house of her childish skull; like a group of friends whose company was both familiar and beloved . . . and yet they were also like a coven of enchanters, at work on transforming the world on which she daily opened her eyes.

Now, as the sound of the carillon distantly chiming the half-hour came in through the window, she got up from the table and went into the shop again. Aunt Marie was sitting back on her stool and knitting fast; there were people busily coming and going across the *plaats*—but there were no more customers to-day, because everything was sold out except a few carrots that had got left over from the day before yesterday and were now very juiceless indeed. Ydette settled herself on her own stool and took out her own work, a bit of lace, and settled down to the long, quiet, hot afternoon.

The hours crept by, without any sensation of weariness or waiting in their passing, and marked at the quarters by the cool, silvery falling of the carillon's notes across the roofs and spires. Occasionally Marie would glance up and sigh and mutter something about *Mother having a long hunt of it for something to eat in Oostende this afternoon, but it was no use, she would go, you couldn't stop her*; then she would settle to her task again.

Ydette endured the emptiness in her stomach, and looked forward to supper-time, and every now and again she would re-fresh herself by a long gaze across at the big house, showing more clearly now, as autumn approached, between the branches of the chestnut tree that were beginning to shed their leaves. She was hoping to get a glimpse of Madame van Roeslaere; that small, thin, upright, elegant figure, in its dark clothes and close feathered hats, was one of deep interest and admiration to Ydette, although she had only seen Madame van Roeslaere in the distance, walking quickly across the *plaats* in the early morning on her way to Mass—"there goes Madame van Roes-laere, she hasn't missed a morning since they got back"—or standing at the door of the big house to say good-bye to Father Jozef or some of them up at the Béguinage who had been there to see her about something.

The figure of Monsieur van Roeslaere was one of almost more mystery and interest to Ydette, not only because she saw him at even greater intervals—usually only of a morning about eight o'clock, getting into the big car driven by Georges Dupont, who lived in the side-turning just across the *plaats*—but because out at the farm they often talked about the place near there where the big foreign flowers were grown, which Monsieur van Roeslaere owned. Ydette had seen its chimneys, standing up tall and black out of the willow trees and the orchards, when she and Jooris were out playing, and often in school, when she should have been bent over her books, she was staring out of the window and dreaming about those flowers that came from the countries far away over the sea. Monsieur van Roeslaere's great height, his bald head and the quick glitter of his glasses, every aspect of him as seen from a distance of a hundred yards away, fascinated her, and when she had been fortunate enough to see his car drive up in the evening, while she was sweeping down and tidying up for the night, she felt throughout the rest of the day a sensation of happiness and content, a kind of soft glow, resting in the hinterland of her mind.

It was well after sunset when Mevrouw Maes's short, sturdy figure was seen coming at a quick hobble across the *plaats*, and with her, unexpectedly, was the tall, striding shape of Jakoba. They were welcomed by the two in the shop with exclamations of commiseration, satisfaction and surprise.

"We thought you was lost, Mother!"

"You been away nearly five hours!"

"Come on, sit down, sit down," and the old woman, without showing any signs of fatigue, let them put her into her usual chair, but she sat upright in it and replied to their enquiries with rather testy mutters as she indicated the carpet-bag at her feet.

"What do you think I got in there? Pork!"

"No!" Ydette and Marie, while Jacoba whisked the empty boxes about, joyfully exclaimed.

"Where did you get it? In Oostende?"

"Oostende! No, that's full of soldiers . . . in Zandeburghe."

"In *Zandeburghe*? You've never been to *Zandeburghe*, Mother?"

"Yes, she has," Jakoba's voice was dour; "me and Klaas was busy with our painting and up she come."

"And what do you think?" Mevrouw Maes continued triumphantly. "Klaartje knew me. After all these years. Didn't he, Jakoba?"

"He knew you'd got a carrot for him," said the daughter dryly.

"And those can go down to him tomorrow," said the old woman, glancing at the withered few on the trestle, and when Jakoba said that he wouldn't thank you for them, she retorted that he wasn't fussy.

"Not fussy! How about all those left-over flowers you used to make me take down to him before the war? Catch him eating those."

"Why should he eat dead flowers? or fresh ones, come to that?" demanded Mevrouw Maes with stout inconsistency. "He isn't a cow." She paused, thinking; Ydette had come near to her, and now Mevrouw Maes put out an arm and drew her to her side.

"Getting better," she said softly, with her firmly-shaped old purplish lips close to the small white ear, "just a little better, every day now."

"More to eat, Granny?"

"Oh yes. Just a very little better, every day. I hope I'll live to see the old times back again."

Jakoba hurled a box into a corner, with the thought that however far the country might travel back along the road to the good old times, she would never find on that road the lost strength of her right arm. Although she was horrifyingly thin, and the skin of her face was parched and yellow from years of half-starvation, the impression of vital energy and force which she had always conveyed did not appear to be impaired—until one saw that her right arm hung almost helpless. She had got into some trouble with the Germans while out working with a gang that was collecting wood for pit-props, and when she had injured it, the overseer had not troubled himself for a day or two about giving her permission to have the bone set.

But she supposed that yes, even in six months, they had got some way back on the road towards the good old times. Klaas and Klaartje were at home again on the bit of land outside Zandeburghe; she and Marie had gone over to the farm and escorted them there a week or so after the end of it all; and although Klaas was even thinner than she was, and hadn't had a full meal for years until the British and the Americans came into Zandeburghe and there began to be food given out and things to steal, Klaartje was all right; although he had more than once been in the gravest danger of being sent off to work in one of those places east, Uncle Matthys had managed to save him somehow, and also to find a bit for him to eat; not enough, of course, but something.

Klaas's shed had fallen in. (He reckoned the noise from the anti-aircraft guns in the pits outside the town had done that; night after night.) But the place was still standing and he was patching it up again. And he had contrived to get hold of two pots of blue and yellow paint and they'd started painting the cart. There had been questions from Mevrouw Maes and Marie, of course, about the bathing-machines, but she had said loudly that *they* had gone for good, and added that it wasn't no use asking *where* or *how*. Father had bought those machines forty years ago to start the business with—Jakoba knew the story backwards, how Father and *maatje* had saved their money to buy them, and gone without tobacco and meat . . . but if Klaas hadn't broken them up for firewood he would have frozen to death. And then him going into Oostende, when the Twelve-mile Defence Zone was set up, and sharing the cellars with those German deserters—oh, *he'd* had a war of it. It was no wonder that when they were kneeling down side by side painting the cart on his bit of land, with Klaartje feeding just near, and the sun warm on their backs, that they hadn't been able to believe it was all over. Neither of them had said anything, all morning, except when Klaas swore to himself in a whisper over the painting from time to time.

Marie was rolling up the carpet. Mist was beginning to waver in white, ghostly swirls along the black, motionless canal, the last light was dying off the windows in Our Lady's tower, and a deadly dampness was stealing out onto the air. The trestles were pushed against the walls, the scales had gone into the kitchen, the wooden box that held the money was already under Jakoba's 'good' arm. Mevrouw Maes had gone on into the house, and already the pork was simmering on the little stove that Marie had lit about six o'clock. Now she was putting out the spoons and forks and three pieces of stale bread on the table; the kitchen smelt good with the four onions, saved from the bag sent in that morning from the farm, which were in the stew.

Jakoba took a last keen glance around, and went through into the kitchen. Behind her, the low mist was beginning to drift across the cobbles and veil the lights in the houses opposite. The three women moved about the kitchen, which, small though it was, the little low fire smouldering on its scanty fuel could hardly warm, and they avoided, by half a century of practice, touching one another or getting in one another's way. The black curtains, not replaced by new ones because the stuff wasn't in the shops, had been drawn across the window, the chairs were pulled up to the table. Marie looked critically around.

Suddenly she darted to the door that led into the shop.

"Ydette! What are you doing? Mooning about . . . you'll get your death. Come on in."

Ydette had been standing between the half-drawn wooden shutters of the arch, her arms wrapped in the warm coat that had been a present from one of those kind ladies in America, staring across the *plaats*. It was dusk now; the lights of the big house glimmered clearly through the soft white mist.

"What's going on over there?" Marie said good-naturedly, but not troubling herself to leave the warmth of the kitchen, which, extending its benevolence as far as the door, made the shop feel the colder by contrast. "What's going on?" she repeated.

Ydette shook her head. She did not think it worth while to say that Madame and Monsieur van Roeslaere had just come home and got out of the car and gone up the steps of the big house, so—"Nothing," she said, and, having closed the shutters and fastened their latch in place, followed her aunt back into the kitchen.

That first autumn of peace, Saturday was the best day in Ydette's week, because that was the day when they went out to the farm.

It would begin with the door of the big house opening on the pealing of seven o'clock from the carillon, and there would stand Marieke, in her dark blouse and skirt and thick cotton apron, her white hair drawn back in its usual tight knot, surveying the wide, sunny, quiet *plaats*, the canal where a few wisps of mist were still drifting, and the people hurrying on their way to work; surveying it with no idle eye, but a severe and critical stare.

"Good morning, Mejuffrouw Joostens."

Ydette, who always stole a few minutes from her task of arranging the counters on Saturday mornings to cross the *plaats*, would be standing—perhaps the 'loitering' with which Marieke had once come sharply out at her was not too far from the truth—at the foot of the steps, pretending to do nothing but take the air. She would accompany the greeting with a respectful movement, between bob and curtsey, which attracted from Marieke considerably less attention than she would have bestowed on its omission.

"Good morning, Ydette," Marieke would say—reprovingly, because that was the form, and then, as if to show that the intonation *was* only a matter of form, she would add, "going to be a nice day . . . or a bad day . . . foggy . . . cold", as she began to turn back to the house, her head full of getting the coffee on, getting the mattresses off the beds a bit earlier, getting Lyntje on to polishing that floor while she went over to Maes' herself this morning for the vegetables, there being too much *geklets* * when the child was sent . . . and Sophie was late, as usual. When she was a kid of fifteen she used to bike in from La Panne; every morning; up at five and all those kilometres to go; and think nothing of it, and now she lived just round the corner at the *charcuterie* she was always late. *She* said it was having little Moritz' breakfast to get; *little* indeed; what harm would even a few *missed* breakfasts do to a boy already as big as an ox . . .

"We're going to the farm today," Ydette would make a highly unsuccessful effort to shout after the unbending figure

* Chin-wagging.

already shutting the door; her voice was of the kind which arouses, in elderly grown-ups, uneasy suspicions of approaching deafness.

"Well, you always do on Saturdays, don't you?" Marieke paused, willing to promote her policy of discouraging, whenever possible, any notions about variation, particularly of an agreeable nature, in the procession of the week's duties. Variety and treats for children, in her opinion, led invariably to trouble and hiccoughs.

Ydette nodded. Impossible to convey to Marieke that it was the *alwaysness*, precisely that, which made the visit so much to be enjoyed. "Here's Sophie," she said.

Marieke stood with the door open, in silence, *about time too* expressing itself in every pore.

"Here I am at last, like the Second Front," shouted Sophie, whose more agreeable characteristics were slowly beginning to revive under the influence of having enough to eat again, and who showed every sign of developing into what people who were only anxious to forget it all were already thinking of as a War Bore.

"So I should hope," Marieke said. "Twenty past."

They would go in, Sophie denying the evidence recently presented by the carillon, and the door would shut.

Ydette went across the *plaats* at a run and resumed her duties. There would be nothing more of an interesting nature at the big house until Mijnheer van Roeslaere left for the hot-houses (she had learned, now, to call the place where the big foreign flowers grew by its right name) at half-past eight.

The morning would pass very quickly, because Saturday was always the big day for customers, and then, usually latish in the afternoon, when the stallholders in the Market were beginning to pack up the coloured tin basins and the bolts of cloth, the boxes of stockings and the saucepans and other necessities which steadily increased in quantity and in quality, every Saturday, as the country began to resume normal trading —when the rows of sabots, painted black and decorated with a carved and painted design of red or yellow flowers, which had been arranged on the cobbles under the shadow of the Belfort since early that morning were being collected, and everything was being packed into the lorries and vans of the traders—the party would set out for the farm. (They were usually sold out at the shop by the time they left, and the few vegetables remaining were carefully set aside, in water, to be offered at a very slightly reduced price on the Monday morning.)

The autumn wind blew warmly across the fields. The van driven by Uncle Matthys' new man Karel (just out of the army, and knowing more about the engine of the van than Uncle Matthys did, and rather fond of drink), went swiftly down the roads which were being repaired by gangs of very young men in grey frieze suits. They would sometimes wave to Ydette as the van passed them. (The wicked Germans. All captured now, and made to work for us. Ydette, prompted by the jeering voice of Aunt Jakoba, would turn obediently away and ignore the greeting.) The immense arch of the sky, in which the white clouds were couched comfortably along the horizon as if they did not want or intend to move, went slowly by; always appearing the same; curving over the farmhouses once again freshly whitewashed, with shutters newly painted green or rust-red; the late afternoon light shone through the yellowing leaves and on the red apples in the orchards. From her place in the van—which seemed to her to be quite high up in the warm air speeding by—Ydette could look at the golden poplars standing tall and motionless, yet moving past like everything else, and the golden-green willow leaves blowing in showers down onto the water in the dykes. Far away over the land, the spires and towers were rising up blue, or grey, or white where the sun caught them, in the clear distances. Thickly, and ever thicker, as though steadily applied by a brush wielded in some benevolent hand, its richness was being restored to the landscape of Flanders.

The van would drive in under the massive whitewashed archway and come to a halt, and when Karel had got down from the driver's seat and gone off on his own affairs, the three women and the child would get down after him; Jakoba climbing out with her usual rough energy, Marie in a dogged way and with compressed lips, Mevrouw Maes very slowly and with the help of a daughter, and last of all, Ydette. They would stand still, and look about them; the sisters curiously—had anything been bought? had there been any changes?—and Ydette and Mevrouw Maes hand in hand, both faces grave with satisfaction as they slowly surveyed the changing flowers of every season and the soft, clear colours, and breathed in the good smells floating in the sweet air.

Sooner or later, someone would pause on the way across some distant part of the farm, see them loitering there, and shout, and the whole party would leisurely come together—and then, while the elders were unhurriedly exchanging their news as they moved into the kitchen, the children would—not 'slip', because there was no hint of secrecy in their manner—but walk off sedately together, Jooris keeping slightly ahead of Ydette with the air of someone having something definite to do, and Ydette following with a briskish air of being prepared to help him do it.

One day that autumn when they came, his eyes looked swollen and red, and when they had wandered off into the orchard and were sitting on their favourite log under the oldest apple tree, he became very quiet, looking down at the ground. Ydette was busy picking the few grasses and flowers that had sprung up again after the hay-cutting, but she glanced at him from time to time, and, when he still did not suggest sailing paper boats in the dyke, or say anything, or move, she at last carefully put her bunch down beside her, and, sliding along the log, put both arms round him and held him close.

He began to cry, pushing his knuckles into his eyes; the tears ran down without check, a child's tears still, although his body, in the shabby clothes too short for him, was beginning to lengthen into the gauntness of early youth. Ydette was neither puzzled nor alarmed by his tears; he was Jooris, and he was miserable; that was enough. She said nothing, but hugged him in silence, and presently he stopped crying save for an occasional fluttering sob.

"I'm going to kill six Germans," he said at last, sitting quietly now in the embrace of the arms almost too short to hold him; "that'll be . . . do you know about it?" turning his tear-stained face to her, and she shook her head.

"They killed my father. You know he was wounded, and he came back here and we hid him away? But you didn't know he went with the Resistance, did you? He used to come back and see us sometimes. . . . That was a secret. Mother made me promise I wouldn't tell—not even you," as she stared at him solemnly.

"But they got him." He began to cry again. "We've only just heard; there was a letter this morning. My mother's been crying all day . . . and . . . and . . ." He turned and pushed his face into her neck, and she felt the warm tears running down; and held him closer. "And she won't tell me what they did to him, but I'm going to find out, and when I'm a man—or before that, when I'm sixteen—I'm going to kill six of them. To get our own back. Killing him like that . . ."

"That's like André Kamiel," Ydette almost whispered at last.

"Yes . . . so I'm going to kill six of them. I'll shoot them. I'll save up what Grandpa gives me until I've got a gun of my own—Jean Wybouw says you can get one quite easily from the Americans—or the Resistance won't want theirs, now the war's over, or there are the deserters—I'll get one easily, and then I'll . . ."

He talked on for a while, and she listened. Their arms were closely around each other now, and sometimes, as if without thinking, he kissed her pale, serious little face, but an hour later they were down at the dyke and she was screaming with excitement while he built a dam. She had washed his tear-stains away with one of Aunt Marie's pieces of clean rag, and when they went in to supper he seemed better, but Ydette saw that Aunt Janine's face was all swollen and red.

Matthys Maes kept Jooris closely to school that autumn; it was as if the old man had a strong feeling that some outer authority must take charge of his grandson, in order that the misery and the childish passion for revenge set working in his nature by the news of his father's death might not take a sinister turn when he grew into adolescence. But although Ydette long remembered what Jooris had threatened to do, and each time that she saw him she wondered if he had managed to get hold of the gun yet, she never heard him speak of the threat again. Sometimes he spoke of his father, telling her of jokes he had made and brave things that they now knew he had done. But the proposed killing of the six Germans seemed forgotten.

She was relieved, because killing Germans would be as wicked as it was dangerous; you weren't allowed to kill people; God said so; and if Jooris had still been meaning to he would have told her, because they were friends, and they did tell each other things.

However, quite soon—as the weeks, and then the months, went on, and dozens of different kinds of sausage began to come back into Sophie's aunt's *charcuterie* and the other meat-shops; and cakes, that gave the impression of having each one been lovingly, lingeringly given their final gloss and twirl by hand, began to come back onto the glass shelves into the silver fili-gree baskets in the confectioner's; and exquisitely-sewn simple dresses began to be shown in the Zuitzand'straat, and the small smart hats were changed in the shops three times a week, and people began to lose their pallor and put on flesh, and Sophie began to talk quite a lot and to kiss Ydette again . . . in no time at all, it seemed very queer to think of a boy who still went to school killing Germans.

Where were all the Germans? You saw them sometimes, but only marching to their work on the roads, or riding back from it in lorries, and when Ydette went with the aunts for a tram-ride on Sundays that ended up by the sea at Zandeburghe or with Sophie's old parents at La Panne, she saw the spiked wire and the concrete forts and the gun-emplacements being pulled down, and the ruins of houses being wheeled away in barrows by the very young men in grey suits; and soon the white hotels were being mended or rebuilt, and the sands were being

leaned of strange twisted lengths of metal and great rusty
bulbous things studded with nuts and screws, and next year,
said Aunt Marie, the tourists would begin to come back.
Drifting steadily away into the Past, like a cloud swollen with
bellowing thunder, like a hideous storm that has left half the
world white and stunned and bloodless, went the war; and
gradually—yet so swiftly, when compared with the endlessness
of the months that had seemed like an enduring nightmare—
the climate of peace was returning: and Jooris Gheldeere was
beginning to be eager to get into the school football team.

Ydette, too, was kept closer to school that autumn than
ever before. This was partly because 'them up at Our Lady's'
had expressed themselves firmly in favour of such a course, and
them at the Béguinage' had echoed their views; and partly
because Madame van Roeslaere had, at last, made time to
walk swiftly across to the archway one afternoon and—meet
her? make her acquaintance?—'make friends with her' would
not truthfully describe what she did, because her manner, as she
stood just outside the shop on that day of late autumn, looking
gently yet keenly at Ydette through the great lenses of her
glasses, was not friendly: it was reserved, expressive of their
being set at certain and clearly defined distances from one
another—nothing so warm as 'friendly'.

Madame van Roeslaere wore a slender coat of pale brown
fur that reached almost to her knees above a narrow skirt of
blonde wool, her black suède boots were made in Italy by a
master, a scarf of thick orange brocade was tucked into the neck
of her coat, her small hat matched it, and she held an exag-
geratedly elongated bag of bright reddish leather. If she was
conscious of the contrast between her own elegant clothes and
the thick and bundly garments, presents from kind ladies in
England and America, in which Ydette and Mevrouw Maes
were swaddled, her expression did not show that she was, and
the two who stood before her—Mevrouw Maes having with
difficulty got her seventy-seven year old body up from her stool
and Ydette, at a sharp muttered word from her grandmother,
having hopped up from hers—were not conscious of the contrast

G

either; if they had been, they wouldn't have resented it; it was only Aunt Jakoba who occasionally muttered something about *roll on the day, when we can buy our own clothes again and chuck the charity-rags into the sea*; and Ydette loved her plaid coat and woollen scarf, for she was one of those children who are always chilly; to be cold, for her, was worse than to be hungry.

Now, her eyes were fixed immovably upon Madame van Roeslaere. Every tint of her clothes, every soft yet defined curve of the white hair lifting itself under the soft yet airy hat, the very way she held her bag and the casual wrinkles of her gloves, was bathed, for the one of the two who could see her clearly, in a romantic glow. Behind this vision, Ydette knew that a delicate blur of dark red and white on the opposite side of the *plaats* was the big house, clearly visible, now, beyond the dark branches of the chestnut tree which had shed all but a few of its last bronze leaves.

"You are often away from school, aren't you?" Madame van Roeslaere said rather briskly, when, the preliminary greetings and the enquiries about Mevrouw Maes' health having been asked, and gratefully and respectfully answered, she spoke directly to Ydette for the first time. As she did so, she made a mental note to tell one of the aunts that the child *must* be told it was rude to stare.

"Yes, Madame," Ydette whispered, staring.

"That's not good, you know, Ydette. Do you stay at home because you have to help with the shop, or because you aren't well?"

"Ydette has very good health, she's never ill, all through the war she wasn't ever ill," said Mevrouw Maes, turning her dimming black eyes in the direction of the vague outline whence came the soft, quick voice. "No, we keep her at home to mind the shop; I can't do what I could, and sometimes I must have a day in bed, and then the girls are busy, it takes such a time, still, getting anything from the shops to eat, and Jakoba's often down at Zandeburghe fixing the cart up and getting a place for those new tents on the sands next summer—so that's it," she ended up.

"You should go to school as often as you possibly can," said Madame van Roeslaere.

"Yes, Madame," in the same softest imaginable tone short of an actual whisper.

"Do you learn English there?" the questioner went on; she was speaking Flemish.

"'Oh yes, Madame."

"Ydette knows quite a lot of English; Madame knows there were some English soldiers in the town last week, and Ydette told them the way when they asked; they were in a lorry; all the other children tried, but Ydette was the only one who could tell them," proudly said Mevrouw Maes.

"That's good," said Madame van Roeslaere. She was almost compelled to turn her eyes away from the steady, unwavering stare of the child's; how lovely they were; too large, of course, in a face that size, but the shape and the colour and the length of the lashes were striking, and she wondered where she might originally have come from . . . really, it was almost embarrassing to be looked at so steadily.

"Do you like to learn English?" she asked.

This time Ydette could manage only a kind of rather awkward ducking movement of her head and a foolish smile. It was the first sign she had shown of belonging to her peasant background, and Adèle actually felt some disappointment, for she had seemed like a little girl of gentle blood dressed up in a peasant's clothes, and now the gesture had spoiled the picture. But of course it wasn't important.

"I am sure you do," she said firmly. "Now, you must go to school regularly, and work hard at your English, and when you haven't missed a day for two months, your aunts can let me know, and I will give you English lessons twice a week.

"You understand, don't you?" she went on with a touch of impatience as Ydette stared and stared without answering. "Work hard, and I'll teach you English myself." She did not know what impulse had caused her to add that rather less impersonal last word, but it had its effect. The palish lips moved uncertainly in the pale face; then there came a kind of pipe—

"Over—at the big house—Madame?"

"Yes. At the big house. So you go to school regularly for two months, and then we'll begin."

She nodded to them, smiled, and turned and walked quickly away.

"There," said Mevrouw Maes, whose hearing was keener than her sight, approvingly, "always so full of *bonté*, Madame is." But she said no more, not being given at any time to the utterance of pious sentiments, and feeling in any case that God and His Saints owed them all something for what they had been through these last six years, and Ydette's dreams, which were still wandering around the appearance, face and voice of the lady from the big house and had not yet directed themselves to the prospect of actually being taught English by her there, were at liberty to proliferate, that morning, undisturbed.

A brief smile or two which Madame van Roeslaere gave to her from time to time when they chanced to meet kept, however, the plan well forward in her mind and soon she was consciously working at her English as hard as she could. But that wasn't very hard, because the day-dreaming, which was the very essence of which her being was formed, drew into itself the energies which might have directed themselves into the more useful qualities—concentration, memorizing, competitiveness and so forth—and even endeavour (and she did work, as far as she could) will not make up for sheer lack of brains.

The teaching nuns, some of whom were clever, accurately judged her intelligence to be of a lowish order; her writing was painstakingly bad, her reading of the kind which compelled you to take a firm grip on your patience, and as for her mathematics —well, to give a fair opinion of Ydette Maes' mathematical faculty you would really be forced to draw upon metaphor and simile—stone walls, swamps, donkeys with their heels dug in, and so forth—and the nuns, who saw no reason why one should be a fool even if one was good, had decided, after some two years of as severe and unremitting a perseverance with her as conditions under the Occupation would permit, that they must concentrate upon the improvement of her soul. They would continue, of course, to teach her as carefully as everybody else in the school was taught. But they came to a decision amongst themselves not to waste valuable time and energy on *hammering* at Ydette, in the hope of better scholastic results, because there just wouldn't be any.

She was stupid. She mightn't look it, but she was, and as for the results of concentrating upon her soul, there was an atmosphere of restrained disappointment about that, too, because she was not exactly a good child. She was not actively naughty or rebellious either, but her prayers in class and her response to instruction in moral enlightenment were rather— and they were *only* rather, so you couldn't even give her a good shaking up about her attitude—negative. She was a disappointment. Her height, which seemed to increase every week, and her eyes, made her stand out from the crowd of children, but her character and abilities did not fulfil the promise of her appearance. The nuns were no longer more interested, now, in Ydette Maes than it was their duty to be: almost unconsciously, during the last two and three-quarter years, they had tended more and more to leave her to God: He, of course, knew what He was going to do with her.

As for what went on within Ydette's head concerning Him: the Three who watched perpetually above the roofs of the city had gradually become identified for her with the Holy Trinity about which she heard the priests talking in Our Lady's church. She felt that the prayers which Aunt Marie and grandmother had taught her to make there (Aunt Jakoba was not one for much churchgoing, except of course to Mass on Sundays) went straight up, up, into the dim, darkened air spiced with the scent of burned-out incense, and through the roof. Once there, they circled slowly round and around the topmost eyes and faces of the Person in the pointed hat. Ydette knew, because Aunt Marie had told her, that her prayers were offered to God and Our Blessed Lord and His Mother and were presumably accepted by them, but to know was one thing (as Marie had already decided when musing upon priests and widows) and to feel was quite another, and Ydette could *feel* her prayers going up through the lofty roof and then slowly round and round that solemn Face one hundred and twenty-two metres above her head. A great number of them must have gone up there by this time, for she was diligent in repeating the Hail Mary and other prescribed forms of intercession and praise, because the sound of the words fascinated her, and so the Person must be quite surrounded by her prayers; up there in the sky amongst the yellow clouds of autumn or the pink clouds of spring, and must always remember Ydette.

She used to walk back from school on those autumn evenings. Some of the children had bicycles; old, battered, patched-up machines which had survived in attics and cellars throughout the war, and a very few of the richest and luckiest had new ones from England or America, but although the shop was beginning to do very well, so well that Aunt Marie had begun to buy fruit and vegetables from another farmer in addition to Uncle Matthys, the money went to buy sheets and blankets and saucepans and cups and there was none for bicycles. But towards *Kerstmis* the aunts told Ydette that she could put away her plaid coat and that scarf, and although she was sorry to see them go, how could she possibly regret them when she was told that the parcel they gave to her one morning on their return from Mass, containing a dark blue cape with a scarlet-lined hood, was a present, actually a present, from Madame van Roeslaere?

"Well," said someone to her one evening early in December, as she was making her way homewards across the *plaats* in the cold, fading light with her carpet-bag full of books almost dragging along on the cobbles, "how is your English getting on?"

She looked up quickly, with a sudden startled smile, and there was the small, upright figure (in dark clothes this time, with something that flashed and sparkled between white hair and each tiny ear) looking down at her; almost on tiptoe, as if Madame van Roeslaere were pausing just for an instant on her way to some affair that had to do with her perpetually-active *bonté*.

"Well?" Adèle repeated. The child looked less dreamy when

he smiled, but what a time she did take to answer! "It looks warm and comfortable," she said, in response to a murmur, which did at length come out, of thanks for the cape, "but tell me about your English lessons?"

"Sœur Angélique says it is better, Madame," came at last; Ydette had been wondering, not what she could say that would be most likely to bring about the English lessons, because she lived almost entirely in the hour and the moment and had scarcely realized, even yet, that she was to have them in the big house, but what would best please Madame van Roeslaere.

"Really better, is it?" Adèle asked in English, and Ydette, after a moment in which she looked blank, laughed and nodded. So she can laugh, thought Adèle; it's a relief; and laughter came into her own eyes and touched her mouth and the pictures of the children all over Europe that pressed continuously and without relief upon her imagination receded a little; just a very little, for a moment.

"That's good. Now we'll start our lessons," she said. "Come across tomorrow evening at six o'clock, Ydette." She added over her shoulder as she turned away, "Lyntje Pieters will be there, too; you know Lyntje, don't you?"

Ydette was still staring after her, walking with head turned sideways and feet moving draggingly along the cobblestones, when she reached the front door of the aunts' house, and had to be asked sharply by Aunt Marie what she was gaping at?

"That Lyntje . . ." said the aunt, when she had heard what the news was, "she must be going on twenty-one . . . *she* doesn't need to go back to having lessons again . . . what's the idea of giving *her* lessons?" She was a little jealous of this division of an interest which she had hoped would be reserved entirely for her foundling. "And she's a rough lot; always playing in the streets," she added.

"She doesn't play in the streets now," said Ydette, after a pause in which she felt a vague impulse to defend Lyntje, the comrade, although certainly a rather unreliable one, of that always-remembered day when Koenraed had pulled up the stones in the road.

"She still stands there carrying on with the boys whenever she gets half a chance. I've seen her."

There was no answer to this, which happened to be true, and Ydette did not understand the full significance of Marie's disapproval because she was dreaming about the big house, and what she would see there tomorrow evening: having grown up in a household where mating and birth were spoken about frankly (although with the decency that was the result of Roman Catholic teaching) she took them for granted; and boys, in any case, were to her still the other members of the tribe; the strange ones, the unknowns, shut away, so to speak, in their own huts at the other side of the village, where they had their own mysteries and their own language, and whence they emerged only to put out their tongues at you or pull your hair. It was true that Jooris was a boy, but then she didn't think of him as one, because he was also her friend.

On that particular Thursday—it happened to fall on the Feast of Saint Damasus but that didn't seem to make any difference—it was resignedly noted by the nuns who taught Ydette Maes that she was attending even less than usual to what was said to her. But they were so accustomed to her dreaminess that they hardly troubled to reprove her; and the few little creatures of her own age with whom she was accustomed to dawdle homeward from school (rather silent amidst their lively babble, and attracted by them, and made attractive to them, only by the same instinct that calls small animals into groups) did not notice that she left them more quickly than usual. She did not go home first to look into the square of looking-glass in grandmother's room to make certain that her hair was smooth and her ribbons neatly tied and her face clean, because she was not thinking about herself, but only of the big house; and when she presented herself at its door, just as the lamps came on in the twilit *plaats*, Marieke's disapproval of Madame's scheme to teach that chit, Lyntje, English in company with Ydette Maes (who would surely soon be getting ideas above her position as the local foundling), was able to find satisfying expression in the observation, "Don't go in with your hair all over the place like that," and a poke, with a knotted, red finger, at a wisp which was escaping from its plait.

Ydette stroked it into place, where it obediently stayed because she had the kind of hair that does what it is told, and stood looking up—expectantly.

"They're in the little back salon; you go on down there, you know the way—and don't kick up the rugs nor walk with those dirty shoes all over my floor."

A moment later Ydette was knocking, so softly that she had to do it three or four times before the clear, quick voice answered, at one of the heavy carved doors.

"You are late, Ydette," Madame van Roeslaere observed, "sit down—there, next to Lyntje—have you brought a book? Silly child—how can you manage without a book? Never mind, today we'll have some English conversation—and don't forget to bring what English books you have next week. Now: Lyntje, try again. '*I'm sorry, I don't know where it is.*'"

The room was warm and quiet, the long, lustrous curtains were drawn over the windows; there was a carpet of rich dark blue and dark yellow on the shining floor, and against one panelled wall a tall cabinet made of gleaming wood that was inlaid with pale red and yellow flowers, contained miniature figures in twisted silver; tiny cups so thickly encrusted with flowers and leaves and bells that they stood out beyond the rims; and some of the old friends of Ydette's early childhood— the monkey fiddlers, and the little man with trousers that were the colour of one of the big plums now being sold over at the shop . . . and all these things, as they glowed and glinted in the soft light, were *beautiful*—that word which Ydette had once or twice heard used by Father Jozef in a sermon, and now used to herself when she saw something that pleased her.

When she glanced at Lyntje, whom she had not seen so frequently since she had gone to service in the big house, she was pleased again, in a different way. The expanse of creamy-pink face was wider than ever, while the small, clear blue eyes still made Ydette think of the wind that blew round street corners in

January. The fair hair, which she remembered as blowing about unrestrainedly, was tidier: Lyntje must have had a 'permanent'; but she still bulged out of her neat brown dress and delicate white apron trimmed with lace, just as she used to bulge out of the ragged old coverings she had worn while the Germans were in Brugge.

Ydette looked at her amiably. Lyntje was familiar: she belonged to the cobbled streets and the stepped roofs and the watching faces of the Three, suddenly looming severely down at you while you were playing; over a sweep of old grey tiles or a breadth of brown wall when you were least expecting them: and while Madame van Roeslaere was making Lyntje repeat words for the pronunciation, Ydette could look at Madame's clothes and face and hair. It was all happiness; it was *beautiful*; and as soon as a word of English was launched into one of Ydette's ears, it went blissfully out and away through the other.

Earlier that afternoon, while the low winter sun was yet shining on Oostende, with a delicate, thin radiance that did not seem the appropriate light for the gross, salmon-pink Edwardian protuberances of the hotels and the coarse, worn, vivid faces that thronged the cafés and the streets, a short, stout, dark boy in a blue overcoat was walking smartly along the *digue*. He had come off the English boat an hour ago, and, having wandered—if the brisk, purposeful pace at which he moved deserves the word—up and down the streets surrounding the harbour and stared avidly into the dingy windows of their shops, and yawned over funnels and masts and cranes, he was now keeping one eye on the interior of the cafés lining the *digue*, while looking for one that he fancied, and occasionally glancing off towards the sea, now rolled far back in low tide. Tiny figures prowled out there, black against the enormous pale expanse of the sands, with sticks, and baskets on their backs; the shouts of a few children playing on the beach came up shrill and sharp through the boisterous air. It was all grey— sands, breaking waves, clear desolate horizon and the sweep of the *digue*, the houses and narrow streets plunging back into the heart of the town—and all bathed in the thin gold light of the setting sun. My God, Adriaan van Roeslaere thought, this is what suits me: there isn't anything here to stop you going as far as you want to, there's nothing to say *no*, you can be alone, you needn't bloody well be doing something useful all the time. I'll come here often. I'd forgotten what it's like.

The afternoon light coming in off the bright, grey, sun-smitten sea was pouring into the café that he finally chose: he sat at a table by the window, and the new paint gleamed and the chairs were covered in bright yellow leatherette, and the succulent paws of big, dark house-plants pressed themselves against the windows. There were stout, warmly-dressed old men smoking small cigars sitting opposite elderly women with the drooping flesh of bloodhounds and glittering, stiff fingers. The look of established prosperity was there again: already: like a wall. His father had told him that it was coming back, but until he saw it, sitting here with the *café filtré* and the dish of pastries in front of him, he hadn't believed it. The air was warm and smelling of coffee and cakes and scent, and he didn't know which he relished most strongly: this, or the rich salt smack of the sea that leapt at you, blowing down the narrow streets and against the hotels of the *digue*, the moment you stepped outside the door.

But he did know that he was never going back to England again if he could help it.

"IF there is a war, and we have to go to England, I am going to send you to school there," his father had said to him nearly six years ago. "It's the school your Uncle Raoul went to during the first world war. It's called The Link House."

Then, on the first evening at the Burlcombe Down Hotel in Sussex, after the heat and the excitement, the waiting, and the crowds, and the thirst, and bawling women, and the endless journey across the North Sea in the steamer lying deep in the water with its load of hundreds of refugees, there had been the small English girl playing amidst the chintzy chairs and the copies of *The Sphere* in the hotel lounge:

"Oh, are you going to The Link House? My brother goes there. But it's going to Wales tomorrow. I expect you'll go too. You'll be all right there, as you're Belgian; The Link House is all mixed up with Belgium."

It was 'all mixed up with Belgium' because its first head-master and founder, the Reverend James Ruddlin, had taken into the school in 1914, to learn with the 'sons of gentlemen' for whom it had been founded in 1902, a number of small refugees belonging to some of the first families in Flanders. Doctor Ruddlin was an authority on Flemish history, painting, architecture and literature, and he felt that this was the best and most substantial way of helping the country, now overrun by the Germans, which he loved second only to his own. He had kept up warm and close relationships with his former pupils and their families until his death at a great age in the mid nineteen-thirties.

When Adriaan had arrived at The Link House, the school had been in all the orderly activity of its evacuation to the West, but his hope that he might, amidst so much rushing about and busyness, be overlooked and able to do what he wanted, was not fulfilled: Mr Ruddlin, the old man's son, the new head-master, darting calmly and (now, as he remembered, Adriaan had to admit it) uncomically, amongst the boys and the suit-cases and the packing-cases, had found time to pay especial attention to him, "because he was Belgian", had lunched with his family at the hotel, and made himself at home with them, to Adriaan's boredom and irritation; and on the day the school left for Wales had seen him, Adriaan, attached as if by a piece of string (indicated, but invisible) to one Michel Pourbus, whose parents had been on their way home to Brussels by air when the news broke and who had landed in England.

Mr Ruddlin had noted every one of Adriaan's determined, and finally successful, attempts to break the invisible string and to avoid the offensively cheerful and excited Michel Pourbus; but the headmaster had been as forbearing as he was kind, and Adriaan had disliked him.

He had wanted nothing from Mr Ruddlin; he wanted nothing from anyone now; he desired only the satisfaction of certain private appetites whose presence within himself caused him no anxiety at all.

He drank some of the *café filtré*, which he had made the waiter take back and reheat, and savoured its bitter taste that was, even after six years, familiar, and remembered with a sullen look in his eyes the sitting-room of the big old house at Port Meredith; he could feel the soft yet uncomfortable surface of the armchair in which he was sprawling; he could smell the three-day-old seaweed in a saucer on the big table, and see the shells of which Everard Ruddlin was making a beautiful and accurate little drawing, annotated in his exquisite minute script . . . yes, and the big microscope, and the three beastly curly black dogs—retrievers?—yes, retrievers—lying in a state of relaxed boredom under the large round table; all mixed up with Nora Ruddlin (reading a book) and Christopher Ruddlin (lost in some old magazines about films) and that little "wet" Pourbus, and perhaps Higgins and Whitcombe and Carlton or some of the rest of the twenty . . . scuffed slippers waving in the air as they lay on their stomachs, wrinkled grey jerseys, mousy heads . . . Mrs R. at the piano tinkling out something by Vivaldi or Scarlatti; and looking straight down on Adriaan through the wide, naked window streaming with rain, a mountain: an unnatural monstrosity of a thing demanding, by its mere presence there, that human beings should do something about it. But why do anything about it when there were plains, which were traversable without the expenditure of much effort?

His dislike for mountains had been increased to detestation during those day-long walks with Mr Ruddlin and the rest of the school. The headmaster would not burden his one assistant, a young man whom defective sight had kept from active service, with the sole care of the twenty, feeling, Adriaan contemptuously supposed, that it was not fair to load him with all that responsibility—and therefore he always went with them himself—*up the airy mountain, down the rushy glen*, as he used to say, quoting from one of those poems about fairies which the English, that race long ago condemned by Adriaan, wrote quite well. Not once had Adriaan been given the satisfaction of seeing the Head becoming foolishly 'hearty' in a way that he could have despised, and not once had he himself been subjected to grown-up teasing because he was fat, and tired out; the troop would arrive home at twilight, satisfactorily drenched and ravenous rather than depressingly wet and hungry, and there was never a superior, yet pleading, "Hasn't been so bad, has it?" from Mr Ruddlin.

The matter-of-fact fair play and the kindness with which he had been treated for nearly six years had not affected in the least Adriaan's boredom with the Ruddlin tastes and habits and with the atmosphere of the school (would he ever forget the sound of those recorders? the anæmic warbling was in his ears yet), and when he remembered the Ruddlins' quick exchanges in their authoritative English voices, he scowled: *have you seen to Betsy's paw; where's the typewriter oil; fetch me that HB pencil from the left-hand bottom drawer of the desk in Room B; go and pick me some cherries, Adriaan, you'll find the bowl on the middle shelf on the left side of the pantry*—they were always *doing* something, and making him and everybody else *do* things too, and they were always bloody useful things, and although, even up until this, his last day at The Link House, he had never ceased from trying to persuade Christopher that it might be fun sometimes to pull things down, hang back from things, just lounge about destroying things, he had never succeeded.

Christopher was so crazy about the cinema that he seemed to care about little else. Old Chris: now, as Adriaan took a large bite of a *baba* oozing rum and cream, he could see the yellow lock falling across Chris' forehead, and the look that came over his face when you tried to stop him doing something he wanted to do . . . and then he saw skinny Nora, who had more than once been known, most monstrously, to boast that she was *cleverer than any boy in the school except Ashton* . . . Mrs Ruddlin, with her big feet and her flat chest . . . thank *God* he hadn't got to see any of them perhaps ever again.

As this thought struck him, he felt at the same instant an intoxicating sensation of freedom and promise and fresh, unbounded opportunities opening before him, and at the same time, surprisingly, that he didn't want *never* to see the Ruddlins any more. It wasn't that he *wanted* ever to see them again, he just didn't want *not ever* to see them again. . . .

A girl came in wearing a fur coat which she opened, as she sat down, to display a beautiful bosom in a closely fitting dress, and he watched her with his bold, yet wary, dark eyes while he paid the bill. He wasn't a child any longer; and it was high time (he told himself as he shut the door of the café and, with a quick backward glance at her long, falling, light hair, strode off through the shells of shrimps and winkles in the gutter) that he got out of the society of children and made a start towards getting what he wanted, in his own way, in his own world.

It was beginning to get dark; the sun had gone, leaving long, melancholy orange streaks between two eyelids of darkest grey cloud far out at sea, the lights were coming out one by one in the scaffolded hotels, the wind blew inshore with great swoops and almost took his breath. He walked very fast towards the station and the train for Bruges, not looking into the shop windows, whose glass might reflect his image, and avoiding mirrors in the cafés (he had taught himself to do that, long ago) because he did not like the sight of a short, fat shape with sloping shoulders and thick features too large for an odd, pear-shaped face.

"That fat, ugly little Belgian."

He had never forgotten that; the overheard sentence spoken by the visitor to The Link House on Prize Day seemed to be burned into him: a scar, shaped like the words, and painful, and burning, and red: but he had taught himself, just as he had taught himself not to look at mirrors, not to 'mind' it.

His pleasure at being for the first time for years in a place where he felt himself at home, was not spoiled for him by a conviction, lying in the hinterland of his mind, that later on he would have to train himself to look into mirrors and not to feel angry at what he saw there. He dealt with *that* prospect by telling himself that a man could always dress well, and if he was also strong and had plenty of money, girls wouldn't mind what he looked like. Yet, again, it wasn't, entirely, that he was *always* thinking about what girls might think of him; that they might find him (*all right, go on, say it to yourself*) ugly and small and fat, because sometimes a rather different sensation came upon him when by accident he saw his reflection in the glass. He would experience a cold and angry distaste, mingled with disgust; it had something to do with what he felt for the plainness of Mrs Ruddlin and Nora, and for the chairs and pictures in their drawing-room, a kind of . . .

But it was no use. He hadn't got the words, and he supposed —here he turned aside from the gutter where he had been tramping along and crunching the tiny shells underfoot as he went, and ran down a long, massive, sloping groin that led onto the darkening sands—he supposed he'd have to admit that he just wasn't *old* enough, yet, to have them. Kicking the grey stuff into loose mounds, and thinking that those big stones could be used to shore up a castle against the incoming tide, he reflected on his age for a moment: at a little over fourteen, it was perhaps excusable not to be in possession of *all* the words in which to pin down one's *every* feeling? Anyway, he didn't care if it wasn't.

"Hullo, Marieke," he said, off-handedly but smiling, to the tall figure that opened the door of the big house to him three-quarters of an hour later.

"Mijnheer Adriaan," observed Marieke quietly, after a pause for inspection, "well, it's good to see you home again. But where have you been, mijnheer? Georges has taken the car down to the station to meet you." Both were determined not to show any emotion in what could have been an emotional situation.

"Has he? Well, if he waits long enough he'll give it up and come back without me." He walked past her, as she stood aside to let him enter the high, square hall where the dim light from globes held in a massive wooden framework fell dimly on the black-and-white marble tiles of the floor. "Is anybody in?" He threw his beret down on a settle and began to unbutton his coat, looking round him with an expressionless face. But it was big and it was . . . stately . . . and it was grand. He had forgotten how grand it was. What was the English word? *Sumptuous.* (He had been thinking in Flemish ever since the boat put him ashore.) It was also beautiful; there was not much chance, now that he was in his own home again, that he would have to experience that mixture of anger and dislike which he felt for his own appearance, when he looked about him here.

"Madame is at home . . . she is giving lessons"—Marieke's face suddenly ceased to be that of the perfect old servant receiving the son of the house after prolonged absence and became cross, concerned and rather sly, and she went on in Flemish—"she's giving English lessons to Lyntje *Pieters*, if you please—she's our parlourmaid now—and another girl, Ydette Maes—a nobody, a little thing the greengrocer found wandering about in the dunes—it's some idea of your mother's about making our country good friends with England."

He looked at her sideways out of his dark eyes. "Seems a

H

funny kind of idea, doesn't it?" They were both speaking Flemish now. "What good does she expect it to do?"

"Yes, Mijnheer Adriaan, that was what I wondered. What good will it do, I said to myself, teaching English to two silly girls, giving them ideas they're better without . . ."

"Where is she?" he interrupted, already bored with what old Marieke had said to herself; it had been amusing to see her face get angry and sly, and he had been pleased with himself for knowing at once who she was, but now *he* was rather angry: hadn't it been enough to have spent six years of "excellent motives" and "service for others" at The Link House? must he come back to find the same sort of thing going on at home? But his mother always had been a doer of good works. She didn't even seem to care about the family money.

"In the little salon, Mijnheer Adriaan. You remember where that is?" and as he shook his head, impatient because he would have liked to walk unerringly towards it, she added, "Across the hall and down a little passage and then the second door; the lesson is nearly finished, I think; Madame said it was to be from six o'clock until seven, and it's nearly seven now, I heard the carillon just as you came in . . ."

He made a dismissing gesture as he walked away; yes, he had heard it, too, as he stood waiting for the door to open; the silvery, remote sound falling from high up in the darkness and spreading itself out across the dim roofs and spires standing up in the winter sky, and it had sent a great shiver down his spine that had made him suddenly, involuntarily, twist himself sideways: plunged, at the sound, back into earliest childhood. He hadn't liked it.

He opened the door of the little salon and went in.

His first impression was that the room was full of rich, dark colours; his next, that it was too hot, the warm air seemed to envelop him as he opened the door; and then the first object which he *noticed*—for the impressions of colour and heat had been instantaneous—was a girl (and immediately he thought of her as a girl and not as a child, although he saw almost at once that she was a child) who was sitting facing the door and looking directly across at him; wearing a dark dress so short and made of so small a quantity of material that on either side of its skirt he could see the dark apple-green damask covering the chair on which she was sitting; with an exceedingly pale face in which he now noticed nothing but the eyes; their shape, their darkness, the drooping of their lids; and legs so long and so thin as to appear really (he told himself at once, angrily) *ridiculous* and *absurd*, like some bird's at the Zoo. She was sitting in rather a relaxed position that—some fussy instinct in Adriaan told him—wasn't sufficiently respectful, either to his mother or to the fact that she, the girl, was occupying a valuable antique chair in a sumptuous house; and on either side of her, on the gleaming brocade, rested her very long, greyish and slender hands. *She looks*, he decided, even as his mother hearing the door open, turned and got up with a quiet exclamation of his name, *like a starved bird*.

"Adriaan! You're early—I told Marieke to tell me—how are you, dear? Quite well?" Lips soft and dry touched his indifferently inclined cheek; he had lowered his eyelids to receive the kiss but he could see the other girl, the fat thing with a bust and dry, fair hair, getting up and making a business of getting herself out of the room at a nod from Mamma. The one like a starved bird was just sitting there and staring at him. He didn't look at her, while his mother was asking questions and he was answering them, but he knew that she was staring. This must be the one they'd found wandering about on the dunes.

"I'm quite all right—no, eight o'clock will do perfectly for me, Mamma, I'm not hungry, I had something in Oostende . . . well, I caught an earlier boat and I wanted to see what it was like there—oh, just wandered about—they're all quite well, I've got my report—haven't the faintest idea—oh yes, I have, though, I believe it isn't too bad . . . how's Papa?"

The answers came out smoothly, while his mother stood confronting him, looking down at him even although she was far from being a tall woman, and he was thinking how well she dressed and how wise she was not to use any paint but that faint colour on her lips. He supposed that he had to thank *her* for his own looks . . . was that starved bird going to sit there for the rest of the evening? Adriaan turned his head suddenly and looked full at her, and then she did look away: across at the cabinet with the Sèvres and Saxe figures in it—ah, he remembered that; there was the monkey orchestra—and his movement seemed to have attracted the attention of his mother, for she turned and said, "You can go now, Ydette; six o'clock on Friday, remember," and smiled briefly at the starved bird before turning back to him.

"What time does Papa get in?" He could keep his eyes fixed on his mother's face, yet see perfectly well what *she* was doing; getting up slowly from her chair, with her eyes fixed now on him *and* his mother, and beginning to sidle out of the room. With violence, he shut his mind down on an infuriating fact: then recovered himself and looked at it stonily: the girl stood on a level with his own head.

When she got to the door, he thought he heard a kind of murmur, but even the intensity with which he was listening for her to say something didn't bring to him what it was: *good night, madame,* probably; nothing more interesting than that, and apparently his mother didn't hear it either, for she did not look round as the door noiselessly shut.

The greengrocer: he seemed to remember an old woman over in the archway on the corner who used to sell cabbages and celery and flowers to them before the war, and wondered if they were the people who had found Ydette? (He had heard the name very clearly, spoken by his mother's quick, soft voice: it was an *extraordinary* name; he put it away and wouldn't say it to himself because he wanted to go on thinking about her contemptuously as *the starved bird*.) While he was looking up into his mother's face (*why must her expression always become sad and nervous whenever she looked at him? what did she suppose, in heaven's name, he had had the* chance *to get up to during the last six years in that horribly boring place, that might give her any excuse for looking at him like that?*) his mind's eye was following the girl out of the house and across the square; she was walking slowly, with her head bent down, and it was so dark that he could scarcely see her; she was walking underneath the eerie sound of the carillon, falling in ever-widening rings of silver out of the dark sky.

"Are you cold, dear?"

"Of course not. I'm rather hot. Why?"

"You shivered. (It is hot in here; we'll go into the salon.) But first I'll show you your room. Adriaan," she slipped her arm round his shoulders as they went down the passage towards the hall, "how much do you remember? Did it all seem *completely* strange to you when you saw it just now?"

He told her exactly how he had felt, *sumptuous* and all, and was amused to notice how her expression gradually changed while he was talking, until she looked almost cheerful. As it seemed comparatively easy to make her look less apprehensive merely by telling her the more ordinary (and, some people might say, the pleasanter) parts of his thoughts, there wasn't any reason why he shouldn't do it, from time to time. After all, what he wanted was to please himself; he didn't want to do anything startling or violent or likely to upset his father's plans for him—("good" day school in Bruges, three years at Louvain University, then a career of some sort in commerce and presumably a suitable marriage and the rearing of an heir to all the sumptuousness)—he simply wanted to be able to please himself in his own way. If his own way was, as he was beginning to suspect with a kind of unholy amusement, very different indeed from the ordinary idea of pleasure—well, that was no one's affair but his.

He really does seem less secretive and more like most boys of his age, Adèle was thinking as she opened the door on the room which she had planned and had carried out for him; suggesting, with its mahogany furniture and navy and white cotton curtains, the cabin of a ship; perhaps he was only going through a difficult stage, a kind of premature adolescence. (*Thank you, dear God, that my prayers are a little granted . . .*)

"What's he *like*?" Marieke was saying severely to Sophie at this moment downstairs in the kitchen; "why, just what he always used to be like, of course—downright spoiled and will have his own way about everything."

She paused, looking severely down into the basin filled with a not-very-rich cream which she was beating up for the dining-room's dinner, and felt pleased with herself for having known Mijnheer Adriaan at once (well, almost at once; at first she'd thought it was some dwarf out of the circus standing there grinning up at her in that haughty way, it had given her quite a nasty moment). They, she and Mijnheer Adriaan, had got back at once into the way they had always had before he went away: him leading you on, and making you say what you knew quite well you oughtn't to say about Madame and what Madame chose to do, and then turning on you . . .

"Different?" She roused herself and resumed the beating of the cream; "why should he be any different? And he hasn't grown, not more than a couple of inches, neither. Different! It would take more than six years in England to make any difference to *him*."

Now that it was deep winter, the nuns let the children out earlier from school. There was not yet enough wood to keep the central heating going for more than a few hours every day, and the Sisters knew that each child would have a better chance of keeping warm at home.

Ydette would walk slowly back through hushed, winding, silent streets. Snow lay light and fragile and silver-white on the stepped roofs and along the black trees, and underfoot it was frozen into a clouded crystally grey carpet. Voices and footsteps and the purring noise of the cars that were beginning to be seen again in the city came softly and flatly back from it; a great patch, that yet looked small because it was so very high up, had been slapped by last night's wind against the side of the Person's peaked hat, dull white in the dark grey-lilac of the clouds. Hushed and cold and quiet were the streets, the canals were broad roadways of white with the sombre trees leaning down over them, the lamplight dimly sparkled on icicle, and frost tracery, and glared back from the slide where the boys had been playing that morning on their way to school. And terror had departed from the air; the hush was the harmless and mysterious one of Nature.

Ydette would go straight to the shop, where an aunt was sitting over the oil-stove, with feet resting on the strip of carpet, waiting impatiently to be relieved so that she could go in and make a drop of something hot for mother; the aunt not on duty would be out hunting the shops for the best of the available food (and that was often very good, nowadays), and Mevrouw Maes would be sitting by the fire in the kitchen, not dozing, but looking steadily through half-closed eyelids into the steady glow of the coals.

After Ydette had been given a handful of hot chestnuts or a juicy, green-brown apple, and answered a few sharp yet in-different questions about the doings of her day, she would take the aunt's place by the stove, and keep watch for half an hour or so while the last late customers came hurrying through the snow to buy what was left, and usually that wasn't much; the shop was still sold right out before they closed the doors. She would be hungry, and far from enjoying that warmth which the Sisters had allowed her to go home early in order to secure, but she liked being there: sitting with her hands wrapped closely in her cloak, alone, watching the lights shining in the big house across the *plaats*.

The snow came on the very night that *he* got home from England. She had not been coming back early from school for long when, one evening when darkness had descended early because of the clouds heavy with unfallen snow that hung motionless above the town, she saw him loitering back across the *plaats*. He must be on his way home from skating with his friends; he carried skates in one hand. He was walking with head down, kicking the snow as he went and cutting a deep furrow through the unmarred surface, for he chose to walk on those parts where no one else had previously gone. There was no one else about, just then. The air was full of glimmering ghostly light thrown up from the ground, and there was the solitary, smallish dark figure, dragging its way along the whiteness.

Ydette got quickly up; she could not be sure that he was coming near enough to . . . but it looked as if he were . . . she bent, keeping her cloak held warmly about her against the bitter air, and felt in a recess behind one of the trestles; then brought out a large apple that ought to have been sold the day before yesterday, when it had arrived at the shop, and a small cluster of fresh Christmas roses; she held them out, admiring them for a moment, then glanced towards the idler in the snow. He was making a wide circle in his progress that would, undoubtedly, bring him past the shop.

She waited, sitting forward on the stool and watching him as he wandered, dawdled on, still with bent head (but she could see that his dark eyes were looking straight at her, from under their brows), and when he was near, so near that she could see the crimson shell of his great ear, sticking out from the beret worn at an exaggerated tilt, she silently held out to him the apple and the flowers.

He stopped shuffling, lifting his head and looked at her. She returned the furious haughty stare with her own mild one; this was the son of Madame van Roeslaere, of the big house. So they remained for a moment, confronting one another silently. Then he came slowly towards her, not looking at what she was holding out to him, but keeping his eyes on her face. He looked down quickly at the apple and the flowers.

"That looks pretty mouldy," he said; "what do you expect me to do about it?" He spoke in Flemish, and she listened with pleasure to the pure sound he gave the vowels: this was the first time that she had heard a young, cultivated voice.

"They're for you," she said, her own voice even softer and more difficult to hear than usual.

"For me? Those? Why, they're stale; you've had them in your hole of a shop for days, I expect. I think it's frightful cheek of you to expect me to take them." He was keeping his eyes fixed steadily on her as he spoke.

He was enjoying this; more than anything that had happened

since he came home. Not even the skating, flying through the air that cut like ice against his face, with the grey, shining canal gliding away underfoot, and the grey sky skimming past over-head, and the shrill shouts of the others bursting out behind him as he flew on, alone and ahead, had been as good as this.

He expected her to shrink away, looking what the English called *squashed*. But she glanced down at the things in her hand, then, looking up at him again, said in a sensible sort of voice:

"No, they aren't. The apple *has* been here for two days but it's a beauty, and the flowers were only cut this morning; Mijnheer Pieters has got a little coke for his greenhouse and he grew them in it."

"Liar," Adriaan said. While the word was coming out he was thinking that it was a childish thing to say and, only because of that, regretting having said it, but for the moment it was all that he could think of. He wanted her to offer him the things again, so that he could again feel the pleasure of spurning them.

But she only stared at him, with eyes the shape and size and colour of which he so well remembered from that first evening in the little *salon*, then, without any appearance of disappoint-ment, put the flowers carefully down on the trestle table and began to eat the apple. She did not look angry or hurt or *squashed*; *he* didn't know how she looked; if it hadn't been quite the silliest idea that had ever come into anyone's head, he would have said that she was looking at him, not as if he were a person, but as if he were a *thing*, and one that she liked to look at.

"Liar," he repeated in his pure-vowelled voice; then, as he turned away, over his shoulder—"and you've got eyes like beetles."

He walked across the square without looking back, but it took the strongest effort he had ever made in his life not to; the figure in the dark cape with her face framed in the scarlet lining of the hood was pulling him as if it had him on a wire, and he could see nothing else but the picture of her, standing by the trestle table and eating the apple with her eyes fixed *like that* on his face.

Any soreness which she felt at the rejection of her offering to the big house was tempered by a recollection that Mijnheer Adriaan was a boy; boys were always rude (except Jooris); they always pulled your hair (with the same exception); they said rude words and shouted at you (only Jooris was always kind). Mijnheer Adriaan had behaved exactly as you could expect a boy to behave: she bore him no ill-will; and her feelings for the big house remained unchanged by his behaviour.

She saw him often throughout that winter: if she had been the kind of little girl that Lyntje Pieters had once been (and was still, for that matter) she would have thought that he came round by the shop only in order to say things to her. And sometimes to shove the piece of carpet aside in passing, with his favourite gesture of rucking things up and kicking them . . . and once, on an evening of lengthening blue light when spring flowers were spread out on the trestles, he launched with his satchel a truly frightening lunge at the oil-stove. He didn't hit it, but it was a near thing. Ydette really was shocked this time, and told the aunts.

"Mijnheer Adriaan tried to knock over the stove, Aunt Marie."

"Oh, did he?" growled Aunt Jakoba, who had just returned from the doctor's with Mevrouw Maes' tablets. "Well, you let him do that once again, only *once*—and I go straight across the *plaats* to his father. And you can tell Mijnheer Adriaan that, from me."

"And you won't be let go there, not any more, not for your English lessons," chimed in Marie.

"No, you won't." Aunt Jakoba nodded her head.

"So you mind and tell him. And if *that's* the manners he's come back with from England, the less you get near him nor talk to him, the better," Marie ended up.

"I don't talk to him," said Ydette, in rather a louder and clearer voice than usual.

It was true: she did not; but it was chiefly because she did not get a chance to get in any words of her own; the gabble which he launched at her on his way to and from school twice a day was non-stop.

"Good morning, beetle-eyes."

The voice with the pure vowels would begin to deliver insults in a quick, formal tone while he was still some yards away and she was forcing herself to move quickly about—struggling against her natural impulse to do every action quietly and slowly—in an attempt to get the shop ready for customers before she went to school: her fingers would be damp with the night-dews off the vegetables and muddy with moist earth from their roots. She would never look up, but she heard the voice, growing louder as he marched past:

". . . do you know what your eyes remind me of? They're exactly like beetles; I don't mean the kind the dirty English have in their kitchens, I mean the kind that live in the garden and sneak into the house in the summer. I've been trying to think for days what your eyes remind me of, and now I know: it's beetles, so now you know, too, and good morning, beetle-eyes."

He never looked at her while he was going through the rigmarole. She would hear the voice dying away, and then she would at last look up from what she was trying to do, and see the squat, square back, dressed in a thick overcoat in winter or in the light clothes of summer (clothes which as the months, and then the years, went on, became ever more expensive and more elegant) receding across the square. Then she would turn with relief to her tasks again.

But sometimes he would stop and stare: just stare, with dark eyes looking out of the face which had little of the smoothness and texture of youth: stand there for perhaps five minutes, following every movement of her hands, which might be embroidering or arranging vegetables or busy on a bit of the lace which Mevrouw Maes could no longer see to do and for which the shop in the Steen Straat paid a good price. Ydette would sometimes look up and return his stare: one 'stared people out' at school, and she was rather good at it. Usually, his eyes fell first. It was after one of these stare-fights that, on his way home one evening in late May, when she was about eleven and he almost sixteen, he suddenly stooped and viciously pinched her leg. The place was sore and blue for days, but she did not tell the aunts, this time, because she thought that if she did, her visits to the big house would be stopped.

Were her eyes truly like beetles? On more than one morning, during the weeks after his return, she would sometimes snatch a moment before she ran downstairs and through to the shop, to study them long and earnestly in the looking-glass in granny's room. The old woman would be dozing, perhaps, in her clean shabby bed, with an appearance of weakness and great age that Ydette did not care to glance at because she preferred the air of competence and dignity which Mevrouw Maes carried while she was awake; or she would be lying still, with her short, thick arms, covered with the brown marks of old age, linked quietly behind her head, and her thick hair, of iron-colour streaked with white, spread along the pillow. Sometimes she watched with a faint smile while Ydette, like a sparrow poised on a branch, stared into the mirror.

Certainly, thought Ydette, her eyes were so dark that they did appear black, and their shape was not unlike that of a beetle, and there was a brilliant little light in each one suggesting the gleam on a beetle's back. She turned her head slightly—and suddenly two tiny images of a long face under a pointed cap were reflected there! One of the Three People who lived in the town was watching her, out of her own eyes! She forgot the beetle as, long and wonderingly with the strangest sensations, she gazed at the minute reflection.

"Good morning, match-legs, do you know what your legs remind me of?"

Almost every morning, during that first winter of his return, she would hear the footsteps, and then the voice, coming through the quiet frosty air. Sometimes she was lucky, and left for school before he emerged from the door of the big house, and sometimes she knew that he must have gone on his way before she came down: that was on the mornings when she was late.

But *he* was very often late for school; far more often than she was. There occurred some weeks in the following summer, when he ran past on the other side of the *plaats* without a glance at the shop; his full, dark face, suggesting something that had been designed for a ballet of trolls, set in sulky lines, and his satchel bobbing up and down on his shoulders as he ran.

But their acquaintance was not confined to the early morning skirmishes. When she went across twice a week to receive instruction in English, which she continued to do regularly, she occasionally saw Mijnheer Adriaan passing through the hall or coming down the stairs, just as she carefully shut the front door after her under the unbending eye of Marieke. Then he would say, in a quite different tone from the one she heard in the mornings, "Good evening, Ydette," or sometimes, if it were Lyntje who opened the door, "Hullo." It was what Ydette thought of as an *ordinary voice*. Lyntje would always toss her head when this happened, and stare at him, but he never looked at her, and at the lesson afterwards Ydette would notice that her fellow-pupil was cross. Rude she dared not be—the girl was not born who could have ventured to be rude to Madame van Roeslaere—but her tone was sulky and she did not smile or look up from her book.

That was a very hot summer: the leaves on the chestnut tree outside the big house were faded and curled into bronze scrolls by the end of July, and the tourists crowded, more and more of them, every week, into the city becoming ever more scrupulously clean and more filled with pretty things to attract them; all along the miles of coast, too, they were swarming into the reopened hotels and wearing their scanty bright clothes along the *digues* and on the wide, wave-smitten grey beaches, or pausing to stare reverently at the splendid canvases that were beginning to return to their place in the galleries of the ancient towns. Only the Belgians, working steadily from early in the morning until late at night to bring back the prosperity of their country, had no time to pause and admire anything. The influx of tourists brought money into Bruges which its citizens spent in its shops, and that summer Marie Michiels seldom drew the shutters across the arched alcove upon anything but empty shelves, while she insisted that Ydette must hurry back from school in order to take her turn at the selling. Ydette would sooner have jumped on her bicycle—new that July, and another sign that the family was beginning to do well—and ridden down to Zandeburghe to help Aunt Jakoba with the bathing-huts and the *excursion à la plage*, but she did as she was told, and dull work though the serving of chicory and carrots and potatoes to the housewives was, she knew that whenever she happened to glance up, she might see someone coming out of the big house.

There began to be plenty to eat again that summer, and, at last, she began to grow. There came a day when Madame van Roeslaere, walking homewards across the *plaats* from a visit to some friends who lived near and accompanied, as she so rarely was, by her son, paused at the stall to speak to old Mevrouw Maes, who was sunning herself there. Ydette, who happened to be standing at one of the trestles, glanced quickly at Mijnheer Adriaan, who was standing at a distance, and who happened to be looking stealthily at her, and knew, then, that she was taller than he was.

She felt distressed, as if it were her fault. He must be almost seventeen; it did seem unfair that she, presumed by the aunts and everyone else to be so much younger, should be the taller.

She looked quickly back at the turnips, and in a moment Madame van Roeslaere, having said good-bye to Mevrouw Maes and given a smile to Ydette—who glanced up to receive it—went on her way. "Good afternoon, Ydette," called Mijnheer Adriaan politely, looking back over his shoulder as they walked off and she muttered a response without again looking up. Her mood was that of the English schoolgirl who expresses her feelings with the word, *Honestly*—!

He was a queer one. You would never think that he said those things to her on his way to school in the mornings. And on the morning following that incident, what he said was really bad; he, too, must have noticed that she was the taller, and he was angry; she bent her head as she tried not to listen.

However, it happened to be a Saturday, and soon she was thinking about nothing but their weekly visit to the farm that afternoon, where she would see all the animals and have a good walk round and a game with Jooris . . . if he had time for a game. He was working so hard on the farm now, and his grandfather made him keep hard at his school work, too, but he still liked to dam a *djik* or climb a tree or throw stones at a bottle, and in spite of being taller than she was—*almost a man*, said the aunts, with a mingling of admiration and disapproval—he still helped her to choose the biggest flowers for the bunches that she always liked to pick, stooping swiftly and pulling the stems from the grass as they went through the orchard. They practised their English together, with shouts of laughter at the ludicrous sounds, but he never got any better at it or much further than *thank you* and *please* and *good morning*. Ydette, however, now knew quite a lot of English, and it was useful when tourists of that nationality paused at the archway to buy flowers and to admire the place (they always seemed to admire it—none of those to whom it belonged could imagine why), and when she helped Aunt Jakoba lift English children in and out of the yellow-and-blue cart down at Zandeburghe.

The summer drew towards its end, and school was over. The holidays stretched ahead. Now Ydette could be down at the huts on three or four days a week; hard at it from eight in the morning until nine at night; getting as many cartloads as possible across the wide, shining expanse of greyish-golden sand and down to the waves before the tide should start coming in, and the close proximity of the sea should make the *excursion à la plage* appear a ridiculous luxury ("*Ride* down to the sea? I should think so, indeed—why, you can *run* down to it in half a minute!") rather than a near-necessity which also happened to be a treat.

The aunts discovered that Ydette was the one who was most successful with the children. They liked to be lifted up and helped to alight by someone nearer their own age than Marie or Jakoba, whose hands were in any case fully occupied with the business at the bathing-huts, and whose welcoming smiles, after some thirty-nine years of it and six of the Occupation, were grown, understandably, rather mechanical. As for Klaas, he was if possible even less popular with the clients than he had been before the war. The smaller children stared aghast at his white stubble and bloodshot eyes, and the mothers and *nannis* anticipated heaven-only-knew-what on encountering that blue, frozen, savage glint. Nothing ever did happen; Jakoba became angry when Marie suggested that it ever might; but you could not deny that he was a liability, rather than an attraction, as he lifted the children out in his huge, trembling hands and scolded them in his rumbling voice when they were nervous or slow. Many an irritable glance did Marie dart at him from the ticket kiosk, at the sound of a louder "na, na, that's enough, come on now, you get down," than usual, but, so far, she had never felt compelled to leave her post and "go down and stop Klaas". In spite of his looks and his manner, Klaas was still all right.

That summer, Ydette was allowed by the aunts for the first time to lead Klaartje down to the sea by herself. She suited her pace to the plodding gait of her charge, occasionally giving him encouragement in a low tone (encouragement totally unnecessary, for he could have done the journey in his sleep—in fact, sometimes did) and glancing from time to time at the children sitting, side by side and quiet from sheer pleasure, along the two benches in the vehicle. Afterwards, satisfaction in what she had successfully accomplished was, however, less strong than her relief that some day she would have made her last walk down to the sea beside Klaas.

She had never, even to herself, said *I'm afraid of him, I don't like him*. But, when he stood near her, *all* of her seemed to shrink away in the effort not to see him and to prevent his seeing her; she could not endure to look at his bent, dirty, slouching body covered in the dark, ragged slops and the torn grey shirt that showed the grey hair on his breast; she was sickened by the smell that came from him and by the hoarse, broken notes of his voice that seemed actually to hurt her ears, and more than all else about him she detested and feared his sly, mocking looks at herself; the way his eyes slid over her while his bluish lips parted to show blackened and broken teeth—then, if they happened to meet her own, slid away.

"You don't want to take no notice of Klaas. Why, it's only Klaas. He's known you since the first day we ever saw you. He was there the day we found you on the sand," Marie, observing her shrinking from him, had said to her more than once. Ydette looked sulky and did not reply. She wished that Klaas were—no, she didn't wish him dead. That would be wicked. But she *did* wish that he would stop slouching down every morning to the bathing-hut and insisting on taking his part in the work of the day. Why couldn't he stay up on his bit of land behind the big *djuin* there, looking after his vegetables, and cleaning out Klaartje's stables—which, goodness knew, could have done with a clean—and leave her and the aunts alone?

But now that she was going to be allowed to take Klaartje down to the sea by herself, without Klaas, one of the most disagreeable details of her life would soon be over.

But as the weeks glided into months, and the months into years, Ydette was now as tall as Aunt Jakoba and wearing her hair in two braids crossed over her head, and Klaas's behaviour towards her began to cause comments from the aunts.

"He don't like working with her," said Marie. Jakoba only grunted, and Marie went on:

"Pushes her away from the cart. Saw him, yesterday morning."

Still there was no reply from Jakoba. The sisters were riding home at the end of the day from Zandeburghe, on the bicycles which had replaced the inherited and carefully tended ones which they had used before the war; *those* had been stolen, ancient as they were, by the Germans. Dusk had fallen, but the roads were lively with the cars of cruising tourists; far away across the darkening grey-green plain the lights of the towns twinkled and glittered; along the coast, a glow went up into the grey-blue air as if from the shining eyes of Pleasure itself. Oh, the country was awake again, all right. But Jakoba,

I

pedalling along with a dour face and her black skirt fastened severely down against the summer breeze, was neither forgetful nor beguiled. Once before, they had thought things were going along as they should. But never again. *She* was never going to be taken off her guard again, and she would never forget what had happened during the six years that *they* had been here, neither. The world was a bad place, and she had been a sinner, and them that lived in it was more like devils than people. Oh, *she* would never forget. But that didn't give anyone the right to turn on someone they had known since they were children.

"Klaas is all right," she said, after a long silence while the new tyres propelled by the thrust of four strong legs sped swiftly through the dust; "*he* says she's stuck-up." There was another long pause. They dipped suddenly into cooler air, as they passed through the shadow cast by a great church, whose clustered saints and kings and burghers and sly little cats with curving backs and angels with eyes perpetually wide-open in holy surprise at the Beatific Vision, were hidden in the twilight. "And so she is," added Jakoba.

"Is what?"

"Stuck-up."

Marie did not answer. She knew that it was true—in a way. Ydette talked as they all talked; she never said a word that didn't belong in the little house in the Sint Katelijnstraat; but wasn't she always pleased to go over to the big house, where Jakoba found nothing to interest people of their kind and where Marie felt guilty and ill at ease? and Ydette's long, long hands —with those fingernails shaped like the almond-nuts that were sold in the shop in October—didn't she make a fuss about putting them into the grey sand they used to use for scrubbing? —and *tall*! she was as tall as the Belfort, none of the neighbours' girls were as tall. She might be one of those great Swedes, or an English girl. From what family, rich as millionaires, perhaps, with two cars and one of those new machines they had in America where you could see the wireless people as well as hear them talking, did Ydette come?

Then the question drifted out of their minds, as it had done so many times before. It was almost certain now that they would never know the answer to it. Hadn't Madame van Roeslaere made all kinds of enquiries through those societies for finding who had been lost in the war (not killed; just lost, as if the war had been a great thing in which you wandered around, unable to get out) and got no answer from any of them? And what did it matter anyway? the shop and the huts were both doing so well that they could afford to keep one extra. Ydette was no trouble, and she was a help down at the huts, and them up at the Béguinage and them at Our Lady's, and even them at the big house all spoke well of her.

"Nonsense," she said at last, in answer to her sister, "she's only Ydette. She's a good girl. And the customers like her."

It was the deciding fact: had the customers not liked her— had *they* found her stuck-up, then it would have been hard for combined affection and habit and the protective instinct to defend her in the eyes of her adopted aunts.

As they wheeled the machines across the dimly-lit *plaats*, not wishing to jar the wheels and bruise their persons by bumping over the cobblestones, there came a series of small, sharp explosions followed by a snort and a roar, and a motor-cycle leapt out behind them and swerved off into the dusk. They withdrew not one inch, although Marie felt the puff of air and petrol vapour hot against her legs.

"Thank you three thousand times, mijnheer, and may God and all His Saints go with you wherever you're going, drat you," she exclaimed, with the eloquence typical of an offended Brugeoise as the sound of the engine died away; she inclined her head in a sarcastic reverence, "It's your poor mother *I'm* sorry for . . . off to Oostende, I'll bet," she added to Jakoba, "in one of those night-clubs you can see photoed in *Match* . . . hullo, Mother, sitting out? that's right," as they came up to their own front door and found the small, dark, shrunken figure of Mevrouw Maes seated in a comfortable chair placed on the cobbles, with Ydette on the step beside her.

"Lyntje's got the sack," said Ydette at once, looking up.

"*Lyntje* has? What for? Marieke said she wasn't doing too badly."

Marie paused with the front wheel of her bicycle poised on the single-stone kerb; Jakoba, who usually disdained gossip, had pushed past the two seated near the doorway and gone on into the house.

"It wasn't anything to do with her work. It was Mijnheer Adriaan. Her mother has just been here . . . in such a state! Where will Lyntje get another job and so on and so forth," said Mevrouw Maes, folding her hands more closely in her soft old knitted black shawl.

"Mijnheer Adriaan! We've just seen him on his motor-cycle, flying off to Oostende or one of those places . . . nearly cut my leg in half, thank him very much," said Marie. "But what for? —Lyntje, I mean—You *don't* mean to say . . ." and she paused, looking at her mother with an expression in which eagerness was mingled with primness.

"No, no," Mevrouw Maes shook her head, "not as bad as *that*, but they've been playing about together, laughing and running up and down stairs, with him chasing her—that kind of thing—not at all the way for a girl to go on when she's in service—and so of course she's had to go."

"And if there was nothing worse than running up and down stairs my name isn't what it is," Marie muttered. She leaned the bicycle against the old plaster wall, and went over to the step and sat down on it, settling herself beside Ydette. "Phew . . . it's hot. Well, I'm not surprised," she went on; "Lyntje always was one for the boys. It's her I blame, not him."

"*He's* been properly brought up. He knows better," said Mevrouw Maes in a tone of reproof. "He's educated—*I* blame *him*."

"P'raps that's why he's been going about with a face like a fiddle lately."

"Perhaps. And that's why Madame van Roeslaere looks so sad."

"Sad! She should look sad. What's she got to look sad about, with their business bringing in all the money it does—

doing much better than before the war—and two motor-cars?"

Jakoba's rough voice joined the discussion as she came out to stand in the doorway behind them. Her mother glanced at her sharply, but the rebuke that she would have given her in former days did not follow: the old woman was very tired, too weary to assert her will over that of her tall elder daughter . . . Jakoba had always been the rough one, the wild and wilful one who never told you anything, nor really cared about coming to church. And yet her mother understood her likes and dislikes and her ways; she did not, as Marie and the rest of the family did, think it crazy that Jakoba should want to walk along beside the angry waves that came thundering inshore when the autumn storms were blowing, or sit in the café with men . . . Mevrouw Maes would never have done such things herself, but she could understand Jakoba doing them. Jakoba, her mother mused, had always needed a man and children of her own. But it was often the ones who most needed them, who didn't get them. . . .

What a long time I've been here, she thought drowsily, as she sat in the comfortable new chair that her daughters had bought for her, and felt the coolness of evening—it was beginning to touch the face of Ydette refreshingly, and to wander, in a breeze so slight as to be scarcely felt by those who sat outside their doors, down the quiet cobbled winding street—strike into her ancient blood with an aching chill; *so many, many times, the light fading off Our Lady's Tower; so many times, the sound of Her bell starting to fall out of the sky. I do thank God and His Mother that I've lived to see most of the old life come back again. But I'm tired; I'm very tired now. And as for the old life . . . as far back as I can remember we've been afraid of the Germans invading us, and there was my own grandmother, telling me how afraid her mother used to be of the French . . . there's always someone to come in on you and frighten you to death, and there always will be in the Netherlands, for all their Leagues and their promises and their talk. . . .*

She stirred wearily in her chair, and Marie glanced up at her. It was time that mother was taken in and helped to bed, but it was so pleasant, sitting here quiet in the fading light and knowing that there was plenty of food in the house and that tomorrow would be like today—ah, God, yes, that was what you wanted after six years of war; just to know that tomorrow would be like today. Let's sit here a little while longer.

"What do you reckon Lyntje will do with herself now?" she asked.

"Mevrouw Halles says she's going to try to get her into 'Priba'," said Mevrouw Maes, awakening, without any signs of a start or confusion, from the doze into which she had been drifting.

"That shop in the Steen where they sell the stuff to put on your fingernails what smells to high heaven," said Jakoba, with a loud laugh; "a nice change from carrying plates and polishing floors at the big house *that* will be."

"And Mijnheer Adriaan's going to college soon, to Louvain," said Marie; "it'll be just as well to have *him* out of the way, chasing girls up and down stairs. . . . You've been over there twice a week, for getting on years now," she went on, turning to the silent figure sitting beside her, whose pale face, and hair braided round her head, were painted in delicate darkness and pallor by the soft, clear light of the afterglow. "Did you ever see any of these goings on? He didn't never chase *you* up and down stairs, I s'pose?" and at the question Jakoba again gave her loud, hoarse laugh.

Ydette shook her head. She was not surprised by what had happened. She had felt, rather than known, for some time now that Mijnheer Adriaan and Lyntje were what she thought of as *friends*, and she had sometimes wished—without wistfulness, as it had been without any jealousy—that she could have been friends with him too. It would have made life easier in the mornings.

"He wouldn't dare do that, not with her being taught English by his mother," said Mevrouw Maes, in her matter-of-fact voice.

"He doesn't never say anything he shouldn't, not to you?" Marie persisted, having suddenly and rather belatedly realized that her adopted niece, assumed now to be aged twelve and some months, stood as tall as many girls of fifteen and more.

Again Ydette shook her head, and Marie, who had been looking at her keenly, let her eyes fall to the slender legs that ended in white socks and childish, stout shoes and thought, with a feeling of relief, that of course Ydette was still only a child; there would be another good two years, yet, before they need start worrying about boys and Ydette, and as for that Lyntje (Sophie was always saying, why shouldn't she have a bit of fun?), see where *her* bit of fun had landed her. Sacked from the big house for messing about with the young mijnheer. As she got up slowly and awkwardly from the doorstep, Marie was experiencing a sense of satisfaction.

"Come along, Mother," she said; "don't you want to go to bed?"

When they had gone into the house, Ydette stayed on for a little while, deliberately lingering over the task of gathering up the folded coat on which she had been sitting, and putting away Mevrouw Maes' chair. The small room beyond the thick, ancient door was almost hidden now in the twilight but here and there its old-fashioned furniture gave back in a faint gleam the fading afterglow; the great white, velvety trumpet of the gloxinia, mottled and spotted with richest purple, glimmered by the small, white-curtained window. The tiled floor was all one smooth flow of dark blue. Ydette sighed, and looked up at the lofty spire of Our Lady's tower. The severe myriad eyes still looked down at her with their air of intent watching, the opalescent glow of a calm day's ending, neither rose nor lilac but a pale and delicate mingling of the two, still lingered upon those remote little archways and mysterious little dark windows, high, high up in the air; bathing them in its fading colour long after the sun had gone down over the dim blue and rust-red roofs and the flat meadowlands stretching away beyond the city's ramparts; everything was just the same. It had seemed the same ever since she could remember.

Oh! for something . . . for something beautiful, loving, far-away, soft as the white sand that trickled lazily through one's sunburnt fingers out in the great dune, on the long days of summer . . . for something . . .

She did not know what. And she had no words for the feelings drifting through her heart.

The feelings—too rooted in her nature and too persistent to be described as moods—passed over, their departure unnoticed, while she briskly addressed herself to pulling the chair over the doorstep, and settling it in its place amidst the other furniture in the dark, overcrowded little parlour, seldom used, and overlooking the few yards of damp garden and the black waters of the canal.

Mijnheer Adriaan! So Mijnheer Adriaan had gone into Oostende on his motor-cycle, had he? the famous motor-cycle that was almost the only one in the city. Oh, Ydette knew all about that; Marieke had told them; it was a present from his father because he had won some prize at school. He was very clever, Mijnheer Adriaan, and Ydette, who knew that she was not clever at all, sighed as she remembered certain lessons which were due to take place tomorrow morning, at which her efforts would undoubtedly call forth sarcastic comments from Sœur Angélique. People always did get cross when they asked Ydette questions about anything—except things like making coffee or selling potatoes or giving out bathing-caps to the tourists.

Even Madame at the big house—Ydette's eyes strayed across the *plaats*—had looked severe and surprised when Ydette had been unable to remember all those dates and names that had to do with the building and history of the Three Towers . . . but it was no use. The Three were as familiar to Ydette as Aunt Jakoba and Aunt Marie and granny; if they ever fell down, she would feel as terrible as she would feel if either of the aunts or granny were to die—but she *never* could remember anything about them, except how they looked. And even if she had been asked *that* by Madame van Roeslaere, she wouldn't have been able to tell . . .

She stood in the doorway with her arms and ankles crossed thinking about all this, and looking dreamily down the narrow lane that curved away amongst the ancient humble houses with their pale fronts and stepped roofs; the lamps were alight now and faintly shining their yellow glow into the air; it was getting cooler.

"Good night, Ydette."

"Star-gazing, Yddy?"

It was Sophie, walking arm in arm with Albert Joos on their way home from their evening stroll round the ramparts, and Ydette looked at them with the lack-lustre expression of a little girl who has more than once been bored by hearing a love-affair discussed in her presence by interested adults, as she shook her head.

"Hear about Lyntje?" shouted Sophie, stopping in full stride and bringing Albert Joos, who was no light weight, to a stop also. "*I'm* not surprised, I can tell you—you and Marieke don't know half what went on—oh, I've seen it—time and time again—pinching her, and that. . . . Well, many's the time I've said to myself—and then I thought, only a bit of fun . . . but seems *they*, them upstairs, didn't think so—but *they* can't do a thing with him. Upsets his mother, too. I've seen her crying. Comes out of her room, face all over powder. I can always tell."

Albert Joos, stout and neat in his black suit and black hat, here gave Sophy's arm a reproving pressure and muttered something which caused her to give a loud laugh.

"But he's getting to the age," she ended vaguely, and began to move on, pulling Albert Joos with her. "So-long, Yddy—grandma keeping well? That's right. Good night."

The sturdy, decided footsteps died away. Now the lane was quiet. There were stars shining round the towers of Our Lady's church, and it was only a little paler than the sky. But it looked ghostly, and as though it were mourning, far away up there in the blue. Ydette stood looking across at the lights shining in the windows of the big house, and thought of Madame van Roeslaere. Crying? She did not believe it.

The people at the big house were not like ordinary people; they did not cry or get cross or hungry or tired; it was a place where everything . . . where . . . everything was . . . good and all right . . . and when she was there, sitting opposite to

Madame van Roeslaere and obediently repeating the English words and phrases at which she had slowly—oh, so slowly, but definitely—become better at remembering . . . there, while she was in the big house, she almost held the beautiful, loving, soft . . . she held it in her hands, the softness of the white sand.

She shut the front door, in the brisk, sensible way that always hid the fact that she was dreaming.

THERE came a morning, some years later, that was hot and clear and cloudless, with nothing relaxed or languorous about it. Summer in Western Flanders gets plenty such; then the massive stone groins of Ostend, covered in plump brown seaweeds that glisten stickily in the glare of the sun, are black with strollers and fishers and idlers; the narrow streets running down to the *digue* that can look, in a lowering twilight, both menacing and secretive, have all their shops open in innocent gaudiness to attract the tourist eye; the town hums and buzzes and buys and sells and eats and drinks in its typical, fierce, marine gaiety; out in the country the green shutters of the farms are closed against the shimmering light, while owners and employees alike work on stolidly through the heat, at what has to be done.

They were busy, that morning, down at the bathing huts at Zandeburghe. Business was even better, this summer, than it had been last year—and that had been very good; if it hadn't been for Klaas—ah, it was sad about Klaas. At least, Jakoba, with unaccustomed softness had been heard to mutter that it was sad, but Marie said forthrightly that it was a very great nuisance, not to say a disgrace, him lying there most days out of the seven with a bottle of something. The fact that many of the tourists remembered him from before the war, made the situation even more difficult.

"And where is the old man who used to help you with the horse?" some mother from Birmingham or Harrogate, returning to Zandeburghe with two children grown tall beyond all recognition for the first time since the war, and buying bathing tickets for them all, would enquire, "not . . .? I do hope they didn't . . .?"

She meant, *didn't shoot him or starve him to death or take him off to one of those places.*

"Oh, no, madame," Jakoba would show her big yellow teeth for an instant, "he's still here. But he's getting old. Old. Oh yes. Like me." A loud laugh, and a bang with her "good" arm on her flat chest, "He can't work like he used to. He's up there," nodding her head towards the high canvas fence which gave to the booth where the tickets were sold some slight privacy, "asleep, I expect," and she would laugh again.

"Oh, I am so glad to hear he's still here. (Rosemary, Neil, the old man is still here . . . but I expect you were too small to remember) . . . er, is he quite well?" The gentle pink face would be smiling with pleasure, the two younger pink ones would be smiling too, because they were having a smashing holiday on the Belgian coast.

"Oh yes, Madame. Quite well. But always sleeping." Once again, Jakoba's teeth.

And behind the wall of canvas, shut away from the movement and the voices and the crowds, on a few yards of sand which, up here out of reach of the transforming tides, had gradually become as soft and as silvery as that of the dunes, with the full heat of the sun pouring down on the body so often drenched and frozen by the North Sea, Klaas lay, with a bottle by his side, drunkenly dozing.

How this arrangement—and an arrangement it was, and they all knew it—had come about, Jakoba and Marie would have found it difficult to say. He had gradually grown more and more aggressive and intractable when working with Klaartje and the cart, and when they tried using him to help at the bathing-huts, his glances and his comments when young girls came to bathe, had caused indignation not unmixed with panic. So they had told him to occupy himself with cleaning out Klaartje's stable, up at the field, and looking after his vegetable plot, and they would pay him as usual for the former task, but that had not kept him away from the bathing-huts for more than a day or two, and Jakoba, who had missed him silently, pretended indignation but was relieved when he came back.

"Na, na," he muttered, when reproached with not keeping

to the new plan, "I don't want no vegetables nowadays, nor not any food neither, the Germans taught me to do without all that—all I want is a drop of something and sit in the sun . . . that's all I want."

The sisters looked rather helplessly at each other. He was standing between them, at the edge of the piece of meadow-land, rougher than most of its neighbours cropped into trimness by grazing animals, and they could see at the far end of it, where the wind blew in from the sea through a gap in the dunes, his lean-to shanty, propped up against the brick wall of an out-house attached to a farm. More than once, it had fallen down during the war and he had shored it up again; with pieces of board from bombed buildings, which prowling deserters had afterwards stolen to light their fires, with petrol tins beaten flat, with sheets of flimsy cardboard, with broken branches from pine trees blown down by winter gales. But it looks smarter now, thought Jakoba, since we put that bit of paint on it left over from the cart.

She stared at the place Klaas called *home*. When he was a child, sixty years ago, he used to live with his family in Door-waden; they had been fisher-people there. Then he had left home and come to live in Brugge; she could not remember how he had first come to work for her family. It was very long ago, and all she could think of now as he stood between them, his head hanging down, sometimes darting a quick sly glance at her, and then at Marie—was that ever since she had known any-thing, she had known Klaas.

"That's all I want," he repeated, in the hoarse broken voice that was like the cry of some bird of the dunes; "sit in the sun . . ."

"You got your bit of land," Marie pointed out severely.

"Might take that away, any time," he muttered.

"How can they? You been there sixteen years and more," Jakoba said roughly, while Marie, alarmed at a remark which implied that he might be dispossessed and have to find *some-where* to go—which might well mean the Maes' finding some-where for him—repeated sharply, "How can they?"

"Don't make no difference. Mijnheer up at Doorwaden—you know he was blown up, all of it was, nothing left but a few . . . I don't know. It was his land, they always said, but . . . there was some papers, but the time those swine got in, in 'forty-three, they took everything—my cup, and my bed . . . and the papers went too . . . everything."

His voice died off into a croaking mutter and he was silent, standing there with hanging head.

The sisters were silent too. Both knew quite well what he meant; he wanted them to go on giving him the sum which he earned at the bathing-huts every week, in addition to that which they gave him for the stabling and foddering of Klaartje, and he was telling them that he would spend it on drink. He was asking that they let him stay in the space behind the booth, shut in by the canvas walls and get drunk.

But they couldn't believe it. That is, Marie could not; Jakoba instantly knew that he must have what he wanted, because . . . and then she knew why.

The feeling was terrible; it struck her like a great blow of pain. But she opened her mouth and gave her loud laugh and said roughly, "Yes. I daresay . . . well, you come on down as usual tomorrow, and we'll see."

He looked at her for a moment, then showed all his broken teeth in a grin and turned and shambled away.

Riding home that evening over the long, straight road to Brugge, under the dark blue sky, between the dewy meadows where the willows hung motionless above the slowly gliding dykes, Marie spoke angrily.

"It's terrible—a man lying drunk just round the corner and all those children—anything might happen."

"Don't be such a fool—'anything'. What, I'd like to know? It wouldn't hurt them to be frightened a bit—spoilt little tourist brats. Besides, it isn't a 'man'—it's Klaas. You know Klaas. You ought to, by now." Jakoba paused, while the two glittering bicycles and the two swiftly-pedalling black-clad figures sped over a hundred yards of road. "There's no harm in him," she ended harshly.

Her sister glanced at her. But she said nothing, because an instinct more insubstantial and vague than the shadow of a cloud racing across the shallows of the sands at low tide prompted her to keep silent.

"It won't be too bad; you'll see," said Jakoba at last.

"Oh yes, it will. He'll get worse and worse. He'll shout. And there'll be trouble with them at the office at Oostende . . . the tourists'll start complaining . . . and what'll *maatje* say? . . . giving someone money to get drunk . . ."

"Shut up!" Jakoba suddenly bawled the words, staring straight ahead of her down the long road, with a face whitey-grey under its sunburn. She shot ahead, bending lower over the handlebars. As Marie, startled, doubled her own pace to keep up with her, she caught the words flung back on the wind . . . "because he's going to . . ." and then, louder still, "snuff it . . ."

"Rubbish—snuff it," she said sturdily when, Jakoba having slackened her pace slightly, they were once more riding side by side, "he'll be going for a good many years yet . . . being a worry and a trouble to everyone."

Jakoba said nothing and her usual grim expression did not change; she only eased her almost-helpless arm where her hand grasped the handlebar, and thought that Marie was a fool. He was going to die all right, and soon.

Silently, she set herself to get him what he wanted, and because of her mute, stubborn opposition to any other plan suggested by her sister, and her fierce insistence that their mother should not be told what was going on, they had gradually drifted into the situation existing on this clear, still, very hot morning some seven years after the war.

About twelve o'clock the mid-day meal began to be served in the hotels and at the cafés whose wicker chairs and glass-topped tables were set out along the *digue de mer* at Zande-burghe. Across the wide golden-grey sands, little parties of parents and children could be seen trailing inland towards dry land and lunch, buckets and spades and water-wings and swollen monsters made of rubber dragging along, with seeming unwillingness to leave the sea, in their wake. Quickly the beaches became almost deserted, as the *digue* became more crowded, and soon there were not enough children clamouring for the *excursion à la plage* to make it worth while taking out the blue-and-yellow cart. The window through which tickets were sold in the office was open (indeed, like the Windmill Theatre, it might be said that "it never closed") and in the dimness within, amidst the coarse clean bathing-towels and gay plastic caps and ancient woollen bathing-dresses, sat Marie, eating her way rapidly through a frugal lunch.

"There you are. I told you he'd be asleep. Now perhaps you're satisfied."

The voice was low and strangulated and English. A shadow moved over the white sand and halted in front of Klaartje. A tall girl, wearing grey flannel shorts and a striped blouse, her pale face crowned by short and not very abundant dark hair, was standing there, with a smaller girl in her hand.

"Let's wake him up. I'm *going* to have a ride in the cart, I *am*."

The tall girl turned her head, sighing loudly. The thick lenses of her glasses flashed in the sun.

"*Really*, what a trial you are. They're all taking their *siesta*, or lunching."

"What's a *siesta*?" Then, without waiting for a reply, "There's someone. Let's ask her. She looks like a programme-seller—you remember, you remember, we saw them at *Giselle*,—come on," and a stout arm pointed energetically.

There was an angry mutter that might have been *shut up*. Then the two, the elder lounging along as if unwilling to follow the younger one's determined pulling, came slowly forward. Nora Ruddlin's eyes were fixed on the face of the girl who was leaning back against the stone wall of the *digue* and eating an apple; the oculist had been right when he had told her that the new glasses would 'sharpen everything up', for the face of the apple-eater came close and near at hand and delicately, alluringly beautiful.

"Oh—I'm sorry to disturb you. Are you—er—in charge of this animal?" Nora asked, in very good French.

Ydette finished a piece of apple before replying. She had been enjoying the pause in the bustle and activity of the day; the rustle of the waves drawing ever nearer as they crept forward with the incoming tide, the black shadow cast by the cart on the sand so soft to the touch and so silvery to the eye, the breath of the farm's own smell that every now and again drifted over to her from the vast bulk of the dozing Klaartje, the cool blowing of the wind against her damp forehead, and, on the negative side, the absence of Klaas. She answered composedly, in a tone just short of disobliging:

"Yes, Mademoiselle. But it is the lunch-hour."

"Oh, you speak English . . . there, Ida, you see, I *told* you they were all lunching."

"We'll stay here until they've finished." The child sat down decidedly on the sand, with stout legs thrust out in front of her, "Go on," nodding at Ydette, "eat it up—we'll wait."

Ydette suddenly laughed at her, and Ida laughed back. Nora, who was not only bored but wishing to dissociate herself from any notion that *she* might approve of this travel-allowance-wasting trap for tourists, this absurd *"excursion à la plage"*, stared aloofly out to sea. Then she turned to her sister. "Oh really, Dogfight, you are a trial . . ." she drawled, and slowly drew her foot in its large white espadrille along the sand. She wished they could have lunched at an hotel; the French bread and the sausage her mother had packed up for them that morning was lying heavily on her chest, and everything in sight was a bore: the sea so large and grey, the sands so devoid of anything to attract the intellect unless, like her father, you were interested in marine biology, and the frightful, frightful hotels along the front which had to be seen to be believed . . . like something off an old postcard . . . and she began to plan an amusing letter about them to Evelyn. This improved her spirits slightly, but what she was really wanting, continually and impatiently, was to be back at School. When one only had another year to be there anyway, it did seem the

K

cruellest waste of time to spend any of the precious twelve months in unwanted and tedious holidays.

But the mere thought of Claregates softened her feelings, and she looked less chillily at the bathing-girl. How odd, to see so much hair, and eyes like that, in the glass when one got up in the morning.

"I'm sorry my absurd junior interrupted your lunch," she said, swept away by one of those impulses towards friendliness which she was apt to regret afterwards, and speaking in the manner which she thought of as *abrupt and charming*. "Please don't hurry, will you—er, take your time—er——" the impulse drew back, like some sea-creature into its shell, and her voice faltered away.

What did the girl think of her? Oh, *the eccentric English mees*, probably, what did it matter anyway?

"You've nearly finished now, haven't you?" Ida was demanding of the Belgian girl, who only laughed and threatened to throw the apple core, which she was industriously eating, at her. And if I do manage to stay in the house for an hour this afternoon, Nora was thinking, out of the glare and all this appalling *outdoorness*, there aren't any books except the ones we've brought, and Daddy meant what he said about strictly bagging the Toynbee first . . . oh *lord*! Here's *Adriaan*, now, as if everything weren't tiresome enough.

Perhaps it was an unconscious wish to see how another girl would respond to the approach of the youth now running quickly down the steps leading from the *digue* to the sands, that caused her to glance again at the Belgian child. Yes, she had seen him all right—and really, *what* a change in her expression, it was quite dopey . . . it was a pity, Nora thought, that people who looked like that couldn't see their own faces: it might cure them. The Belgian girl was standing up now, and it did not please Nora that she displayed a height at least two inches greater than Nora's own. But they were both taller than that ghastly little Adriaan, which was something.

"Hullo, Nora; hullo, little fat Ida," he said, coming up to the group with his usual casual bounce, and then his eyes just moved towards the bathing-girl, not really looking at her, and, he said pleasantly, "Hullo," before they came back to Nora. "Look, can you come for a drive?" he went on. "I've got the car—it's only the second-best one, but you'll have to put up with that—on the *digue* and I've collected your parents; your father wants to go and look at a house in Ghent."

"Oh . . . yes, thank you . . . we'd like to." Nora, thinking that at least it would be better than an afternoon on the glaring sands, turned to Ida, who was circling round Klaartje and staring up, with an expression on her freckled face not unlike awe, at the lofty satin slope of his rump. "Dogfight, come along . . . we're going for a drive."

"Where's Christopher?" Adriaan went on, taking out a case and lighting a cigarette and keeping his eyes fixed rather determinedly on Nora's face.

"Need you ask? 'Shooting', as the mysterious jargon has it, the belfry, I imagine, or 'shooting' something, anyway."

"I've got a new projector to show him. I hope to make him vomit with envy . . . What's *Les Alouettes* like? Bloody?"

She looked curiously at the stocky confident figure, dressed in sharply-creased sailcloth jeans of light rust-red and a T-shirt of shrill lime-yellow. Really, it was rather beastly, how he always said spiteful things in strong language. His vocabulary was as ugly as his face.

"It's rather *intimidating*," she said; "the salon's full of velvet sofas and polished tables, we're almost afraid to breathe in there, and Mummy's decided to lock it up for the three weeks we're staying here. *Most* peculiar, velvet sofas in the middle of the dunes . . . but you've seen it, haven't you? You must have, you arranged it all with your family's friends and everything."

"Yes I did, and a bloody bore it was . . . I just wanted to make sure that you thought the place was godawful," and he laughed. "Come on, they're waiting up there, and I'm in a hurry."

"Dogfight! *Marche!*" Nora called, turning her head. When she turned back once more to Adriaan, she was just in time to catch his eyes fixed, but absolutely *fixed*, on the Belgian girl's face. She was dusting sand off the floor of the cart with a hand-brush, and not looking at him, but he was staring at her with the *oddest* expression. Dear me, thought Nora, experiencing an uncomfortable mingling of excitement, curiosity and firmly-rooted distaste. It must be 'the usual thing'. But the child couldn't be more than fifteen (he, of course, must be getting on for twenty, so, she supposed, in his case it was more under-standable, however peculiar his taste might be); the girl would only have been in the Fifth at Claregates, and if her dopey ex-pression and his very odd one really meant that something of 'that kind' *was* going on between them, Nora thought it was rather disgusting.

Dangerous for the Belgian child, too. Because Adriaan was horrid; he always had been, ever since he used to tweak Nora's hair (not in a handful but just one hair at a time, so that it really hurt her and had more than once set up a kind of neuralgia) when they had all been children together at Port Meredith.

A solemn, noble feeling began to stir in Nora. She looked seriously at the Belgian child and thought in a sensible off-hand way that if ever she should need rescuing from Adriaan, she, Nora, would help her. Then, glowing slightly, she turned to her sister.

"Dogfight! Come on," she called, impatiently now.

Ida came dawdling round the side of Klaartje and said, with a determined look that matched her square, freckled face, "I'm going for a ride in the cart. You've finished your lunch," accusingly, to Ydette, "come on."

Ydette, who was slowly re-tying the strings of the white apron that had caused Ida to compare her to a programme-seller, looked at her and smiled.

"But first we must find some other children to make the ride," she said soothingly, "if *mademoiselle*," with a polite, but not shy, glance at the elder sister, "will wait here with you, I will go to see if other children are coming."

"There isn't time," Adriaan cut in loudly, his dark face red-dening, "I'm in a hurry." He added, more quietly, to Ydette, "You heard me say that *mademoiselle*'s parents are waiting up on the *digue*." Now he was looking full at her, but Nora thought that although his voice had sounded angry, his face did not look it. "You'd better tell *mademoiselle* that you can't take them in the cart."

Ydette hesitated, glancing first at Nora with a questioning expression. Then slowly her eyes came back to his, and rested there, dreamily.

"Of course, there isn't time," said Nora with authority. "Come on, Dogfight, don't be a bore, Mummy and Daddy are waiting."

"There *is* time, there *is* time," Ida exclaimed passionately. "I've been waiting all the morning to go in it, I got up es-pec-ially early and I was good all the time in the Bank while we changed the tra-vel-ling cheque, and now you say there isn't time. It's *not fair*."

This fatal verdict, prelude to many an exhausting argument, landed threateningly amidst the elders and caused Nora to give a loud groan; but Adriaan turned quickly and said something to Ydette in what Nora, whose father spoke it fluently, knew to be Flemish.

"Tell her the cart isn't going," he said; "go on, tell her, I'm in a hurry."

His eyes bored into, rather than rested upon, her face; it would have been better if no-one else had been there, but at least for a few minutes he could stop trying *not* to look at her. He couldn't even guess at what she was thinking. There had come the usual change in her expression, when she looked at him. He knew it so well, having seen it during the past seven years that had passed with such extraordinary swiftness, and had changed so slightly her face, merely elongating and slightly rounding her body; he had seen that look in the light cast by winter snow, and in the windy, leaf-scattered glow of autumn evenings, and always he looked for it when he chanced to meet her, but still he did not know what it meant; the steady, bright, dreaming look. It maddened him.

Ydette turned docilely to Ida and knelt down beside her on the sand while the other two watched, and began to talk to her almost in a whisper; presently Ida nodded in a grudging way; suddenly she flung her arms about Ydette's neck and bestowed upon her a strangling embrace. Then, portentously, she nodded.

"Mind—it's a secret," she said, in a tone mingling confidence with warning, and Ydette smiled and nodded too.

"Well, that seems to have 'taken care' of that," said Nora, sighing loudly, "*now*, perhaps, we can get up and relieve the alarm of our waiting parents."

She nodded pleasantly at Ydette and turned away; it did occur to her that she might say something about seeing her again soon, but she resisted the impulse; no doubt they *would* see her again, and many times, for Ida was already announcing in her most passionate tone that she *liked* that girl, she *liked* her, and Nora herself—she confessed it—found the Belgian rather interesting.

She was accustomed to such sudden, brief attractions for younger girls, which passed as rapidly as they came; something maternal and protective, something in her that was chivalrous and perhaps fated to wither, unless it found an outlet, was stirred from time to time by the face and personality of some newcomer—and, because of this latest interest for which she slightly despised herself, the holiday at Zandeburghe already promised to be a little less dull.

Now definitely in Adriaan's charge, the party was walking as smartly as the soft, heaped, sliding sand would permit, towards the steps ascending the sloping stone wall to the *digue*. She said casually to him:

"Do you know that rather unusual-looking child?"

"*Know* her?" he said violently. "Of course I *know* her; her aunts keep a greengrocery on the corner of the *plaats*, just across from us."

"Well . . . I was only wondering . . . she is rather unusual-looking, don't you agree?"

She was well aware that she was trying to pump him, but, although she was a little ashamed of herself, she could not resist the faint, distasteful yet enjoyable excitement that came upon her at the idea of 'something' between those two. She also told herself that if she was to be in a position ever to help that long, dreamy-looking child to 'get out of some hole with Adriaan' she must know how he felt about her. At present it seemed that the mere mention of her put him into a temper. But *that*, Nora remembered from former days, had *never* been difficult.

"Is she? You think so, do you?" He stood aside to allow her to go up the steps, which she did awkwardly, made self-conscious as usual by any action which pointed to the fact of her being a girl, and she and Ida waited at the top for him while he came bounding up. He really does look much older than he is, she thought, perhaps it's because he wears his clothes as if he didn't care about being fat and small and ugly. As he joined them, he went on:

"Her looks might come from anywhere, I suppose—I mean, she might be anybody. She's a foundling—isn't that the word? Yes," as Nora nodded, "a foundling."

"Dear me. How very romantic. What's her name?"

"Ydette," put in Ida importantly, who was marching along beside them with her chest, in its striped jersey, stuck out, "she told me her name, Ydette Maes. That's what we were whispering. I told her mine, too—Ida Ruddlin, The Link House, Ashbourne, Sussex, England, Great Britain, Europe, the world——"

"Yes, all right, very interesting." Nora's tone was crushing, because she wanted to hear more about Ydette. "Is she a war orphan, Adrian?"

"She was found just before the war—or when it had only just started, I believe. But I really don't know all the details," he answered, while he thought how often he had 'pumped' people—the shop-keepers, his mother, her old friends, even the Sisters at the Béguinage when he was dragged along to grin and stare at the floor while his mother jawed with them—he had cunningly, casually encouraged all the locals to relate, over and over again, the scanty details that were known about the finding of Ydette in the big dune. "My mother will tell you—if you're interested," he went on, "Ydette is a protégée of hers; she taught her to speak English."

"I thought she had an unusually good accent."

"Did you? It's a wonder if she has—she's a bloody fool at everything else—half-witted, practically, or so everybody round here says . . . and my mother says that the only thing for her to do when she does go out to work is to get a job packing the flowers at my father's place; you don't need brains to do that; any ass" (he gave it the long *a* and grinned as he spoke) "can do it. It's mostly done by women. And the little swine will be able to keep her hands beautiful."

"Dear me, does she make a fuss about them?" Nora screwed up the blunt members which were thrust into the pockets of her shorts and flushed at the memory of those repeatedly made, and repeatedly broken, vows to give up nail-biting.

"How in hell should I know? Females always do and hers are very long and . . . bony," he ended quickly. He must pull himself together. Nora was a fool about everything that mattered (she was clever academically, but with a woman that neither mattered nor counted), but even she might detect his desire to talk about Ydette if he kept on doing it; she would see through the contempt he put into his voice and discover what was behind it. And what was behind it? He was damned if he knew.

"Oh, there *is* Chris," he said, relieved to change the subject.

The three elder Ruddlins did not appear to be as tall as they actually were, while they waited in the van Roeslaeres' car, but that was because they were sitting down and their long legs were folded; Christopher's seemed as if his knees might at any moment touch his chin, and the books piled on Everard's lap were pushed uncomfortably high against his chest; May, although not, of course, a Ruddlin by birth, suggested in her elongated gawkiness that she had both been chosen as a Ruddlin's mate for that reason, and had, during twenty years or so of being one, become longer and leaner than she was naturally. They were all sitting quietly and they were all silent: Everard was looking down into one of the narrow lanes of old houses leading from the *digue* into the town; Christopher was staring off to sea with his eyes screwed up ("thinking about long shots," decided Nora, as their party approached); and May was reading, with the wisps of hair to which she had long ago become resigned, making shadows, as they blew about, on the pages of her book.

"Here we are," observed Nora, in whom there was an occasional impulse, that was not a family characteristic, to make unnecessary remarks, "did the Belgian Mrs Mop turn up, Mummy?"

"Yes, and most efficient she is. Speaks some English, too."

"That's a blessing. So now we shan't have to rely upon Daddy's doubtless rather rusty Flemish," said Nora, surveying the accommodation in the car and feeling relieved that she would not have to sit next to Adriaan, who was going to drive. The car was so large, white and opulent as to appear to English eyes slightly vulgar, but at least there was plenty of room.

"My Flemish is decidedly rusty," said Everard, turning away from his long gaze at the tall pale houses in the narrow lane, "but then it's a long time since I've used it."

May looked up from her book. "How long? I was trying to remember this morning."

"Sixteen years," he answered decidedly, "I was last here in the autumn of 'thirty-seven."

"Here? I thought the delights of Zandeburghe were new to you," said Nora.

"So they are—or almost. I was at a place called Doorwaden, some distance inland." He turned round to see what Adriaan, who had disappeared round the back of the car, was doing.

"You were getting material for the additions to Grandpapa's history, weren't you?" asked Nora.

Her father nodded without turning round, and at that moment Adriaan slammed the boot, with that violence of movement which was sometimes startling in him, and came round to the front of the car.

He offered no explanation of the delay in starting, and it was only Christopher, whose interest in cinema and pre-occupation with the techniques of camera work and habit of looking about for unusual 'shots' made him unusually observant of detail, who had noticed that 'van Roeslaere' had done nothing with the boot but stare into it for five minutes.

He meant to keep us waiting, he decided; he's annoyed because Papa and Mama van R. have told him off to keep an eye on the old English friends and visitors and make himself useful to them; he didn't like having to meet us at Oostende yesterday, it stood out about a mile, and I'll bet he'd had to drag himself away from somewhere disreputable to do it, too. . . . He certainly doesn't improve with time. But I'm damned if I gratify him by taking any notice of his goings on. He's an odd one. *And then some*, thought Christopher, who affected the slang of the 'twenties.

He had the Ruddlin slenderness and height, but had inherited the rusty-golden fairness that had been his mother's in her youth, rather than his father's dark eyes and hair, and he was—although they seldom referred to the fact because they were not a family interested in looks—exceedingly good-looking, with straight features and good teeth and bright hair that fell in a straight Hitler-lock over his high white brow. He had a naturally brusque, rather managing way with him that his two years in the Army had developed; it broke out from long silences, and implied a capacity for getting things done in the best and quickest way; he wasn't in the least inept; he gave an impression of being very interested in one thing, which kept him thinking about it during those long silent withdrawals of himself from whatever happened to be going on—as, in fact, he was; he might, when he grew older, seem just a little intimidating. He was rather clever, but not so clever as Nora, who cared for him better than anyone else in her world. He was nearly twenty-two, to her seventeen.

They settled themselves into the car, and it rolled off: down one of the narrow lanes of tall, pale grey houses with white shutters and decorations of plasterwork in elaborate Edwardian scrolls, leading into Zandeburghe and away from the dazzling

grey sea. There was a light like the reflection thrown by water
upon a white ceiling in these lanes; diffused, very bright, extraordinarily calming and yet filled with excitement; and Everard
Ruddlin, sitting beside his wife with the soft straight wisps of
her rusty-grey hair blown every now and then against his cheek
by the wind, thought that it came from the vast hidden presence of the sea. He turned his mind away from the knowledge
that his own excitement, and his inward sense of pain, were
caused by something more than this strange, nostalgic light.

"What tempting things they do put out for us to spend our
precious travel allowance on; it's disgraceful," May said
briskly, as the car ran past shops displaying the pretty jewellery,
the bright scarves of imitation silk, the mouth-watering sweets
each with its indescribable air of being hand-made down to the
last crystallized violet. "Nolly, you and I will have a prowl
round here later."

"You know I hate shopping, Mummy."

"Yes, in England . . . but these shops really are entrancing."

"*All* shops and all shopping," persisted Nora, "except book-
shops."

"And shops for seeds and plants and gardening tools," said
May, stifling a pang of regret that she would miss the opening
of the zinnias and the early dahlias at home . . . but of course,
if one allowed oneself to become a slave to a garden . . .

"Now . . . now you have a *char*-woman, Mummy," began
Ida, who had been preparing herself to make one of the long
speeches which she occasionally delivered, "will you be able to
—will you be able to have a nice holiday? I hope you will,"
leaning forward from her seat on her father's knee, and smiling
graciously.

"Have you been worrying about her health?" asked Nora in
her snubbing elder-sister tone.

"Never mind, Dogfight, it was very kind of you," said her
father, putting his chin for a moment against the curly hair, and
feeling through it the warmth of her large, squarish head.
"May, did you lock up the house?" he asked.

"I didn't think it necessary. No one else seemed to be doing it. And then the woman who's got the bungalow just over the dune, a Miss Rogers, says that it's like the country at home; no-one bothers to lock up. She said she was going to lie outside her front door sun-bathing all day and would keep an eye on *Les Alouettes* for us."

"That was very kind indeed of her, wasn't it," said Ida loudly, "is she a nice woman?" and May laughed as she answered, "Yes, I should think so. Rather talkative but quite nice."

"Oh dear."

"What's the matter now, Nolly?" asked Everard, reminding himself that Nora was clever, and conscientiously helped her mother in the house, and did not *deliberately* get on his nerves.

"Need we get 'all matey' with forlorn English spinsters alone on the 'Continong'?"

"She isn't at all forlorn; she's rather smart and seems to have come here for the sun-bathing, rather than to sight-see; I left her lying in a hollow of the dune wearing a very smart yellow-and-black bikini."

"More suitable for Le Zoute than Zandeburghe," said Everard, "or so I should have thought."

"Yes," said Adriaan, as he sent the car along the road, now out in the country, that led towards Ghent, "Le Zoute for smarties, Zandeburghe for stodgies."

"The stodgies being us. Thank you," said May, "how well you've kept up your English."

"Thank you, Mrs Ruddlin," he said with mock politeness.

And your unpleasantness, thought the wife of his former headmaster; disagreeableness is too mild a word for you. Nevertheless, the thought was unaccompanied by condemnation or dislike, for it had been a fact, acknowledged by the Ruddlins for years now with mild amusement, that she accepted Adriaan just as he was, without feeling either; she was just brisk about him, as she was about dust on top of the wardrobe and answering awkward questions, and she invariably said that he would 'probably grow out' of his unpleasing mannerisms and qualities. But Everard Ruddlin, who had always felt

strong repugnance towards his pupil which he had always perfectly controlled—he hadn't even fallen over backwards with
trying to be fair to him—thought that it was too late, now, for
Adriaan to change his spots.

The car rushed on, with a low, luxurious humming that was
full of latent power, and its driver amused himself by driving
just a little too fast in the hope of frightening the women . . .
but, he thought irritably, that if they *were* frightened they
wouldn't show it. The Ruddlins were a very stiff-upper-lipped
lot, and *never* had he known people who took their pleasures so
unrelaxedly and with so much reserve; Everard's interest in
marine biology and the history and art of Flanders was prac-
tical and intellectual rather than æsthetic, and May played her
Vivaldi and her Scarlatti and Bach with perfect touch and sensitive interpretation and never a word more about what she
played than a 'rather charming' or '*really* very delightful'. As
for the feelings fostered by lounging languidly about, or gossiping amusingly and maliciously, or responding with sensuous
pleasure to experience—such feelings simply never seemed to
get within the Ruddlin ambience. They make me think—
(thought Adriaan gloomily, as he sent the car by a twist of his
wrist down one of those Continental roads so straight, and extending so far into the distance, that they produce a hallu-
cinatory effect of leading into permanent escape)—they remind
me of the smell of that soap, Lifebuoy, that we were all soused
with every day at Port Meredith. They're so bloody *healthy*.

And, for the next three weeks, he had been told to keep an
eye on them and drive them about and see to it that they enjoyed their holiday . . . his parents seemed to take it for granted
that he wouldn't *mind* doing it; would in fact even *like* it, simply
because he had lived for six years with the Ruddlins during the
war; his people had assumed, too, that he would have nothing
better to do with three weeks of his long vacation, which had
just started from the University of Louvain, than to run around
wiping the noses of the Ruddlins.

He was particularly affronted by the squareness and plainness of Ida. (He was simply not *going* to be lured, by their

silence on the subject, into enquiring why she had been nick-named Dogfight.) Her appearance was an insult, her manner to him noticeably offensive, and he did not agree with the prophecy made by his mother during the previous evening, when they had been discussing Nora: "That poor child, she is being over-educated and her hair-cut is deplorable: I shouldn't think that she will ever marry—but no doubt May has told her that that doesn't matter. The little Ida, now, she still has a chance to grow up attractive; I feel sure that May will do better with her."

Not if present omens are borne out, Adriaan was thinking. Dogs: she'll live in the country somewhere and breed dogs, but I'll bet that's all she ever will breed.

Behind him, the silence which he thought of as that typical-Ruddlin-chewing-over-something-*interesting*, had been broken by fuss about what they still called sweeties.

"Hungry, Dogfight?" her father was asking, and, at her answering emphatic nod, "feel in my pocket, then—not that one, the other, on the left—and you'll find something."

Nora reached over his shoulder and helped herself from the bag which Ida had taken from his coat, then passed the bag to her mother and Christopher, but Adriaan, on being offered a damaged but once highly superior piece of tinted sugar, shook his head.

"Are you afraid of getting fat?" Ida's tone was sympathetic. "I'm fat but I don't mind. Nora minds getting fat. *She* says she's fat but *I* don't think she is, do you?"

"Really, Dogfight," sighed Nora; ten years of acquaintance-ship with the young man in the driver's seat did not enable her face to keep its ordinary colour, "how can that *possibly* be of any interest to Adriaan?"

"It's extremely rude to ask people if they mind getting fat," Adriaan said forbiddingly, half-turning his head to look at Ida's bulging cheek and staring, sobered eyes. "As it happens, I'm like you. I'm fat but I don't mind."

"You've lost weight, as a matter of fact, since last year," May Ruddlin said.

He shrugged, without answering, and the car went on down the straight, narrow lane between fields glowing in summer's most placid green, with the whippy branches of the willows scraping along its sides. Everard crunched the last of an expensive piece of Bruges confectionery between some teeth which had recently been substituted for his own, and looked up to meet his wife's smile.

"How do they feel?" she asked.

"Decidedly easier; less like wooden ones," he said.

"They look very nice."

He shook his head in mock resignation. "But they do," May insisted, "it was more than worth while spending so much on them. I shan't; when it comes to my turn I would sooner have the shrubbery turned completely out, re-dug and re-planted with exciting things; but I do think it's been worth it for you."

"What are you talking about?" asked Ida, twisting round.

"Daddy's lovely new teeth."

"Mummy says I must look nice, and have teeth costing a lot of money, or new boys wouldn't come to the school. But I think they would, just because I'm so nice myself, don't you?"

"YES! Have you got your new teeth in now? Let me see them . . . which are they? Those? That one, and that one, and that one——"

"Steady on," said her father, joining in the laughter, while he put aside the small, blunt finger that was investigating his gums, "you—make them sound like a mouthful. There are only three of them."

"Four," said Christopher, amidst more laughter.

"I meant four." Everard bowed his head to the correction of family amusement, "but I can only feel three now, thank heaven; they did feel like a mouthful, at first."

While they were talking and laughing, the car had been entering, and was now travelling down, a broad quiet track that apparently led into the heart of a region where the usual features of the landscape seemed to be in some way heightened and intensified.

Perhaps the solitude of its farms, separated by wide distances and half-concealed by rich masses of orchard trees, deepened the placid, sunny silence brooding over meadow and poplar and willow; were the slowly-running streams a little clearer here, reflecting more pellucidly through their screen of bordering leaves the tremendous sky? The poplars strayed across the meadows in a wayward procession, their tufty elongated shapes familiar from Flemish paintings; the sheep couching in the shady grass, cows and horses drowsing motionless in the shadow of the apple boughs, with tails switching lazily against the flies, glowed with the rich cinnamons and soft greys and glossy blacks of archetypal animals; it was like going on into the very heart of Flanders: yes it was like that; and there— there on the near horizon, coming up sweetly and austerely out of the wandering lines of the poplars and the silvery masses of low willow, and smitten into whiteness by the powerful light of the afternoon sun—there was the tower of the church.

"Door-waden."

It was Ida's, his daughter's, voice, reading out the name that absolutely went through his heart. She was half turning back to look at a sign-post that was already receding into the distance.

Well, here it was. He must get ready for what might be coming.

"Door-waden," she said again—and again he felt the stab— with surprise and dismay, for although he had expected to feel *something*, he had never expected to feel so much. After all, it was sixteen years ago.

What was she clamouring about now?

"I want to go there. I want to go to Doorwaden. Can we go there, Mummy?"

May, now, full of lively interest.

"Yes, do let's . . . I'd like to see it," turning to him, "your letters made it sound so charming. Is there time, Adriaan?" but the thick brown neck, where the black hair grew low, did not turn, so presumably he had not heard.

"It *was* charming," said Everard, trying to keep his voice normal, "but I doubt if it looks very charming now; our bombers were very busy up and down that coast in 'forty and again just before the invasion . . ."

He mustn't sound too irritable, nor yet too regretful; he mustn't sound *too* anything, because (oh, it was horrible) any excess of feeling in his voice or manner might *arouse suspicion*. And all the time that he was keeping his voice and manner ordinary, he felt as if he were weeping inside; asking May to understand, and forgive, and be kind to him. If he had known that coming back was going to be as painful as this, he would never have come; he would have made any excuse not to. He hadn't wanted to, anyway, but had not put forward strong objections to the Van Roeslaeres' suggestion that they should take a house for three weeks near Bruges, because he had supposed that he would have to go back to Flanders some time, and he might as well get it over this summer as any other.

Oh, couldn't May keep quiet?

"But is it on the coast? I thought you said that it was inland."

"So it is, about five or six miles. But it used to be on the coast, before the sea withdrew and left it high and dry, as so often happened to these little Flanders towns. But that was some hundreds of years ago."

"Why did we bomb it, then?" asked May. The children were quiet, Ida staring across the meadows at the tower of the church, and Christopher and Nora occupied with their private interests—which did not often include the war that had ended seven years ago.

"Well, the Astrid Canal runs quite near it and the Germans had parked their invasion barges all along there. Then, just before our invasion of Europe, we pasted it again."

" 'Pranged' is the correct term, I believe," put in Christopher.

"Pranged, then. So it may be rather knocked about," said Everard, noticing with increasing relief that Adriaan was making no attempt to turn aside from this road which, Everard knew, only skirted the region of which Doorwaden was the centre. Nowhere did this road approach nearer to the little town than some two or three kilometres, and if they could only get as far as the point where it turned off to join the main

Bruges—Ghent one, he thought, he would be safe . . . for that afternoon, at least. But there were going to be nearly three weeks of this to be got through.

May was staring across the meadows now; the tower of the church was almost opposite, and he had to turn to look at it. Another stab, although he had seen it so often in memory during those first months after his return to England, he knew now that he had not been seeing it clearly in his mind's eye. Because he had forgotten how beautiful it was. It absolutely hurt him to look at it.

"The church is still standing," May was saying, with a persuasive note in her voice. "Let's just go quickly through there and see how much of it's left—can we, Adriaan?"

"The church *is* still standing," said Adriaan suddenly—and Everard was waiting so intently for what the young man's contribution to the situation was going to be—would it be helpful or would it make things worse?—that he missed the subdued grumble from Nora about *bomb ruins being quite the dullest thing imaginable*, with which he usually dealt severely—"it *is* still standing, but it's about the only thing there that is," Adriaan went on, "I drove through the place a week or two ago and it's Doorwaden la Morte all right now. *Quite* a sight to see." He blew a long, insolent, sonorous note on the horn as they rushed through a quiet village.

"But I want to see the church . . ." moaned Ida in a die-away voice, "I want to see it, I want to see it—is that it, that tower-thing sticking up out of the trees? Let's look what it says in the guide book," and she sought about in the recess for maps and other objects between seat and hood, and for the next few minutes was quiet.

"We won't go there this afternoon," Everard, seeing that this was the critical moment, said with decision, "I want to have plenty of time to see this house at Ghent. And I'm sure the sight of poor old Doorwaden would be depressing."

"There's time, you know—*if* you want to go there," said Adriaan carelessly. He had been idly balancing between his wish to do old Ruddlin out of a leisurely inspection of the house at Ghent, and the wish to side with May and Ida against him; now he came indifferently down on the side of depressing him with the sight of a ruined place which he had formerly admired.

"*No*. Not this afternoon," said Everard sharply, feeling his sweating forehead cold in the wind, cursing silently.

"There!" Ida shouted suddenly. " 'The at-ten-tion of vis-it-ors is par-tic-u-lar-ly drawn to the un-us-ual steps of the Town Hall.' "

"Good God, can you read?" demanded Adriaan, startled into turning round to look at her.

"Of course," was the chilly reply.

"I could read when I was two. How old were you when you could?"

"Two." After a pause, during which they looked at each other and the words *so sucks* trembled on the air, she turned away and moaned, "I *want* to see it, I *want* to see it, I *want* to see it——"

"Do shut up, Dogfight, you're being a bore," said Christopher. "There are much better things to see in Ghent and we'll have a super tea there."

"I want tea now. I want it in Doorwaden."

"You can't want it, it's only just three o'clock."

"I *do* want it, I didn't have a proper lunch."

"You had sausage and bread and butter and *Reine-Claude*," said her mother.

"That isn't my idea of a proper lunch . . ."

The car turned into the main road. It swung out into a thoroughfare whose smooth, wide, perfectly-kept surface stretched away into the seemingly endless distance, between splendid chestnut trees lifting their load of late summer foliage into the hot sunlight and on either side casting deep cool shade along the road; and Adriaan, smiling with the first sign of pleasure that he had displayed that afternoon, accelerated. They sped away, towards the forested slopes of the distance.

Everyone was interested by the change in the scenery and there was an exchange of remarks about the landscape, the cultivation of the fields on either side, and *that sort of thing* (thought Adriaan) between the elder children and their mother; he listened contemptuously, and Everard, in a moment, slowly let out a long, stealthy sigh of relief. Hardly did he dare to let it come, but he thought that—for this afternoon at least—he was probably safe . . .

Oh—Doorwaden—with the afternoon light that has hardly yet begun to decline into the west falling sleepily across russet bricks and grey cobblestones and little dark panes of glittering glass—the sky, that seems to hold perpetually in its blueness the pausing, benign depth of five o'clock, glowing above the roof-tops at the end of every street—the grass of the meadows outside the town coming into its narrow alleys; straying capriciously in, and settling undisturbed between the stones of the tiny *plaats* surrounded by the tall, richly-carved, ancient houses—and five miles away, across the meadows and the white sandy hollows of the dunes, where the coarse dark grasses bow in the wind or bleach in the sun of summer, the sea that retreated from Doorwaden more than three hundred years ago spreads itself in foam along the lonely shore.

Sea-colour is in the sky above the descending stairways of the stepped roofs, where the black daws and silver pigeons perch and balance; on days when the wind blows inland its voice sounds through the quiet streets as if sighing faintly through the convolutions of a shell left high on the dunes when the waves have withdrawn; on days when the town is veiled in rainy mist, the smell of saltness and the taste of it comes in, blowing on the wind, past the dim old ruby and garnet-red houses that seem to have fallen asleep. That last day of all—*when the delicate dark face is wet and streaked with tears*—the sun has gone down; last light is fading off the grey-and-red roofs, now coolness is wandering through streets that have soaked up the sunlight of the long summer hours—later on that evening, the train will pass Doorwaden, on the way home to England—a little town that you go past in the night—nothing more than a cluster of lights shining faint and few, like mournful stars across the black fields, but in the house the curtains will be drawn, as usual, over the window looking out on the willow tree——

"Here we are, Mr Ruddlin." The car came gently to a stop; he looked up at tall grey-and-white buildings, people passing, afternoon sunshine, little trams painted a light dingy yellow, and Adriaan's bored face, "Ida's demanding tea—do you want to drive straight to a tea shop or see the house first and then——"

Everard addressed himself, thankfully, to the settling of the question.

"I like it very much at Zandeburghe, do you think we shall come here again next year?" Ida asked, while Nora was supervising her going to bed on an evening some days later. She was sitting up with a glass of milk in one hand and a biscuit in the other, spinning out her supper with an expertise due to long practice, and her hair (emphatically "curly" hair, rather than the more poetic and languishing "curling") stood out round her face after an enforced and inadequate combing. "Do you like it here, Nolly?" she went on.

" 'This side idolatry.' "

Ida dealt with those answers of her sister's which she did not understand by repeating her question; she now said patiently, "Do you like it here? Do you like it better than at The Link House?"

"Of course I don't like it better than at The Link House, ass, and you do know I don't like anywhere much, except School."

Ida's eyes, kept open with difficulty in a face already burned crimson by wind and sun, stared at her drunkenly over the milk which she was sipping, and the glass began to tilt.

"Look out——" Nora swooped and made a dramatic rescue, "you'll spill it all over the bed and we shall have Monsieur Ruisdael 'fit to be tied'."

"Is Mon-sieur Ruis-dael a friend of Mad-ame van Roes-laere?"

"You know he is—she told him about us, and he let us this house. Now hurry up, if you want to read *James the Red Engine* —although how you can like that baby book, when Daddy lent you his Violet Fairy Book especially to bring on holiday, I cannot think."

"I DO like the Violet Fairy Book, I took it down to the beach this morning while you were still asleep, and Ydette read me some of it."

"You oughtn't to, then. You'll get it all over sand and stuff. You know Daddy's very precious with those books."

"There are hundreds of them, all different colours—the Red Fairy Book, the Grey Fairy Book, the Blue Fairy Book——"

"Yes, I know; now *get on*, or no *James the Red Engine*."

"And it didn't get all over sand and stuff, because Ydette took great care of it, she wrapped it up in her apron, and we sat on the sand and she read it to Klaartje and me. Of course I know Klaartje can't understand. But Ydette said—she said he likes to hear us talking. He likes *the soundings of our voices*, she said."

"What else do you talk about?" asked Nora curiously.

She was not going to let her gratitude to Ydette—for coming strolling along the dunes with the cheerful Ida in her hand, on that first morning when Nora, oversleeping, had awoke in mild dismay to find her sister's bed empty—to lead her into an acquaintanceship which could too easily develop into an encumbrance. She was pleased to observe, as the holiday progressed, that Ydette's manners and her behaviour seemed to match her strangely fascinating appearance, but she herself never went beyond the cool good-morning nod and the casual word of thanks for having taken Dogfight off her hands for odd half hours.

"What do you talk about?" she repeated, as Ida remained silent, sipping with eyelids almost closing over her eyes.

"We talk about—we talk about the children. The children that go in the *excursion*. There's a *very* naughty boy called Tarmy——" her sister said slowly, at last.

"Called *what*? Now come on, put that down, you don't want any more, you're only playing with it."

"Tarmy. He's an American." Ida allowed her to take the glass, and settled herself among the pillows.

"Oh, *Tommy*."

"No, it *isn't* Tommy, it's *Tarmy*, I heard his mother calling him, and it's *Tarmy*."

"Oh all right then, it's Tarmy. Have it your own way." Nora was bustling round the room, pulling curtains and straightening coverings.

"Do you think Simon Broughton will have a new mouse next term? His old one—his other one—it was called Julius Cæsar —it was very sad—it died of a mys-ter-ious illness." Ida's voice was becoming slower and more repetitive and *James the Red Engine* was already drooping from her hand.

"How on earth should I know whether Simon Broughton will have a new mouse next term? Now no longer than ten minutes, remember. Good night."

"Quick! Let's have a pillow-fight!" Ida suddenly flew upright, wide awake.

"Oh I daresay. Very nice, but I'm going downstairs." Nora poked her quickly in the patch of plump brown flesh showing between pyjama top and trousers, and, leaving her chuckling, went quickly out of the room.

The house called *Les Alouettes*, property of a business associate of Hubert van Roeslaere's, was a small building of two storeys, and it stood with half a dozen others of the same type which their owner, eager to take advantage of the reviving tourist trade, had had built amidst the dunes. It was covered in rough-cast painted pale pink and had simple white-painted doors and window-frames, but it was furnished more elaborately than might be expected in a house built for letting to summer visitors, and although the wooden stairs were uncarpeted save for the thin film of silver sand which the occupants brought indoors in their comings and goings throughout the day, there were thickish curtains with pelmets at the windows and May Ruddlin had—as Nora had said—already decided that she would not be bothered with telling her Belgian daily-help to brush sand out of that carpet and those chairs in the *salon* every few days. Although the *salon* commanded the view of the vast North Sea and all the changing panorama of the beach from its windows and the kitchen ones looked out only upon a steep wall of white sand a few feet away, the family ate in the kitchen.

There was a small verandah and porch on the side overlooking the sea, with steps leading down onto the dune, and here Nora found Christopher and Adriaan, lying in deck-chairs and laughing about something: by the fact that although they continued to laugh nothing was said by either of them to initiate her into the joke, she suspected that it was one of Adriaan's. It wasn't necessarily *an indelicate story* (this was Nora's phrase for a dirty joke), because Christopher had told her that the telling of such was, rather surprisingly, not one of Adriaan's almost countless unpleasing habits, but it was probably an anecdote about one of his own experiences—and that might very easily be indelicate; in fact, from the expression on Christopher's long, fair face, which matched that on Adriaan's pear-shaped, swarthy one, she was pretty certain that it was; and the silence that descended upon the verandah after she had gone over to a seat in the farthest corner—having waved aside with an impatient and embarrassed mutter Adriaan's polite rising to his feet and offer of his own chair—convinced her. She took up one of the copies of *Girl* and *Eagle* with which Ida had armed herself against possible boredom on the journey from England, and began with a superior expression to turn the brightly coloured sheets while the young men smoked and looked out to sea.

But she was fretting about Chris. Was he going to take her for a walk after the parents had been driven off to dine with the van Roeslaeres? They had not had a walk or a good long talk since they got here. In fact, he had been rather cool and casual: *beastly*, Nora called it, in an honest reversion to the language of ten years ago, she must have done something, she supposed. I have been awful, this last year; she *always* seemed to be doing something to annoy him. But it wasn't her fault; she was never aware of doing anything that he might not like, and she had to be herself, didn't she? it wasn't *her* fault that frightful arguments always developed about the kind of girl he *did* like and the kind that Nora was: and the type he seemed to enjoy being with was the very worst type imaginable, in the verdict of Claregates; the type that got into such a state for weeks before the End of Term dance, with endlessly talking about what it should wear, and who it should bring as a partner, that all sensible people (which included herself and Evelyn Berrow and Hilary Perowne) were bored stiff. And he was "always" hinting, since he came back from that first term at Cambridge, about her clothes and the way she talked and her manner; covertly criticising; being almost catty.

A heavy, dull sensation of muted pain began to creep over her as she sat slowly and intelligently studying the pages of *Girl*.

He would probably go off and spend the evening with Adriaan.

It felt worse when she disliked the person with whom he 'went off', because then disapproval—and in the case of Adriaan, fear of a bad example—was added to—well, a perfectly justifiable resentment at being 'out of it'. Adriaan couldn't help being a bad influence for even the best-brought-up person. And one of the worst things about it all was that it seemed such a short time ago—and it *was* a short time, it was less than a year—that she had had Chris almost to herself, to share her interests and share his (heavens! the times that she had forced, compelled herself to comment brightly and intelligently on his holdings-forth about films—which she certainly did like very far 'this side idolatry') and help her with her work at school. (But she prided herself that she so seldom had to ask him for help.) And now she was beginning to realize that he had given her that masculine society which she enjoyed and badly needed, but which she was not getting from other young men because, with them, there was always that embarrassment and shyness and sense of being—oh well, let's face it—a failure.

Males, 'chaps', that tiresome but (worse luck) necessary other half of the human race . . . at any hint of well, sex, between herself and one of them (oh, she admitted that so far there hadn't been even a hint)—any question of *that* 'tiresome business' caused her to curl up inside herself like a hedgehog. She was not interested. She found the subject (briskly explained to her, at the age of thirteen, by her mother) tedious and strange beyond all words and more than a little repulsive. An emotion that was both within you, and able to attack you from without; a *fact*, that was likely, almost certain, to upset the cool, orderly, satisfying procession of your days.

But the masculine mind—ah, that was something else again! She delighted in exercising her own brain with that of a young man, and she did not resent it when his mind was better than her own, in fact, she came away from such exchanges soothed and stimulated, and full of satisfying pride in her own powers; feeling none of that dull, resentful conviction that she was the victim of some fundamental and unchangeable *unfairness* which always afflicted her at the School Dances.

Those dances! It was her one quarrel with Claregates. Then she suddenly remembered the sensation that she had caused in the middle of the Winter Term, when she had taken Ashton as her partner; Ashton, in his first term at Cambridge and already making his mark there as an athlete; six foot one and a half, dark, straight-featured, curly-haired, and so clever that her father said his taking a first in Greats was as near a certainty as anything could ever be . . . people's eyes had nearly fallen out of their heads . . . and it certainly had been decent of him to wear tails and a white tie . . . people had treated her with surprised respect for weeks afterwards.

She felt a little more cheerful suddenly. She sat up, dropping *Girl* on the floor, as her parents came out onto the verandah.

"How elegant you look," she said, but it was to her mother that her eyes turned behind her thick glasses; her father's looks and appearance gave her, as usual, nothing but satisfaction, but Mummy so seldom bothered to make herself look nice.

"It's quite pleasant to be in evening dress again," said May cheerfully, looking down at the pea-green taffetas of her billowing skirt, and the shoes which just did not match them, "and look . . ." she put up a capable freckled hand to her lips.

"Why don't you use it more often?" said Nora. "It really 'does something for you', as the Americans say."

"Haven't time. I leave it to Daddy to fascinate the parents.

Now, Adriaan, we're ready . . . are you coming too?" as Christopher got up.

"We're going out somewhere after dinner," said Adriaan, "my mother did tell me to ask Nora and Chris to come along, but I forgot."

"Well—" exclaimed Nora, "I must say, you are the absolute —extent, Adriaan."

"It wouldn't have been any good, Nolly, you would have had to stay with Dogfight anyway," said her mother. "I'm quite sure Madame van Roeslaere will ask you another time."

"You can come now if you really want to," said Adriaan as they made their way down the steps. "Can't you ask the lady in the bikini to keep an eye on Ida?"

"There isn't time," said Everard rather impatiently, "we're rather late now."

"I may as well walk up to the dune and see the last of you, anyway," Nora said; she did not particularly want to dine with the van Roeslaeres, but that was no thanks to Adriaan, she might have been very disappointed, and she felt heartily sick with him. He had 'forgotten' on purpose. He really *was*—and why should *she* be the one to stay stuck at home with Dogfight? Why shouldn't Chris?

She glanced away towards the sea, lying far out under the sunset which cast a pathway of dim, rosy light across the placid, gently-moving, neutral-coloured swell. The glow was carried inland by a continued reflection across the wet sand, where a few dark figures strolled or loitered, too far off for the sound of their voices to break the evening quiet.

"There's Ydette," she observed, her eyes now fixed on two figures strolling beneath them at the foot of the dune.

"Ida's 'case'? Where?" Everard looked in the direction to which she was turning, but he never wore his long-distance glasses when dining out and he could not see the strolling figures clearly. "That tall girl with the soldier?"

Nora nodded. "She is very tall. But she's only about four-teen, and it does look—I mean, children of fourteen in England don't usually go about with young men."

"They grow up so quickly over here," said May Ruddlin. "I agree with you, Nolly, it does look vulgar, a child of that age. But of course, girls of that class . . . especially abroad . . . and perhaps he isn't her boy-friend, they may be related."

"That's Jooris Gheldheere, his father has a farm out at Sint Niklaas, near the hothouses," Adriaan's voice was quiet and toneless; his eyes were fixed on the two figures now passing immediately below them, "and they aren't related—unless of course she's a bastard of the old man, the boy's grandfather. She might well be. No-one knows who she is."

"She's extremely photogenic," said Christopher suddenly, "I was watching her the other day while she was chattering with Dogfight."

"Is she? How can you tell, dear?" May asked, passing over Adriaan's little contribution to the conversation with the technique first developed in the early days at Port Meredith, and known in the family as *not-taking-any-notice-of-van-Roeslaere-it-only-makes-him-worse.*

"You can tell, if you know anything about it—she's remarkably photogenic."

They were leaving the path of firm white sand that led along the ridge of the dune now, and beginning the descent that led towards the road, and the bathing-hut girl and her 'escort' (as people at Claregates would call him) had dropped out of sight. Nora walked along with compressed lips and a critical expression, and Adriaan was wondering why he hadn't hated the spectacle of that brat—that bastard-foundling—walking with the lout from the farm. Usually, when he was interested in a girl, he hated everybody whom he saw her with; a black, hot hate that was a damned nuisance. But when he saw the bastard, the brat with the eyes, laughing down there (they were laughing, he had seen and heard them) with young Gheldheere, he hadn't felt hatred; he had not felt what he had known, in the other cases, to be jealousy. There had only been the old, familiar, irresistible desire to look, to watch her.

Of course there couldn't be jealousy, when you hated a face as he hated Ydette's, yet when he had heard Christopher's idiotic remark about her being photogenic, he had wanted to snarl, *Leave her alone. You try taking pictures of her and you'll be surprised what'll happen to you.*

He plunged down the slope, kicking out sand in every direction and causing May and Nora to exchange resigned glances, and all the way down he was struggling with the impulse to dare the danger, to sneer at Christopher: *you ought to film her, some time.*

"Are you coming along?" he said to him, instead, while he was unlocking the door of the big white car that stood parked in a hollow of the overhanging bluff, and Christopher nodded. "Yes, thanks, I may as well."

"All right, then. We'll drop them at the house and go; we can be in Oostende in fifteen minutes."

"I expect we can, with you driving . . ." and they grinned at one another. As he climbed into the car after his mother, Christopher was thinking that although Adriaan might be a peculiar little swine he was good company; he always had been; his malice was endlessly entertaining, and when he was annoyed his vocabulary was something to hear; he was never boring either, a quality which strongly recommended his society to Christopher.

Nora stood on the edge of the dune and watched until the car was out of sight, not wistfully, but because she had nothing else to do. How very good looking her father was still; she was only now beginning to realize that his height and his grace in movement, and his clear, dark eyes and the dark hair beginning to turn to a grey almost silver, were all helped by his fortunate passions for drinking cold water and going for long walks. When she had been twelve or so, his charming looks had been to her a part of his goodness and his kindness, and she had thought of him as personifying the "Intellectual Beauty" of Shelley's hymn. Now she knew that beauty was accidental; her father's appearance was just as much a matter of chance as her own unabundant hair and the weak eyesight inherited from her mother and the skin that nothing (not even long walks and cold water) could really improve.

I wish I were an American.

The surprising thought came up suddenly out of nowhere, as she turned away and began to walk moodily back towards the house. Out of the corner of her eye she could see the lights beginning to twinkle and flash out among the pink-and-white stucco hotels along the *digue* at Zandeburghe, and beyond the white curve of the dune, which stood up, rounded and silvery and touched here and there with dark fringes of grass in the clear twilight, there wound away a long curve of dim land stretching into the distance, glittering and sparkling all along its length. The pleasure-towns of the Belgian coast were lighting up for the evening; the dancing-places and the cafés, the restaurants and the *bistros* and casinos, the promenades under clipped trees, and the cinemas, the strolling-grounds for the 'girls of that class' who grew up so quickly, the places where people chattered and held hands and kissed. *If I were an American girl, something would have been done about my skin,* she thought.

As she began to descend into the broad hollow in the dune where the group of houses was situated, remembering that there was a new book on Physics waiting to be begun in preparation for next year's work in the Upper Sixth, she saw Ydette and her escort crossing the lower part of the sands.

They were walking at a short distance apart, still laughing, and looking at one another. Nora could not honestly say to herself that their laughter was vulgar. If it had not been for the adolescent ring in their voices (and even that sounded neither self-conscious nor hysterical) she might have taken it for the laughter of children; the old words that used to be spoken about laughter, *hearty* and *sweet*, came into her head as she listened. The young man was even taller than Ydette, and Nora now realized that the impression of smartness which she had received from him was due to his uniform; a dark beret cut across his hair, fair as the sand of the dunes, in a hard and audacious line that no civilian hat ever achieves, and his long thin body was set off by battledress. His face was red and he had a long nose; that much she *had* observed. No film-star; not a patch—if you thought about such things—on Ashton. It was a very Flemish face; she had noticed—or rather, had had them thrust upon her because their owners were selling her something or taking a ticket from her or explaining the way to her, for by nature she was unobservant as well as shortsighted—scores of similar faces, all up and down Bruges and Zandeburghe and Brussels and Ghent, ever since the holiday had started.

She stalked over the verandah and into the house, and as she shut the door she heard the laughter that was childish and hearty and sweet ringing on; in her mind's ear; through the lively, darkening air now twinkling with the lights of the pleasure towns; over the wet, shining surface of the darkening grey sands.

As she paced beside the large, nodding head of Klaartje on the way down to the sea, on a day when the Ruddlins' holiday in Belgium was slightly more than halfway through its course, Ydette was feeling a little sad, but not—not really—surprised. This was not the first time that tourists had shown friendliness to her one morning and a cool manner the next, and perhaps (she thought) she had almost been prepared for such an attitude on the part of Mejuffrouw Nora, for hadn't she thought of her, from that first moment when she had looked up and seen her standing there with the little Ida in her hand, as *the cross girl*? It was only when Mijnheer Adriaan had come up, and Ydette had learned that the two visitors were friends of the van Roeslaeres, that she had looked at them with anything more than the friendly, but business-like, glance which she gave to all touristry, and it was only because of the connection with the big house that she minded Mejuffrouw Nora not saying good-morning to her, or smiling good-bye when she came to take away Ida after her daily ride (a treat which Ydette, secretly defying the aunts, had more than once contrived for her to enjoy without payment).

The two girls, the cross one and the little one, had stayed at the foot of the dune as usual for a little while this morning after Ida's ride was over, the cross one reading her book (what a big one, it must be something to do with lessons) and the little one digging in the sand; occasionally she ran over to bestow on Klaartje, as he rested between his excursions to the waves, a series of pats smart enough to startle a smaller horse but felt by him no more than the feet of an alighting fly. These visits, however, had ceased towards twelve o'clock, when Ydette saw Ida checked in the act of running towards her, and held for a moment, straining unwillingly away, while a warning and a lecture were evidently being delivered. Then Nora returned to her book and Ida had to content herself with an occasional frantic waving of her spade in Ydette's direction. It was unkind of the mejuffrouw. Why shouldn't Ida come?

It didn't matter. Quickly, as the morning passed away, Ydette lifted the warm, small bodies up in her arms and settled each child comfortably on the low benches in the cart.

"All right? Comfy?" (She had found that in one of the English books lent to her by Madame van Roeslaere and she always used it to the English children.) "*Allons!*" and down to Klaartje's head she would go, and take up the leading string. The children sat in two rows, smiling in anticipation or looking rather apprehensive; some eyes would be fixed in delightful expectancy upon Klaartje. Could that mountain really be going to move?

"Gee up! Getalong!" A gentle tug at the reins, and they are off; Klaartje not so much moving forward as launching himself, like some majestic ship, upon the waters of activity perpetually surging about his own majestic calm; and the cart crunches slowly across the glittering grey sand, making broad deep tracks and a series of deep, hollow, romantic shapes that might have been left by a giant.

We are getting nearer; now the waves are very loud. Shall we go right into them? Oh, if the cart went right into the sea with us in it!

But it doesn't, of course. Precisely at the edge, where the tracks of hoofs and wheels begin to blur away the instant they are made, there is another jerk on the rein, and Klaartje allows himself gradually to decline into a halt.

For perhaps five exquisite seconds the cart pauses at the extreme limits of the land, while the entire expanse of the North Sea (and perhaps never in its history has it been farther from being referred to as the German Ocean) pours itself into our eyes: they are filled with it: our backs are to the land and we can't see anything but greyness and sparkle and glitter, and then some of us begin to feel bored—why doesn't the cart go on, why doesn't the horse turn round?—and some of us sneeze with the salt taste and the dazzle of it all, and Ydette, who has finished slowly counting under her breath, gives the third tug at the rein and slowly, satisfyingly slowly, while everyone enjoys the peril of the situation and the slurring of the wheels in the sand and even a certain reluctance to turn round (too manageable to be called obstinacy, but thrilling in its hint of worse to come) on the part of Klaartje—we are set towards land again.

Just before twelve o'clock, when all the Belgian world thinks about nothing for two hours except its lunch, the tall, fair young man, the brother of those two girls, came walking quickly across the sands.

"Hullo, Ydette. Lovely morning, isn't it?" he said, surprising her by stopping beside her as she was about to sit down and begin on her sausage and bread, and smiling at her; his eyes were screwed up against the glare of the sun; his teeth looked very white, and his bright hair was blowing about in the wind; his grey shorts showed long brown legs, and his dark blue coat had a device of shields, rather like those on the wall of the big house, on one pocket. "Had a busy morning?" he went on. Kind, friendly voice: her heart warmed to it.

"Oh yes, Monsieur. But so busy. All the children who came at the weekend—so many, they all want to ride."

"I expect they do. And how's the horse standing up to it?"

"Standing——?" She was puzzled; the English taught her by Adèle van Roeslaere had included some idioms, but not many.

"How does he like being so busy, I mean—he's not getting tired—not falling down under the weight of so many children?"

She nodded—and Christopher saw with pleasure, mixed with an eager satisfaction, how her face responded to the change of her mood as she tried to understand what he was saying: the smile vanished, and a solemn and—well, actually it was rather dumb, but it wasn't in the least unendearing—look replaced it.

He lingered for a few minutes, chatting to her; out of the corner of his eye he was perfectly aware that Nora had looked up from that enormous tome she was crouching over (who but

Nolly would read Toynbee on the beach, in the middle of a seaside holiday?) and had her eyes fixed steadily on them . . . let her stare; it was about time that Mistress Nora's irritating interest in every female he talked to and went about with was taken in hand . . . but just now he was wondering if it would be too soon to ask this child if she ever went to the pictures?

But he decided not to risk it; after all, he had nearly another ten days in Zandeburghe during which to lay his foundations, and he mustn't scare her off . . . looking critically and coolly, but always with that sense of pleasurable excitement, at the face of ivory and darkness lifted to his own, he didn't think it likely that she was going about yet with boys; she *did* look such a child, when you saw her in close-up; in spite of her height, but he didn't want her to think he was trying to 'get off' with her. Above all . . . yes, that above everything . . . he didn't want to get in the hair of those old battleaxes of aunts, or whatever they were.

He was just about to make his farewells, quite satisfied with his ten minutes' manœuvres, when there came a raucous hail from the direction of the *digue*:

"Y-dette! Y—dette!"

"Yes, what is it, Aunt Marie?" shouted Ydette back, in Flemish and with a most ineffectual attempt to make her soft voice carry as far as the square black shape standing on the skyline.

"Jooris—he just came by on his bike—got a bit of leave last night—he said don't forget you're going to the *molen* next Sunday," shrieked the distant figure, "says he'll treat you to a *roomijs*."

"No, no, I'll remember."

She turned back to Christopher, smiling.

"What was that in aid of—what was that about?" he asked, then paused. "Didn't she like you talking to me?"

"Oh no, Monsieur." Ydette looked rather shocked. "My aunt tell me that my friend will take me a walk next Sunday to the *molen*."

"*Molen?* What's that?"

But, although smiling still, she shook her head; her English did not extend to the word *mill*, and Christopher stored it away, to ask his father the meaning.

"Is it a boy-friend?" he asked, in a teasing elder-brother tone, and awaited the answer with considerable interest; for, if she *were* going about with boys, it would be easier to ask her to come to the pictures with him; on the other hand, if she were more emotionally developed than she looked, and had one particular boy-friend, it might make his foundation-laying far more difficult.

But she was in fits of laughter.

"That seems to have gone well," he observed, smiling with something more than sympathy (really, when she laughed her face was enchanting). "What's the joke?"

"Boy-friend! But of course no. He's—he's—it's Jooris. I'm not . . ." she hesitated, her expression changed, and he watched fascinated . . . "I'm not . . . I don't . . . I'm not *gaan met* any boy," she ended gravely.

"*Gaan met* . . . is that 'going with'?" he asked, guessing, and she nodded. But she still looked grave, and when he smiled his good-bye and went off, he only succeeded in getting a very slight smile in return.

But what a charmer, he was thinking, as he walked quickly across the sands to the solemn figure of Nora, sitting with a rather straight back above the ponderous volume of the Gibbon of the 'fifties and keeping her gaze fixed dolefully upon her approaching brother, and what angles and bones! This could be one of the really big ones. And it's only three years to wait. In three years she'll be eighteen. If I let her slip through my fingers I shall never stop cursing myself . . . but I'm not going to. *I've found her*, and she's going to be *my* find.

"Well," he said coolly to Nora as he came up, "what's the matter with you? Toynbee given you indigestion?"

"Was I looking as if I had indigestion? I'm sorry if it affronts you," rearing her long neck disdainfully, "no, as a matter of fact I'm feeling slightly sick . . . I was sitting here perfectly inoffensively, reading and keeping an eye on Dogfight (who *will* keep on charging down to worry Ydette), and an old man came round the corner," glancing at the curve of the *digue*, "and—well, he—it sounded like a *hiccough*. Oh, all *right*," disgustedly, "I know it's very funny, but if you could have *seen* him—he had on one of those round caps the old things wear over here, and he was practically in rags and he was kind-of wagging his head and he looked absolutely *mad*—as a matter of fact, I think I've seen him before, I think he's the one who sweeps down the plank walk outside the huts every morning and collects the rubbish—but really—if you could have *seen* him, Chris—why doesn't somebody *do* something about people like that?"

"They do, in England. It's only because it's over here and you aren't used to it," he said drowsily, having arranged himself at full length beside her on the sand.

"Well, I wish somebody *would* do something about him."

There was silence for a little while. Nora read diligently and even assimilated what she read, but beneath the words that appeared so large and clear under the powerful glass of her spectacles, and the intellectual concepts which they conveyed to her brain, there ran through her nerves a series of shaken and disgusted and pitying impressions, a kind of shamed annoyance, because she felt pretty certain that the old man's sly, lingering leer, directed towards herself, had been caused by the fact that she wore a skirt, and was sitting alone. *Really* . . .

Presently she tapped the page and said, in a tone at once authoritative and musing:

"I suppose you could apply Toynbee's theory of Challenge and Response to human beings, couldn't you?" No reply. She went on with slightly more self-consciousness, "I mean—I was thinking about someone like that old man, the idea, I mean, of Toynbee's theory being carried out in each individual person . . . I was just thinking, the challenge *he* had to meet must have been very definitely too much for him. Don't you agree?" A pause. "Chris—— Did you hear what I said?"

"Yes, but this isn't the kind of morning to talk about that kind of thing." He opened one eye and, seeing that she was looking distinctly mortified, went on, "When you get up to Oxford——"

"*If* I do," she interrupted tartly.

"Oh, I'm pretty sure that you will, and so is Ashton (there, I saved that up as a tit-bit for you) . . . when you get up to Oxford, you'll have plenty of people to talk about that kind of thing with."

"But I want to talk about it with *you*! Damn Oxford. Chris, why have you been so peculiar to me lately?"

"Haven't been peculiar. Don't know what you mean."

"Well—we always used to—I only meant by 'peculiar' that you never seem to want to talk to me about anything nowadays and——"

He did not answer, having learned, through a certain amount of experience which his good-looks had brought him, that it never did to relax his rule of not talking to a girl when she was showing signs of making a scene; and he had found that its application usually worked. He supposed that it would do equally well with a sister, and evidently it did, because when he cautiously opened one eye again, Nora had returned to her book. Her lower lip did look a bit sulky and her eyes a bit shiny but there wasn't any need to do anything about that, and he shut his own eye and went to sleep.

But Nora was now reading Toynbee without any intellectual concepts reaching her brain at all. It simply wasn't possible that he could be getting a crush on Ydette?

But that would be *too* extraordinary. She was only a child.

Or was she? She was taller than Nora, she went about with a soldier who must be at least twenty, and, let it be remembered, she was a foundling and no-one knew exactly what her age was. She might be seventeen—from a distance she looked it—and in that case there wasn't any case why a distastefully furtive and unsuitable *affaire* shouldn't develop between her and Chris.

Not if I can help it, thought Nora, with eyes flying sternly backwards and forwards across Toynbee's closely-filled and informative lines. Oh, Ydette was *nice* enough, she supposed;

she had seen, while Ydette thought herself unobserved, how carefully she had made Dogfight sit beside a small and gentle French child, whose legs and arms of stem-like thinness instinctively inspired the protective instinct, rather than beside the large and aggressive Tarmy (who seemed bent on carrying out the original mission of the Occupying Forces to which he belonged, in his own well-nourished but shambling person); such niceties might be wasted upon Dogfight, who was more than capable of taking her place, in Nora's opinion, in this world, and who rather enjoyed the shoving-contests which sitting next to Tarmy involved—but it did show a sensitive and kind nature on the part of Ydette.

Yes, but a flirtation with Chris would be in the last degree unsuitable and extraordinary and a bore, and if Nora could prevent one, she was going to.

How very tiresome sex was. And sisterly jealousy didn't come into it; it was a case of sheer—sheer *suitability* and duty, and she would begin at once by assuming an even cooler manner towards Ydette.

They happened to meet late that evening, when the Ruddlins were on their way back from the restaurant in Zandeburghe where they always had their evening meal, and Ydette was about to mount her bicycle for the ride home with the aunts.

The three were assembled with their machines at the top of the yellow ladder leading down to the sands, which bore the name "Jan", painted on it in bright pink letters. (There had been a good deal of family argument before this apparently simple effect had been brought about, some people pointing out that 'Marie and Jakoba' was a bit of a mouthful, while others said that tourists—who, inexplicably, like that kind of thing—would be pleased by the unusual name *Jakoba*. However, Mevrouw Maes had asserted her maternal authority by announcing that her husband's name should be used—if the new bathing tents *must* be advertised in this outlandish fashion—and "Jan" was also an easy name for the tourists to remember. So "Jan" it was.)

As Ydette saw the Ruddlins approaching, an expression of

pleasure came over her face, warming to a dreamy beam of welcome as they drew level with the Maes party—then, as Nora passed her without a word or a smile, it was replaced by a humble expression which seemed to ask, *what is it? what have I done?*

The lady members of the party had not even noticed her; even the little Ida had been absorbed by something her father was saying as she hung on his hand; the tall young mijnheer did smile, and even bow, but that brought its own disadvantages; and Ydette's soreness of heart was increased by a lecture from sharp-eyed Aunt Marie, who noticed most that went on, about the imprudence of smiling at the tourists before they smiled at you; followed by the dismal and well-known story of some bathing-tent keepers out at Le Zoute who had become very thick with a party of Dutch tourists that had ended up by buying the pitch just next to them and taking all their trade.

"And the young mijnheer was talking to you this morning," Aunt Marie went on, "I saw him myself. You want to be careful about such things."

"What things?" Ydette's voice was sulky, as she fastened a scarf round her head to keep out the evening wind.

"You know quite well what I mean. We don't want any more goings-on like that Lyntje and Mijnheer Adriaan—and look at her now, twenty-six and not married, and stuck in that "Priba" all day selling red stuff to put on your mouth . . . see what it leads to, talking to young mijnheeren . . ."

"I'll do that for you, Auntie," Ydette interrupted, and deftly tied the side of the basket that had worked loose from the handle-bars of her aunt's machine, to the accompaniment of not entirely grateful remarks about strength, young wrists, unrheumatic fingers and so on.

Ydette's heart was sore as they rode away into the dusk. She decided that after supper she would go over to the big house and help Marieke.

The old woman's eyes were beginning to find difficulty in detecting the dust, and the maggots in the peas, and the wrinkles in the sheets, which they had inexorably pursued for more than sixty years in the service of Adèle van Roeslaere's family, and she was glad, now, of a young pair to help her.

"Is Sophie still here?" Ydette asked of her, as she followed her across the black-and-white tiles of the wide, lofty, silent hall towards the kitchen premises at the back of the house.

"How did you know she was here?" demanded Marieke, without turning round.

"I saw her come in. About nine, it was."

"Then if you was keeping such a sharp eye on us, you can tell me if she's gone out again," retorted Marieke crushingly, and Ydette's spirits, which had lifted as they always did as soon as she felt the atmosphere of the big house around her, went down again. This was certainly not being a good day—what with snubs and scoldings—and there were also certain memories aroused by the question of the young mijnheer that morning— was she going with a boy? No—and heaven forbid that she should—after last Sunday: she could still feel the disagreeable warmth of Antoine Jonckheere's face pushed against her own, and his great arms squeezing her waist—and just as she *wanted* the aunts to look round in the dimness of Our Lady's porch, where they were still gossiping with his mother and elder sister, of course *nothing* would make them—and everyone else at Mass had gone home—and she had really had to *fight* him to get away. A great boy of going on eighteen, he ought to know better, and she had been feeling so cool and fresh and good inside her clean dress.

Sophie was still there; she was sitting at the table shelling peas (four pounds of them, company expected for lunch tomorrow), and opposite her sat young Moritz, now a great thing of nine, poring over an American comic. They greeted Ydette; she settled down at the corner of the table where she usually sat, and applied herself to what was now recognized as one of her tasks—the scraping of salt from a large block into a jar from which it would be taken to flavour the day's cooking. Marieke disappeared completely into a cupboard in a far corner, where she became noiselessly absorbed in something to do with the table-glasses, and quiet settled over the kitchen.

It was a very large room, but the massiveness of the thick, straight wooden beams separated at intervals of about a foot and crossed transversely in the centre by a truly enormous one, which formed the ceiling; and the size of the red-and-brown tiles faded by age which covered the floor, so detracted from its proportions as to make it seem almost cosy. Ydette's eyes wandered comfortably from time to time while she diligently scraped the salt, taking pleasure in the small bricks of a dark rose colour lining the immensely wide recessed fireplace, where a modern stove for cooking and heating water now silently burned; and the row of plates, gaily coloured in coarse blues and yellows, that were ranged along the carved wooden shelf above it—a fad of Madame van Roeslaere's, this, which Marieke had only learned to take for granted (never to like) over the years. There was a window of small panes of white and coloured glass, divided by leaden strips, above the door that led into the rest of the house, and another of the same type which overlooked the small garden paved in stone, its flowers wreathing the large terra-cotta urns, now hidden by the darkness; from where she sat, Ydette could see the moths flitting past outside in the blackness and the lamp faintly shining in its place on the brick wall across the canal.

Presently Sophie, who had been glancing irritably from time to time at the pensive face opposite, said, without raising her eyes from her diligently moving fingers:

"You been seeing a lot of young Jooris these last weeks?" and, as Ydette, after a pause, slowly nodded, "He got a regular girl yet?"

This time Ydette—again after the pause which usually followed on any question put to her while she was in one of her dreaming fits—doubtfully shook her head. She followed this up with "I don't know".

"*Don't know*," Sophie (who was out for blood this evening) scornfully mimicked; "you go out there every Saturday, don't you? Don't you see him with anyone or hear him saying he's got anybody?"

After a third pause—during which a rather hopeless expression began to descend, like the falling of a wettish cloud over a peaceful landscape, on Ydette's face (*why must people always* . . .?) —she answered, "I don't know," again, and, the salt crock being filled, got up and went over to Moritz, and rested her chin on his shoulder while she began to look at his comic. He, solid as a sack of cement, moved about quarter of an inch with the intention of making her more comfortable, and the red face and the pale one rested side by side, absorbed.

Sophie did not want people to be absorbed, this evening. In a moment she began again.

"I s'pose you and he'll be thinking about sweethearting, next thing, then".

"Who?" said Ydette slowly, looking up.

"You and Jooris. Sweethearting. Go on, Yddy, don't be so green, you must be going on fifteen, you know what sweethearting is, or you ought to by now, with your Aunt Jakoba . . ." her voice went off into a mutter, which ended "and Klaas."

"Klaas?" said Ydette, and this time she looked a very little cross.

"Yes, KLAAS." Sophie got up from the table and crossed the kitchen and hurled the colanderful of empty pea-shucks into a capacious receptacle standing in a corner. "You're dopey this evening. She and him used to be sweethearts."

"Aunt Jakoba and *Klaas* used?" said Ydette; she was wide awake now, and staring at Sophie with her mouth open. A rare and unexpected sound now broke the tranquil silence of the kitchen; it was Moritz laughing, but as he continued to keep his broad red face bent over his comic, it was not possible to tell whether he was laughing at that or at what his mother had just said. However, as Ydette usually liked to join in when anyone happened to be laughing, and as the notion just suggested by Sophie really was very funny, she began to laugh too.

"Oh, you can laugh," persisted Sophie, meaning to go on being irritable and spiteful but feeling herself being won, by the sight of other people laughing, towards cheerfulness and good nature, "but they was. Years ago, before I was born and you was even thought of. Everybody says so."

"It's so funny . . ." giggled Ydette, making a silvery, silly, helpless sound; "they're both so old . . ."

"Oh, and I s'pose me and Albert's old, too?" Sophie sat down again, leant her arms on the table and permitted a great sigh to come up through her substantial bosom.

"He's sixty, isn't he?" asked Ydette, pleased at an opportunity to change the subject and speaking in a respectful voice.

"No he isn't sixty, he's fifty-three, and I don't know who puts all these lies about . . . very nice age, fifty-three is, for someone thirty-four . . . but I can't make up my mind. Wish I could."

Ydette returned to studying the comic paper, having grown accustomed to hearing Sophie express this wish during the past three years, and Sophie, becoming irritated again by this seeming lack of interest in her affairs, resumed: "And there's just a nice difference with you and Jooris . . . and a very good thing it wouldn't half be for you, too, him going to get the farm when his grandad dies and everything and you a foundling and not having nothing . . . if I was to give you a bit of advice it would be go on and get him."

"Get him?" said Ydette, coming up slowly from the pages spread before her on the table—whose coarse lines and jejeune words presented to her eyes colourings and impressions far more delicate than those which she actually saw, because they were passed through the filter of her imagination; she looked at Sophie—the big face, once pink and now a blotched brownish red, the scars that years had faded to faint white and purplish marks on her forehead—and heard, echoing in her mind's ear, the booming voice that was beginning to grow a little hoarse. That face and that voice were amongst the earliest things Ydette remembered.

"I s'pose you think you're going to pull it off with him, don't you?" Sophie continued.

"What?"

"Catch him—get him—tie him up—marry him, girl," Sophie said with increasing impatience.

But at that moment there came a clink, faint but distinct, from the cupboard. It sounded as if someone had accidentally tapped one glass against another. It was only a tiny sound, but it caused Sophie to wink at Ydette and pull down her mouth. Her next remark came in a lower voice.

"No—but don't he always take you out when he gets a bit of time off from that place where they're making them into soldiers—weren't you out with him on the sands at Zandeburghe, other evening? Someone I know saw you, so don't try and say you wasn't. Holding hands!" She wagged a great finger.

Ydette neither coloured nor looked down, but stared rather blankly in silence.

"I s'pose you know what sweethearting *is*?" said Sophie, really exasperated by the sight of so much obtuseness, and Ydette silently nodded.

Yes, she knew; no one could live for thirteen years in the Sint Katelijnstraat and not know; and you couldn't live there for six years with the Germans in Brugge and not know how babies came—and a lot of other things as well that sometimes you wished you didn't know. (But you hardly ever thought of them nowadays; they seemed to be going away.) And those things about babies—she also knew things about Snow White and the Seven Dwarfs; the two sets of facts were lodged together in her mind—quite comfortably, except that she rather preferred the facts about Snow White.

"Don't you?" suddenly roared Sophie, and immediately there came a rather more decided clink from the cupboard, followed by a loudish cough.

"Yes, but——" Ydette found difficulty, as so often when asked a direct question, in bringing the words forward into her mouth, "Jooris isn't . . . Jooris and me . . . we don't . . . he . . . we aren't like that," she ended, on a triumphant note and with a smile that, nevertheless, did conceal a slight feeling of trouble and doubt. Holding hands? But they always caught hold of each other's hands; he helped her up and down places.

Sophie contented herself with muttering (one eye on the

distant cupboard) that if they wasn't now they soon would be, and shortly afterwards heaved herself up, collected Moritz with the kind of gesture between a scoop and a cuff that might have served a mother-bear and took herself off. Marieke emerged from the cupboard to utter a word of warning to her about being on time tomorrow because there was going to be plenty to do, and, after they had gone, sat down at the table with a bit of lace. Ydette, full of relief now that the trouble-maker had departed, took out her own bit from her apron pocket and settled herself opposite, and they worked in silence.

Yet she could not sink deeply, this evening, into the peace of the big-house kitchen. The words 'going with' continued to drift through her mind.

She had been accustomed to hearing them, ever since she could remember. But tonight, now, she was *thinking* about them; she did not like them . . . never had . . . and it was funny that twice today someone should have asked her if she and Jooris were *gaan met* . . . first the young mijnheer down on the sands, whom she liked because he was kind, as well as because he was a friend of them here at the big house, and brother to the little Ida . . . and now Sophie . . . and then there was that lump Antoine last Sunday after Mass . . . and Aunt Marie, telling her not to talk too much to the young Englishman because they didn't want any more of that Lyntje–Mijnheer Adriaan business . . . the entire day seemed to have been filled, in one way and another, with *gaan met*, and if Nora Ruddlin and Ydette had been able to confer on the subject that evening, there was no doubt that they would have agreed on their verdict: *sex is a nuisance.*

Ydette was not the kind of young girl who decides to put a disagreeable matter out of her head and then does so; she could only wait, passively as the meadow under the hail, until gradually the disagreeable sensation connected with the words, and with what had been said, drifted away. They did not drift away entirely, but gradually, as she wove the thread about the pattern and dreamed of the life that was going on in the rooms beyond the kitchen door and its leaded panes the colour of golden syrup—she became at peace. The clock that was set in the middle of a big blue-and-white plate ticked quickly, Marieke straightened her shoulders now and then and looked up as if she ought to have sighed, but did not—everything was just as it always had been in the kitchen of the big house. Ydette began to think about next Sunday, when she would go for a walk to the mill with Jooris, and about the ice-cream he had promised to buy for her.

And even a long nose in a red face can look agreeable when you have known the owner since before you could talk, and have laughed for years and years at the same jokes with him.

Ydette had heard with dreamy dismay and fear the gloomy prophecies of the aunts when Jooris had gone off to do his Military Service a year ago; *they'd* got him now; that was the last anyone would see of *him*; he'd come back so changed you wouldn't know him; no more going to Mass; the kind of floozy that hung round those camps wasn't the sort that a respectable woman could talk about—and so forth.

But he had come back looking and talking and behaving exactly as he had gone away: presenting himself, on the afternoons when he had to pass through Zandeburghe on his way back from leave spent at the farm, at the foot of the ladder with "Jan" painted on it, with trimly poised feet, a smart salute and a flash of beautiful teeth, to the admiring eyes of Ydette and the aunts. Ydette remembered with a happiness that always made her smile, the strolls they contrived on these occasions to take across the sands; particularly the evening ones, when the wind off the sea swept across the grey reaches that reflected, in a dim goldy glitter, the rising moon. Their feet sank deep, and with every step, there shone out in a green glow the light of the sand-worms they were disturbing; the smell and sound of the waves blew over them as they walked—the waves, spreading like dim white lace across the dark grey shore. Jooris always told her such funny things about Sergeant Lebrun—saying he would buy some stuff for the Sergeant to make himself an apron like Ydette was wearing . . . and that kind of thing . . . and when they at last turned homewards, in obedience to that imperious bellowing from the aunts within range of which they were moderately careful to remain, he always helped Aunt Marie onto her bicycle (Aunt Jakoba would never let him) and stood there at the salute when they all three rode away. No one was so . . . so *good* as Jooris; it was good, too, that by the time Sunday afternoon arrived, all thoughts about *gaan met* drifted away.

She had intended to be half an hour early at the statue of Koenig Albert in the park near the station, where they were to meet, so that she could sit for a little while enjoying the sight of the strolling Sunday crowds before he arrived, but she had twice been delayed; first, by Aunt Marie, who had caught her just as she was coming out of her bedroom and demanded why, in the name of everything that was decent and respectable, was she going to walk about the streets with her hair done in that extraordinary fashion?

Ydette, assuming that blend of inward obstinacy and an outwardly soothing manner which she instinctively kept for such contests of will, explained that she had seen a girl with her hair done like that last Sunday at Mass. This silenced Aunt Marie, except for a few receding grumbles like the tide going out about it making her look nearer eighteen than fifteen, but then Aunt Jakoba, sitting in the doorway enjoying the afternoon sun in company with granny, had laughed so loudly and with such an expression that Ydette, fearing something about 'going with', had given a hasty kiss to the old woman and hurried away.

Crossing the *plaats*, something much better had happened; the little Ida had come running to her across the cobblestones from a group standing round the white car outside the big house, and demanded to know where she was going. Ydette had told her: to the *molen*; for a walk with a friend, but, on Ida's asking what the *molen* was, and being apparently prepared to settle down for a long explanation, Ydette had gently sent her back to her family (they were all there, the father and mother, the tall, kind, young mijnheer and the cross girl, and just then Madame and Mijnheer van Roeslaere and Mijnheer Adriaan came out of the house to join them).

Ydette had gone on her way, happy because Adèle had given her the smile for which she had been looking; enjoying the feeling of the thick, tidy plume of her hair confined by its broad black velvet ribbon, and falling in a pony-tail to nod gently against the thinly-veiled skin of her back; enjoying the feeling of the familiar streets and towers and roofs lying all about her, smiling dimly and anciently in the sun. She heard the little Ida asking questions of her brother in her loud voice, but she was too far away now to follow the sound of the quick English.

How dark the shadows were round Mijnheer Adriaan's eyes! How he had stared! But she did not care; he was part of the happiness of being recognized by the big house, and by its friends.

She had not been sitting near the statue of Koenig Albert for more than a few minutes, before up came Jooris, his trousers creased as sharply as the blade of a knife and his beret set at such an angle that it was miraculous it did not fall off his head, and she was pleased to be greeted by a very smart salute; she was unaware, as they walked away—with him already talking at a great rate about the health and progress of every animal on the farm, whence he had just come—of the benign glances that followed them. But Jooris did notice (his clear, light blue eyes did not miss much), and the wooden stare with which he met such unspoken comments concealed some amusement; Ydette looked so much older than she was, and he, being now fairly describable as a young man, was of course associated in the public mind with sweethearting. It was a joke, the idea of being sweethearts with Ydette.

But as they went through the cool green shadows of the chestnut trees which are planted all along the rampart walks, he began to feel a little differently about the joke. It must be the way she had done her hair. He wanted to glance sideways at it as they went along; he couldn't keep his eyes away for more than a few minutes from the demure, dark, glossy waterfall, bound with that broad ribbon of a different kind of black, and

N

although she was walking beside him in silence, staring ahead
into the patterns of leaves and sunshine with the look on her
face that she always had when they went for a walk, she seemed
almost like another person.

At last he said: "You've done your hair differently today."

"Yes," she answered, turning to him with a little placid surprise, for they were not in the habit of making remarks to one
another about their appearance, "I saw a girl at Mass with it
done like this, so I bought a quarter of a yard of ribbon at
'Priba'—you know, that shop in the Steen. Aunt Marie
doesn't like it; she says it's extraordinary."

"I like it," he said quickly, and before he knew he was saying
it, then seemed about to say something more. But he did not;
he went straight on to an account of a recent crisis in the short
life of one Soldat, a pig at the farm, to which Ydette, who knew
all the animals there and the life-history of every one of them,
listened with a rather conscious interest.

Indeed, they both turned to the recital with something not
unlike relief: Jooris because he did not like feeling himself compelled to say to Ydette the kind of thing that he said to the girls
he and his military friends talked to in cafés in Brussels and in
Oostende; and Ydette because, for one incredible and dis-
maying instant, she had thought that she detected in his
stare, in the tone of his voice, and what he had said—the un-
welcome and surprising presence of—*gaan met*. But when he
went on to tell her about poor Soldat, she gradually became
certain, or almost certain, that everything was all right.

It took them nearly three-quarters of an hour, at a comfortable pace, to walk round the wide quarter-circle of the southern
ramparts from the Sint Janshospital almost to the Kruispoort,
and then they made their way towards the First Mill, with the
object of taking a look, from the modest eminence on which it is
situated, across the city.

The mill that stands, idle now but famous, on that part of the
ramparts called the Kruisvest is one of two survivors, all that
remain out of twenty-four that once stood round about the
city and ground the grain for its bread. From beside it, the

greater part of the roofs of Bruges can be seen, and as there are but few shops in the ancient quarter of the town which is situated immediately beneath it, the long, silent, cobbled streets that wind away into the maze of softly-coloured old houses seem to extend into the heart of a city concerned only with beautiful, ancient and useless ceremonies; such as the sounding every now and again of some bell with sides worn thin and note made tremulous by the passing of centuries, and the passive spreading out of red, grey or silvery corroded roofs to the great face of the sky.

While Jooris was helping Ydette to climb the mound where the mill stands, from one side, another party was hastening up it from the other.

"*Will* you stop *bellowing*, Dogfight?" Christopher Ruddlin was saying exasperatedly. "I've *told* you why I want to catch them; I want to film Ydette, and if she hears you roaring about it she mayn't want me to. She and the boy-friend are only just on the other side there; it's the greatest luck we've managed to get here at the same time as they have, and now will you kindly shut *up*?"

"Look, Dogfight," Nora put in soothingly (the prospects for the afternoon were quite bad enough, without bickering being added), "you asked me what med-iæ-val meant the other day— I can't explain it to you now——"

"Why can't you ex-plain it to me now?"

"Because I *can't*, I tell you, there isn't *time*—but there's a mediæval city for you. It must have looked just like that," nodding towards the view becoming ever more panoramic as they climbed the mound, "in the Middle Ages. Mustn't it?" to her brother.

"I expect so. Oh good, there are some other people up there as well; I shall want them."

"Oh damn, I should say," observed Nora, holding down the skirts of her new yellow dress from the assaults of the wind.

"I am not you, and I've told you hundreds of times that places in films are only *backgrounds for people*."

"But *I* should have thought that as you're making a film

about Bruges, the places were *at least* as important as the people *in this case*, because, speaking architecturally——"

"It isn't a film about *Bruges*, that's only an excuse to get some shots of Ydette, and if Adriaan doesn't turn bloody-minded and refuse to let me use his projector, I shall show them to you before we go home—I've suggested to him that we give the van R.s a film show one evening just before we do go—and then you'll see."

"I know who you mean when you say the van R.s, you mean the van Roeslaeres," Ida said coldly, and went on, "It was me—*I* found out she was—she was—coming to the *molen*, I know *you* knew she was going, too, but if *I* hadn't asked her *this afternoon* where she was going—I mean, we shouldn't have—I mean, because you wouldn't have known *this afternoon*, I mean, at *that very minute*, she was going, I mean——"

Christopher's gesture, as they reached the summit of the slope and came face to face with the pair they were trailing, was so furious that she stopped abruptly.

"Hullo," said he heartily, smiling at Ydette, then looked at once at Jooris with a friendly, open glance, "you having a Sunday afternoon walk? So are we. Lovely day, isn't it?"

"Yes, Monsieur," she answered softly. But her face was alight with pleasure, and Ida went over to her and took her hand.

After she had spoken, there was a silence in the group lasting for perhaps half a minute. No-one seemed to know what to say next; the wind blew with a kind of boisterous playfulness into the young faces, and the ancient roofs glowed in the light of the sun or darkened beneath the passing shadows of the clouds. Nora was looking at Ydette: for an instant a feeling which was unfamiliar came over her as she met that soft stare; a kind of desire to protect, to share something . . . an odd feeling. Then it had gone; she felt nothing but impatience, and distaste with the situation.

She avoided looking directly at Jooris, partly because of her disapproval of Ydette's going about with him, but even more because his air of youthful manliness, his look of confidence and health, embarrassed her: she was not accustomed to the society of youths whose masculine qualities were more noticeable than their intellectual and social ones. But for an instant or so she felt his eyes resting upon her face and, when they left it again, she was glowing with irritation.

"You're just the people we wanted to see," Christopher was saying lightly; "I'm making a film about Bruges"—he held up his cine-camera—"and I want you to be in it—with some other people, of course—perhaps those ladies"—lowering his voice and nodding slightly towards two stout parties wearing top-heavy hats who had paused and were staring idly at the group—"would let me film them. You'll be in it, won't you?" winningly, to Ydette.

She did not answer at once, and Nora and Ida were just wondering whether they were to witness the unprecedented sight of *Chris having to ask somebody twice to do something for him*, when Jooris demanded, "What's he saying?" in the Flemish in which he was most at home, and she explained. Shyness and excitement (the friends, the friends of Madame van Roeslaere!) had made her incapable of answering, and she was glad to have a moment to recover.

"All right, if you want to. I don't mind," said Jooris, when he understood what was being proposed, "but I mustn't miss my train, mind."

"No, no, of course not. But you *won't* miss it . . . it won't take long, I've seen the American tourists making films like this, it isn't big ones, you know, it's only the little ones, that rich people show in their houses." She turned to Christopher and nodded, smiling with pleasure—and, just for a moment, he couldn't take his eyes off her. Jooris was also looking at her, and oddly enough, as Nora's eyes moved from her brother's face to the other boy's, she experienced no conviction that her fears about Christopher were justified. The two young men were not wearing the same expression; Nora's only experience of the love-look in action was on the faces of Juniors suffering from a 'rave' at Claregates, but there was nothing like that on Chris' face. About the young soldier, she was, however, not quite so sure.

Nevertheless, when Christopher turned briskly to Nora asking if she would try her French on the two Mrs Noahs in the top-heavy hats, with a request to be allowed to include them in the film, her mouth was sufficiently down at the corners to make him file away, in that corner of his mind not at work on the filming of Ydette, a note that there was a ticking-off coming up for Mistress Nora.

"Can I be in it, can I, *please*?"

"No, Dogfight, I can take you whenever I like, I've got *hundreds* of you already, and I've *told* you," lowering his voice, "it's Ydette I really want; the others are just an excuse. Now go right over there and stand in that corner *out of the way* and *stay put* and," in a burst of generosity because his own wish was about to be gratified, "I'll buy you a really smashing cake for tea."

"Are we going to have tea? Oh, super! But Mummy says tea isn't ne-ces-sary when you're abroad; it's ter-ri-fy-ing-ly expensive, she says."

"Never mind all that now—and *don't* come out with it when you hear me suggest tea later—this is my affair and I'm paying. Now"—slightly raising his voice—"are you ready? All I want you to do is just to stand over there and look out at the city. That's all. *Don't*," he added hastily, "for heaven's sake try to act or anything, will you? Well?" turning enquiringly to his sister, who had been haughtily speaking exquisite French to the two Mrs Noahs, "No luck?"

"None at all," she said, indicating the slow departure of the two, with heads lowered as if they were cows retreating from a terrier; "I think they're like savages, they probably think that if you make a film-image of them it'll cause them to *withah away* . . . haven't you got enough without them?"

"I want some contrast and I don't want Ydette to feel self-conscious—oh, splendid, she's got someone. All right, off you go."

While he was speaking, Ydette had gathered in three small girls who had wandered up to the summit of the hillock, all with fair plaits twisted round their heads and all wearing short

check dresses, accompanied by their little white dog,
explaining to them what they were wanted to do. Th
lowed by Jooris, who had his hands in his pockets and s
rather amused, she went with a serious, obedient expressic
her face over to the corner which Christopher had indica
While the little girls made their dog dance, and Jooris star
very hard at the distant tower of the Jerusalem Church as
warning it to behave itself, she looked steadfastly away across
the roofs of the city.

There was no sound but the soft whirring of the camera; the
wind blew across the gulf filled with spires and clouds and light,
bringing its hint of the distant sea, and Ydette forgot that she
was being put into a film, as she looked steadfastly at the distant, severe and watchful face of the Person in the peaked hat.
Nora, lounging bored and yet reluctantly interested in her distant corner, looked across at her as she stood quietly in the
brilliant light, and the thought went idling through her mind that
she reminded her of someone. But she could not think whom.

The curiously intent little moment, which seemed to mean
something for the Ruddlins and for Ydette, was suddenly
broken by a mutter from Jooris: "How about that ice-cream?
it'll be getting cold." Ydette turned quickly at this and laughed
out loud, and Nora heard Christopher, who had moved nearer
for a close-up, give a kind of surprised little grunt of satisfaction.

"Thank you very much," he said, turning to them both with
a bow and a smile, when the little girls had been told very
firmly by Ydette, on his instructions, that there was absolutely
no chance of their ever seeing the film and had gone giggling
away down the slope. "I think that ought to come out qu'
well. Now how about some tea?" He looked at his watch.
just four. I 'feel like a cuppa'; how about you?" to No
wagged a listless head in fulfilment of a promise to
up' in anything that he might suggest, which he h
from her earlier that afternoon, and——

"Oh yes!" cried Ida, acting innocence '
turned to Jooris and explained what was
looked at him in eager enquiry.

"Do you want to go with them?" he asked. He felt rather disappointed, because he liked to have her to himself when they went for a walk, but if she wanted to go with these English people—and they seemed all right, as tourists went—then he would go, to please her.

She said nothing, but her nod expressed how much she did want to. All right, then, said Jooris very quickly in Flemish, they would go, but he was going to pay for their tea and he would see to it that she got her ice-cream and he would pay for that, too. He wasn't a beggar, and Belgium wasn't a nation of beggars either, though she *had* had to take goods from the Americans, and he wasn't taking any money from the English, not he, and so on . . . and while he was talking, his eyes, with their expression of honesty and hardness so characteristic that it might have been shining up from the very bedrock of his character, rested with a slight decline of amiability upon the face of the hopefully waiting Christopher. Yes, oh yes, thank you, Jooris, that would be all right, said Ydette, and turned smiling to the young Englishman. Yes, they would be pleased to come.

He thought how much more graceful were her manners than those of the average Belgian peasant girl, and reflected with complacency that this might be due to some strain of the finer blood suspect in the mystery of her origins; that unknown heredity which was responsible for the close grain of her skin and the length of her limbs and the delicacy of her features. He also thought, with something like glee, how well all this would sound in the advance publicity some years hence . . . except that it *was* rather too like something cooked up by Publicity anyway; it was perhaps a little too typical of a new film-star's origins. But everything was going beautifully, so far, and as he gathered his party under his wing and led them down the steps in the direction of 'a decent place' which he said he new, his charming face was alight with satisfaction and good-ill towards all the world.

But in a moment the expression became a little modified. re was Nolly, at it again, pumping and patronizing Ydette;

do you go to a Church School or a State one? what class a
dear me; how much longer are you going to stay at school.
what are you going to take up when you leave? . . . Take up . .
God, thought Christopher, wasn't there enough talked
thought about Education in the Ruddlin household all
year round, without carrying it over into the Long Vac? . . . a
couldn't Nolly see that Ydette was the one kind of girl for who
education, in Nolly's sense, would never have the faintes,
importance?

But Nolly would never believe that such a girl could exist
(thanks to that new-fashioned feminist type, Hilary Perowne,
whose friendship was having such a painful influence on his
sister), and the clearly enunciated words in the superior young
voice continued to echo back from the old, quiet houses on
either side of the cobbled street, which seemed to have fallen
asleep from sheer boredom while listening to it. As the party
marched on through the quiet quarter near the Jerusalem
Church, Christopher could see the young soldier looking at
Nora as if she were some kind of a curiosity—and God knew
that she would be, unless Oxford knocked the nonsense out of
her and *that* wasn't very likely. And in spite of that dress having
cost quite a lot (he had heard his mother saying so) in a smart
shop in Bruges, it looked somehow all wrong on Nolly. But
then her clothes always did.

His irritation was increased by her behaviour while they
were all choosing their cakes in the tea-shop. "What a very
'elaborate confection' *you've* chosen," to Ydette, "are you in the
happy position of not having to worry about *dieting*; alas"—
(alas, fathead!)—"everything that *I* eat goes straight to *fat*
I'm just going to choose this *very* modest and meagre
portion," with two ill-kept fingers hovering over the dr
cuit which she finally selected. He was so irritated
that he said to his younger sister, who was car
magnificent mound of pastry and cream, "Tak
yes, go on, I mean it," and met her awed
Chris-to-pher, *super*," with a smile of appr
Ydette was in such a state of dreamy plea

much by the pretty surroundings as by the company she was
—that she had not understood what Mejuffrouw Nora had
been saying, in those long words she always used. But she was
meekly pleased to be taken back into favour again. She did not
wonder why this had happened, but, if she had, she would have
concluded that it was because Mijnheer Christopher had been
taking the film. He would not have done that if he had not
liked her, and of course the sister would do as her brother did.

"This is better than Fortes," announced Ida suddenly. She
had been taking a long stare, while making the most of her
enormous *baba au rhum*, round the light lilac-coloured walls of
the shop, the white woodwork and the floor tiled in black and
white, and enjoying the coolness and shade in which the
customers sat while being comfortably aware of sunlight and
radiance outside, "*I* like it better than Fortes."

"What, better than your beloved Fortes at Brighton, that
you said was the best place you'd ever been to? Oh Dogfight,
Dogfight!" and Nora shook her head at her sister reproach-
fully.

"What's the mat-ter? What have I done?" demanded Ida,
ceasing to eat, and beginning to turn red, while she stared
indignantly.

"Nothing, nothing, it's all right," Christopher said impatiently.

"Is Nora cross because I said I liked it better than Fortes?
I do like it better. I shall like it better if——"

"Yes, yes, all right; for heaven's sake *shut up*; Nolly didn't
mean it. Ydette," Christopher turned to her authoritatively,
"I'm probably going to show this film at Madame van Roeslaere's house before we go home on the thirteenth. Would she
let you come and see it, do you think? I'd like you to come."
He paused, for just a fraction of a second; the eyes of everyone,
even Ida, were fixed upon him with considerably more interest
than any of the previous conversation—which had been con-
ed to a few grinning remarks about Army-life exchanged
ween Jooris and Christopher, and comments upon the cakes
the weather—had evoked, and he was wondering just how

much he must watch his step—"I'm very keen for you
you see, because I think you're the kind of—well, I thin
probably film very well." (That was clumsy; but all the
were beginning to make him nervous.)

She was leaning forward a little, looking at him with t
gentle, bright, soft stare that he already could see described
critics all over the world as her 'characteristic look'; setting a
new type for girls to follow in Mexico City and Birmingham
and Durban. But it was quite plain that she did not understand
what he had said.

"I mean you're very photogenic," he said, conscious now of
the young soldier's eyes fixed upon him very keenly and using a
word, out of nervousness, which she certainly would not understand, "you've got the kind of face that can be photographed
perfectly for the films—the very best kind of face for—a film
actress," he ended up, with an excited laugh that did not, he
felt, make his remark sound any the less surprising. But he
couldn't help that: he *was* excited, and, he believed, with
excellent reason.

"My brother thinks that you could become a star—a *vedette*—
on the films," said Nora suddenly in French, wanting to fulfil
her promise about 'backing him up', and she leant towards
Ydette, "He thinks you could become a *very great* star indeed;
one of the greatest. Would you like that?" She tried to make
her voice soft, alluring and winning.

But the effect, if there was one, was spoiled. Jooris laughed a
loud and disbelieving laugh, got smartly up from the table,
looked at his wrist-watch and said something to Ydette. She
looked at him slowly, as if she did not see him, and did not
answer. He spoke again in an impatient tone, still laughing,
and Ydette turned to Christopher.

"He must go," she said, "he has to be back—with the other
soldiers." She got up from her chair, with an air of taking her
own departure for granted that silenced Christopher's protest.
and Jooris began to make stiff little bows round the company
he spoke his farewells.

"Will you be able to come and see the film, Y

Christopher was determined that the party should not break up without getting from her a definite promise.

"I do not know, Monsieur." She looked tranquilly at him, and he could not be sure whether she wanted to see herself in the film or not—much less whether Nora's remarks about being a star had sunk in.

"Well, you can ask Madame van Roeslaere, can't you?" he went on, really brusquely, "or shall I?"

"*I* will ask her, Ydette," said Nora soothingly; "I'm sure she'll say 'yes', so don't worry about it any more . . . and as soon as we know which evening, we'll let you know. There, that's quite clear, isn't it?" (*It is indeed,* she thought as she finished her sentence, *and now have I "backed him up" enough, for one afternoon?*)

Ydette only said "Thank you, mademoiselle", and then everybody became taken up with an argument in broken English with Jooris, about paying for the Belgian guests' tea; it did not last long, and both the young men were perfectly polite about it, but Christopher was quite surprised and not pleased to find, at the end of it, that he had accepted a little pile of coins.

"So far, so good—I suppose," he said, leaning back in his chair to watch the two walking quickly away across the cobblestones, between the houses now softly reddened and gilt by the light of the declining sun, "They're nice children."

"She is. I thought him rather a lout," Nora said; whatever private world those two might be walking away into—and it did look as if they were walking into one, and as if they shared it—she was certain of one thing—that it was a world both crude and narrow.

"Oh *lord,* Nolly," her brother said impatiently.

"Well, I *did* think he was one. He laughed when I said you thought she could be a star—he probably understands quite a lot of English, they all do here, it seems—and that will put her off even considering the idea, if she's—keen on him."

"Oh well, I shall have to deal with quite a lot of family opposition, I expect, in three or four years' time. But I shall simply play up to the old girls' greed. They're bound to be money-mad; peasants always are, and if they think Ydette's going to make a lot, they won't be so set against the idea."

"Have you got it all planned out?" she asked casually; she thought that, having backed him up, he might at least take her a little more into his confidence about the scheme, which seemed to her (and she had some difficulty in concealing the fact) as wild as it was unlikely ever to take shape in action.

"Of *course* I haven't 'got it all planned out'. How could I? when I don't even know yet whether I'll get my degree, and that's going to have such a big effect on what sort of job I'm going to get. But I do know that if Ydette were handed over to the right people, and had the right grooming and production, she could be made into a very big star indeed. I'm *certain* she could. I've got a hunch about it—and you know that my hunches are usually right." Nora nodded reluctantly. "And I'm absolutely determined to keep in touch with her for the next year or so. I'm *not* going to lose sight of her. Adriaan can write and tell me how she's getting on (of course, being Adriaan, he'll probably think I'm interested for just the obvious reason, but I can't help that). And one of us ought to write to her, too, fairly frequently."

He turned to Ida, who, ignoring the conversation, had been carefully scraping her fork round and round the surface of a plate from which every trace of cream had disappeared some moments since, and silently sucking it, "*You* can do that, Dog-fight. You'd like to write to Ydette, wouldn't you? Well, wouldn't you?" impatiently, as she stared at him in bilious silence, and at last she vaguely nodded.

"It seems a pity . . ." Nora began slowly, looking down the length of the quiet street where the two had disappeared, ". . . to think of her leaving school, and spending the rest of her life between helping at that dreary little shop and with those touristy bathing-tents, or perhaps stifling away packing orchids for old van Roeslaere for about two pounds ten a week . . . she ought to be trained for something . . . get a really good job . . . perhaps go abroad . . ."

"She is abroad; what do you mean?" demanded Ida loudly, coming suddenly to life.

"That's a very old joke, Dogfight (no, I can *not* explain it now, I want to talk to Chris) . . . but perhaps she'll marry. She might marry Adriaan," she ended, with an uncharacteristic giggle; the picture was irresistible.

"Marry *Adriaan*? What on earth are you getting at? There isn't anything going on there, is there, for God's sake? That *would* just about . . . besides, it would be . . ." Christopher checked himself on the verge of the out-dated expression *a damned shame.*

"I don't think there is anything 'going on' . . . now. I did at first, because of the very peculiar way they looked at each other, but . . ."

"How do you mean, peculiar? The usual thing?"

"I don't know anything about the usual thing," coldly, "but she looked singularly 'soppy' when she saw him, that first day down at the *excursion*, and he really *does* stare at her, his eyes nearly pop out of his head."

"They do that anyway; they always have—so you don't think he's up to anything, now?"

"I don't know, Chris. I only don't think so. She . . ." Nora hesitated . . . "she really is rather nice, you know. Sweet, like a kitten or a pup . . . I can't imagine her 'carrying on' with him."

"It's a bit hard to imagine anyone doing it, who wasn't very hard up for someone or else crackers, but I understand from him that people do—and quite a lot." Again Christopher checked himself; he had no intention of directing his sisters' attention towards Adriaan's grimy little love affairs.

"There was a—there was a girl in Ashbourne who got married," said Ida suddenly, "I saw her do it, she had a super white dress and an en-or-mous bunch of flowers and—oh, super," waving her arms about; "you could do it, Nolly, if a young man asked you to—I could, anyone could, Mummy says. It's a thing girls do—can do in England."

"So they can in Belgium, half-wit," said Nora, "but," returning obstinately to her original point, "it does seem a pity about Ydette and her education—and she may not want to marry . . . some people do prefer spinster's delights . . ."

"What?" said Christopher, very rudely. Something in the elaborate, drawling, superior manner irritated him suddenly beyond his powers of control—and here was as good a place as any to launch the ticking-off.

"Spinster's delights." She glanced at him in surprise, then (oh, fatal! . . . but the sheer injustice of talking to her 'in that tone' when she had been backing him up so nobly . . . and in front of Dogfight . . .), "What's the matter?"

"You are." He hesitated for an instant. "I may as well tell you here and now that if you don't drop that frightful affected way of talking, you're likely to be one—a spinster—yourself."

"Well. Is that such an appalling fate?"

"Not necessarily. But even a girl with a brain needs at least the opportunity of leading a different kind of life from a woman don's. We all think they're rather frightful."

"How frightful for the women dons. Dear me. I wonder how they can manage to get through their work, under the appalling disability of—of—being thought 'pretty frightful' by——"

"Oh leave it, Nora. I'm serious. It's you who are silly," as she repeated something about 'silly little boys'. "I didn't mean to tell you this but—Ashton thought you were the absolute end."

She was quiet, and did not move.

Ida's head was moving backwards and forwards, as she glanced from one face to another, like that of a spectator at Wimbledon. That had shaken Nora, Christopher thought. Ashton, whom no-one could possibly call a silly little boy, Ashton, with whom Nora had had such long arguments, and against whom she had held her own so well.

In a moment she said, "I didn't like him much, you know," which surprised him into exclaiming, "Didn't you?"

She shook her head, looking down at the table. "Not very much. But then——"

"Then what?" He still kept his tone full of asperity, but

he was not unfair; he would listen, if she said anything that was not mere haughty nonsense.

"I never do like men much," she said.

"Why on earth not?" demanded he, with a hearty amazement which the next instant he regretted; "you *can't* not like us, we're half the human race. You like me, don't you?" (That slipped out, too, but somehow the whole conversation was beginning to move away from the lines which he had originally laid down for it.)

"That's different. I mean men who aren't relations."

"That's part of what *I* mean, Nolly. Men can always tell when women don't like them, and they resent it. If you really didn't like Ashton (and I must admit that I'm surprised, *I* thought you did, you were always playing tennis with him and talking to him), naturally he thought you were the end."

"Did he say I was the end?"

"Of *course* not. Can you imagine him? It got back to me through someone else."

"How?"

"Oh, some old washerwoman or other—I can't remember, if I ever knew—but why did you hang round him so much, if you didn't like him?"

"If I did 'hang round him', as you elegantly put it——"

"There you go *again*, Nolly, that way of talking—it sets people's teeth on edge; don't *do* it, you don't know how grisly it sounds. Why can't you be natural?" And he added, causing her heart to sink even further, "You take a superior attitude towards Ydette, I've noticed—if your manner was like hers, it would be—a damned sight more graceful," he ended vaguely, but with energy.

The bite seemed to have gone out of the contest; he had a feeling that he hadn't quite succeeded in what he set out to do, and now Dogfight, confound her, was looking scared. He got up and went across to pay the bill, feeling slightly ashamed of himself.

Nora sat quietly at the table, continuing to stare down at the check cloth. Oh, she could have told him of 'spinsters' delights' that were satisfying enough; the long, quiet afternoons when she and Hilary and Evelyn were sitting at work in the gallery above Hall, with sunlight falling across the pages of their books; the peaceful hours as like to one another as were the Georgian stone slabs in the paved garden, yet each, like the stones, with its own slight and enjoyable divergence from the pattern—the joke of that particular afternoon, the faces that broke into exactly the right sort of shared smile, the voices of girls and women—creatures who lived in the same kind of body as oneself and about whom one *knew* instinctively, without doubt or fear—sounding orderly and controlled and yet fresh— in the distance; and the atmosphere of the great, calm, sober place!—brimmed with learning, filled with idealism—oh yes, she could have told him.

But what was the use? when, although he was her brother, he was also a male, and therefore would never understand?

But, as usual, the mere thought of Claregates had exerted a calming effect, and when he came across to them, announcing amiably that if they were ready, he was, she accepted his placating tone without hesitation. They all walked homewards without further disturbance, and Nora assured him, as they ran down to the sea for a late bathe, that she would ask Madame van Roeslaere if Ydette might come to see the running through of 'her' film.

Ydette and Jooris came upon a fine prospect of the Belfort as they walked quickly towards the wide Market, but this evening, although she looked upwards as usual at the elongated, fantastic, yet strictly ordered, shape soaring against the blue of the sky, it seemed to her (as can sometimes happen to us when we meet, on a day that has held wonderfully good news for us, the oldest friend who has the strongest influence) that its power came to her through a sunny mist. She could still see the inside of the tea-shop, and taste the cakes which Jooris had bought for her; but more clearly than anything else she could see the eager faces of the Ruddlins, telling her that she had a face like a film star's.

o

It was a completely new, strange and just-beginning-to-be-gratifying thought. No-one had ever spoken to her about her face since the days when Mijnheer Adriaan had said those things about it, on his way to school every morning. She felt triumphant, as she walked silently beside Jooris, her long legs almost keeping pace with his stride. (Beetles indeed! Just let Mijnheer A. try that on with her now!) But of course, he would not say such things, now. He was almost grown up. He sometimes spoke to her in rather a rude voice, and he always stared so hard that sometimes she wondered what was the matter with him, but for a very long time now there had been no insults.

Jooris, who had been glancing from time to time at her dreamy face, suddenly stopped in his stride, and drew himself upright.

"Now! The *roomijs*," he said, and, wheeling smartly about, marched in the direction of one of the more expensive cafés, which had tables and chairs set outside, under a striped canvas awning.

"Oh Jooris! Thank you . . ." Ydette was almost running now to keep up with him. "I thought . . ." (really, this afternoon was just one good thing after another).

"Did you think you weren't going to get it?"

"I thought—when you said you'd got to catch your train—we shouldn't have time."

"I said *that* an hour before I really had to. Didn't want them hanging on while we had our ice-cream." His voice was rather curt, and she glanced at him tranquilly: didn't he like the young English people? But it was not Ydette's habit to ask questions which might lead to a disturbance of the peace.

"Here we are." He pulled out a comfortable armchair of scarlet cane-work and held it while she settled herself, then sat down opposite. "Now." He indicated the menu, on a board outside the door of the hotel, "You choose."

"Aren't you going to have one?"

"No. Beer for me." He beckoned sharply to a lounging waiter.

As Ydette slowly spooned up the sweet, icy stuff flavoured with chocolate, she felt that the afternoon could scarcely have ended better; with the sun touching the soaring tower of the Belfort to a last gold, and the sky almost directly over her head containing one of those stupendous curving trains of cloud, faintly resembling thousands upon thousands of minute human heads glorified to a misty supernatural whiteness and sweeping halfway across the heavens, which always made her think that they might be angels. It was the week of the Fair; and the great square of the Markt was almost filled up by red-and-yellow booths and a *carrousel* playing the latest American music so loudly and stridently that it almost drowned the noise made by the crowds of giggling girls and boys strolling past, playing, and shouting to each other; and at the other side of the square, directly by the low, massive archway leading into the gateway of the Belfort, the woman who sold fried goodies in her coffee-stand was cooking away for dear life and adding the smell of hot fat to the clamour and noise and confusion . . . but Ydette saw the Belfort, and the far-off train of angel faces, and tasted the elfin sweetness of the food in the heavy spoon.

Presently she looked up, and found Jooris staring at her. She looked down again at her ice without having done any more than smile at him in thanks for the happy end to the afternoon. In a minute or two she looked up again, and he was still staring, so she asked placidly, "Have I got some ice on my face?"

He shook his head. Then he seemed about to say something, but stopped. Ydette went on peacefully eating.

When she next glanced up, he said at once, with his eyes still fixed on her, "What was he saying? Something about you being like a film star?"

Ydette gave her soft giggle. "Yes. Just fancy!" There was no reason for saying anything more, so she industriously scraped the spoon round and round the already denuded glass in silence, but when he did not speak, she went on, "and the mejuffrouw said he thinks I could be a really big one——" She giggled again.

"It's because you've done your hair that way," said Jooris quickly. "Have you done it like that before, when he was anywhere about?"

She finished the last trace of ice off the spoon, sighed, slowly put the cup down on the table and leant back in her chair and smiled at him like a replete child.

"This was the first time," she said.

He said nothing to this, but suddenly looked severely across at the fantastic cockerels and horses swirling up and down, up and down, as they went by on the revolving *carrousel* with its screaming, laughing load. He was thinking, for the first time in his life, about Ydette's face.

It wasn't really pretty; at least, not what he called pretty, not like Angéle's face, who worked in a hairdressers' shop in a side street off the Boulevard Anspach in Brussels; Angéle, now, really was pretty, with a French figure and a smile rather like Marilyn Monroe's—she was a nice girl, too; he had been to Sunday dinner with her family. But he did not like her face (he came to that decision instantly, although he had never made the comparison before) as much as he liked Ydette's. The only time he had ever been reminded of Ydette's face when she wasn't there had been that time he and the others went to the *bioscoop*, and there was a close-up of a giraffe and everyone had laughed. *That's like Ydette*, he had thought, and had gone on laughing with a kind of warmth in him. He liked (he was thinking it out now, to a conclusion)—he liked Ydette's face better than any face he knew: better even than his mother's.

Ydette was looking at the cockerels and griffins and the royally maned lions careering by: not wistfully: just admiringly, and suddenly he leant towards her and smiled.

"Like a ride?"

"Oh, Jooris!" She got up at once, smiling, eager, with not a word about whether he could afford the money, as an older girl might have asked, or about the risk of being sick after that huge ice; yes, she was still completely a kid, and of course she wasn't going to get any ideas into her head because of something a stuck-up English boy from Oxford College had said, and, after all, if anything did come of it, if the Englishman did try to start something when she was a bit older, he, Jooris would always be there, and he would see—yes, by God and His Saints he would —that she didn't get hurt.

He looked steadily at her as she hovered, smiling, poised on tiptoe and ready to mount, while the lion which she had marked for her own steed came slowly round and drew to a standstill in front of them. Half of his feelings were clear and decided, and made him feel good; and then there was something else—a kind of pain, a kind of impatience and wanting and sweetness that wasn't clear at all, and made him feel rebellious.

He put his arm round her to help her up, and felt the soft waist and slender bones that had been familiar to him ever since he had carried her round the courtyard at the farm when she was two years old—and all at once everything was all right, and they were just having the last treat on an afternoon that had been—(in spite of that rather disturbing new way of doing her hair, and what the young English fool had said)—a pretty good one.

During the Ruddlins' last week in Belgium, the weather changed. It continued warm but became very rough; the sea tore forward onto the beaches with a crash and a rolling fury of foam, and all along the miles and miles of dunes that fringe the coast the sand spun and drifted under the wind, with a sound so shrill and insect-like that only in the hollows of the dunes was it audible; broad patches of magnificent blue showed for an instant across the heavens and were gone again; then the sun positively leapt out, and all the hinterland spread wide behind the dunes lightened and darkened, lightened and darkened, under the racing shadows of the clouds.

On the evening of a certain day of this weather, about seven o'clock, Klaas opened the door of the shack in which he lived and stood there, swaying, and looking out at the rapidly clearing sky and the glimpse of livid, white-ridged sea visible between the dunes to the west. Half an hour earlier, Marie and Jakoba had brought Klaartje up from the beach and stabled him in the shed which stood at a little distance from Klaas' hovel, for they knew that in this wild weather only a few hardy bodies, racing down in raincoats from their hotels, would venture to bathe: there would be no tourists hopping in and out of the wavelets *this* evening, and who would want to make an 'excursion' down to such a sea? the sisters might as well pack up and go home.

Klaas had been down to the huts that day; almost sober, for once, and had even made himself of some use; as they bicycled homewards along the deserted roads with heads bent into the pushing wind, Marie had been saying that he seemed better, and might be good for a year or two yet . . . if you could call it *good* . . . and Jakoba had said nothing; and then they had got themselves into an argument about just how old he *really* was, and when exactly their father had first come across him. . . . Ydette had stayed at home to take care of Mevrouw Maes and would have the fried potatoes and the coffee waiting, with perhaps a bit of fish, as it was Friday, and they were looking forward to it.

Klaas stood for a little while in the windy sunset; wild beams were striking down on the land far away, whitening a tower, throwing a fading forest into a great glow of bronze, dazzling the eye. His mouth was full of the sound and taste of the sea and the wind blew rough and warm through his ragged clothes. Muttering to himself, he drew the door to and did some complicated twistings and fastenings and turned an old key in the rusty padlock; then he pulled his round cap down over his head and set out at a kind of stumbling run aross the rough grass towards Zandeburghe.

Later that evening, Everard Ruddlin was sitting in the window of the dining-room at the big house, smoking, while, at the far end of the room, his elder daughter and his son and Adriaan van Roeslaere were assembling the implements for the film show.

Leaning back comfortably, he stared out of the window, leaving behind him the young voices raised in suggestion or in quick argument, and wished that he were back at The Link House.

The holiday, spent by him in frequent expeditions to towns and villages famed for some beautiful ancient building or object, and in day-long walks with his wife through the quiet—too quiet—countryside, had seemed to him endless, and it hadn't done him a bit of good; he felt almost as on edge and as strung-up as he had been when he arrived here, and all he wanted now was to get back as quickly as possible to The Link House, and immerse himself in work again. He wanted to leave behind him for ever that sickening faint sensation of pain—suggesting the deathly scent that hovers perpetually about the corridors of a hospital—which had haunted the air of Flanders for him ever since he returned there.

He was going to take good care that he never returned *again*. The experiment (and he had not been entirely unwilling to come, it hadn't been altogether a question of May's persuading him into coming) had been a mistake, as well as painful—*God*, it had been so *painful*! He felt sore from the pain; and from this eerie sensation, which he carried within him all the time, that something had been spoiled and made cheap. And there was the sense of loss! loss of someone he had known and loved (and he *had* loved her, oh God in Whom he didn't believe, he *had*), someone he had known for only three weeks out of his entire life. Dead, perhaps, ten years or more, and he could still feel so much . . .

"Do you mind if I just move these chairs, Monsieur van Roeslaere?"

"Not at all, not at all, I don't mind, Christopher. So . . . and what about the curtains? Must they be drawn?"

"Of *course* they must be drawn; if they aren't, you won't see a thing." Adriaan's voice, at its sourest and most furious: he had been sulking about something all through dinner.

"Really, Adriaan, we cannot draw them yet; with this heat—in spite of the wind—we shall all not be able to breathe." Madame van Roeslaere, out of courtesy to her guests, was using her rather rusty English. "You want to shut out all the air."

"I don't 'want' to do anything, even to show Chris's film—particularly; but if the curtains aren't drawn, the delicacy and drama of his camera-work won't get full justice done to it."

Everard glanced down the room; really, Adriaan's voice and manner sometimes sounded as if he would end up in that hinterland known to Christopher and his friends as *round the bend*: Everard himself knew, from six years' teaching and handling of him, that Adriaan's brain and health were far too stable to make such a catastrophe at all likely, but certainly his manner could be most odd . . .

"Oh, la la! I'm sorry," said Adèle, with a rueful smiling grimace at May Ruddlin that did not quite serve to mask the painful flush running up into her thin face, "by all means, then, please to draw them."

"Not yet. Just before we start, we will." Christopher's voice, sounding calm and deep as it always did just before a showing of one of his films. "Nora, come out of there and give me a hand, will you?"

Everard, not wishing to continue the train of thought in company with which he had been staring out of the window, saw his elder daughter emerge slowly from the niche between a Dutch cabinet and the tall porcelain stove, where she had successfully half-concealed herself, and go, too quickly, down the room. As he watched her, his irritation mounted; really, she did move badly; she would simply have to be sent for a month or two to one of those places where they taught girls to move and walk; it wasn't fair to her, to let her go out into the world with that blend of scholar's crouch and hockey-girl's tramp . . . but what would May say? "Oh, you attach too much importance to these things, dear; they don't matter *nearly* so much now that girls are properly educated . . ."

But they did matter, to him. May had never known how responsive he was to grace and beauty. She suspected it; she sometimes teased him about it, bless her. But she didn't know how strong it was in him: an appetite, a thirst: *and what harm it might have done . . .?*

The pain crawled over him again. He turned quickly and looked out of the window.

He could still hear May's voice, earlier that day:

"Oh . . ." on a funny flat note, as they turned a corner amidst the heaps of ruins which ended on the banks of the broad, quiet Astrid Canal.

"Nothing of it left," he had managed to say, looking at the mounds of pitted and broken old bricks, and the stumps of foundations still imbedded in the sandy white ground.

"The whole place has simply vanished. . . . Was there a row of houses here?"

"Yes. Very beautiful houses," he said.

"It *would* be this kind of town that would have to go, wouldn't it? . . . poor old bricks . . . it seems sad to survive for four hundred years, and then come to such an end . . . but isn't the colour still lovely?"

He had suddenly tucked her hand into his arm, desperate for comfort.

"You're such a nice person, May," he said briskly.

"I am?"

"You are," with a laugh and a little pressure.

"Because I was sorry about the bricks? But anyone would be . . . oh look, everything isn't quite dead; there's the root of a tree, and it's budding. What is it?" She moved a little nearer, peering with her shortsighted eyes, "A willow? yes. A weeping one, I do believe; look, there's a shoot already starting to bend over." She looked up at him. "Was there a willow in the garden of 'your' house, can you remember?"

"Yes. Yes, I believe there was."

"Bless it," she murmured, looking at the shreds of green; she was moved to tenderness by plants and flowers as other people are moved by children, "I hope they'll let it stay there if they rebuild."

They stood for a moment and Everard looked interestedly about him at what had once been Doorwaden. Then she had said, "Perhaps this *is* 'your' house, then . . . I suppose the poor old man must have been killed. I had his name on the tip of my tongue a second ago . . . Monsieur—it began with a B, I'm sure . . ."

"Did it?"

"I'm almost sure it did. But I can't remember . . . I wonder what happened to him."

"I haven't the faintest idea. I did ask Van Roeslaere about . . . the people who were living here but . . . but he didn't know anything; of course, Doorwaden is some way from Bruges, but I thought he might know something: the hothouses are only about four miles from here, of course. But he didn't."

"Had he any family?"

"The old man? A daughter." *That* had slipped out before he could stop it.

"Poor things . . . why does it seem so much sadder because one knows a little about the people who lived here? . . . I wonder what became of her. Was she married?"

"I don't think so."

"Was she young?"

"Middle twenties . . ." and then he couldn't stand any more, and had turned abruptly away, saying, "Let's be getting back. It's rather sad here."

"It is indeed. What was her name?"

"Who? The girl? I can't remember; I don't even remember what she looked like," (he was driving himself, as if with a whip) "I was out a great deal, walking, and looking at places, and taking notes, and only used the house for eating and sleeping."

He had to resist the impulse to wipe his forehead, and then he had to stop himself from going on talking; from adding something about *thinking it must have been a dreary life for her, the daughter.*

But he had never thought that, not even at the beginning. It had seemed to him that she and her father lived in the middle of an idyll, so quiet and so beatified with domestic peace their lives had been, with every detail performed as if it were a small, well-loved ritual, and hovering above it all—small, quiet house, shady garden where vegetables flourished beyond the shadow of the weeping willow, the freshness and the cleanness of everything—were the great virtues which shaped both their lives, and which were never spoken of, perhaps never even by them perceived—duty, and piety, and content.

Out-dated virtues. The present generation thought them dull . . . when they thought about them at all . . . the pain came back, having been kept successfully at bay for a minute or two by generalizations.

And into that idyll *he* had broken, with his own confusion and the rebellion and unfocused passion that had suddenly overwhelmed him after his father's death.

There had been that sleepless twenty-four hours after the funeral: when he had wanted to get as far away as possible from the school and his work there under the guidance of his father in his wonderful and awe-inspiring old age, away from May and the children and everything that he loved most; he had felt that he never wanted to see again everything that he had cared for and worked for . . . and May (but May had been wonderful . . . if rather puzzled . . . she had been wonderful) had told him firmly that he was run down and must get away. Why not go to Flanders, and stay for three weeks—a month— six weeks—as long as it would take him to get really well again? She had spoken as if *it* had been an illness.

So he had gone, taking with him the notes for the final chapter of the book that his father had been constructing on Flemish history and Flemish art, and its influence upon Europe, and he had wandered off the boat at Ostend, and through the shabby marine and industrial quarters on its outskirts, then taken a bus out into the country and ended up, late in the June twilight, he remembered, in Doorwaden: at the house of the Brandts . . .

. . . This room was very beautiful, the panelling was almost the colour of a nutmeg, and the coffee-pot and cups had probably been made by Chinese craftsmen to the order of some Dutch ancestor of Adèle's who had been an administrator in the East Indies. How thin Adèle had grown: those incongruous hands of hers, which should have belonged to a beautiful

woman, looked disproportionately long and white as she waved
them about while saying something to May, as the two sat
together, chatting, at the other end of the room. She had made
herself ill, he and May agreed, with worrying about Adriaan's
soul. That was exactly what her trouble must be, because
Adriaan was doing well at the University, and his habits,
although too luxurious, in a boy of his age, to be anything but
alarming to an elderly couple inclined to a brisk asceticism in
their way of living, were not so wild as to give genuine cause for
anxiety; no, it must be his soul, and certainly, if his face provided any reflection of that (to Everard) hypothetical item, it
must be in some peril.

Peril of what? (Everard's thoughts played determinedly on,
keeping pain and memory at bay.) Hell? What did that mean,
in contemporary religious terms of reference? Being shut away
utterly and for ever from what "people whose minds were so
orientated" called God?

He himself had never felt the faintest need for a religion;
never a whisper or a warning from anything outside his own
brain and his own conscience had ever come to him: he lived
by a set of personal ethics, based upon one bequeathed to him
by his father, that had served him and the School very well—
until the three weeks in Doorwaden when he had been insane.

Sitting by the window, looking out across the sunset lights
in the *plaats*, he was supposing that he never dared to let himself wander back, in thought, to the weeks in Doorwaden,
because they had been the most fully lived, and the most—he
could not think of a word that should not profane them—the
truest days that he had ever experienced. It was difficult, so
difficult as to be almost impossible, to realize that those days,
beautiful, and calm, and filled with the radiance of love, had
been 'wrong'.

But it was the harm! It was the harm that he might—that
he almost certainly had done to her and to the life that she had
lived before he came! It was the thought of *that* which had
haunted him, day and night, ever since he came back to
Flanders; staining everything; spoiling his memories; cheapen-

ing and soiling and destroying . . . if only he could have known that no harm had come to her and her life, if only (the hopelessness of the wish! the utter hopelessness of it) he could forget that when they said good-bye, on the last evening, she had been crying.

He glanced round with leisurely half-smiling interest towards the upper end of the room, and saw that the screen was now set up; they were all gathered about a table, arranging the projector. It was a relief that soon there would be something to take him away from his own thoughts: until this holiday, he had never really understood the state of mind that makes people go to the pictures to be 'taken out of themselves'; he felt as if he would like to walk out of himself and slam the door and never come back . . . really, how badly Nora wore her clothes; that was a pretty dress, but, on her, it hardly looked it.

Nora, at that moment, was thinking how fortunate young men were to have a costume for the evening which was as correct and easy to wear as a uniform; how well Christopher looked in his dinner jacket, and even Adriaan appeared less hideous than usual, though surely something could have been done about his ears while he was a baby; pads, or something? But no doubt Mamma van R. had believed that their angle was due to the *Will of God*.

Nora had been slightly shocked, as well as mortified and disappointed, when Madame van Roeslaere, gently but decidedly, and with no appearance of regret, had told her that it was impossible for Ydette to come to see the film.

Madame van Roeslaere had shaken her head, when rather casually asked (too casually, May Ruddlin had afterwards told her daughter; Nora must remember that, in some respects, Continental life retained some of the formality that English life had lost) if "it would be all right if Ydette came along too?" and when Nora had looked surprised at the refusal, and tried to coax a little (an accomplishment in which she was far from being proficient), Adèle had said with firmness:

"You must remember, you enjoy playing with Ydette, and

your mother allows Ida to behave with her almost as if she were her younger sister, but *we* have to live with people of that sort after you have gone home. It would make awkwardness for Ydette, if she had been here as my guest. She would not know —how shall I put it? yes, '*where she was*', she would be embarrassed, and begin to get thoughts, perhaps, in her head. She is a good child but she isn't a bit intelligent. (The nuns at the school have been quite in desperation over her.) And . . ."

But here Madame van Roeslaere had broken off, and said no more.

And Nora had not dared to reopen the subject; she was quite sensitive enough to feel that to do so would have been exceedingly rude, and she also felt—in spite of her contempt for Madame van Roeslaere's passive attitude to 'the Will of God'— a kind of curiosity and awe concerning her religion, and the way in which it so plainly moulded and dictated her attitude towards every detail of her life. Nora knew no one else who lived thus, and, as she would have put it, "it fascinates me, in a grisly kind of way".

"So much for Christian charity," said Christopher, rather awfully, when his sister reported back to him, "why didn't you say something about us all being the same in the eyes of God . . . *that* would have floored her."

"*I* don't think it would," Nora said.

"Well, never mind, can't you get round it somehow? get Adriaan to ask her—no, that won't do, damn it, *he's* in the dog-house for not turning up at Mass for the last six Sundays— how about Papa van R., can't you get at him?"

"I don't think I can, Chris, it really would be rather awful; Mummy would be furious, and so would our papa."

"Yes, I suppose they would, and I see what you mean. But I don't mind telling you frankly that this has rather finished the van R.s with me; I'm no Communist, as you know, but any attitude more likely to make for Communism I *never* came across—and so utterly absurd, too; Ydette would—well, she'd be outstanding *anywhere*. I shall laugh like a drain if she's world-famous in another five years or so and the van R.s are tumbling over themselves to say they knew her when she was unknown. They'll be sorry enough, *then*, that they wouldn't let her sit in their ruddy *salon* for half an hour and drink a cup of coffee."

Then he withdrew himself into preparations for the evening's performance, which so engrossed him that he left it to Nora to break the news to Ydette.

"But of course, Mademoiselle," said Ydette placidly, when Nora, crimson and mumbling, had stammered through the rudiments of a sentence in which the words *not convenient* were repeated two or three times, "it is all right."

"Don't you mind?" said Nora, relief at the calmness with which the blow had been received making her even more tactless than usual.

Ydette indulged in a very Flemish shrug; yes, she minded; she always liked a reason for going to the big house; but she was not at all sure that she would like to sit on one of the chairs that she had so often helped Lyntje to dust, in the presence of Mijnheer van Roeslaere's evening clothes and his twinkling eyeglasses of gold wire and crystal, and the tall young English mijnheer who had said such strange and thought-provoking things about her face, and under the dear but awe-inspiring eyes of Madame, and of Mijnheer Adriaan, staring. No.

"I do not mind at all, Mademoiselle," she said, with more decision than her soft voice usually carried, and she smiled at Nora.

"Oh . . . good. But I'm sorry," Nora said, remembering to give to her own smile its prudent touch of reserve as she turned away, "well, we'll tell you all about it afterwards," she concluded.

When Adèle had checked herself on the verge of her sentence, she had been going to say that there was another reason for not inviting Ydette to the big house as an evening's guest; she knew that Adriaan was interested in her protégée.

She had noticed his prolonged stares in that direction, and had marked how 'touchy' (as the English would say) he was on the subject, and she was really afraid that something might come of it . . . occasionally, her mood growing darker as she brooded over the state of his soul, she wondered whether something had not already come of it? secret, apparently accidental, meetings, long talks, perhaps even kisses.

To her sorrow, she knew that Adriaan was capable of doing such things (since the dismissal of Lyntje, Adèle had not employed a young woman in the house) but she also believed that Ydette was not. She was a good child, and still only a child; and Adèle had seen enough of her to know precisely what her character was: gentle, rather more sensible than it appeared to be, docile and conscientious and sufficiently devout—her chief fault appeared to be that 'dreaminess' (another expressive English word); she was *vaag*, as the Flemish put it; sometimes took a long time to come back from wherever she was wandering when you spoke to her; found it difficult to concentrate, and so on. But that wasn't a serious fault, and hers was not the kind of nature that took its owner to meet a young man of superior social position in secret, and permitted kisses. Ydette was a good child.

All the same, better to remember Adriaan's interest in her, when it was suggested that she come to the house as a guest.

Adèle looked at May Ruddlin, sitting beside her in the evening light with the skirts of that pea-green dress sprawling across the exquisite, carefully mended tapestry of the couch; animated, busy, cheerful, did she never think about the darkness lying outside the circle of a contented human life? Wasn't she ever tortured—or puzzled, *tortured* was of course not the word to use in connection with May—puzzled, then, to 'square up' agonizing facts with the Will of God? What about all those who had never had what mankind called *a chance*?

Yet of course we all had a chance; *the* chance; it was as if we went staggering, stumbling, blind with pain and thirst, past a well of such coolness and depth and refreshment that . . .

"She will be delighted with it," May was saying, looking down at the copy of *Les Malheurs de Sophie* in her lap; "it's so kind of you . . . do you notice that children of Ida's age read far more babyish books than we did?"

"Don't the parents wish to shut away everything that is

frightening from children, because real life has become so frightening? and so the children read only sweet, baby books, like the Beatrix Pottaire?" Adèle said.

"I shouldn't call *The Tale of Mr Todd* exactly sweet," and May's loud laugh rang out, and Adèle said, "Ah, ah," nodding and smiling in understanding while she clasped and unclasped her lovely white fingers, on which it was beginning to be difficult to keep the rings from slipping up and down and falling off, so tiresome . . .

May was feeling rather glad that Adèle could not see Sunday evening supper at The Link House, with the cold scraps of food from the week-end's meals, from apple-tart to beetroot chutney, spread out on the dining-room table for the feeding of the young people who dropped in, every week—students living in Ashbourne, sons and daughters of old friends in the neighbourhood, acquaintances of Nora's and Christopher's—drawn there by Everard and his charm for the young . . . of course, entertaining at the big house was much more *elegant*, but it wasn't nearly so much fun, May decided, and wondered how Dogfight and her baby-sitter, Miss Rogers, were getting along?

"And in two days you will be back with your family of seventy little boys," Adèle was saying.

"Yes, in the thick of it. But I love it, you know."

"No one could live such a life if they did not love it," Adèle assured her, looking at the red face of her old acquaintance. It was like that of a good, kind horse; an intelligent horse, that was quite ready to listen to your troubles—always provided that you didn't 'go on' too long about them, and that you would take its advice when you had finished. She turned away, and stared down the room: at Adriaan.

He was still looking very sulky, and his mother allowed the breast of her elegant dress to rise in a quivering sigh as she recalled his expression, and his tone, as he had flung at her the single word "Why?" just before dinner, when she had shaken her head in reply to her husband's jovial enquiry as to whether the little Ydette was coming to see herself as a film-star?

"Because it's not suitable to ask her, my dear," Adèle had

P

said, in answer to that "Why?", and she had used the most final and the firmest, yet the lightest, tone in all her large repertoire of dismissing tones. He had had, thank goodness, enough manners not to say anything more, but his look! a thunder-cloud, a black miasma, surrounded him throughout dinner, and she had wondered if everyone had guessed the cause of this latest 'fit'?

Then she wondered if *she* really knew it? Apparently he was sulking because the greengrocer's adopted niece wasn't invited to 'drop in' and see a film made by a visiting English friend, but was that the real reason? With Adriaan, she could never be certain what his reasons were, because he had never formed the habit of talking freely with his father and herself; his anger this evening might be based on some dangerous Communist nonsense about class equality, for all his mother knew; might be as easily explained by politics as by love—for certainly there was no trace of what Adèle had been brought up to recognize as love in the brooding gaze which she had seen him fix upon Ydette.

Unsatisfactory boy! Cause of silent grief, of imploring prayers! yet loved, of course; oh yes, still so deeply loved. Her eyes were fixed upon him now, in a wistful stare; her little black thing, her weazened baby, born to her late in life: and such a delight to Hubert and herself in his infancy, when he would lie warm and heavy in her arms for hours at a time, his small, placid eyes fixed raptly upon flowers or the light, anything that was brilliant or strongly coloured. Yes, he had been a good baby; it was only as he grew into a little boy that the sulks and the obstinacy and the frightful, perverse, stubborn self-will, the unshakable insistence upon having *his way* no matter what anyone else wanted or said or did, that sometimes made Adèle literally shudder—because she knew what, in the eyes of her Church, it implied—had begun to show itself. It had been like an invasion by an evil spirit. Or hadn't it been more like the gradual awakening and uncoiling of one that had always been there? asleep, securely lodged and implacable inside that dark, pear-shaped head and thick, ungainly body?

"What on earth does the shape matter, so long as it does its job?" Christopher Ruddlin's voice was as charming as the rest of him, thought Adèle.

"I don't suppose it does 'matter'; it's just bloody hideous," and Adriaan darted a venomous look at the projector, now arranged in position on a *boule* table which had been carried in from the hall to accommodate it.

"Fitness for purpose implies beauty, surely?" said Christopher; he was still feeling sore that Madame van R. had not finally relented from her incredibly snobbish and out-of-date standards and allowed Nora to walk across the square with a last-minute invitation for Ydette. But he had already learned that it did not increase one's popularity, nor the likelihood of one's getting on in life, if soreness were publicly displayed. For example, something had upset the old monster (his own name for Adriaan) just before dinner, and they were all being made very much aware that it had. What was the matter Christopher neither knew nor cared. Adriaan was in a stew about something again: but then he always had been, ever since the Ruddlins had known him.

"For four hundred years"—he was now holding forth to the luckless Nolly, who could not be blamed for looking as bored as she did, even though it wasn't good policy in public—"people have relied on themselves to make their own amusements in this room—oh, playing the lute, cards and so on, how should I know?—and now *we* have to rely for *our* entertainment on *this*," and he launched a kick at the table supporting the projector, which received the blow from his elegant evening shoe without a tremor.

"Steady on!" Christopher said with some indignation; "really, you go on sometimes as if you were right round the bend."

"Perhaps I am."

"Well, good luck and everything, but you might remember the rest of us aren't. Now. We're ready. Can we have the curtains drawn, please, and will you all sit down?"

Everard, as the person sitting nearest to the windows, got

up and began to pull the long draperies of red brocade over the small, clear panes with their inset lozenges of red and blue and syrup-yellow; when he came to the last one, however, he looked out, and found the prospect of the *plaats* in evening light, at which he had been looking without seeing it, so beguiling that he stopped to gaze for a minute before hiding it from his view. Behind him, the room was now in almost complete dimness, and he heard the whirring sound begin as Christopher started the projector; in his present mood, it irritated him faintly, and when, having drawn the last pair of curtains, he turned back to the room, he did not join the circle seated before the projector but went across to his former chair and sat down there, at the same time casually moving aside the curtains nearest to him so that, without letting any light into the room, he could continue, through a narrow slit, to look out at the square.

He had seen so many of Chris' films: they were all exceedingly well photographed, even interestingly so, and composed and chosen and all that, and Christopher was going into the film business, somehow, when he came down from Oxford: it was all settled, and Everard no longer found the subject very interesting. He felt more interest in his youngest daughter than he did in either of the elder children; he admitted that poor old Nolly, satisfactory as her brains and character might be, definitely got on his nerves, and when he saw Christopher so confident about what he wanted to do in life, and so likely to be able to do it without parental opposition or even criticism, he experienced a mixture of wry feelings (envy? regret? nostalgia?) so confused and disagreeable that he never voluntarily indulged in them. Like some other feelings, they were banished without an instant's hesitation as soon as they reared themselves up within.

He turned away from the quiet evening, and looked at the screen.

A view of Dinant, bold and rugged against a sky filled with the bellying purple shapes of threatening clouds, was opening the performance, and there were admiring exclamations—but Everard's eyes moved, in a moment, to the chimney-breast above the fireplace, crowning, with its milky brown wood lacily carved into light medallion and elegant swirl, the tiles of the grate itself, where 'Chinamen' (that was exactly what they were, seventeenth-century Europe's conception of the Chinese), carrying hods of faggots or posturing with fans, were pictured in faint darker blue lines on tiles of palest dawn-blue.

He looked at the screen again, and saw the gipsies that he and Christopher had talked to during their three-day trip to the Ardennes. The room was dim, but he could see everyone plainly: Hubert van Roeslaere and Adèle sitting side by side in the white-and-gold chairs with arms that had been brought in from the *salon*, and gazing indulgently; Nora, lounging back and looking critical; Adriaan, staring at the screen with a sneering scowl (bless the boy, when did he mean to start grow-ing up?); May, sitting upright and gazing delightedly like a child—good old May, how she did revel in any entertainment, however simple; Christopher, the impresario, was manipulating the projector and making occasional comments on what was passing across the screen.

"That's all of that one," he was saying, as the flower-market at Brussels passed from the screen amidst cries of admiration from May; "now *this* is the one . . ." his voice died away, as he manœuvred with the projector and exchanged low-toned remarks with Adriaan, then it rose again, "this is the one I really want you to see. This is Bruges."

And indeed it was; the Market, in all the strolling bustle and animation and life of Saturday afternoon; with the native Brugeois and his wife walking between the stalls hung with gay cottons, and pausing to inspect a sky-blue jug from amongst rows of them set out on the cobblestones, and the stout girl inside the Belgian version of a coffee-stall that stands almost within the dark archway below the Carillon tower, frying her oily-smelling goodies, while the bright summer sky smiled over-head, and the huge pastel-coloured cars were edging their way round the sides of the square, and the tourists and the cyclists were circulating, and the children marching back from school—oh and there, wending his way through it all, with shy eyes lashed like a doe's looking determinedly downwards, a young friar clad all in brown, with rope-bound waist and sandalled feet.

"Oh lovely, Chris! What a nice thing to have! We can show it to people on Sunday evenings——"

"That really is a triumph," generously, from Nora.

"You should come here in three years' time and take the Festival of the *Sanguis Christi*, the Holy Blood," said Hubert van Roeslaere; "now that is something to see, the Belfry floodlit, and the procession through the streets, and the play they act in the Markt—oh, it's a spectacle." He himself did not quite see what all this enthusiasm for a completely ordinary picture of Saturday afternoon in the square was about; there had been a market there on Saturdays ever since the Belfry had been there; it was nothing out of the ordinary, just some stalls and some people.

"Chris thinks the *Sanguis Christi* is commercialized and a bit vulgar," said Adriaan's voice, very maliciously, and Everard saw Adèle van Roeslaere turn her head in the dimness, with an uncontrollable kind of movement, to look at him.

"If it had been going on this year, of course I should have filmed it; it's a superb spectacle, and that's a very good idea about coming back in 1957 (*you really are the ruddy extent*)." The last part of Christopher's reply was uttered in an angry whisper.

It had only taken a few seconds for this exchange to occur, and the shots of the Market and Belfry were only now leaving the screen. The camera then took the audience along curving alleyways lined by small pale houses with stepped roofs; it went tracking across cobbles rounded with age and gleaming moist and dark after a shower; lingering, as if pensively musing, on the Bonifacius bridge, and looking down into the water gliding beneath; then, after wandering, as if scarcely interested, over the steeply-rising roofs of the Choir immediately below, it suddenly soared straight upwards until it caught and held the heaven-piercing summit of the Sint Maria Kirke, and the beholder almost gasped, experiencing such a giddy sensation of height as to be almost bodily, after the sensation of enclosedness while the camera had been loitering in the small, shady, walled garden below.

Everard was as familiar with all these places as he was with the High Street at home, and, while admitting the impressiveness and majesty of that perpendicular peak of sombre brick, he had been wishing that the addition of its four pinnacles in 1872 had never been thought of, when he heard Christopher's voice, saying with a note of excitement in it that made it sound suddenly boyish, "And here's my star."

The scene had changed to a long shot of the old mill, one of the two that still stand on the ramparts, and as Everard watched, it moved forwards until it took in a group of people gathered just below the structure; there was one, a very tall, dark, young girl wearing a light summer dress, who was standing quite still in the brilliant light, against the distant roofs of the city and its tremendous sky.

"Ida's bathing-hut girl?" Everard asked, on a questioning note; but of course he knew who it was; he had to say something aloud because—and the pain absolutely leapt at him and hung there clawing, like something alive—*she was so like Margarith.*

He had realized, almost from the first time of seeing her, that she belonged to the same tall, dark, slender, physical type; it was common enough throughout the Low Countries, where its presence might be accounted for by intermarriage between conqueror and conquered during the Spanish occupation of four hundred years ago; but this was more than a resemblance in feature and large eyes and delicate mouth; more awe-inspiring yet, it was one of individuality. When, under the stare of his incredulous eyes, this child turned suddenly towards the camera and laughed, she might have been a younger, a more light-hearted Margarith.

Murmurs of interest and admiration were all around him.

"How awfully nice she looks," from May.

"But she is handsome!" from Hubert van Roeslaere, with the intonation that used to be called '*gallant*'.

"She isn't really, not when you see her close to." Nora, this time, cool and deprecating. "She's too thin and her eyes are too big."

"You can't be too thin for the screen." The white glare showed Christopher's absorbed, gratified expression, and lit up the face of Adriaan, who was standing very still and looking steadily at the picture.

"But she must see herself, she is a budding 'starlet'." Hubert van Roselaere was good-naturedly insisting. "Is she coming in to see old Marieke this evening?" to his wife.

"I don't believe so——" Adèle was beginning rather repressively, when Everard, who had found himself absolutely unable to look at the face on the screen for another instant and had turned away and resumed his study of the *plaats*, uttered an exclamation.

"What is it?" Adèle said nervously, starting and turning.

"There's something wrong—he's fallen down—an old man. I think he must be ill," Everard said, and as he spoke, the laughing young figures on the screen disappeared abruptly into dimness as the film ended.

Everyone hurried across to the window, where Everard was now holding aside one of the curtains and admitting the strong evening light.

There was no one moving in the *plaats*, but, extended on its stones, about halfway across to the arched niche at the far corner where the shutters were drawn down over the shop of the Maes' sisters, lay the body of a man. It was dressed in dark trousers and a heavy blue upper garment which looked like a fisherman's jersey; the group now gathered at the window could see his round dark cap lying beside him where it had evidently been knocked from his head as he fell, exposing his thin, silvery hair.

"Do you think we ought to——" suggested Everard, pity for the figure sprawling there mingling with his relief at having escaped from the unbearable sight on the screen.

"Of course. Adriaan——" began Adèle warmly. But Christopher and Adriaan were already halfway to the door.

"I wonder who it is; there's something familiar about him," May went on, and then Nora exclaimed:

"Oh! *I* know—it's that poor old thing who helps down at our bathing-cabins sometimes—Klaas, I think they call him. He's a horrid old man but I hope he's all right."

They watched the young men hurrying across the square. Christopher reached the prostrate figure first, and, removing his dinner-jacket, rolled it up and placed it gently under the lolling old head.

The eyes were shut. His breathing was stertorous, and the smell of drink came up strongly from the thick, patched, dirty clothes still carrying in their dim and faded rags some of the blueness of the sea; the big hands, knotted and veined and scarred, with hooked nails of violet-black, were clenched, as if in a silent rage that matched the expression on the bluish old face.

"I think he's a goner," said Christopher in a low voice, and Adriaan nodded. "Shall I go and knock up the old girls?" he asked.

"I suppose you'd better, but what we really ought to get is a doctor."

"Here comes your father—perhaps he'll go over to them while I go and find one." Adriaan got to his feet, and stood awaiting Everard, who now came hurrying towards them.

When he got his first glimpse of the face resting on the pillow improvised by Christopher, he received his second shock of that evening, and it was doubly shocking for being of the same nature as the one that had already shaken him—*he thought that he knew this face:* it was old, wrinkled, its individuality already partly destroyed by that mysterious uniformity which illness bestows on the human countenance, and he associated it with Doorwaden and the hidden weeks in his own life. Hadn't there been someone, a loutish older man, of whom she had gone in a kind of disdainful fear? He could not even remember a name in connection with what might only be some distortion of the memory, and wasn't it much more probable that his trembling nerves were repeating the blow they had already received, and causing him to imagine a likeness where there was none?

So he reassured himself. Yet he could not banish that haunting impression of *familiarity*, and as he knelt beside the heavily-breathing body, listening, without taking in what was being said, to the quick exchanges of his son and Adriaan, he was trembling.

"Don't you think I'd better go across to the old girls' house?" Christopher was saying. "The poor chap was probably on his way there."

"Yes . . ." Everard pulled himself together, "that would be best. Adriaan—you had better go for a doctor—I expect you know the nearest one?"

He himself did not want to be there when the child—the young girl who looked like Margarith—came out of her aunts' house, but it was the obvious suggestion to make.

Adriaan repeated a name and address (the doctor lived on the other side of the Steen *straat*, where most of them in the city set up their plates) and was relieved to scramble to his feet and hurry away. As he crossed the square, he saw Christopher knocking at the door of the little low greyish house next to the archway.

"What is it? What do you want? The shop is shut—we have no more to sell," announced Marie loudly and indignantly as she flung open the door at his imperious summons. "Is something the matter?" she went on, suspicion mingled with alarm as she recognized the young English mijnheer who often bathed from their tents. Well, at least it couldn't be anything the matter with Ydette, who was at this very moment peering over her shoulder at the visitor. And *moeder* was upstairs safe in her bed with Jakoba sitting beside her . . . so it must be something wrong at the farm.

"It's the old man who works for you"—Christopher jerked his head over his shoulder—"he's ill—can you come? I think he's rather bad," he added.

"It's Klaas—he's fallen down!" cried Ydette, who had been staring across the *plaats*, and without hesitation Marie said, "I'll get Aunt Jakoba."

While she was hurrying up the tiny flight of stairs as quickly as a prudent regard of their highly slippery state would permit, Christopher and Ydette confronted one another in silence. Remembering the scene afterwards, Christopher found that he had learned something from it about himself. He had stared, with fascinated eyes, past Ydette's pale, frightened face into the little room beyond; a tiny space filled with tender shadows because the light was guarded and dim, a gleaming doll's-house staircase winding up and away into them; a glimpse of old, blue, faded tiles covering the floor, and the long, velvety trumpets of hothouse flowers glimmering out of the dimness—he had hardly been able to tear his eyes away. Afterwards, he realized that it had been unnatural to be so absorbed by a mere background when people were suffering, and felt ashamed. But it had not been until afterwards. Ydette was saying:

"Is he very ill, do you think, monsieur?"

"I'm afraid he is, yes," he said, "but don't go over there——" as she started forward, "he looks so bad—it's really—rather—I expect the doctor will be here any minute now."

They stood undecidedly together for a moment, then he heard voices inside the little dark room, and saw the old woman coming back again, accompanied by the taller, sterner sister. *She* took no notice of either himself or Ydette, but pushed past them and went straight out across the square towards the dark shape lying on the stones. Reaching it, she knelt down beside it.

Ydette did not at all want to go across to Klaas. She felt sorry for him, of course, but she was far more frightened than sorry. But in a moment the question was settled for her by an imperious beckoning gesture from Aunt Jakoba, which Ydette instantly obeyed.

What frightened her most when she looked down at Klaas was his poor bare head; she had never seen him before without his greasy, round cap, and now there was something shocking in the blowing of his grey hair in the wind; it was dirty, too, and his, and the rough way the wind tugged at it, made her so sorry that she almost began to cry. He was exceedingly ill; she knew

that at once, by his pallor and even more by his confused and
wild expression. His eyes went wandering from face to face—
first to the Englishman's, who was kneeling beside him and
re-arranging for greater comfort the jacket rolled beneath his
head, then to Jakoba's, who was sitting back on her heels on the
other side, with both hands lying slackly at her sides as if in
unfamiliar helplessness, staring at him, and last of all, to the
face of Ydette herself—where his blood-veined eyes lingered
with an expression of mocking malice.

The blue lips sucked in and out and Everard Ruddlin bent
nearer. "Can you get some brandy—cognac——" he was beginning to Jakoba, when there came a hoarse, mumbling mutter:

"*Met die manierin von van dame* *—yes, just the same. I know—
wasn't good enough for her—*met die manierin van een dame*—just
like your mother——"

The eyes closed again. Everything was quiet for a minute;
Ydette's stomach seemed to be contracting, and it was cold and
she felt horribly disturbed; she felt sick. Had she heard, really
heard, *that*?

She glanced as if for help, at the English gentleman; he was
almost as pale as Klaas, and staring down at him with a puzzled
look, and suddenly Jakoba startled them both by beginning to
sob—loud, noisy, uncontrollable sounds that seemed to tear up
from her chest. Everard looked at her helplessly, and a woman
amongst a little group of neighbours and passers-by that had
quickly gathered, leaned forward, muttering consolingly, as if
to lift her up. But Jakoba writhed away.

"Here's the doctor," someone said.

"And a Sister; that's right, they've brought one of the good
Sisters——" this was Marie.

The doctor was hatless and wore a dinner-jacket. He stooped
beside the heaving old body. He felt the pulse, put his hand
inside the rough jersey over the heart, and after a minute
shook his head. A sigh went round the tiny crowd.

Inside Klaas, the thundering of his heart had become con-

* Ladyfied; stuck-up.

fused with the thundering of the sea. He could feel it dashing against his breast and shaking him from head to foot, as its waves had done so often in the past; part of him knew what was happening, but another part *was* the sea, the violent, grey, cold sea, salt and stinging and strong in each drop of spray, that was the earliest thing he could remember. Crash! the great waves burst and spread through him in circles of icy foam, crash! it strove against his sides, that were old, old, old—couldn't do what he used to—and now he felt against his body the strength and warmth of Jakoba's, and under his feet the grit of the damp sand at evening, and then just for an instant of time he saw, as clearly as if it had been in a picture-book, Jakoba, naked, downy with the coarse strength of her youth, like in a picture book or a woman in one of the paintings in the city's art museum . . . the picture faded. He was alone again, and when he opened his eyes there was that brown, wrinkled, distorted face bending over him with the others . . . Jakoba . . . but not the big white woman whom the sea was drowning, even as it was drowning him. And Margarith Brandt's brat . . .

"You . . ." he said again, struggling to say something to the dark young face above him, the stuck-up chit, the reminder of Margarith's fear of him . . . the bastard-brat . . . but the waves were bursting on the long, grey, twilit shore, the waves were breaking, and thundering inside him, bursting and breaking and carrying him away. He thrust something angrily aside that they were holding out over him, something he could just dimly see, and then he felt the cold foam, rolling over him and turning him round and round and round, driving him down like a piece of sodden drift-wood into the deeps of the icy sea . . .

The doctor only glanced towards the nun, but at once she unhurriedly placed on the breast covered by the blue jersey the crucifix which the old man's last movement had been to push aside, and, clasping her hands, began to say aloud the prayers for the passing soul. The doctor stood upright. "I'll go back to my house and telephone for the ambulance," he said. "Will you stay here with him?" to Marie, who was more shocked by the sight of Jakoba sobbing in public than by the death of Klaas, and she nodded. The nun, too, was now kneeling on the cobblestones and calmly praying aloud, saying the prescribed words, above the deathbed spread on cobble-stones in the open air.

Ydette, stiff from prolonged crouching, stumbled when she tried to stand up, and had to be caught by Christopher and lean for a minute against him. She was still feeling shocked and sick.

"Bear up," he said to her almost in a whisper; "he was very old, you know, and it's all over now. Better to die than live on, a sick old man."

She glanced at him piteously. The dreadful thing was that she could not be *quite sure* what Klaas had said to her just before he had died.

"He said—he said . . ." she muttered, trembling.

"Oh, I shouldn't take any notice—people often get queer in the head before they die, especially when they're as old as he was. I don't expect he knew what he *was* saying. Don't let it worry you, anyway, Ydette dear."

The brotherly pressure of the arm about her waist was comforting and she rested there for a moment, feeling strength and calmness coming into her, as it always did when she was with anyone connected with the big house. But in a minute she gently withdrew herself from the embrace and stood upright because his father was looking at them with an expression that showed displeasure.

"Christopher, I think we ought to go back," Everard said suddenly.

"I couldn't agree more." Christopher knew quite well what turn his father's thoughts had taken, and it annoyed him. "But I do think we ought to just—are you quite sure you can manage now?" he said gently in French to Marie, who had knelt down beside the nun and was telling her rosary. In response she only nodded, and he, seeing that the other sister, the rougher type who had seemed so much more 'upset', had got up

and gone back into the little house and was apparently in no
more need of consolation, turned again to Ydette.

"Now it's going to be quite all right," he said. "I mean, you
haven't got to worry about anything now except comforting
your aunts. If I were you, I'd try to persuade them to have—a
—a glass of wine. It's good for shock." (If he had been at home
he would have suggested tea, but presumably in Belgium wine
was the more natural thing.) "And do try not to feel too sad,
you know."

Then she surprised him. "I am not sad," she said, nevertheless keeping her eyes fixed on his face and away from the bluish,
calm, infinitely far-off and unreal one lying at their feet, "I—I
did not like him."

"Oh," was all Christopher found to say; he more than understood; in fact if she *had* liked the poor old guy it would have
been surprising. But of course, you could mind about not
minding . . . "Do you think I might take my jacket now?" he
said.

"But of course, monsieur. I will ask Aunt Marie for her
shawl."

"Here's the ambulance," said Chris. He was feeling rather
like a glass of wine himself; this was his first sight of a dead body
outside the cinema screen, and for some reason his reactions to
the spectacle had been different.

When the black shawl had been rolled and arranged by the
nun with tender yet detached care under the ugly old head, and
the ambulance men were approaching, Christopher, as he put
on his jacket, glanced for the first time at Adriaan, and was
surprised to see his pallor.

"Come on—let's get out of this—I've had enough of it,"
Adriaan muttered, loudly enough to cause Christopher to
frown at him, and then without further speech they withdrew
themselves from the little group. Christopher, taking a last
look at Ydette, felt no more fears for her. Now, as the ambulance men expertly lifted the body of Klaas into the vehicle,
an atmosphere of orderliness, even of peace, had descended
upon the little group left standing there that was soothing to

Christopher's jarred young nerves; he was confident that it must also soothe Ydette.

"How hideous he looked," said Adriaan suddenly and violently, as they walked away across the square. "It was an outrage."

"Well, really, Adriaan. Poor old bastard—he couldn't help it."

"I'm not saying he could. I'm saying he looked so hideous that it was an outrage."

"On what? Your exquisite sensibility?"

"People oughtn't to be allowed to look so ugly."

A very unkind retort occurred to Christopher, which only his feeling for the situation compelled him to suppress.

"So he is dead? I'm not surprised; I've thought he was looking very ill for months now," said Adèle van Roeslaere, meeting them in the hall.

"And he was drinking heavily, of course," her husband added.

"He was drunk when he died," Adriaan said, "he was muttering rubbish to himself."

"I wish you'd tell that to Ydette," Chris said, "she seemed upset by something he said."

"I will leave the delightful task of consoling the greengrocer's foundling to you, my dear Christopher."

"Oh, do for pity's sake stop being such a b.f.," muttered Christopher, and then Madame van Roeslaere earned everybody's gratitude by suggesting that they should have a drink.

It arrived on a silver tray carried by Marieke, who showed no tendency to look either grief-stricken or agreeably excited by the scene which she had been watching from her attic window, and they swallowed it gratefully. The evening had passed extraordinarily quickly, and yet it seemed a long time since they had been sitting in the dimness exclaiming with admiration at Christopher's film of Bruges.

He himself, warmed and soothed by the brandy, was now able to think with satisfaction of the impression made by the screen appearance of Ydette, upon the audience.

"Didn't you think Ydette looked wonderful?" he said to Nora, as they were rushing back in the car, with Adriaan driving, towards Zandeburghe.

"I wouldn't quite say 'wonderful'. But I do see what you mean about her being photogenic. When she's on the screen one doesn't look at anyone else."

"That's exactly it. And that's star-quality."

"It really *is* rather exciting, I suppose, isn't it? What are you going to do about it?" Nora drawled; she was still congratulating herself on having escaped any close contact with the deathbed of the poor old bathing-hut-man, and she also felt confident, now, that Christopher's interest in Ydette was not sentimental.

"Not as much as I hoped to, I'm afraid," he said, lowering his voice because of his father's silent presence on his other side. "I *had* hoped to get her to come to a movie, with Dogfight for chaperone, once or twice, but there isn't time now—these things need leading up to, if you want to avoid misunderstandings, of the obvious kind."

"*Dogfight!* I don't see what use *she* would be." Nora's suspicions revived somewhat. "I would have chaperoned you, if you'd asked me."

"It's too late now. They'll be in a tizzy for days about the old boy's dying and if I asked Ydette to go to a movie I should think that would just about finish me with them. No, all I can do now is to keep in touch with her—Dogfight can do that, she's got a thing about her already, and you know how she gets into a stew and bores us all stiff round about October with her annual fuss about Christmas cards. She can put that to some use this year by sending one to Ydette. And I shall get news from——" He nodded towards the squat and silent figure at the wheel.

"What about?" it enquired, having observed the gesture reflected in the driving-mirror, and thereby causing Christopher some confusion, "what am I to give you news of, my dear Christopher? Ydette Maes?"

"I should like to know how she's getting on, from time to

Q

time, yes," he said stoutly, recovering himself. "I think she could be made into a really big star one day, she's got all the possibilities——"

"Except sex appeal." Adriaan's voice sounded even more sardonic than usual.

"Oh . . . well . . . perhaps not . . . I don't know—she's very young still . . ." (What a *hopeless* person Adriaan was in any situation requiring a little tact; couldn't he *feel* that Christopher's father, sitting silent on the other side, was stiff with disapproval and suspicion?)

"She always will be," the sardonic voice pronounced; "if you're counting on that Beauty-and-the-Beast, Snow-White and the Dwarfs atmosphere she carries around with her suddenly disappearing when she's eighteen, and being replaced by the normal thing, you're going to be disappointed. Like to take a bet?"

"Christopher may be disappointed for other reasons than a little girl's failure to develop sex appeal." It was Everard's voice at its most schoolmasterly and biting. "He may fail to get his degree."

Neither young man made any response, Christopher because he was embarrassed and Adriaan because he thought that it would be more amusing to let the acid sentences ('a squashing', as they used to call it at Port Meredith) fall into an unbroken silence.

Everard regretted them as soon as uttered, partly because they were so unnecessarily severe as to sound spiteful, but even more because he did not want to give any impression of being other than mildly interested in Christopher's plans for his 'star'. Everard felt that if he were ever to be questioned about his own views on the plan; if ever he were asked to express an opinion about Ydette Maes—he might do something irretrievably silly—lose his temper, and roar out something about a man wanting to keep *some* of his life to himself, or even begin— overcome by the almost uncontrollable misery that he had felt from time to time since the afternoon's sight-seeing with May at Doorwaden—to weep.

And although he did not permit *that* thought to come out into the open, he was disturbed by the knowledge that his son was interested in the girl who so resembled Margarith. Anxiety about such situations was sometimes called 'vulgar', yet he knew from his own wretched experience that their 'vulgarity' did not prevent their developing, and ending in mutual misery and regret; indeed, they grew and developed just because they *were* 'vulgar'; in the accurate sense of the Latin; they were situations 'common' to mankind. How extraordinary, how eerie, if his own experience were one day to be repeated in the life of his son!

He tried to dismiss the thought; it would be years before Christopher possessed any power to 'do' anything for Ydette Maes—if he ever did—and thank God the day after tomorrow they were all going home.

The car bounced and bounded on, Adriaan taking pleasure both in shaking the nerves of his passengers and in showing off his driving, and Nora, who was prone to car-sickness, also consoled herself by reflections about their return to England. The holiday hadn't been much of a success, so far as she was concerned, but of course she was getting rather beyond the age for family holidays anyway. . . . The best things in it had been Antwerp Cathedral—that really had been a cause for saying 'Laus Deo!''—and getting to know Ydette.

She admitted it at last; she was fond of Ydette; oh, only as one would be of a puppy or a kitten, of course; Ydette wasn't the type with whom one could have a friendship; friendship was reserved for people like Hilary and Evelyn, who possessed brains. Allowances must be made, of course, for Ydette's having been educated (if it could be called educated) at a Church school, and for her having grown up in what has been called 'the most Catholic city in Belgium', but even when those allowances had justly been conceded, Nora could not feel that Ydette possessed, as she herself and her friends all possessed, a clear, logical, scientific and historical conception of what the world *is*. It made Ydette very difficult to talk to and to understand—really, Nora would not have been surprised to learn that she believed in fairies! Presumably she believed in angels, and, if angels, why not fairies? Yet Nora, in spite of all these difficulties, liked her.

Nora's thoughts began to play about the subject of education, and suddenly, while she was sitting there being banged about and bounced up and down by Adriaan's driving, there came overmasteringly upon her a conviction of her own intellectual capacities that actually heated her blood: warmth spread throughout her body, accompanied by such a feeling that she was able to achieve any task connected with learning to which she might apply herself that she felt a sense of exultation. This must be, she decided, what people meant when they said of something, "It's marvellous"—and it was, too; she had never felt it before, it was like being slightly drunk. Her next feeling was one of pity: for people like Ydette, who, being unintellectual, could never experience it.

"Don't forget to tell me how my starlet's getting along, when you *do* write," said Christopher to Adriaan as they stood on the deck of the Channel-boat some days later.

"Are you really serious about all that?" Adriaan's light tone successfully masked, he thought, the dismay which caused a downward plunge in the muscles of his stomach.

"I really am. I think she can be made into a new Garbo . . . always provided, of course, that she's teachable. So much will depend on that."

"It will indeed. And I will bet you any money that you like that she isn't," said Adriaan, very spitefully indeed.

Christopher shrugged. "We'll see. Anyway, we shall be over again this time next year, and I shall be able to see how she's shaping."

The silent, ugly laughter on the other's face, at the unintentional double-meaning, was the last thing that remained with him as the bells and siren sounded, and those who were seeing the passengers off returned to the quay, and the vessel drew away from the port of Ostend.

Slowly the coast of Flanders—the wide grey sands where the

yellow waves were breaking, the long stone groins, the fringe of white and pink hotels—began to grow small and dwindle into the sea-mist. Everard stood by the rail, watching them recede. *Margarith. Margarith. I don't even know if you are alive or dead. Good-bye, my darling.*

A FEW days before Christmas of that year, when the gliding movement of the dykes had been stilled by the fierce frost creeping across the flat sea-plain unprotected by any hills; and the water lay in streaks of cloudy white between the old houses of the City and across the dim fields, and the polders in the open country shivered in the relentless wind, there arrived at the house in the Sint Katelijnstraat a Christmas card from England for Ydette.

It represented two sly but bold-looking robins who, judging by their bloated silhouettes and comatose stance upon the snow-covered bough which supported them, had been generously anticipating their Christmas dinner. In the background, a church had attracted through snowdrifts some eight or nine feet deep a congregation in stove-pipe hats, muffs and crinolines, whose footprints were lightly and neatly outlined on the white background. In one corner a cluster of bells tied with frosted ribbons in which a sprig of holly was thrust rang out the notes of 'Silent Night, Holy Night!' evidently to encourage a coach drawn by eight horses, rearing spiritedly in spite of being almost saddle-deep in snow, which was careering away into the distance, beneath a sky promising yet heavier downfalls. Inside was written,

Dear Ydette—To wish you a Merry Christmas and a Happy New Year. Hopping you are quite well and your aunts are quite well. Please remember me kindly to Madame van Roeslare when you see her and pat Klartie for me. Christopher says remember about being a film-star.

            With love
              from
                  Ida Ruddlin (I hope you remember me).

The Link House,
    Ashbourne, Sussex, England.

Yes! Ydette remembered the little Ida. She admired the Christmas card, and stood it up on her tall old wardrobe with her few other small treasures, and sent off in return a card carefully chosen from the shop in the Markt near the corner of the Steenstraat, showing the Holy Child and His Mother, containing just her name and a polite little message in French.

The year glided by, and next December there came two more fat robins, engaged this time in dubiously watching the cavortings of a small dog with a curly tail who had evidently buried a bone six feet deep in snow. The message said:

Dear Ydette,

Christopher says don't forget about being a film-star one day and he really means it. What do you think!! Exciting news!! He is engaged (fiancé) to a girl, Susan Ryder, who lives near us. She's *rather bossy*. I am to be a bridesmaid. Mummy is having a very pretty dress made for me, white net with sort of yellow rosettes on it and my flowers will be yellow roses. They are going to be married next year. Nora sends her kind remembrances. Thank you for your pretty card last year. I hope you are quite well. With love

from

Ida.

So he was *fiancé*. Ydette, who was not at all disposed to feel sentimental about Christopher Ruddlin, heard the news with emotions which could all have been applied equally well to a brother. As for being a film-star—he said that he 'really meant it', but she herself could neither believe that he did, nor could she believe for a moment she could ever become one.

What did film stars *do*? She had never thought about the matter. They were not real people, to her; she saw the girls at the packing-station, where she now worked at despatching Monsieur van Roeslaere's orchids, reading magazines with photographs of Marilyn Monroe and Kirk Douglas and all the others, but such magazines did not interest her, and she never bought them, preferring the French *Elle*, in which there was often a serial story which she could enjoy. And in the same way she enjoyed the films and the stars, watching with wide eyes, completely absorbed, as a child might have been, by what was happening on the screen. The film stars were 'real' people to her in quite another sense from that in which they were real to her fellow-workers at Sint Niklaas. They lived in her mind, fellow-dwellers with that Person in the peaked hat who had watched her throughout her childhood, and the delicate white sand out at Zandeburghe, and the big house.

They were not real people who had villas outside Hollywood, and earned astronomical sums, and frequently got divorced. And how could you imagine yourself becoming one of those figures who moved and lived, for your pleasure and delight, in your own mind?

But although she did not take Mijnheer Chris' idea seriously enough ever to consider that her life might, in a year or two, be completely changed by it, she took it seriously enough to make a habit of going to the cinema much more frequently than either the aunts or Jooris approved.

For the first time in all her life, Ydette was now doing something (in going twice a week and sometimes three times to the pictures) which Jooris did not like. The pictures! what a waste of precious spare time, when you might be playing football or sitting with friends and neighbours drinking in some cosy café where the tourists never went, gossiping about the market price of chicory or bacon! The pictures! a waste of hard-earned money, sitting in the dark watching a pack of idiots acting lies! He was willing—more than willing, he liked very much—to take Ydette for an evening stroll along the ramparts and end up at a café in the Markt eating an ice-cream, but although he had himself taken her to the pictures once, it made him feel so cross to see her sitting there, staring up at the screen with that look on her face as if she were a hundred miles away from him, that he never asked her again. And as for what the young Englishman whose little sister still wrote to her had said about Ydette herself some day becoming a star, it was such nonsense, and it made him so angry even to think about it, that the subject was never again referred to between himself and Ydette.

He supposed, and hoped, that she had forgotten all about it.

Dear Ydette (said the Christmas card showing a chastely-coloured and embossed shield, with a pair of gates and a Celtic cross and some swans all worked into a design about the letters C.G.S. on a dead white ground, which reached Ydette a few days before the fourth Christmas since she had seen Ida Ruddlin). How are you? I'm in my first term at Claregates, my sister Nora's old school, and having a *wizard* time. What are you doing? I've decided on my career, I'm going to be a P.T. Instructor (teaching people how to do exercises). I expect the horse that used to be with you at Zandeburghe must be dead by now. But I hope not. Can you imagine—this time next year I shall be an Aunt! It makes me feel very ancient. Chris says next summer he really *will* write to you about being a film star. *Do* write to me when you have time.

With love, yours very sincerely,
Ida Ruddlin.

"Dead, indeed!" was Marie's vigorous exclamation on hearing the card read aloud, "why should he be? Thanks to the Saints, he is in excellent health and stronger than ever."

But she sighed as she watched Ydette's tall, slender, black form going up the stairs to her room to put the little card away with the others. 'Death' could only remind them all, now, of old Mevrouw Maes' passing, last summer. It had been peaceful, but they missed her painfully. Her hand had ruled the orderly little house and the widowed dutiful daughter and the wild, secretive, rough one, throughout some fifty years. Now the place continued without swerving upon its peaceful, useful, frugal routine, a household of schooled women, but they all missed the old woman's frequent glints of gaiety and imperiousness as much as they did her controlling touch. Mother gone, Klaas gone (not that *he* was much loss, but he was a part of the old times vanished for ever) and Ydette as silent and—and (Marie had no word for 'dreamy' and had to use *vaag*)—as I don't-know-what. Marie was more than a little disposed to believe that these twice-weekly visits to the pictures were responsible for Ydette's dreaminess and her strange refusal to 'go with' with any of the local boys . . . the pictures, and working all day shut away from God's good open air in Mijnheer van Roeslaere's packing department.

But Ydette loved working there.

However greatly the weather in the outside world might vary under the rays of the sun, or the winds almost blow her and her fellow workers from their bicycles as they rode to work in the morning, the climate in the hothouses out at Sint Niklaas remained the same: warm, still, silent and faintly scented with moist earth and young growing leaves whose shapes, as well as their odours, seemed to have only a distant cousinage with the lively green things blowing about in the hedges.

This unchanging climate through which sweet smells crept and wandered, where white stars that were flowers shone gently in the distance at the end of long corridors, under a roof of glass white as milk which shut out the changing sky—this mild and orderly jungle into which she went every morning had become what the children call *my best place*, in four years, to Ydette.

The long shed where she worked at packing the orchids, with the other girls and women from Damme and Bruges, was of course neither so warm nor so quiet as the hothouses, but it was clean in a rough, rustic way that she liked: the clear windows looked out on the whitewashed glasshouses, the neat gravel rides and small lawns bordered by ordinary cheerful flowers, and the tall chimneys with their plumes of smoke, while the wooden floor and the benches were scattered with the soft brown fibre that went into the crates large and small. It gave out a dry, spicy scent that was a perpetual gentle stimulant to her dreaming fancy. When, as she did perhaps twice a day, she was sent alone or with some companions on an errand that took them into the houses themselves, this not-quite-sweet smell seemed to have prepared her, with its vague prophecy, for the almost unendurably regal scent that walked the places where the orchids were growing.

Drip . . . drip . . . drip . . . the beads of water condensing throughout the hours fell with an intermittent musical ringing from the broad leaves and the milky glass of the roof, like the sensation of placid growth made audible; and sometimes, while she lingered behind for a moment when her errand was finished, and her companions were going back to the packing-shed, she almost expected some tremendous mystery to be revealed: when, turning unexpectedly around some corner, she came with a quiet gasp of indrawn breath on a plant with sombre leaves broad as her own breast and pink, curved flowers hanging motionless in their own swooning scent, she seemed to confront the spirit, the revelation, towards which all the hush and the warmth and the mysterious broken dripping of water were leading. Yet there was nothing there but growth, a complex, yet serene, mysterious activity going on under her eyes.

Then there were the long, hushed walks, lined with green, fernlike fringes that hung gently over the damp, narrow paths and seemed as if they should nod to and fro in a warm wind, but which never did, because no wind was allowed to blow there; and in some of the houses there were the orchids growing in brown, hairy masses of root and leaf and fibre suspended from the wall, as if in their native tropic; these were knotted, contorted entities, unmistakably *people*, who looked at her without having eyes, even as the Three Towers had looked when she was a child, and each time she encountered them on her visits to the orchid-house in which they lived, she seemed to know them more intimately. These—the imperious yet subtle scents, the long vistas of green fern and blunt leaves in varying stages of growth, the coiling beings with a score of brown fuzzy faces who clung to the warm moist walls, the scent of damp earth and, every now and again, the sudden appearance of some flower like a star in shape and a jewel or a rainbow in colour, which presented the culmination of long, warm, silent years of growth —these were now her day-long companions. When she was with them, she was under a spell as strong as that imposed by the white sand and the big house in the recent years of her childhood.

What the neighbours, and the aunts, and the people who lived at the big house saw, now, when Ydette Maes rode away each morning on her bicycle to work, was a tall young woman who last May, on the date that she had been found in the dune, had celebrated her nineteenth birthday. She was usually dressed neatly but not prettily, and local opinion was as united about the stuck-up-ness of her silent manners as it was divided about the pleasingness or otherwise of her looks: those eyes! so big and beautiful—or such an outlandish shape—she was too thin—she had a figure like a film star—she was a queer thing, after all no one knows where she came from, she might be any-one—she was only Ydette and we've known her ever since she could walk.

"Yddy doesn't like a bit of fun; that's the worst of her," would say Sophie (now married to Albert Joos and his *charcuterie*, which was so unfortunately situated as to be a rival to that one belonging to her aunt in which Mrs Sophie had spent most of the war); "she's as dull as a dyke these days." And she would add to Jakoba or Keetje or whoever happened to be her gossip: "fact is, she ought to get married and have a kid, there's nothing like it," and the gossip would look at Sophie and reply, rather dryly, that it seemed to suit her, anyhow.

Nora and Ida were the only members of the Ruddlin family who ever discussed Ydette at any length, during the next four years, and although—as was natural between an elder sister now out in the world earning a living and a younger one absorbed in the small universe of school—they did not often mention the girl who was no more than an interesting foreign acquaintance, her name (always introduced by Ida) did come up from time to time, when Nora was staying the week-end in Sussex and in-cidentally grudging every minute spent away from the flat in South Kensington which she shared with Evelyn Berrow and Hilary Perowne.

Ida's rather rudimentary imagination had been stirred by Christopher's talk of his ambitions and hopes for Ydette; naturally, the difficulties in the way of their being realized did not occur to her. And, above everything else, it was her sense of fairness that had been aroused; she was a natural partisan; a taker of sides and a hater of domestic or social injustice, and his failure, as the years went on, to 'do something about Ydette', gradually led to Ida's being in a state of permanent indignation about 'unfairness', and not slow to accuse her brother of practising it.

"What do you expect me to do—fly her over here and arrange an interview with Jon Burke?" demanded the goaded Christopher on one of these occasions: he was going through an unusually prolonged spell of being in the red while awaiting a substantial rise in his salary, and he was also beginning to be rather disturbed by his young wife's extravagant tastes.

"I don't know who that is——"

"My dear Dogfight! He's only the greatest living producer. Even the Russians have admitted that—or as good as."

"Well, why can't you arrange an interview?"

"Because I can't—I'm very small change indeed compared to Jon Burke. And although he *does* like Ydette's type—the Fairy Princess type—and although he does always like to pick them out of little back streets or hill villages in Greek islands, or from decaying suburbs in Irish towns—you have to be careful with Burke. He's tricky."

"Why is he tricky?" Ida was leaning forward with stout elbows planted on the knees of her tweed skirt and unmovably staring at him.

"Well, he won't stand for the least hint of a gimmick about one of his 'waxlets', as he calls them——"

"What an extraordinary name. What on earth does it mean?"

"It's like 'starlet'—he calls them 'waxlets' because the type he likes best are as soft as wax and he can mould their potentialities into what *he* can see they can become. He likes them innocent and dim—and Ydette is all of that—but teachable too. (I say, do you understand all this?)"

"Yes, of course. Well, why can't you make him see her?"

"Because I *can't*, I tell you. To start with, he's in America directing a very important film involving millions of pounds, and besides, I'm far too busy just now myself. If only he were over here I might manage a shot at it, but as it is, it's quite out of the question."

"If he could have an interview with her, would he want to make her into a 'waxlet'?"

"How do I know? He can be very tricky indeed. And the one thing that puts him clean off a girl is any suspicion of a gimmick. I should have to get Ydette under his nose very, very carefully—it would really be best if he were to meet her at a party or at a friend's house—if he thought I was trying to make her interesting or dramatic or unusual he'd be off like a scared rabbit. He loathes tricks, especially publicity ones."

"Well, I think you ought to *try*. It isn't fair—making me mention you every time I sent her a Christmas card and then not doing anything about it. Nolly and I *both* think it isn't fair."

"You and Nolly!" Christopher waved her away with the newspaper.

This reverse had no effect upon Ida beyond increasing her conviction that unfairness was, as usual, being perpetrated. She continued—having now developed a strong and obstinate desire to stand as Ydette's champion in an unjust world—to goad Christopher whenever she saw him, and at last she succeeded in arousing Nora—who disliked being involved in any affairs beyond her own, but who shared, in a more sober way, her sister's passion for fair dealing—to taking action.

"Good heavens, what are you doing here? Why aren't you at school?" demanded Christopher, opening the door of his flat in Bloomsbury one Saturday morning in the summer of the year that Ydette was assumed to be nineteen, and quite failing to keep a note of dismay from his voice as he saw both his sisters, dressed in chaste light summer suits, confronting him on the doorstep.

"I've come up to see the dentist; it's Half-Term and I'm staying with Nolly," said Ida instantly, in whom four years had not lessened the capacity for righteous indignation. "*I know, you thought I'd got some disease, and you and Susan would have to have me. Well, I just haven't. What are you doing? Do-it-yourself?*" for Christopher's very old pullover and trousers were splashed with whitewash and in one hand he had a roller-brush.

"Yes. Susan's down with her mother for a few days, so I'm doing our bedroom. Come in. Everything's in a hell of a mess and I can't give you any lunch. I'm going out, almost at once."

"We don't want any; Nolly's going to take me to a nice place she knows in Fitzroy Street."

"Good God," said Christopher absently. "Well, come on in, and don't fall over that bucket."

The large, square, light rooms of the mansion-flat in a block behind the British Museum looked desolate and rather bare in the light of the July morning. Susan's taste, like Christopher's, inclined to the 'contemp.', and contemp. does not look at its best unless completely uncluttered.

"I've brought these." Nora held out a large bunch of damp and thorny roses, wrapped in tissue. "I thought Sue would be here."

"Oh—thanks—no, she's been rather fat and sorry for herself, so we thought a change was the thing for her. I'll put them in something." He looked irritably about him.

Nora, who had not seen him for several months, thought that he was getting 'rather fat' himself, the charming sturdiness of his early twenties was being replaced by a John-Bullish thickness, with more than a hint of heaviness to come. The back of his neck was already a rich, dark red.

His job as personal assistant to one of the more important directors at Commonwealth Associated Films made long, rich lunches and a great deal of drinking simply a part of his daily routine. He was as lucky as hell, he knew, to have the job, just as he was lucky to have the flat, and Susan, and her eight hundred pounds a year that had just made possible their early marriage, and which also made all the difference between feeling that the rat-race was at any moment going to be too much for him, and being able to sit back occasionally and draw his breath without a sensation of guilt. But he still kept, in some part of him that had remained unchanged, the desire to help create a film that was both true and beautiful. Only, the last four years had passed so quickly and had been so full . . . and he sometimes wondered whether the anonymous carvers and masons who had helped to build, say, Chartres or Louvain, had had to endure the snake-house miasma which existed at Biggin Hill Studios; was it the price that must always be paid for being associated with the co-operative making of a work of art, or had the building of the cathedrals taken place in a less competitive atmosphere?

"We've come to talk to you about something," said Nora, sitting down.

"O God," was Christopher's response to this. "Nothing I've got to *do*, please. I've quite enough on my plate already—new picture, and a baby coming, and everything costing as much as hell. What about?"

"Ydette," said Ida importantly. "We think it *isn't fair*, the way you've made me send her a card every Christmas telling her not to forget about being a film star, and then *you* don't do anything. It isn't *fair*."

"She's probably forgotten every word about it," irritably. "I haven't, but this last year has been so damned busy——"

"Oh no, she hasn't," Nora said, in the light, cool voice that matched her clothes. "I'm certain the reason she goes to the pictures two or three times a week now is because of what you said to her."

"*Does* she go to the pictures two or three times a week?" staring. "How do you know?"

"Adriaan."

"*Adriaan? He* hasn't been writing to you, for heaven's sake?"

"Not to me," said Nora. "To Dogfight."

"Writing to *Dogfight*? Adriaan?"

"Well, you wouldn't do anything about Ydette so I had to do something myself. I got his address out of Mummy's book and typed a letter asking him for the latest information about Ydette Maes," Ida said.

"I hope he ticked you off good and proper," said Christopher, staring.

"Oh no, he didn't. He was quite decent. He told me he's living in Brussels now and doesn't often go home, but he does see Ydette occasionally, and he said he was sure it was your going on (he wrote 'going on', his English really is very good, you know) about her being a film star that made her go three times a week to the pictures."

"That's good hearing, anyway," rumpling his hair with a painty hand; "shows she's interested."

"Yes. She works for his father now, packing the orchids for export, out at that place Sint Niklaas. And she isn't engaged or anything."

"You and Adriaan ought to set up a private enquiry agency." But he was not really annoyed; in face, he was rather impressed by her enterprise. "What else did he say?"

"Nothing much, except that he supposed your ideal of beauty must be the giraffe, since you admire Ydette so much. Oh, and he said she still goes around quite a bit with someone—a young man, a farmer—called Jooris Gheldeere," she said, pronouncing the name carefully, but as it was spelt.

"He seems to have kept a pretty good eye on her, even though he doesn't often go home."

"He always did," Nora reminded him; "don't you remember how they used to gaze at each other? I thought it was a case."

"And don't you now?"

"I imagine if it had been, something would have occurred by now—since Adriaan is involved." Her tone was dry and had an inflection of distaste. Christopher looked with a little brotherly malice at the long, thin figure sitting on the sofa surrounded by the unmanageable sheets of the morning's newspapers. The tan dressmaker-suit was fashionable in cut and made of the last drip-dry, uncrushable material; the lipstick was the new bright coral pink and put on with no amateurish hand; her hair was cut by someone expensive and good—but already, poor old Nolly, she looked like a spinster.

"Well, what are you going to do about it?" Ida had been

R

standing with her legs in their neat, drab socks planted well apart while she critically studied a drawing by Gwen John above the mantelpiece; now she turned round and questioningly fixed her severe, light hazel eyes on her brother.

"I suppose I *could* get her an introduction to Burke," he muttered, again ruffling his hair; "he's over here, at the moment, doing a picture for us, in fact. Nothing would be simpler, really; I do know him slightly. This is the moment—if ever. Some years ago he was working nearly all the time in America, and I wouldn't have had a hope of getting him to see her (although she *is* just the type he likes best). I'd have had to work like stink pushing her around introducing her to a lot of people who might be no use to her anyway. Yes, now's the moment, if I'm ever going to do anything. But it's so inconvenient personally. I've got such a hell of a lot on my plate, with Sue in the last stages and everything—I can't possibly ask Ydette to come here now."

"Why can't you?" demanded Ida.

"Because people would think it very peculiar and rude if Sue wasn't here to be Ydette's hostess, and Ydette would be nervous and shy if she were here all alone with me," he said firmly, avoiding Nora's eye, which had grown wary. "No, here is definitely out."

"Couldn't the parents have her?" suggested Nora, almost praying that another and even more obvious solution might not occur to him.

"I shouldn't think so for a minute; you know what Father is about putting people up——"

"I do indeed."

"—and she's bound not to be an easy guest. Besides, he seems to have *gone off* anything to do with Belgium, in a decided sort of way, these last years. I suppose it's the reaction, after Grandpapa having soaked him in it ever since he was a child."

"Can I go and ask Mrs Deane to make us some coffee?" asked Ida.

"Not now; she's fussed with my Do-it-Yourselfing, and I

don't want to upset her. And you're always swigging coffee. Be warned by the Three Wise Virgins—they all drink too much coffee."

"They drink beer, too, though," Ida instantly retorted. "Hilary *knows* lots about beer, and she says it's good for your complexion; brewers' men always have lovely rosy faces, she says."

"Hilary's rustication has had a most unfortunate effect on her," Christopher muttered. Then he ran his fingers once more through his hair, that was beginning to lose its fairness and natural lines of growth owing to firm treatment with brilliantine and brush, and stared fretfully out of the window.

Nora almost held her breath. She disapproved strongly of bribery, but she had been compelled to resort to it to restrain Ida from suggesting, as she had wanted to do, that Ydette should stay with Nora and her friends at Imperial Court. Now, she tried very hard to prevent the idea from floating around in her own head.

But it was too late.

"Of course!" he suddenly cried, and it is not too much to say that Nora blenched as she heard, "You've got a spare room. She can go to you."

"I *would* have her," she began slowly, marshalling her defences, "but it doesn't quite rest with me. Evelyn and Hil have both been working so hard this year (so have I, for that matter) and we all *need* the last two weeks of the vac. to settle into our routine again. It's really most important for Hil. You know the state she gets into about exams."

"Yes. She's a shining example of my theories about women being over-educated——"

"Need we go into that now? I know your views on the subject. If you have a daughter, you may feel differently."

"I shall welcome the chance to educate a girl *appropriately*, for once, and so will Sue . . . but let's get this settled. You and Dogfight have decided something has got to be done about Ydette. Right. I can't have her here; so you must have her or else nothing will be done this year. Now: yes or no?"

"Oh Christopher, you know how I detest being bounced into things. . . ."

All the same, by the time they were sitting over lunch in a much better restaurant than the one Nora herself had had in view, she knew (although they were still arguing and she was protesting) that not only would she persuade Evelyn and Hilary into sacrificing four days of their much-desired peace to a Belgian peasant whom Chris wanted to make into a film star (and Hil! who so despised films!), but that Ydette would almost certainly three weeks from now be occupying the spare room, sleeping under the quilt with the Jacobean design worked by Mummy Perowne, and keeping her unguessable-at personal possessions in the little bow-fronted lowboy that the three girls affectionately called Tubby.

And so it came about. But it did not occur to either Christopher or his sister to draw a contrast between the world into which Christopher hoped to launch Ydette, and the one in which she had grown up.

"Ydette! Hi!"

She was just mounting her bicycle. She turned, and looked dreamily in the direction whence came the sound of her name, while the other workers leaving the packing-sheds glanced with casual interest at Jooris, who was leaning out of the van; Friday was the day that he always met her and drove her home; what was he doing here on Wednesday? And—"It's not Friday" was her first remark, as she came smiling towards him, wheeling her machine.

"I know that, silly. But I was passing near here anyway and I thought you'd like a lift."

"Thank you." It was pretty, the way Ydette always thanked everyone for doing things; it annoyed him that his mother and the neighbours were inclined to laugh at her for it. He opened the doors at the back of the van and lifted in the bicycle, while she was settling herself in front, in the seat next to the driver, drawing her skirts aside rather fastidiously from some old pieces of sacking that had somehow collected on the floor.

While he was arranging the bicycle he was not thinking about what he was doing. This was a most unusual state of mind for Jooris, but it was in keeping with the extraordinary feeling that had come over him twenty minutes ago while he was driving back to the farm with a roll of wire-netting which he had been to fetch from a neighbouring village.

He had been thinking that when he saw Ydette on Friday he must tell her they wanted her to spend a week of her holiday, which started next week-end but one, with them at the farm, as she had last year. And then, exactly as if he had suddenly become violently thirsty or hungry, he had wanted to see her: then: at once: without waiting for an instant.

The craving had been so strong that he did not even think it strange; he could think of nothing else, and feel only that. Without hesitation he had swung the van round in the direction that would take him to Mijnheer van Roeslaere's hothouses, then he had looked at his watch; yes, she would be coming out in about fifteen minutes' time; he would just catch her.

And now, as he shut the doors and shook them to make certain that they were fast, he was acting only from habit. He could see nothing, think of nothing, but Ydette: coming towards him just now across the wide pale road bordered by old willow trees covered in yellow leaves, under the vast quiet sky where violet-grey clouds whispered of rain: a shape as slender as a nymph, with hair looking black, so black, in the clear, fading light.

But it was only Ydette! He gave the doors a last masterful shake and marched round to the front of the van.

"Looking forward to your holiday?" he demanded, having cleared his throat, when they had been rushing along for some minutes.

Ydette reflected. Was she? Why must he drive so fast? she wanted to go slowly, and notice the country going by, and if it had not been for this smell of petrol, she could have breathed in all the cold, rich scents of autumn. That was why it would really have been better to have gone home as usual; it was good to see Jooris, but she always enjoyed the ride home; unless, of course, it was raining hard, or snowing.

"Are you?" he repeated, and swung quickly round a rather sharp corner.

"I don't know," she said at last.

She had what seemed to her good private reasons for this answer, but she had to remind herself that he did not know them.

"*Don't know!*" he repeated (what was the matter with him this evening? His face looked different).

"I don't mind being at the packing-sheds," she said, after another pause, and her mind—as it always did in these days when anyone showed the slightest sign of being difficult, or cross—slid off into thoughts about the pictures; she was going to see a film after supper.

"Yes, but you want your holiday, don't you?" This evening, for some reason, he was violently anxious that she should be like all the other girls whom he knew in Brugge and the villages roundabout. "Everybody likes holidays. Didn't you like it at the farm with us last year?"

What a question! What *could* be the matter?

"Of course I liked it, Jooris." She turned round the full gaze of her eyes—and instantly extraordinary sensations were running all over and up and down and through him; as if he were aching with cold while still warm with the full blaze of the sun; and it was all even odder and more disturbing than that.

He said nothing more for a while, and Ydette was relieved. She did not like this talk of holidays. In her bag she carried the exciting, disturbing letter from England which had kept herself and the aunts sitting so long over supper last night, and so long at breakfast this morning that she had nearly been late for work in consequence. And she had almost made up her mind to go to England. Now, she did not want to tell Jooris about it all; why, she could not think, for, as much as she liked talking to anyone, she liked talking to him, and she had always been able to say more to him than to anyone else in the world. But she just felt that she did not want to tell him.

"Like to come again this year?" he said suddenly.

"Where? To the farm, do you mean?"

"Where else could I mean?"

"Oh yes. You know I should. It was so good last year, with the little pigs, and picking the pears. . . . Thank you, Jooris." But now her heart was sinking. He was driving faster than ever, with such a red face. . . .

"All right, then. When'll you come? Mother said the second week of your holiday would be better, because she'll be bottling the plums and pears all the first one."

Ydette wondered if she should say something about being willing to help with these tasks, and then realized that while they were in progress she would be in England. She said, thankfully, "Oh yes, that will be very good. Shall I come on the twenty-fourth, then? Thank you, Jooris, and please tell your mother thank-you for me, and your grandad."

She began to feel easier. Perhaps she would not have to tell him, after all, about going to England. He was sure to find out that she had gone, of course, but she did not mind that; what she minded was having to tell him herself, face to face.

And then, with his next words, it looked as if she would have to tell him, after all; for he said, in a tone more like his usual one, "What are you going to do with yourself the first week? Do that old embroidery of yours all day and sit in the pictures all night?" He was going to suggest that they should spend a day in Oostende together.

Now was the moment. Ydette tried to answer in the same tone, "Yes, I expect so," and laugh, but she could not. She sat there as if dumb, and in a moment he turned and looked in surprise at a face that had turned the deep pink of an apple-blossom bud.

"What's the matter?"

But there was no answer; she only looked at him imploringly.

"What is it, Ydette. What's the matter? Why are you looking like that?"

The mutter that followed gave him to understand that she was not looking like that.

"Yes, you are. . . . It must be something . . . I only asked you what you were going to do the first week of your holiday, and you——" He began to stare at her suspiciously. "What *are* you going to do?" The idea of another young man, a rival, struck him suddenly, with furious pain. A *rival*? But it was only Ydette!

"Come on, now. You're going to tell me." He braked, and drew the van in carefully to the side of the road. He would have the truth out of her if they stayed here all night.

It was so quiet, now, that Ydette heard the soft twittering of birds in the willows, settling themselves for the night, and she noticed, through her distress, a branch drooping above the gliding water of a dyke, and felt that she could almost see the dew gathering on its long, lemon leaves. The solemnity and deep hush of the Flemish countryside at twilight brooded over fields and sky.

She was not angry with Jooris, nor was she experiencing even a reflection of the strange, strong feelings that were shaking him. She only did not want to tell him that she was going to England.

"Come on, tell me," said he, and suddenly put his arm about her waist, and held her. It was an exceedingly strong arm, with muscles hardened by years of work in the open air from early morning until dusk, and she did not like the feel of it there at all. Certain thoughts about certain places, a number of exquisite pictures and powerful reveries that she had carried deep within her and yet, at the same time, outwardly surrounding her, ever since she could remember, seemed to shrink in fear as she felt that iron clasp. *Save us*, she could hear them whispering; *we are in danger*.

She drew away from him, straining back against the side of the van.

"I'm going to England," she said quickly, "at least, I think I am . . . the sister of that young man, Mijnheer Ruddlin, you remember, four years ago, he made a film of us on the Mill. . . . Well, she's asked me to go and stay with her in London. And I think I shall . . ." Her voice wandered off weakly, because he looked so strange, and it was strange, too, to feel a young man's arm around her waist and know that it was the arm of Jooris. And he was so warm! he seemed to be keeping the chill of the evening away from them both by his mere breath.

"What do you want to go there for?" he asked at last, and slowly pulled his arm away.

"They *asked* me," Ydette piped, with indignation beginning to arise. In all her moments of fearing to tell him that she was going, she had never supposed that he would *mind*. "They *asked* me," she repeated. But it was very clear that he did mind.

"There's nothing for you over there, not a thing."

"He says he'll show me Buckingham Palace, where their Queen lives, and——"

"He?" It was a pounce, and it made her start.

"Mijnheer Ruddlin——"

"So he's the one who's asked you to go."

"His *sister* wrote to me," said Ydette patiently. "I'm going to stay with her, in her *appartement* (a 'flat', they call it), and——"

"Do you want to go?" he asked quickly, and—without his saying a word—the arm came back; not quickly, this time, but in a slower and somehow a much more alarming way (*Oh save us, we are in danger*), and this time Ydette began to feel rather confused, because she did not seem to mind it being there any more. She took her time about answering his question, because really there was such a lot to think about. But all that she could *feel* was the arm: hard, warm and somehow—for all her confusion—comforting.

"Yes, I think I do want to go," she said at last. "I should like to see Mejuffrouw Nora again and perhaps the little Ida. And the Queen."

"And the Queen! Does he know her, then?" But his tone was not so mocking as the words, and when he had spoken them, silence fell. He continued to look at her, and when, glancing away from the gliding water at which she had been staring, she turned to him and met his eyes, she did something that afterwards seemed to her the strangest event of that extraordinary drive: she quickly shut her own. At once, thoughts about kissing rushed into her mind, and she could think of nothing else, and in an effort to drive them away, she screwed up her face as if she were about to take some medicine.

The next thing that happened was that the arm was withdrawn and she heard the engine start up.

She opened her eyes. She had never seen Jooris looking so cross.

"There was some rubbish about your being a film-star too, wasn't there?" he said presently. "That afternoon we all had tea in that place, I mean. Does his sister say anything about it in her letter?"

"She says he—Mijnheer Ruddlin—may be able to get me a job with Mijnheer Burke."

"And who's he?"

"Oh, a very big man in the pictures," vaguely, "he chooses the people to be in them or something, I don't know. But he's very important."

"Well," said Jooris with energy, "now I'll tell you what *I* think will happen about all this. You'll go to England and stay with these people because you want to. Right. You won't enjoy it. . . ."

"Why? Why shouldn't I enjoy it?" she cried, roused to indignation at last by his crossness and the way he had been going on with his arm. "I *want* to go to England, I *want* to see the Family Ruddlin again." And indeed, stimulated in some way by his disapproval, she now longed to make the visit: he had made up her mind for her.

"Why? Because you aren't the sort that enjoys being away from home and all the people you know, that's why. And then this Mijnheer Burke won't give you a job, and you'll come all the way home again, and a whole week of your holiday will be wasted. That's all."

She was longing to ask him if he still wanted her to come to the farm, but she did not dare. So these two old friends drove on in silence.

The country was left behind now and they were going

quickly through the outlying suburbs of Bruges. The Three Towers stood up dark and thoughtful against the deepening grey of the sky, and beneath Saint Saviour's Cathedral the old houses with their tiled roofs, peaked windows and stepped gables were shining with homely lights. Ydette tried to think about the film that she was going to see after supper.

The van swooped across the *plaats* and, whirling round in front of the greengrocery, screeched to a stop.

"Great God, Jooris, what a way to drive!" exclaimed Marie. "What's the matter? Is Grandad dead?"

"Wasn't at six o'clock. Can't say what's happened since then, of course," came snappishly from round at the back of the van. He lifted out Ydette's bicycle and set it, with considerable emphasis, down on the cobbles.

"And you've brought Yddy home. . . . That's right . . . now she'll be in good time for the *bioscoop* . . . Yddy . . ."

But Ydette had gone quickly into the house.

SITTING motionless in the corner-seat which a young man had found for her on the boat-train, she was still under the spell of her first sight of England.

The *Koenig Leopold* had moved onwards through low, rippling waves seemingly too indolent to lift themselves up from the great, mild, gleaming plain of the sea, and the balm, the freshness, which began to descend upon the passengers had seemed in some way the beginning of England, revealing herself, quietly and strangely unsubstantially, yet how majestically! in these her first watery outposts and bastions. The sun had gone down into a great mist of heat, and through the calmness beginning to descend on empty ocean and cloudless firmament the ship had glided on to the accompaniment of her own water-music.

Ydette had stood throughout the voyage by the rail, looking out over the fading, coloured mists in the west and now and then down into the clear dark sea traced under with luminous white foam; near at hand, the water talked strongly and ripplingly to itself; far away, it was radiant and silent.

And presently she had begun to see something looming up out of the transparent mists that were the faint colours of a ripening peach.

It—they—there was more than one of them—were high, pale objects which at first also appeared transparent, or in some way unsubstantial, but as the ship drew nearer she was able to see that they were cliffs; towering masses of white rock rising from a beach which, to eyes accustomed to the Flanders coast, appeared small as a toy. It was scattered over with big white boulders, and the waves breaking on it were mere ripples. Along the summit of the cliffs ran a thin line of a mysteriously deep and dark green. She could see one or two tiny figures walking briskly along up there, in the quiet, fading blue sky, and even make out a bounding little dog. The ship had shut off its engines, and was now sweeping onwards into this scene—which looked still, and far-away, and strange, as if it were a picture— in almost complete silence; they were approaching the hoary walls, overgrown with dripping masses of seaweed, of a small harbour within which the peaceful water stretched itself in an unrippled expanse of peach-pink.

The men waiting on the quay for the ship were not shouting or rushing about, the air was as hushed as if it were falling asleep, and Ydette felt as if England, the unknown country of the insubstantial cliffs and those small white and grey houses climbing undramatically up the dark green hollows and cling- ing to the roads and fields that led up, up, up to the mass of great grey stones on the summit—England herself was com- manding Ydette, and the ship, and the men on the *quai*, in an old, strong, calm voice to be quiet, to be at peace, and to behave.

When she was not dreamily regarding these sights and sounds, she was going over in her mind the final scenes at home: her parting with the aunts and such of the neighbours as had been told of her impending visit to the English tourists who had kept in touch with her for four whole years.

She had received from the aunts, more particularly Aunt Marie, warnings about not losing her passport, her clothes or her money: that there had not been warnings about avoiding graver dangers was perhaps due to the fact that Ydette had never been one for going with boys.

As for Nora Ruddlin's remarks about her getting a job with this *bioscoop* man, aunts and niece alike did not take it very seriously. Ydette had felt throughout all Christopher's deft hints about her possible future career on the films—that the idea was ridiculous, and impossible, and just one of a young Englishman's mad whims. The particular pleasure offered to her temperament by the cinema, the dreamlike quality, the shadowiness, the exaggeration of the people and places which it presented, had been far more the cause of her frequent visits there than any wish to follow up the hints and promises thrown

out by Christopher. Something in Ydette's nature 'took to' the
dream-world of the cinema 'like a duck to water', but if Christopher had been able to return each year to Bruges and learn a
little more about her, he would very soon have realized that her
relation to the world of stardom was—at present, at least—the
entirely passive one of admiring spectator. But year after year
there had always been good reasons for his not going.

Now, as she sat watching the dim fields, bordered by black,
encircling woods, sinking away into twilight, she began to see
the faces and hear the voices which she had left behind in
Brugge more clearly than she saw her fellow passengers, and to
think more about the Sint Katelijnstraat (they would just be
having supper, and the lights would be shining in the big house)
than of England going past in the dusk. The large fields in
which grew nothing but grass seemed to her a waste of good
land—for there were but few animals grazing in them—and
almost every little house had a strange contraption of wires
springing from its roof which must, she supposed, serve some
useful purpose but which was so unfamiliar to her that it added
to that atmosphere of mystery with which England had seemed
to her to be imbued. It was so big, so untidy, so wooded and
quiet. The train stopped once or twice at little stations where
the tall, slender trees, laden with dim, fragile leaves and revealing between their stems the blue-green labyrinths of a wood,
came crowding right down to the railway line and looked
silently in at the windows, causing her to turn uneasily away.

And always at the back of her mind was the memory of
Jooris' face as she turned away from him that evening; sullen,
heavy, and yes, cross. In all the seventeen years that she had
known him, he had never been cross with her—and how Ydette
did mind people being cross! And now she was miles and miles
away from him, and sitting in this rather dirty English railway
carriage that was carrying her still farther away with every turn
of its wheels; drawing ever nearer to the station named Victoria, where Nora would meet her, and she was growing more
and more unhappy every minute.

I was a fool to come, she thought, with the severe common

sense which persistently tempered her dreaminess, and which was pure Flemish.

What a huge, echoing place was 'Victoria', crowded with thousands of people hurrying in every direction, while far-off, hollow voices boomed indistinguishable sentences in a tongue that certainly was not English, high overhead in the vast, curving roof. Ydette took down her suitcase and her carpet-bag from the rack, and, firmly clasping her large, sensible umbrella, stationed herself, with murmurs of apology to her fellow travellers, at the window. Now she could see the long, grey platforms, stretching away into the distance and losing themselves under the clear, colourless lights in the roof. She had never before felt so lonely.

She looked carefully over the heads of the hurrying crowd before she descended from the train, and to her intense relief saw Nora Ruddlin standing at the far end of the platform. She had never felt at ease with Christopher's sister, but at least, amongst these thousands of strangers, here was a face that she knew; and in a moment her long, limp hand in its black glove was being wagged up and down with a rather determined heartiness.

" 'So this is London'," said the young lady who stood beside Nora; her voice sounded as if she were smilingly telling a child a secret, and Ydette, looking down on this small, slender person from her greater height, was bewildered by the contrast between her dress, which was that of a peasant from the Austrian mountains, and the intellectual expression in her eyes. "I expect it all seems very strange to you, doesn't it?" Evelyn Berrow continued, "but you will have lots of exciting things to tell them when you get home, won't you?"

Ydette, feeling more ill at ease and unhappy every moment, managed to nod, and then Nora exerted herself to find a taxi and got them all into it; in a short time they were driving through the hot, quiet streets of Kensington, which Ydette, too shy to look at her companions, stared at in silence.

The other two had been murmuring together. Now Evelyn's soft voice addressed Ydette.

"I was thinking . . . perhaps we ought to warn you just a wee bit about Hilary—Miss Perowne (she's the friend Nora and I share the flat with). She may seem—well, sometimes people who don't know her find her the least little bit *difficult*. She's a darling, really. Only she gets so tired, especially just now when she's working for an examination, and when she's tired she's inclined to be a little *alarming*—oh, and one thing we really *ought* to tell her about, oughtn't we?" turning to Nora, "is not making a noise. Your room is next to hers and she's a *terribly* light sleeper, and lack of sleep upsets her more than *anything*. So if you *can* just remember not to hurl your boots about," Evelyn laughed, "it would be all to the good."

"She is ill?" Ydette asked after a staring pause.

"Oh for heaven's sake don't say that! It's the one thing no-one's allowed to say, or there really *will* be an 'atmosphere'. No. You just remember to be *very* quiet in your room and everything will be all right."

She smiled, with her head poking forward and a soft wisp falling down from her fashionably cut hair.

Nora had been listening to Evelyn's remarks with rather less than her customary approval. She loved Evelyn with all her heart: it was impossible to imagine even a husband being closer to her in spirit than was Evelyn, and one of the qualities which she most doted on in her friend was that simplicity which she privately compared to crystal, and fluids like spring-water and new milk. But somehow, when she saw Evelyn with Ydette, she had an uneasy and disloyal feeling that Evelyn's simplicity rang false—or appeared to. This did not make her any fonder of the Foreign Visitor in the dowdy black coat. She sighed, and explained to Ydette that Christopher was exceedingly busy, but was coming to the flat soon after breakfast on the following day, and would take her out to see London.

Ydette heard in melancholy silence. These endless, wide, grey streets where the coloured lamps were just beginning to burn under the fading sky made her feel very sad, and when they stopped at the large red-brick block of flats and climbed the echoing stairs to Number 30, she was well in the grip of homesickness. And although she had never been one of those girls who consciously prefer the company of the other sex, she was beginning to feel oppressed by the continuous company of strange *mejuffrouws*. The one who opened the door to them was more frightening than either of the others; Nora seemed an old friend, compared with this small white face and large green eyes like a cat's that looked crossly at Ydette through horn-rimmed glasses. Oh yes, she was cross, very cross, and Ydette knew it; there was no hiding it from her when someone was cross, and although the latest one shook hands, and said in French "How nice to see you, Ydette. Welcome to England," her thin, white fingers felt so bony and cool, and her voice was so light and sharp, that Ydette did not feel welcomed in the least.

The flat, too, was alarming; the rooms were almost as large as those at the big house and everything seemed either very dark and shining or very pale and looking as if it would break if you touched it. Ydette sat on the edge of a chair, clutching a cup of coffee that did not smell or taste like the coffee at home, crumbling an alien biscuit and not cheered by the incomprehensible remarks called to one another by the *mejuffrouws* as they moved quickly about their domestic affairs between the rooms:

"Chris has been very *masterful* about all this, hasn't he?" "Oh, we're congratulating ourself; we think our fortune's made." "Not our fame?" "Oh, I *do* do us the justice to think it's our fame, rather than our fortune, that we're after." "What do you think of the 'find'?" "The intelligence is in inverse ratio to the size of the optics, I should imagine." "Good heavens— that takes me back to the Upper Fourth—I haven't called them that since we were all in it." "*I* think all this is in rather bad taste."

The last remark was made coldly by the cross young lady in the glasses, who up till now had not said a word, and when she had said it a silence fell. Then they began to talk about bedrooms and breakfast and baths, in a way that Ydette could understand.

s

She declined their offer of a bath for herself. She made a habit of using creams and lotions; she took concern over many matters which troubled her workmates not at all; but a great splashy bath all over oneself on a Thursday night, even when one did not have to go out to the public baths for it—no. So they all crisply bade her good night, and in a few moments more she was alone at her bedroom window, looking rather fearfully out at a distant cluster of towers rising in unfamiliar silhouettes against the greenish, moonlit sky, and struggling with a strong impulse to cry.

"Where are you taking her?" Nora asked Christopher, after breakfast on the following morning, when Ydette, having timidly greeted him, had gone to get her scarf and coat—"to the studio for lunch?"

"No, I'll do that on Monday, if everything goes well. How's she liking it?"

"I don't really know. She hardly utters. She seems a bit under the weather, but of course, she may be shy of Hil and Evelyn. What do you think of her?"

She spoke without apprehensions about his probable answer; her former fears of his becoming entangled with Ydette had vanished—simple Nora!—on his marriage.

"Oh, she's perfectly ravishing . . . to look at. I can't keep my camera-eye off her. I never saw such angles; I can't wait for her to have a test. But I don't feel nearly so easy about the other necessary qualities—teachability and temperament and so on—and there's one vital thing I'm almost sure she's short of, and that's sex appeal."

"I suppose that's very important?" his sister said.

"It is and it isn't—I mean, it needn't take the obvious form (that sounds like a corny pun); it *can* be something else than hip-waggling and cleavage, but it's got to be there in *some* way. And I rather doubt if she has it at all."

"These are deep waters," said Nora, with a caustic wag of her head, and then Ydette reappeared, her scarf carefully tied under her chin, somewhat lifted out of a pensive mood induced by the exchange of largely incomprehensible remarks at breakfast, by seeing Mijnheer Chris again, and hearing his warm and friendly welcome.

That day he took her in his fashionably shabby little car to the places that he was certain she would want to be able to tell the aunts that she had seen: Westminster Abbey, Piccadilly, St Paul's and finally Buckingham Palace, where they were so fortunate as to catch a glimpse of the Royal children driving through the gates. She appeared to enjoy it all, and ate, with less caution than he had expected her to show, an ample luncheon at a Chinese restaurant. But not once during the day did she become animated, or show a glimpse of the positive, endearing quality which he remembered as giving attraction to her personality when she was a child, and which he had always thought of as typically Flemish. She was pensive, she drooped; more than once she sighed unromantically through her nose; she went off into brown studies; and when he sounded her about getting a job of some sort in a studio, she merely shook her head and answered that they expected her back at work on the nineteenth. Did she like it there? Oh yes . . . and then she was quiet for fifteen minutes.

You might almost call her moody . . . and Christopher had small patience with moody girls; Susan had won him finally because she could offer the imperious gaiety and hard good sense which all her rivals had lacked. Perhaps 'pensive' was a better word (for Ydette was not exactly moody). But if she were going to be pensive as well as lacking in sex appeal, her chances of ever becoming a star were remote indeed, for pensiveness was in the doghouse, together with chastity, piety and reticence. He began, as the day went on, to feel that his little scheme was really rather ridiculous; flimsy, even impertinent. But not yet had he felt the dismal conviction that it would never come to anything at all.

He brought her back early to the flat after a nice little dinner during which he had cautiously told her something of Jon Burke, the man who had made that picture about Greece which she had liked so much, *The Violet Crown*. He ventured to tell her that she was the type that this famous Mr Burke most

admired, adding that he might even be at the studios when she
was taken to lunch there on Monday!

Ydette, spooning up ice-cream with a most melancholy expression, answered only, "Thank you, Mr Christopher."

It had not been a satisfactory day, and he was nearly a hundred and four pounds overdrawn at the bank.

"ARE you all right?" Nora stood there in her dressing-gown, when Ydette opened her door in response to a tap, half an hour or so after the flat had retired for the night; "I thought perhaps you might be . . ."

She could not quite get her tongue round 'homesick'.

"Thank you; I am very well." And indeed, at the sight of that face, now greasy with night-cream but endearingly familiar, and those clever eyes that had looked upon the aunts, and Madame van Roeslaere, and even Klaas, to say nothing of Klaartje and the Three Towers, Ydette's own face widened into a smile that absolutely fascinated Nora; causing an imagination not usually given to flights of fancy to present her with images of grateful giraffes and complacent honeysuckles.

"Not lonely?" She forced herself to utter the word which must never be used of feelings or people but only of landscapes.

"I wish all were here," confided Ydette, "my aunts, and all who are at home."

"It would be rather a tight fit, wouldn't it?" said Nora, and the essay at Christopher's style of humour when talking to Ydette was rewarded with another delighted smile.

"Well," she said, preparing to withdraw, "I just thought that I would make sure you have everything you want."

"Thank you, Mademoiselle."

"I think you might manage to call me Nora, don't you?"

Ydette smiled, but did not answer. Her eyes rested gently on Nora's, and the latter suddenly felt a strong wish to protect her.

Without knowing much about the world of the film-makers, the little that she did know, through the conversation and habits of Christopher and his friends, made her suspect that his 'find' would not be happy there; that she might even find it impossible, if she went into it, to be good. (By 'good', Nora meant the keeping of personal integrity and the abiding by certain standards of conduct which had been very carefully thought out.) *A word of warning might be dropped*, she thought.

But it was late, and she was tired, and she really did rather shrink from entering into explanations that might keep them whispering there until one o'clock; besides, wouldn't it be distinctly unfair to Chris to prejudice his starlet against a film career even before she had started on one? But she did lean forward and gently kiss Ydette.

"Sleep well," she said, smiling, and noiselessly shut the door.

Mejuffrouw Nora, so clever, to kiss her! This was the first time that anyone not an aunt or her granny had kissed her since she ceased to be a little girl (here her thoughts hastily shied away from the memory of the last time she had thought about kissing): and, comforted, and feeling less lonely, she fell asleep.

Saturday, however, was worse.

Her spirits had fallen steadily during breakfast, for Nora had returned to her usual manner, and ate in silence while looking for the most part absently out of the window, and the two other girls had chattered away in long words and very fast, scarcely interrupting themselves to shove the sugar at Ydette (they seemed surprised that she drank her coffee with sugar) or to push the bread at her with brief smiles. She was not used to long conversations at any time, least of all during the times when one was eating, but she did not like feeling so out of it all. And she would have liked Mejuffrouw Nora (no, she could not drop the mejuffrouw, it was no use) to talk to her.

After breakfast the white mejuffrouw with the big eyes went into her bedroom with a great pile of books and shut the door, and Mejuffrouw Nora and the Austrian-dress one went out together.

Christopher arrived a little later, disliking the hot weather and irritable because Susan had come home unexpectedly, very lively, and demanding to be taken out. He wanted to take her (she was one of those girls who look very beautiful in the last stage of pregnancy, and he was proud of the respectful admiration she attracted when they walked abroad) and he had planned to make Nora entertain Ydette that day. His annoyance, when he found that his sister had gone creeping off into the country with Evelyn, was considerable. He had to telephone Susan and break it to her that Ydette must make a third for lunch.

If Evelyn and Hilary had alarmed Ydette, Susan puzzled and irritated her. She thought Susan's dress—an elegant olive-coloured modification of the sack line—as ugly as it was revealing, and her quick, high-bred voice contemptuous. Susan, after saying a few nice things to her with the flashing smile due to a possible future star discovered by Susan's husband, talked entirely to Christopher, who occasionally asked Ydette if she would like another pineapple-juice, but simply could not resist the fascination of his wife, and hardly took his eyes off her. It happened to be a day when Ydette was looking almost plain, and he knew with resigned annoyance that Susan was wondering what all the enthusiasm had been about.

In the afternoon he drove them up to Hampstead Heath, and they trailed silently about in the thundery heat, looking at London spread out in the valley, and lack-lustredly admiring the rose-garden at Kenwood House. By the time they were having tea in the Old Stables there, he felt as though the day had been going on for six weeks, and the sight of Ydette's expressionless, milky face and black crescents of lowered eyelashes, as she sat winding her long pink tongue unhurriedly round the 'lolly' she had with quiet obstinacy insisted on buying, was almost unbearably irritating.

In fact, she was enjoying one of the few moments of peace which she had experienced that day, largely because she had been able to secure this object, which, while satisfying her longing for an ice-cream, did not remind her too painfully of the kind she was accustomed to eat with Jooris. All her thoughts, now, were either of what they might be doing at home, or occupied with counting the hours until she got back there, and although England was beautiful, she did not like it because it was unfamiliar.

Susan, feeling belatedly that she had been neglectful of her

wifely duties towards Christopher's career, exerted herself in
the car on the way home to charm Ydette. She sparkled; she
asked interesting questions; she made sensible remarks (neither
too frivolous nor too plainly taking it for granted that Ydette's
life might soon be entirely altered) concerning the possibility
of her getting a small part in a film directed by this Mr Burke,
and she told Ydette what a lot she might then be able to do for
her family.

Ydette did not make any reply.

"I think it would be a good idea if you got to bed early tonight, Ydette," Christopher said, very masterfully indeed, as
the car stopped outside Imperial Court. "If I were you I
should just have some—er—some milk or something and then
tumble in."

"Tomble——?" She was standing there, looking about
seven feet high in her long black coat, staring at him.

"Into bed, I mean." He was conscious of Susan's far-from-
stifled giggle. "Here—I'd better come up with you, just in case
all those wretched—in case none of the girls are in."

The door, however, was opened by Hilary, with an even
whiter face than usual. No, they hadn't really disturbed her;
she had only been resting; not asleep; she had been working all
day and had rather a headache; it was this wretched Biology on
Monday that she was rather dreading; it was her weakest subject.

Christopher, who saw no reason why a young woman should
require a Research Fellowship with the Nature Conservancy,
murmured, "Oh, is it?" and the atmosphere was not lightened
by Hilary adding that she was taking Biology to help her with
the theme she was working on for her Ph.D.

Ydette had wandered into the kitchen and was staring fearfully at the electric stove. Feeling rather like a good Pagan
leaving a Christian to the lions, Christopher repeated his
advice about milk or something and went quickly away.

"For God's sake kiss me—I'm starting to loathe women," he
said to Susan as he shut the door of the car.

"Poor love. Let's go and have daiquaris somewhere."

"The O. is up to a hundred and four. I told you. (How lovely you smell. I suppose that cost the earth, too.)"

"(No, it didn't, I pinched some of Mummy's 'Joy'.) Never mind, Ydette's going to make our fortune, and we'll soon be rich."

The evening passed exceedingly quietly at Imperial Court. Hilary worked in her own room, and Ydette, having brewed herself some milk under Hilary's snappish instructions, slowly had a bath and went to bed. Nora and Evelyn, returning sunburnt and peaceful about eleven o'clock, found both their doors shut.

Nora had been asleep for perhaps two hours when she was aroused by a light, imperious tapping, and when, in answer to her sleepy call, her door opened, Hilary was revealed, looking younger than she did during the daytime because her hair was in two plaits, and exceedingly cross.

"Can you come and do something about that Belgian creature? She's crying," she said.

"Oh lord," said Nora, feeling for her dressing-gown.

"Exactly."

"I'm terribly sorry, Hil—has it been keeping you awake?"

"I'd just got to sleep when it started."

"Oh, I *am* sorry." And indeed she felt it, and rather apprehensive too, for a broken night upset Hilary as did nothing else.

"I'm sorry," she repeated, getting out of bed, and feeling miserably guilty.

"Don't you bother, I can manage," she whispered as she turned the handle of Ydette's door.

"No, I'll come too; I can probably manage better than you would," and to Nora's relief, Hilary smiled. Nora smiled too, and opened the door.

At once the sniffling and the sobbing, which had certainly sounded rather unrestrained, stopped. The room was dark, but the subdued glow from the hall showed the bed and a surprising quantity of dark hair, presumably damp with tears, scattered all over it. Hilary and Nora were both conscious of the same distaste, and Nora's voice was brisker than usual as she said:

"Ydette? What's the matter?"

An alarmed heaving, and the long, white shape surrounded by showers of black sat up. There was a gasping interrogative sound.

"Is there anything you want? Are you ill?"

They thought, although they could not be sure, that she was shaking her head.

"Well, if there isn't anything you want and you don't feel ill . . ." began Nora. But she felt rather unkind and was relieved when Hilary interrupted, in the voice she had been accustomed to use on juniors who had a 'rave' on her.

"I expect you're rather homesick, aren't you?—miles away from your family—especially if it's the first time you've stayed away from home. But *do* cheer up, Chris is going to take you over the studios on Monday, and that will be fun, won't it? And tomorrow you can have a nice quiet day."

Silence. The head was apparently bent down into the showers of hair.

"Won't it?" Hilary repeated, winningly.

"Yes, Mademoiselle." They caught the whisper.

"And you *mustn't* cry any more, because I've got a *terribly* difficult examination on Monday, in my very weakest subject. And if you cry, you'll keep me awake," Hilary ended on an appealing note.

"I am sorry, Mademoiselle." Now they thought that she was busy with her handkerchief; she was moving her hands about near her bent head.

"So now you'll go to sleep, won't you? . . . Do you think you'd feel more comfortable if I got you a Disprin?"

A shake of the head. Hil was being marvellous, Nora thought.

"Sure? All right then . . . now you go to sleep, like a good child."

"Yes, Mademoiselle."

They waited a moment, but there was no further movement or sound. She only sat there, with her head bent.

"Good night," said Hilary firmly, and they withdrew.

Outside in the hall she opened both eyes widely upon Nora. "How very surprising. One would think that we were nine rather than nineteen."

"Ydette *is* very childish in some ways," said Nora. Although Hil had been both tactful and kind, she felt irritated with her. "It's one of the things one likes the tiresome little creature for."

" 'Likes'? Don't you mean that one feels superior, and therefore pleased with *her*?"

"No. I mean 'likes'. You must get back to bed, Hil; you'll be dead tomorrow. Thanks most awfully for managing, and I'm terribly sorry about letting you in for all this." She gestured helplessly with both hands. "It's only until Tuesday, thank heaven."

"It does prove, though, doesn't it, that girls *must* be educated?" Hilary said thoughtfully. (She never noticed when you were irritated with her.) "You know, she makes me feel quite *bad*—all that wetness, and softness, and helplessness—it's revolting, in some queer way. Don't you agree?"

"Hil, you're trying to start a discussion," said Nora, not welcoming one at this hour, and unable to feel quite as fond of Hilary as usual, "we really must get back to bed."

She lay awake for a little while, trying to hear whether Ydette was still crying. But there was complete silence throughout the flat. She felt sorry for Ydette; sorrier, actually, than she did for Hil.

But of course, Hil's exams were rather more important than the fantods of a Belgian peasant.

Nora fell asleep.

Sunday was spent more quietly than either of the preceding days, but Ydette did not find in it much refreshment. And by evening—it began to rain about three o'clock, an event pointed out by her three hostesses as being typical of that peculiarly bright kind of late summer day in England—she was feeling more depressed than ever.

After they had all risen late, and dawdled over breakfast in a way that to Ydette seemed rather shocking, Nora took her to Westminster Cathedral and left her to go in alone to hear Mass, promising to call back for her.

This left Ydette with at least a clear conscience, but the familiarity of the service only emphasized the strangeness of her surroundings; she could not keep her eyes on the altar and off the unfamiliar faces on every side, and would even have been glad to see the rusty cape of the old woman who performed certain humble tasks connected with prayer-books and candle-selling at Our Lady's, much as she usually disliked that sour and toil-hardened countenance. Nor could she, she felt, say her prayers properly when they did not go straight up through the roof to circle about the head of the Person in the pointed hat. They seemed to fall back again, as if baffled. And when she came out again, into the strange streets of very tall buildings, full of solemn-faced people idling past the closed shops and cafés, and saw Mejuffrouw Nora standing aloofly awaiting her at the corner, and realized that it was only half-past twelve—her heart sank indeed.

The sinking was shown so plainly on her face that Nora's subconscious misgivings about the situation suddenly took shape, and she resolved to talk to her. Firmly announcing that they would lunch out today, she took a taxi to Soho, where they found a restaurant that was open, and soon Ydette was looking more cheerful as she confronted a large piece of fried veal. (Nora noted the exact price of the latter, determined that Chris should pay both for it and for the taxi.)

"Now," she began, determined to waste no time, "that's better, isn't it? I'm afraid you haven't been enjoying your visit very much, have you, up until now?"

Ydette neither looked startled nor made any attempt at denial. She kept her eyes down, and Nora in a moment was compelled reluctantly to recognize the expression creeping over her face. Sulks, now. That was all that was needed.

"You must find it all rather strange," she doggedly continued. "London is so big, and this is the first time you've been abroad, isn't it? And of course, I and my friends are always so busy—I'm afraid you've been rather lonely."

"No, Mademoiselle," Ydette said, after a pause just long enough to be rude. She still did not look up, and, apparently uninterested, continued to masticate veal.

"What do you really think, Ydette," Nora, feeling surprisingly rebuffed, ignored her own sensations and leant persuasively across the table, "about this plan for working in the cinema? Do *you* believe you can become a star? My brother believes it, you know. He's absolutely convinced that you can, if you want to. Has he ever talked to you about *acting*?" But as she spoke she knew that *acting*, where a 'waxlet' was concerned, didn't come into it. Jon Burke preferred malleable, teachable girls, Christopher had said, without the histrionic temperament.

Ydette shook her head, cutting up a piece of veal.

"Well, I don't suppose you would have to do much of that—anyway, not in the accepted sense." Nora paused, and called home her straying vocabulary. "It would all depend really on whether this Mr Burke thought he could make you into the kind of person he wants. Would you like that?"

Ydette suddenly looked up. Her expression was slightly desperate. Nora—so clever, and older, and rich, with a big flat and a very good job teaching French in a smart private school, the friend of those two frightening mejuffrouws—how to make her understand the miserable loneliness, the silly longing for the streets and towers and light of home? How could she possibly know how frightened Ydette was about Jooris; that she might have made him so angry that he would never ask her to the farm again? (She knew, of course, in her calmer moments, that this idea was ridiculous, because the farm had always been there and so had he, but she could not dismiss, in her lonely fits, the recurring fear.)

She tried to answer.

"I like to work at packing the orchids, Mademoiselle; I like it there very much. Monsieur Chris says that I could be a *vedette*. But——"

"*You* don't think you could be?—is that it?"

"I cannot——"

But here her small supply of words failed. What she wanted

to say was that she could not possibly imagine such a thing happening to *her*—the body and spirit that had grown up for nineteen years with those vague friends who were yet now so painfully absent; the Three Towers, and the white sand of the dunes, the big house, and the orchids out at Sint Niklaas. But the words would not come, and frustration brought back her sulky expression.

"I don't know, Mademoiselle," she ended.

Nora, a believer in the restorative powers of reflection, time, sensible behaviour and all the other resources of civilized people, decided that she could do no more. She felt as if she had been trying to open a stubbornly-shut window that looked out on an unknown landscape; a little bruised, very baffled and curiously hurt, as if the window's obduracy had been directed against herself. The odd thing was that she did not feel cross with Ydette. She still only wanted to protect her. She looked at the strikingly foreign figure sitting opposite, and felt really rather hopeless. She also began at this precise moment to look forward to tomorrow evening, when (if nothing came of her visit to the studios with Christopher) Ydette would be gone. But one thing she *was* going to say; whether Christopher liked it or not; it was her duty to say it, and she would.

"Well, I won't worry you any more now," she said, leaning forward again. She struggled with reserve and managed to get out something of what she wanted to express. "But—you know, I like you very much, Ydette, I always have, we all do—Chris and my sister and I—and I want you to have what Chris calls 'a great, big, lovely success'. So I think I ought to warn you that if you *do* get a job with Mr Burke—you may not like the cinema studios and the people who work there." She paused.

"They want only money, I expect," said Ydette placidly; her sulky expression had been replaced by one of pleasure, and Nora wondered why.

"Yes, that's what it is," she said, surprised by this unexpectedly penetrating judgment. "That does sometimes make people rather . . . but you'll like Mr Burke. He's an artist."

No more was said. She gave it up. She finished her luncheon, conscious that her last remark had been more optimistic than truthful. Did simple people always like artists?—artists, who could be rude, ruthless and selfish? Wouldn't the kind of person whom Ydette would like resemble more a dog or a horse or a child?

Nora wished that she were sitting peacefully at home with *The Observer*. She paid the bill, collected her protégée and took them back to South Kensington by another taxi through the quiet Sunday streets. She had said her say; her conscience was clear; but she could not feel that any good had been achieved at all.

Monday morning came; fresh, sunny and clear. "*Sweet day, so calm, so cool, so bright*," hummed Evelyn, standing at the window.

"*Must* you sing?" demanded Hilary savagely, where she sat amidst text-books and notes at the breakfast table.

"Sorry; it is maddening, I know." Evelyn slipped back to the seat whence the glow of the morning had tempted her. Hil had never really recovered, she thought, from that business in their last year at Oxford, when she had got herself into that extraordinary scrape with Peter Bayford in Jugoslavia and been three weeks late for the beginning of term—by her own fault, on her own admission, and had consequently been rusticated. Jugoslavia and Peter and Hilary had all been in the *Daily Express*, with photographs, and to this day Hil had never told them exactly what had happened.

Evelyn had no wish to be *obvious* in her suppositions or inquisitive in her thoughts. She took some marmalade made by Mummy Perowne, and turned brightly to Ydette.

"This is the great day, isn't it? Are you feeling excited?" she brightly asked.

Ydette's lugubrious shake of the head was interrupted by the arrival of Christopher, so nervous that he had cut himself while shaving, and irritably playful in manner.

"Hullo, *girls*! Everybody happy? Hilary, surely you're too much of an old sweat to have text-books for breakfast before an exam?"

"I can't help it; I can't sleep; you know I'm no use at any-thing when I can't sleep; I go absolutely to pieces," she said crossly.

Christopher shrugged, Nora looked conscious, and Evelyn pitiful, and then Ydette reappeared, in coat and scarf and wearing an expression of apprehension mingled with stubborn-ness that caused his heart to sink.

"Cheer up," he said to her, when, their farewells having been made and luck wished to the unresponding Hilary, they were driving away; "look here, you know, you mustn't look like that. Jon Burke doesn't go for sullen girls. You just think how lucky you are—you think of the hundreds and thousands of girls in England and Italy and America and France—and Russia too, I expect—who would give absolutely anything to have the chance you've got. You're one girl in hundreds of thousands —in millions, really—who's had the luck to have this wonderful chance, and now what I want you to do is just to be *natural*. Don't feel afraid (no-one's going to be cross with you) or try to be any different from what you always are. Just enjoy your-self, and everything will be perfectly all right. Will you do that, Ydette, to please me?"

He had never been more aware of how completely brotherly were his feelings towards her as he made the plea. As he looked into the lovely dark eyes with their feathery black canopies he did experience a momentary inward quiver, but it was because he had suddenly realized *how much* a director would have to do to her in order that those eyes might learn to convey the passions and desires of what the world calls maturity. And there was not going to be any help from *her*. . . . She . . . he certainly had put off facing this fact until the last moment . . . she definitely wasn't teachable.

Oh well, Burke had tackled even more hopeless propositions, possessing the right kind of face, before now. (At least, Chris-topher hoped that he had.) He said no more, but drove as fast as traffic would permit towards Kent.

The studios of Commonwealth Association Films, which they reached just before twelve o'clock, filled what had fifteen years previously been some excellent farming land, then divided into five or six large meadows. These were now occupied by buildings: some new, of white concrete well designed and well built; others dingy, and displaying the truncated angles and inferior materials of the 'thirties. There were also the lofty, rickety-seeming, barn-like structures where the actual shooting was done, and small sheds, cloakrooms and offices; and the whole was surrounded by gravelled walks and beds of flowers looking as if set down by nurserymen rather than planted by gardeners. In the near distance were the surprisingly high and green Kent hills. There was nothing shabby or going-downhill about the place. It exuded prosperity, and even paid some tribute to Beauty and Craftsmanship; the wrought-iron gates through which all visitors must enter were as graceful as they were well made.

"Now—what would you like to see?" Christopher said to her, when he had parked the car; "we've got about half an hour before lunch. Mr Burke usually lunches at half past, and I want to be certain of getting a table near the one he always has, so we must be in there in good time. But we can stroll around a bit, if you'd like to. Don't you think it all looks interesting?"

Ydette merely nodded, while seeming doubtful. She was in her natural state of being unable to say what she was feeling. That did not matter at home, where no-one ever asked her what she felt, and where in any case her feelings were usually pleasant. But here——! The stark-white buildings and squat little sheds were ugly. The sky seemed to be sitting on top of you. The hills were pretty, but she never had been one for hills, preferring to any picture of mountains the placid levels, through which the eye could wander here and there recognizing a spire or a farm, of home. And when she thought about the places she had seen on the pictures, where beautiful and wonderful people lived, and remembered that it was *here* those films were made—she felt so bewildered that it was actually painful; her mind seemed to be aching inside her head.

"Let's go and look at the Pacific Ocean," Christopher said.

She did not know what on earth he meant. But when they

T

were standing before the enormous tank of water which filled all the foreground and was backed by a tremendous sheet of metal, chemically stained to a tender, tremulous and unchanging blue, that represented a tropic sky, she actually turned pale.

"This is where they take the shots for scenes at sea," Christopher volubly explained; "they can whip up quite a storm, with various machines, on *that*, you know, and if they want a blazing hot day, there's the sky. It's been up there for two years now and it's as blue as ever. Pretty good, isn't it? Look at the reflection in the water."

Ydette looked; it was an exquisite colour, the more so for the background of common greys and greens and browns behind it. Then she gazed up at the smiling incorruptibility of the sheet of tinted metal; unchanged, undimmed or damaged by the rains and fogs of two winters, looming with a kind of incongruous beauty and permanence over the dull scene. Something about it frightened her very much.

"What?" said Christopher, turning.

"It is frightening," she said in an almost inaudible voice, and turned away.

"And there are the models they use if they want a long shot across the tank," he said, thinking that her present expression and pallor were not becoming and hoping she would have cheered up by lunch-time; "they're exact models of the people acting in that particular scene. Look, there's——" and he named a world-famous male star who was one of Ydette's favourites, and indicated one of several little figures that had been dumped on a bench beside the tank.

"No!" said Ydette, after a quick, fearful glance.

"No?" he repeated, amused. "Don't you like them?"

"No—no—no. They are——" She had an expression of absolute distress and her lips were trembling as she struggled hopelessly to say what she was feeling.

"Yes, I suppose they *are* a bit startling, if you haven't seen any before." He casually drew her arm into his own, and felt it shaking. "If you were given to practising black magic, they'd be very useful, I feel. But you don't know what I mean, so let's come and have some lunch, and do cheer up. Just think—in a few months you may be able to buy your aunts a washing-machine."

He had chosen this contemporary symbol of delight as being the one most likely to ravish the senses of the aunts: it was perhaps as well that Ydette was now feeling too frightened, confused and wretched to bring out the ungrateful "They don't want one" which was trembling on her lips. But she knew they didn't, because Aunt Marie had often said where on earth would they put one if they had it? and electricity costing so much, too . . .

"There's no need to be frightened," he went on; "*you* haven't got to do anything. Just be perfectly natural and enjoy your lunch. I'll do the rest."

"I am not frightened," she said, with an intonation and expression that was suddenly all stubborn Flemish, "I am hungry."

"Splendid. Come along, then."

They passed several people on their way to the restaurant, who hailed Christopher. But those glances of startled interest at Ydette, followed by longer ones of professional appraisal and topped up by a look of envious respect at himself as discoverer of a potential new 'big one'—these simply did not occur. Bryan Martin did give Ydette a once-over but, with his reputation with women, that didn't count. For the first time, Christopher began to wish that he had never carried his plan any further than the day-dream stage.

He also began to blame Ydette. Why must she look so uninteresting just *today*? His colleagues no doubt supposed she was some wholesome Dutch lassie whom he was escorting to an *au pair* job with his aunt. And why must she be so unexcited, so almost shocked, by the studio devices which he had been showing her? Really, he was inclined sometimes to think that she was very slightly mentally deficient. An incipient neurotic, perhaps. But if once she became a 'big one', that might easily be an advantage.

However, as they sat down at a table actually next to the one always occupied by Burke, he realized that none of the people who had ignored her held any important status in the studio. None of them possessed sufficient imagination to see what possibilities lay in that profile, those cheek-bones, eyes and length of neck. Let Burke once get a look at her and *his* reaction, Christopher still felt almost sure, would be very different.

The restaurant awed Ydette, yet she liked it. None of those to which she had been with Christopher or Nora had been as grand as this, with its walls and ceiling dappled in cloudy gold and a plushy gold carpet covering the floor. And at tables near to them there were surprising hats above vivid faces to look at; there were even one or two that she had seen on the pictures, although she did not recognize them until Mijnheer Chris pointed them out to her. She could not really enjoy her first mouthfuls of English roast beef, because she was wondering when this *bioscoop* man would come in and look at her, but undoubtedly she did begin to feel a little better. The picture of that blue sky, uncanny as some enchanter's mirage against the everyday background, was beginning to fade.

Christopher, finishing his own roast beef with an eye on the door, was not feeling better. He had to keep telling himself not to become agitated; nothing solid was actually at stake. But it was useless; for although hundreds of thousands of pounds couldn't exactly be regarded as lost if Burke didn't like her looks, they would undoubtedly be set in circulation if he did. And there were certain to be pickings, as there was certain to be the prestige attached to him as her discoverer.

He did not calm himself by hastily beginning an explanation (long meditated but frequently deferred) about the reasons for Ida's not coming to London to see Ydette: half term and its excursion to town was just over; work for summer examinations was in full swing; there were tennis matches at the school, and so forth. But in fact, his father had severely forbidden Ida to go, saying that fares mounted up and Christopher's friends were not suitable for someone aged eleven.

He had wondered why Everard's voice had sounded so annoyed, but it was probably only part of his father's general reaction against Belgium which seemed to have set in ever since that holiday at Bruges.

Ydette listened with a dejected expression. The photograph of Ida on Nora's table, in shorts and shirt and racquet, several inches taller, well-developed and frowning menacingly against the sun, looked almost totally unlike the square and friendly child of four years ago and she wasn't really sorry that this stranger had been unable to come. But it was another sad little thing to happen; another thing to increase her loneliness.

And suddenly loneliness absolutely burst within her, like something starting to cry. She turned cold with it, and actually glanced up at Christopher in desperate appeal.

"What on earth's up?" he demanded, staring. "Are you feeling ill?"

She shook her head. But the fatal lump was coming up in her long throat, and at that precise moment, and no other (it would be, Christopher thought savagely, staring at her), there was a stir at the entrance to the room; heads turned, there wasn't exactly a murmur but people were whispering, and then, in a kind of procession, down the long room came Marcus Elver, Frank Page and Jon Burke, followed by a very large American publisher in a suit of the very finest dark wool that could possibly be dreamed up and bought, and wearing on his wide yellow face an expression that seemed to be saying: *go on, amuse me. Make me want something that I can't buy. Convince me that someone exists who isn't buyable and rotten. Go on, I'm waiting. Not that I should care if you did.*

They approached, wafting before them a smell of cigar-smoke and alcohol, and as they settled themselves at the next table, Burke just caught Christopher's eye and gave him a tiny nod.

So far, so good. But it was plain to Christopher that they had been having one of their rows, in which the American had presumably been the guest-artist. They gave their orders in a glum undertone, and, being served, proceeded to shovel the food in, or somnolently pick at it, according to their natures. People accustomed to venerate the artistic temperament would have said that their creative urges were being frustrated: others, accustomed to nursery behaviour, might have murmured *sulks*. But whatever explanation was given to their overclouded looks, anyone would think twice about choosing this occasion to introduce someone to them.

"What sweets, sir?" the waitress asked.

Christopher, in an extraordinary mixture of hope and rage that had the curious effect of making him feel as if he were watching the scene from somewhere a long way away, took the menu. Out of the corner of his eye he could see Ydette's pale face, her head well lifted and her large eyes fastened sadly on his own. Her head and her braids well displayed, anyway, on top of that ravishing white giraffe's neck. But how odd she looked, how—almost silly. The typical queer, laughable foreigner.

And then, as he picked up the menu, he saw Jon Burke lift from his plate his long, rangy head with its thinning, bright hair and look round the room. His eyes, with the one famous drooping passerine lid, travelled slowly past the humorous faces and the challenging hats as if they were not there, and came to rest—on the face of Ydette. His glance alighted, and it lingered. The glance became a stare.

Christopher almost began to tremble. He said casually, "What would you like, Ydette?" forcing himself to keep looking at the list he held before him—but then, because in spite of all the bad luck beforehand, the unlikely, the so-desired thing had after all happened, and the most famous director in the Western World was sitting six feet away, with eyes fixed on the girl whom Christopher had first seen as a potential star four years ago on the sands of Zandeburghe—he added in an excited little burst of kindness:

"How about ice-cream? I know you like that, don't you?"

She sprang up from her seat, made a loud sniffling, choking sound, bent her head and, blundering out from between their table and Burke's, made her way clumsily but quickly down the length of the room and almost ran through the swing doors and out of the restaurant.

"Here!" Christopher exclaimed, springing up, "Ydette . . .!"

Heads were turning, every face in the room, with expressions of amusement, surprise, irritation, was turning to watch the hasty flight; then back to the table where the girl had been sitting. And Christopher saw Jon Burke drop his eyes indifferently, then bend forward to re-arrange the table-cloth, which had been dragged awry by Ydette in her passing.

Christopher began, without any haste and after a bewildered shrug at the waitress, to make his way down the room and after her.

I know just what he's thinking (his furious thoughts raced as he moved composedly between the tables): *he thinks it's a put-up job; that I told her to sit down under his nose and make a scene so that he couldn't fail to notice her. It's the one thing that would make him angrier than anything else—the one fatal thing—a gimmick, a story for the admass press—something contrived. The one thing that'll make him absolutely determined never to think about her, or me, or her face, again.*

When I get hold of her I'll kill her.

But when he did get hold of her—standing as if unable to go any farther beside the immense tank of water reflecting the chemical blue sky, and staring out across it with a kind of horror on her face—he wasn't just angry with her any more. The whole idea had failed stone-dead; perhaps it never could have succeeded anyway, and now the only thing to do was to get her back to Bruges as quickly as possible.

"Hullo, Ydette," he said with simple, deadly kindness, slipping his arm through hers. "What was the matter? Were you frightened?"

She shook her head, and then she turned and looked at him. In a minute, he laughed and gently shook the arm he held.

"It's all right, velvet-eyes," he said; "come on, let's go home."

They did not talk as they walked back to where he had parked the car. The fact was that he had suddenly felt so fond of her—exactly as he was of Dogfight and that poor ass Nolly, and as he had never, not even in their early days, felt of Susan—that he couldn't feel the faintest anger with her any more.

WHEN they got back to the flat in the late afternoon, tired and silent, they found it empty. But stuck against the telephone was an urgent-looking note in the spiky hand of Hilary: "Christopher: I've been trying to get you for three hours. Susan telephoned at eleven to say that the baby has started and she's gone into hospital. Can you *ring them at once please?* she said it looked like being quick."

"Oh my God, that was all that was needed," Christopher said. He looked distractedly around. "Shall we have a drink? No—better not, I suppose; 'young father reeking of rum greets newly-born' wouldn't look too good, I suppose. Look here, Ydette, Susan is having the baby. I must go round to the hospital at once. You can look after yourself, can't you—make tea and that sort of thing? One of the girls is sure to be in soon."

She nodded. Her face was so pale as to be almost greenish; the white-tinted, unearthly green of certain orchids. He hesitated in rather a distraught way for a moment; he felt that something should be said or done to make her look less stricken. But all he could think about was Sue—darling Sue, being hurt. He went on rapidly:

"I shall probably be tied up there for hours, so I don't expect I shall see you again. I'm awfully sorry about everything; I'm afraid you've had rather a rotten holiday, too. Don't mind about the film-star business; it was just an idea of mine; it probably wouldn't have come to anything anyway."

He broke off, remembering that they had sat in almost total silence during the drive home, and feeling that some explanations about the absolutely fatal thing she had done ought to have been given her, to account for his sudden abandonment of the plan.

But he simply couldn't spare the time now—and it was surprising how much trouble could be averted—and to what extent a fuss would settle itself—if you just didn't *talk*, and left things alone.

"I really must go," he said. "Nora's got your ticket, hasn't she?" as Ydette slowly nodded, "and she'll see you off to-morrow morning, of course." He crossed the room and stood by her where she drooped at the window, "and don't worry, will you?" She did not move or speak, and suddenly that feeling came over Christopher again of being so awfully fond of her.

"Oh cheer *up*, poppet," he said and gave her a kiss and a great hug. "I shall see you again, of course. I'm—I'm awfully *sorry*," he said, and went out without looking back.

"I hope it will all be good with the baby," Ydette said just as the door shut, but he did not hear.

She turned to the window. The brilliance of the early morning had again ended in rain, and she looked out on broad, wet, deserted streets, in which a few figures struggled with wind-tugged umbrellas, and towers and spires, strange to her as any in Turkey or Latvia, stood up darkly against a lowering sky. She saw Christopher hurry across the road, hail a cruising taxi and drive away, and she was just turning back to the room, with a deep sigh, when she heard a key turning in the front door. Dismayed, swallowing a rising lump in her throat, she stood looking towards the sound. A mejuffrouw!—Oh, let it be Nora!

But the white-faced one came in, walking so quietly and looking so pale that Ydette actually felt frightened. When she saw Ydette, she stopped and looked slightly sick; there wasn't any mistaking her expression. There followed a pause.

Then the telephone bell rang. Ydette looked across at it; not without interest, for there was one at the big house and they were all over the packing-plant, but it was a detached interest, for she had never used one.

In a minute, as she did not move, Hilary went across and snatched off the receiver.

"Empire 4646. Who? Oh—yes, she's here. Hold on, will you?"

She held it out to Ydette. "It's for you. A man," she said.

"A man?" staring. "Is it Monsieur Ruddlin?"

"No, of course it isn't; I know Chris' voice. Here, will you *take* it, please? I've got to go out again; and I should *welcome* the chance of getting ready if you'll just *take* it, please." She slightly shook the extended receiver.

"I do not know any man in England except Monsieur Ruddlin," Ydette said. Cautiously she took the receiver and, holding it a good distance away from her, addressed—by luck— the mouthpiece.

"I am here," she said softly. But there was no distant answering cackle, and in a minute she looked at Hilary. "I think he has gone away," she said.

"Oh. Well, put it back, then. Put it *back* on the *stand*," as Ydette hesitated, then, in that tone which expresses reasonableness pushed to the last limit before it explodes in fury— "look here, do you very much mind if I leave you now? I'm late as it is—and I'm pretty sure I've come down heavily in my exam this morning, thanks to next to no sleep for three nights on end."

"I am sorry, Mademoiselle." Ydette carefully replaced the receiver; she did not quite understand, beyond knowing that something had gone wrong and feeling that she was being blamed for it, and she was too agitated to wonder about the man who had been on the telephone.

Hilary snatched open the door and went out, slamming it after her.

Ydette's throat ached intolerably. She had been so distressed, so frightened by the tone and the look, that most of her usually quite adequate English had deserted her, and she had only known that she was being violently blamed. Her sense of guilt, of being ungrateful and stupid and therefore unwanted, was unendurable. And the ice-cream! the dreadful moment when the thought of it and the sound of its name—and Jooris hundreds of miles away and cross with her—had made her cry in front of Mr Burke! Monsieur Chris did right to be cross Oh, he was cross all right; he had been very kind, he hadn' said anything, but she always knew when people were cross

It wasn't that she had ever truly wanted to have a job with a picture-company, and all that stuff about her one day being a star was just crazy English nonsense—but she liked the Ruddlins so much! and she had wanted to be with them, and to please them, and now everything had gone wrong and it was all her fault.

She sat down heavily—*plumped* would not be too strong a word—on the fragile sofa, which skidded slightly along the parquet under her impact, and put both hands up to her face.

A subdued, decently muffled sound crept out on the air. The large, chaste faces of the white dahlias in the Venetian glass goblets looked as if they disapproved. It continued.

Suddenly the door opened and Hilary's head came round, wrapped in a stole.

"Sorry," she said; "I lost my temper. Overwork."

Then, as she saw and heard, in a tone of disgust, "Oh *lord*—I can't cope, really I can't," and she withdrew.

Ydette settled herself to relieving her grief. The clock ticked on and the dahlias stared.

Suddenly the front-door bell rang imperiously, long and loud. She ceased crying, and fearfully listened. Oh, who? Some English friend of the mejuffrouws? Monsieur Chris back again? She kept very quiet. If she took no notice the person might go away.

But in a moment there came another ring, louder and longer. It sounded as if someone were standing there with bad news, and now she was afraid not to answer it. She did not want to do more wrong things and make more mistakes. She got up, and went out of the room and down the long hall.

She opened the door in the middle of the fourth furious ring. She was drooping, damp-cheeked, smarting-eyed; and at first she could scarcely see, for the afternoon light that filled the well of the staircase was rainy and dim and her wet eyelashes were entangled. But when she did see who was standing there, she gasped, and her woebegone face broke into a wide smile.

"Oh mijnheer," she said, grasping his coat sleeve with both hands, "I'm so glad—I'm so glad. You've come to take me home!"

She spoke in her broadest Flemish, and it was in Flemish that Adriaan answered. All he said was:

"Oh, hullo, Ydette. Yes, I suppose that's what I'm here for," and for a moment he made no attempt to come into the hall. He carried a small briefcase, and had a light overcoat across his arm; rain-drops were on his pear-shaped face beneath his dark, thinning hair.

"I am so pleased . . . so pleased . . ." she said in her very softest tone, "come in, mijnheer—do come in."

"Are you alone?" he asked, throwing his coat and case down on a chair. "They're all out, are they?"

"Yes, mijnheer." Her tone was now more respectful. She had not been able to hide her delight at seeing, so utterly unexpectedly, someone from home, but now that he was actually here, in the mejuffrouws' room, sitting on the most comfortable chair and looking around him with his familiar expression of superciliousness, she felt more conscious of his status as heir of the big house. She stood before him, very long in her black dress and white collar, and with her lovely hands linked. He was lightly touching his forehead with a handkerchief.

"Sit down, sit down, for God's sake," he said.

But his tone was not cross—and it was almost the first voice that had spoken to her for three days without an impatient undertone. She did not resent the apparent rudeness, because, although this was now the voice of a man, and neither musical nor amiable in tone, it was familiar in sound; and familiarity, the sense of home, of something long known and long accepted, was what she yearned for at this moment. How often in the past had this grating voice, with its soft, clear consonants and flawless vowels, so different from the voices of anyone else she knew, broken the quiet of winter mornings in the *plaats*, carrying, for Ydette, a charm and authority exceeded only by the voice of Madame van Roeslaere herself.

He was staring at her. "Why on earth did you ever come?

And you've been crying." (He used the Flemish equivalent of *blubbering* or *howling*.)

"Monsieur Chris wanted me to—and it was my holiday, so . . ." She broke off. Impossible to tell anyone, and especially not Mijnheer Adriaan, how the spell exercised by the big house extended to the friends of its owners.

"Well, you were a fool. But then you always were, weren't you? Haven't I always told you you were a fool?" banteringly.

"Yes, mijnheer," and she smiled.

There it was again, the soft, bright, bemused expression on the face that was irretrievably stamped into his mind's eye; so deeply impressed there that whenever he was attracted by the face of another woman, *this* face (whose tiny gradations separating cheekbone from brow, and upper lip from chin, effortlessly built themselves up into purest beauty) immediately floated before him, often chilling him in the full heat of anticipation and pursuit. It's as bad as God, he thought suddenly, meaning that her face had a similar power of laying something delicate and questioning upon the heated pulse. But now, as he sat opposite to her, where she drooped before him in the last light of the rainy summer afternoon, for almost the first time in his life he felt no resentment against her.

"You'd better tell me all about it," he commanded roughly, leaning back, and she began to tell him.

If there had never passed between them any words but those mocking insults which he had paused to throw at her on his way to school, she might have felt some difficulty in talking, in spite of her veneration for what he represented. But there had been those other occasions—when he had been constrained by the presence of his mother to speak to her courteously, or when, passing her in the corridors or on the stairs of the big house on a day when she had 'come in to help', he had felt himself compelled to be polite because he was then in a sense her host, 'the young master'—and these were the times that she now remembered. Indeed, they returned to her so strongly that she felt he was indeed 'the young master', sitting listening in silence while

she tried to make him understand her unhappiness; extending
to her by his attention, and his mere presence there (so strange!
Why, *why* had he come?), some of the kindly protectiveness and
the interest in her small affairs which she had always enjoyed
from his mother.

She spoke slowly, and occasionally he had to help her by
asking questions, for no amount of distress or loneliness could
ever have made Ydette eloquent. Indeed, watching her as the
words came slowly from the pink, unformed, child's mouth, he
doubted whether any passion whatever could have unlocked
that tongue. He was thinking more about her than about what
she was saying. She was a fool; oh yes, there wasn't any doubt
about that. But perhaps only in a certain kind of way. A fool
about the things of the mind (hadn't she, he had always heard,
been very stupid at school?), and perhaps a fool about people
(imagine sucking in Chris' stuff about being a film star—yes,
and what exactly had Chris really been up to?) and slow on the
uptake.

But was she finally and completely one? Could a face that
suggested some very early version of one of the oldest of the
fairy-tales, belong to an utter fool? *What* was floating through
the brain behind that exquisite surface? What thoughts might
the heroine of 'Beauty and the Beast' be imagined as thinking?
He remembered Jean Cocteau's film, and for a moment his own
thoughts played about its images. Then another train of
thought began to emerge, but vaguely, and from so far at the
back of his mind, that it did not come upon him clearly until
Ydette was well into her story and very haltingly trying to
explain something of what she had experienced at the studios of
Commonwealth Associated Pictures:

"And there was a whole street, mijnheer . . . a whole street
of houses . . . where you could walk or a car could drive. But
. . . just fancy! those houses, they had no backs! Not like streets
that have been bombed . . . all in ruins, I mean . . . but really
. . . I mean, they were made, those houses, like that. Oh, i
was—I don't know—I was frightened!"

She paused, and he said impatiently:

"Well. You knew that the houses you see on the screen weren't real ones, surely?"

She was silent for a moment. No, he thought, studying her, she didn't know. She believed that every place she saw, in every rubbishy third-rate film, was a real place—and probably that 'real' people were walking about in it, too. She believed that it was another world somewhere. He smiled.

"It must have been quite a shock," he said, but he felt that his dry intonation was wasted.

"Oh yes, mijnheer," gratefully, and lifting her eyes to his, "it was so strange. And there were the little images too that Mr Christopher showed me. Little figures of the stars . . . when they . . . I didn't understand what they do with them quite . . . but it's for something to do with a long way away . . . and there was a big tank of water, with a blue sky. The day we were there . . . this morning, why! it was only this morning . . . there was sunshine, but not like that . . . the sky was blue, blue, always blue." She shuddered as if at the taste of something bitter, then murmured something, and was silent.

Now why is she so upset? he was beginning to wonder (endeavouring, with a sense of condescension, and for one of the few times in his life, to put himself into another person's place) what might seem horrifying to such a girl, brought up as Ydette had been?—when his attempt was checked by the soft but imperative stealing upon him of an exquisite sensation.

As it invaded him, he was so charmed by it that he neither wondered whence it came nor in what part of him—senses, heart or spirit—it was unfolding. It was not completely unfamiliar, but never before had he felt it so strongly. He had felt it when he stood in the Louvre, looking at a statue of the goddess Diana with a young deer; once it had come upon him on an evening at home in late summer, when he had happened to glance down one of the canals, where St Mary's tower was reflected out of a golden haze on the dark water, while every bell in the city was chiming for a fête. And once again, he now remembered, when he was looking at the portrait of an Englishwoman painted by the Italian, Annigoni.

But it had never come so strongly before, never like this. He felt quite at peace beneath it, disarmed, content. He wanted nothing but to continue looking at Ydette. And while he looked, a line came into a head which had never been in the habit of quoting verse: *Beauty, helpless as a flower*. And then— *Beauty and the Beast*.

So that's it, he thought without emotion; she is perfectly beautiful, and that's what I want. I've always wanted it and only just found out what it is. But I don't want Ydette. This has nothing to do with *that*. It's much more difficult to satisfy— if it ever can be satisfied. Perhaps it can't. And I'm the Beast, I suppose. All right. I don't mind being the Beast, if this will only come to me sometimes, and if I can do something for it.

Rarely, rarely comest thou, spirit of Delight. I'm in a mood for English poetry this afternoon, it seems. That's Shelley—I ought to remember *him*, after all those tedious English Literature classes with old Ruddlin at Port Meredith. And with the recollection he tried to 'pull himself together'. But the exquisite peace, ignoring him, persisted.

If I can serve it in some way. That was an odd thing to think. Nevertheless, he did feel a desire to serve; it was even faintly painful, and as the feelings which had been storing themselves within him since his rebellious and insolent childhood gradually welled away under the soft calling of the Spirit of Delight, he began to know that he could never insult Ydette again or pretend to have for her that hatred which had actually been his strong resentment at being charmed. And now, he supposed, he must begin by doing what he could for *her*.

He stirred, sighing faintly. When there were twenty-seven years of arrogance, self-will and malice behind you, it was not simple to start 'helping' anyone. However, you could always do the easiest thing, and that was to spend some money.

"I'll take you home," he said shortly, breaking a silence the length of which neither of them had realized; "that's what you'd like best, isn't it?"

Her expression became sedately radiant. "Oh yes; thank you, mijnheer."

"You don't seem very surprised." *He* was; he had rather expected protestations about ingratitude to Mr Christopher and so on.

"No, mijnheer." Her smile broadened.

"Why not, Ydette? Weren't you very surprised to see me this afternoon?" He could not resist the impulse to find out, if possible, just a little about what was going on in that head.

"Oh yes, Mijnheer Adriaan. But——"

"But what? Come on, tell me; we've known each other a very long time, you know." He kept his voice light; rather mocking.

"I . . . thought . . . perhaps Madame had asked if you would come, to see if all was right with me," Ydette said.

"My mother? No, she didn't ask me to come. She knew I was coming, because I told her, but I didn't know myself that you'd come to England until I came home on Friday, and then I was in such a state"—he checked himself, then went on, "I *was* rather worried about you. I thought you might come to some harm. So I came over to make sure that the Ruddlins weren't doing awful things to you."

He laughed uneasily: even his coolness found the change-over from contemptuous mockery to brotherly protectiveness a difficult one, and his embarrassment was increased by the recollection of his mother's surprise and concern when she saw his agitation, and heard his final decision to go after Ydette. *She* thinks I'm in love with her, he thought, and so does papa. Well, I'm not. But that'll be a bore too: explaining.

Ydette had not laughed. She said seriously, "Do you think that they will be cross, Monsieur Chris and his sister, if I go home with you?"

"I expect so, but a bit more won't matter," he said with the impudence which was his form of cheerfulness. "Chris is pretty fed-up with you anyway, I expect, and you say these awful women—Nora's friends—are too, so 'in for a penny, in for a pound', as the English say. At any rate, they won't be *worried* about you."

"No, they will know that I am with you," Ydette softly said.

U

"Oh, is that such a guarantee?" sneeringly. "I haven't such a good reputation as all that, you know. They may think I'm going to make love to you. But I don't suppose you'd like me to, would you?"

The words were no sooner out than he was mentally rapping the claws of the Beast for uttering them. (The fact was, the Beast had rather bad taste.) It wasn't a question, quite, of 'profaning' his new feeling for Ydette (if indeed it was actually felt for the girl herself at all) as of a kind of irrelevance in saying such things; they didn't seem even to touch the edge of the Spirit of Delight's robe: they belonged to another—a by no means to be despised but an utterly different—world. He experienced a disagreeable sensation, which unfamiliarity prevented him from identifying as shame.

"Good lord, mijnheer!" Ydette had gone a deep pink, and she gave an embarrassed laugh, "good lord . . ." she let it go at that. Her sensations were rather as if one of the demons in a sacred painting in the City Art Gallery at home had made the remark—a demon whom she feared, but who was at the same time dear to her because of his homely associations. In a moment she had dealt with the situation by taking it for granted that she had misunderstood what he had said.

"We'll fly," he said, beginning to bustle with the telephone directory, and ignoring her murmurs about return tickets; "you go and get me some coffee, like a good girl, and I'll fix things up . . ." He was looking forward to leaving a note that would properly rattle that ass Chris, and Nora and her snooty friends as well. You did not get out of the habit of malice in three-quarters of an hour. Nevertheless, he had changed, and he knew it. Faint excitement fluttered in him, as if it were the promise of something later on to be explored and delighted in— he suddenly thought, while awaiting a reply from the Airport, that he would buy himself a fierce *tachiste* picture for the walls of his flat in Brussels. . . .

By great good fortune, there were two seats on the evening flight, a series of recent crashes having resulted, among other things, in a series of cancellations, and there was just time to drink one cup of coffee and scatter a few crumbs of cake, like some sacrilegious manna, on the lustrous surface of the mejuf-frouws' carpet, before setting out.

While they were drinking it, in a silence on both sides of almost complete content, it seriously occurred to Adriaan that he might marry her. She was docile, and well disposed to him in spite of his years of rudeness to her (and *how* damned rude I was, he thought remorsefully, glancing at the placid face poised above the Georgian coffee-pot), and her very lack of relations and background was in many ways an advantage. And he would possess for ever the face and body that could call up for him the Spirit of Delight.

Then he dismissed the idea. Her lack of even rudimentary intellect would soon drive him crazy, there would be endless scenes and tedious explanations with his family, frightful junketings and parties with hers, and probably a crack on the head one night from that tough footballer, young Gheldeere—who was, Adriaan supposed, more likely to marry her than anyone else.

That she might refuse to marry someone from the big house never once occurred to him.

Ydette, apart from some misgivings about their hasty de-parture, was entirely reassured and content. It seemed quite natural to her that the big house should extend its protective care over her even as far as England and in the shape of Mijnheer Adriaan—and he was being so much more polite and kind than she ever remembered! But then, hadn't she always known that he was 'like that' really? As if anyone from the big house could truly be cross and unkind! And, too, she had successfully made coffee with that uncanny electric saucepan.

"Feeling better?" he asked, glancing at the clock as he felt for a cigarette, when the cups were put aside.

"Yes, thank you, mijnheer."

"We can get a car from Brussels; mine's at home this week-end."

"Yes, mijnheer."

"You don't think the old ladies will be frightened by your coming home er—rather unexpectedly?"

"Oh no, mijnheer. I sent them a postcard of the Tower of London on Saturday. They know I am alive and well."

"I see . . . I hope that reassured them. Coming home with *me*, I meant. Won't they mind that?"

"Oh no," eagerly, "of course not, mijnheer."

"Oh come off it, Ydette." The Beast raised a tentative paw. "You must know I've got quite a name at home—girls and so on."

"People always say bad things," she answered in a low tone, "but my aunts will not mind."

"Oh indeed? Why is that?" He was jeering now.

"You are from the big house, mijnheer."

The tone, the expression, kept him absolutely quiet for a moment. Then he said:

"It means a lot to you, doesn't it?"

She looked enquiring.

"Our house—the big house—you . . . well, it means a lot, doesn't it?"

"Oh yes," with the confident look of a child, "yes, Mijnheer Adriaan." Then, as if feeling that more should be added, but as always, unable to say what she felt, "It has . . . ever since I was a little girl, it has been *there*. And Madame, so kind, so good to me."

"Yes . . ." he said, thinking angrily of that goodness, and how he had thrust aside, almost ever since he could remember, his own knowledge of it and his love for it, "I expect, in one way, you feel you kind of belong to us, don't you?" he casually continued.

What followed literally astounded him. A kind of joyful blaze illuminated her, her face sprang into smiling life and confusion and joy. Then he saw her eyes brighten with tears. Drawing in a quivering breath, she whispered:

"Yes, yes. Oh yes. That is it. I belong to all of you at the big house," and made no other movement than a knotting and an intertwining of her long hands. She looked down, and he saw the tears—the first of joy that he had ever seen—fall from her eyes.

He was extremely dismayed. Great God, he thought, she believes she's related to us in some way. *That's* why she's always looked at me like that. *That's* why she's taken it for granted I should come over and rescue her. What a fool I've been. It's the inevitable thing. We're the only gentry she knows, and she's a foundling and so obviously a cut above the Maes, and my mother's always been so kind to her . . . it's all happened perfectly naturally: she probably thinks I'm her half-brother—except that I'll swear she's never worked it all out anything like so clearly. It's all mixed up inside that marvellous little head with the *bioscoop* and the stories of the Saints.

But it oughtn't to go on. It isn't fair to her or to us. And if ever any kind of a story did get around (with a touch of pride) it would dishonour the name.

Thinking his way as he went, with the greatest caution, for what he was about to do was as if he should awaken a sleep-walker in full, dream-burdened stride, he easily began:

"And you do belong to us in a way, because my mother has always been . . . fond of you, Ydette; she thinks you are a very good girl. And you know that my father thinks well of your work." (*Yes, and giving her a job in the factory, too; that must have seemed so significant to her.*) "As for me," and here he really did pause.

Must the Beast apologize to Beauty? Well, not perhaps to Beauty, but to the spirit that lived within her. "*I'm* a bad lot," he ended impudently, "but I know I've always been damned rude to you, ever since we were children. I'm sorry. It was just because I liked so much to look at you, and I didn't want to show it."

He held out his hand (he almost thought of it as a paw, in contrast to the one which she slowly put into it), and so they sat for a moment. He felt nothing but the agreeable softness and the coolness of her skin. His eyes were fixed on her face.

"So I expect you do feel like a kind of 'daughter of the house'," he went on, and then, with a sudden lightning intuitive leap into the heart of the illusion, "my mother did have a daughter once, you know, but she died."

"She . . . died? I thought . . . Sophie Bouckaerts said . . . that you lost her, that she was lost."

"That's what Sophie meant. She meant that we lost her through death. Yes, that was my sister Suzanne," hurrying on, no longer looking at her face, "she's buried in the family grave out at Les Fleurettes. I can just remember her—a little thing with very fair hair, almost silver. She would be in her late twenties now, about nine years older than you." He paused: he had been speaking slowly and rather deliberately, yet without any unusual emphasis, because he wanted what he was saying to sink in, but did not want to give the impression that he was out to shatter the illusion of a life-time. And still he did not care to glance at her face.

In a moment Ydette said:

"There is her grave, out there at Les Fleurettes?"

"Yes. It's in a small churchyard, attached to the church there. Next summer, if—if you'd care to see it—it's a pretty little place—I'll drive you out."

"Thank you, mijnheer," she answered after a pause. "It—it is kind of you." And she added, in a tone and with an expression that just for an instant made her appear like an older woman, "Poor little girl."

He did not answer, but laid a light kiss—perhaps a little hot and bristly, but what could you expect from a Beast?—on the hand he held. More than poor little Suzanne, he thought, would from now on be buried out at Les Fleurettes. Then Ydette said suddenly, as if driven by some very strong feeling:

"Mijnheer Adriaan . . ."

"Yes? What is it? Tell me, Ydette—I came over here to rescue you, you know." He was so full of remorse, in spite of his relief at having done the necessary smashing, that he could not speak warmly enough.

"Well . . ." she made an effort that paled her face . . . "it is . . . do you remember the old man who died? Old Klaas?"

"Of course; very well. He died four years ago, in the *plaats*, on that evening when the Ruddlins dined with us and we saw Christopher's film. What about him?"

"He said . . . while he was dying he said . . . something."

"Oh? People often say queer things when they're ill. What did he say? Something frightening?"

"Not really frightening, but . . . I . . . I minded so much." He leant nearer, for he could scarcely hear what she was saying. "I . . . was beside him, and he looked up at me and he said that I was just like my mother, and then something about '*not good enough for her*', and '*ladyfied*'."

"Oh, he was wandering," Adriaan said firmly. "I don't expect he knew what he meant himself. He probably didn't recognize you, he got you all muddled up with someone he'd known years ago."

"Yes . . ." she breathed, her face beginning to show hope, "but it was so queer . . . and he always used to look at me so queerly too, as if . . . he didn't like me . . . and was making fun of me."

"Old types like that always hate the young," said he; "it's only envy . . . I shouldn't give it another thought—why didn't you tell your aunts, if it worried you?"

"I don't know, mijnheer. I minded so much . . . I could not, no, I could not." She was desolate again. Not even to Mijnheer Adriaan, who by now appeared to her as a kind of father confessor with whom she felt perfectly at ease, could she relate that she had feared some outburst from Aunt Jakoba about her own relations with Klaas in the past, that Ydette would so much rather not hear. And not even to him could she confess the horrible suspicion which had weighed her own spirits down for four years, existing side by side with the other day-dream about the big house, and now, since he himself had just destroyed that vaguer and happier hope, most miserably reinforced.

But he seemed to possess the power of reading her mind.

"Look here," he suddenly said, giving a sharp and admonitory wag to the hand he held, "don't you go getting any absurd ideas into your head about that shocking old type being your father. It's utterly ridiculous. We probably won't ever know who your parents were (it's my belief they were both killed in the very first days of the war, while they were on their way with you to the coast), but one thing I am *quite* certain of—and it's that that terrible old man wasn't anything at all to do with you. Be your age, Ydette. Can you *imagine* him producing someone like you? Besides, people would have been sure to hear about it; you know how they gossip."

"It is true," she said after a pause; the reassurance was as welcome as it was sweet. "And I did not truly think . . . only sometimes I remembered . . ."

"Well, don't remember any more." He moved her hand again. "And now we really must go, or we shall miss the 'plane. (Never flown before, have you? You just hold on to me, I'm not nervous.) Now go and collect your things and I'll write a note to the Ruddlins and then 'phone for a taxi."

Humming to himself, he hunted out some elegant paper from the girls' desk. Always at the back of his mind there lingered the taste, stronger than mere memory, of the visiting Spirit of Delight and his half-formulated wish to serve it. And he no more suspected how much that spirit was to transform him than did the Prince in the story, when first he fitted over his ugly face the mask which was to mould and change it at last into its own lines of purest beauty.

The note he finally left was a masterpiece of alarming vagueness, signed with so intricate a monogram (Adriaan had rather a taste for, and skill in, the minor art of lettering) that it took the girls, aghast and guilty at the empty flat and the meekly washed-up cups in the kitchen, nearly ten minutes to puzzle it out. "A.V.R." Who on earth——? The man on the telephone, of course; but *who*? It was Nora, at last, picking up the note with the slightly brusque and indifferent air which she had worn since the discovery that her guest had flown, who identified Ydette's rescuer.

Long did the mejuffrouws sit up that night, going through Hilary's Biology paper and wondering what exactly had hap-

pened to the Belgian creature? Hilary and Evelyn both carefully refrained, over the coffee and shortbread, from saying that
Ydette was just the type who *would* have a shady man up her
sleeve; Evelyn even tried not to *think* it; but their opinion was
plain to see, in spite of themselves; and Nora, for once, was not
grateful to them for their delicate tact in not blaming her for the
spoiled week-end. Even less was she grateful for their tolerant
concessions to 'the Belgian creature's' lack of education, and
her immaturity. But then, Nora always had been inclined to
a fondness for Ydette.

Before eight o'clock the next morning, Ydette was sitting in
Madame Maes' old chair, in charge of the shop.

It was a still, early autumn day, with the cobbles of the
plaats still damp from yesterday's rain (so they had had rain
here, too!), and while the water of the canal looked nearly
black, the walls and roofs of all the buildings surrounding the
plaats displayed every shade of grey from lightest pearl to darkest
slate. Ydette's eyes dwelt with a delicious sensation of homecoming on the subdued, familiar tints; already the red brick
and gaudy advertisements, which were now, unfortunately, her
strongest impressions of England, were beginning to fade from
her memory.

Oh, the peace, the pleasure, of home! the joy of seeing it all
again, from the moment last night when Aunt Marie, wrapped
in a variety of hastily-caught-up garments, had snatched open
the door in answer to her niece's knock with the forthright
statement that anyone coming home so late and unexpectedly
was enough to kill them all from shock . . . but Ydette had
scarcely heard, being so occupied with taking everything in:
the gloxinias, the red armchair, the photograph of Queen
Astrid and the bowls set out on the table for breakfast.

The relief of not having to sit through another meal with the
mejuffrouws, eating their horrible damp English bread and
drinking their unfamiliar coffee while trying to understand
what they said in their quick, cool-sounding English voices!
Even the rather disturbing information that Jooris had been in

for a cup of coffee that very evening, and had sat like a dumb stone off the beach for best part of an hour without giving a bit of news to a body who might have liked to hear it—even this (though the stone part certainly was alarming) was heard by Ydette with pleasure. And the aunts had shown neither amazement, nor suspicions of a certain kind, on hearing that Mijnheer Adriaan had been so good as to fetch Ydette home; and by aeroplane, too! They had assumed that he had gone on some hint from his mother that there might be perils in England about which they, the aunts, knew nothing. It was very good of them at the big house to show so much interest, let alone spending the money. As for Ydette's ever being a star—a fine idea *that* was. Aunt Jakoba had laughed until she cried, telling Jooris about it.

"What did he say?" Ydette had demanded, pausing in her filling of the kettle for that nightly hot wash about which the aunts rather proudly teased her.

"Not a word. (I told you, he sat there like some great stone off the beach.) But he turned red."

"Turned red?" faintly.

"Quite red. Like as if he was going to burst a blood vessel. (*Rage*, we reckoned it was.) But never said a word, not a word."

"Oh." It was almost a sigh. ". . . When's he coming again? Never?"

" 'Never'! What sort of talk is that?—off the pictures, I suppose. He's coming at eight o'clock tomorrow morning with the van—that Karel's fallen into a dyke again and hurt his leg this time. What was it like on the aeroplane?"

"I don't know. Rather hot. I was asleep."

"Trust you! You get a free ride on an aeroplane and you go to sleep! And so you aren't going to be a star after all. Just what I expected—though I can't get over you crying like that in front of the gentleman—what he must have thought of your manners, *and* them that brought you up, I don't know . . ." Marie went across to her niece and felt her shoulders with her big, hard hands. "Cold, are you?" she muttered. "What a time to come home. . . . But you always were a stupid girl. 'Be thankful she's a *good* girl, for clever she is not', them up at the Béguinage has always said to your Aunt Jakoba and me. Never mind. Go up and get your sleep now; no need for *you* to be up tomorrow before seven."

"No; that's good." It was a drowsy murmur, lingering comfortably with Marie's promise of the humblest imaginable treat to come, in the quietness of the small, ancient room.

Freshly washed and carrying her best shoes in her hand, Ydette yawningly climbed the tiny flight of stairs. The little window of her bedroom was, naturally, tightly shut, but she could see the stars through it, and, almost indistinguishable against the dark autumn sky, the blacker mass that was Our Lady's Tower. The calmness of it all, the comfort of again going to bed surrounded by the mild, familiar faces of home; the chipped basins with their border of green leaves downstairs on the table; the old wooden clock in her room whose loud, fat ticking she no longer noticed, her narrow bed with its counterpane of coloured woollen patches knitted by grandmother, the faded blue paper on the wall—everywhere she looked, there was something good to see. And tomorrow morning Jooris was coming. That 'going-red' needn't be taken too much notice of; really, she could as sooner imagine one of the old apple trees in the orchard at the farm getting really cross with her, as Jooris.

She felt lighter in spirit, as if some load that had been weighing upon her for years had rolled away, as she knelt beside her bed, but she was also so sleepy that it was only the familiar hard pressure of the floorboards through the worn little mat under her knees, that kept her from falling asleep while she was praying, lovingly and long, for Mijnheer Adriaan's soul.

In her narrow bed, in the next room which she had shared with Marie for the better part of fifty years, Jakoba had lain awake in the darkness. A shouted conversation up and down the stairs had soon informed her that their niece's late and unexpected return was not brought about by any disaster, and, neatly disposing behind her head with a flick of one hand, the long plait whose greyness was now beginning to be touched with white, she prepared to sleep again. But she heard the bells chime one, and then two, and three.

All that day she had been thinking, on and off, of Klaas; perhaps because it was getting near the time that he had died four years ago. She still missed him, the more because she could not tell anyone that she did; she could not even mutter to her sister, because Marie never spoke of him without thanking the Saints that he *had* gone—with his 'drop-of-something' and his sulks—and congratulating them upon having a much more satisfactory helper in Sophie's young Moritz, who now devoted all his spare time (a commodity in which, he saw to it, he was rich) to helping the Maes sisters down at the bathing-huts.

Jakoba resented young Moritz' presence: who was he, to be young and strong and alive, when better people who had once been as young and as strong had grown old and died? More and more, as she herself grew old, Jakoba liked her own solitary habits; she liked among other things to pedal along the road to the sea with her face set in a certain expression that she need not trouble to change into a smile (God knew that she had to smile often enough, during her day's work at the huts) and the flat, rich, untroubled countryside going by, looking just as it used to before the Germans came.

Sometimes, as the stiff figure in its dark clothes passed swiftly along beside some field where a blue-bloused shape was bent over the rows of cabbages or hoeing with a slow and steady movement between the crowded stems of the wheat, an old man would glance up and wave to her, or perhaps stand with a hand shading his eyes to watch her out of sight; she always knew who they were, the name of each one, and the exact number of his years, these silent figures, and always returned their greetings. They were her living Past. The sight of them gave—or seemed to give—her back some of the strength, and the appetite for life, which grew a little, just a very little, less with every year.

Jakoba turned restlessly in her narrow bed.

Well, she had been a sinner, there wasn't any getting out of that, and one day she would have to pay for it. But there had never been another like Klaas. He had always been *the* one.

First come, last lov—but the word refused to shape itself, even in her thoughts.

She wondered just how much he had known about the parentage of Ydette? A good deal, Jakoba sometimes suspected, from hints that he had dropped from time to time. It had all been mixed up in some way with Doorwaden, anyway, where he had lived as a child, but now he was dead and they would never know anything more. Jakoba had grown tired of questioning him . . . and often she had thought that his hints were nothing but teasing and spite. He always had hated Ydette. He could be very cruel, Klaas could.

Yes, very cruel. But before she fell asleep two terribly bitter drops had wrung themselves from under Jakoba's eyelids and dried away on the leathery skin of her cheeks.

It was almost eight o'clock. Ydette had set out the trestles and trays ready for the vegetables and fruit; the children were idling across the *plaats* on their way to school; their voices rang through the still air, and some of them waved to her. The carillon had already sounded the quarter.

She sat upright in the chair that had always been Mevrouw Maes', expectantly, but with her hands—that would never, now, wear jewels, or pose for a photographer—linked soberly on the lap of her apron.

Her eyes were fixed placidly on the front of the big house. Marieke had already, some half an hour before, been out for her morning inspection, and they had exchanged the restrained gestures of greeting to which Ydette's (supposed) years of discretion had now promoted her.

Everything was just as it always had been and, Ydette imagined, it always would be—for not only had she absorbed all that Adriaan had said to her yesterday without its making one shade of difference in her feelings towards the van Roeslaeres, but she made no allowances for these sudden transformations in a nineteen-year-old female life which may be brought about by a passionate and determined young man.

Really, I might never have been to England at all, thought

Ydette, staring with peaceful devotion at the big house. It's *so good*.

The carillon for the hour, silvery, joyful and fresh, came floating across the roofs, and as it died away the lesser bells of the city took up the sound, far and near, until the air was crossed and criss-crossed again with voices of ancient harmony.

And here was the lorry. Turning the corner into the *plaats*, it swung bumping across the cobbles and drew up in front of the shop. It carried an unusually fine load this morning; a mass of large, rich brown swedes, two or three sacks of scarlet string packed to bursting with golden carrots, and a pile of stiff green and white celery. There was also a box of large dahlias, so bright in their yellow and white and pink that they seemed to make an actual glow above themselves in the grey air. And the lorry was a nice, gay, sharp green.

Sitting amidst all this rustic colour and autumn ripeness was Jooris, red-faced indeed, but only with the morning's chill, his very blue eyes smiling out from under a smart English velvet cap. His arrival was heralded by a scent of roots and fresh earth.

When he saw Ydette standing inside the arch by the empty trestles he saw at once that everything had happened exactly as he had told her it would; the picture-man had not given her a job, she had not enjoyed herself, and so she had come home again, and four whole days (not quite a week, she had been lucky there) of her holiday had been wasted.

But now that she was home, he was going to see to it that she did not stray away again. She always *had* been rather silly, Ydette. How long had it taken him to make her understand that the chickens in the yard at home would not hurt her? Ten years, was it? That showed you what she was like. All the same, 'home' was where he was going to take her (after he had unloaded the van, of course, and filled up those empty trays) to finish out her holiday in the place that they both liked best.

It would be a surprise for his mother and grandfather.

But he would be prepared to bet that neither they nor anyone else in all the city of Brugge would be surprised at the next thing he was going to do with Ydette.

"Hullo!" he called, waving, and—

"Hullo!" she called back. She stood there, looking at him.

If, somewhere deep within her spirit, there were the faint voices of certain childhood dreams and reveries calling to her . . . the lonely whisper of the wind over the white sand of the dunes, the watching eyes of Our Lady's tower, the noble façade of the big house, the scent of the orchids out at Sint Niklaas, and, farther back yet, the drooping leaves of a great willow-tree . . . she did not hear their cry for aid. *Save us, we are in danger, we are threatened, we are vanishing, like mist in the sunlight.* . . . But she was listening to an older and a stronger voice, and smiling as she heard.

The bells had stopped now, but their echo was floating on, over the roofs of the city, out towards the distant sea.

"Right on time, aren't I?" Jooris said. "Had your breakfast yet? Or how about an ice-cream?"

For further regular information about

FORTHCOMING NOVELS

send a postcard

giving your name and address

in block capitals

to

THE FICTION EDITOR
HODDER AND STOUGHTON LTD
1, St Paul's House, Warwick Square,
London E.C.4.